Broken Shelves

Unquiet Mind book three

Roso,
Let Sam Rock
your world.

Anne Malcom

Broken Shelves
Unquiet Mind, Book Three
By Anne Malcom

Copyright 2017 Anne Malcom

ISBN-13: 978-1977562623
ISBN-10: 1977562620

Cover Design: Simply Defined Art
Edited by: Hot Tree Editing
Cover image Copyright 2017
Interior Formatting: Champagne Book Design

Dedication

This is for me.

Because I've done a lot. Become a lot. Been through a lot.
And I'm still here.

And I'm pretty awesome.

People think you're weird when you acknowledge   your
self-awesomeness.

Which is good, considering I'd always rather be weird than
whatever passes for normal these days.

And to everyone reading this, don't be afraid to acknowledge
your self-awesomeness. Be weird. It's fun.

Prologue

Everyone thinks there's a moment in your life when it all changes. "It" being life, love, you, *everything*. At least that's what books tell us. The second Romeo locked eyes with Juliet, he *knew* he'd met his love and his destruction. As with Cleopatra and Mark Antony, Lancelot and Guinevere, Tristan and Isolde—the list goes on.

Despite what most people say, even the most fiercely independent, our fragile human souls wish for that.

Really, though, life is made up of all sorts of little moments, not one singular catalyst.

All those little moments create the human equivalent of the "big bang" in which your universe is created by a little thing called love. And it creates almost as well as it destroys. Up until then, you're living in someone else's universe, one made by your mother, your father, the friend you secretly want to be because she seems to have *it*.

Whoever makes that life before, it's not really important. What's important is that it isn't yours. When you think about it, really think, life never really is, though. Even at the moment of the big bang it's not yours. It's someone else's.

The person who belongs to that collection of moments.

Astrologists may disagree regarding matters of the cosmos, but a little closer to the ground, the big bang doesn't exist in isolation. That's not how it works.

According to this girl.

The big bang—*my* big bang, at least—was the moment that everything aligned. All my moments, all those stolen moments, collected and stored in the secret corners of my mind, exploded from their space. From the safety of their shelf. And a universe was created.

My universe.

Made of him.

And that moment was long after that friend of mine had created her own universe. Had lost it. Then found it. Then almost lost it all again.

My moment was when she was celebrating the fact that maybe it wasn't really lost ever.

It couldn't be.

My moment was at the compound of an outlaw—or more recently rather *inside* the law, or as inside as they could get—motorcycle gang watching my friend get married to the man who didn't just consider her the creator of his universe. The way he looked at her, you could tell he was certain she created the sun, stars, and the earth itself. He would fight the astrologers to the death if they dared dispute his belief that she created the cosmos.

She, my friend Lexie from high school, turned out to be one of the most famous people in the world. The lead singer of the most famous rock band in the world, Unquiet Mind.

But right then she was just Lexie. Just a girl getting the universe in her hands.

In the form of a wedding ring.

And as it happened, so was I. Not in the form of a wedding ring, though. Mine was in a locked gaze.

I was gaining a universe, but I was losing something else.

Everything else.

He took it all.

And I let him.

Chapter One

It started with a glimpse. That's all it was.

The big bang was the connection with eyes I'd met a thousand times before, what seemed like a thousand years ago in high school.

I'd seen them a thousand more in my mind's eye when I perused the shelves I kept them on.

All my Sam memories.

My traitorous eyes locked with his in a bold rebellion from my mind. I didn't make eye contact. Not with grown-up people, at least. The miniature ones were fine, but certainly not men standing in the same breathing distance as me. Certainly not attractive men. Who just happened to be one of the most beautiful on the planet, as decided by *People* magazine and who also happened to be in one of the most famous rock bands on the planet. Oh, and the man who used to be the boy I was irrevocably in love with in high school, who didn't even recognize me.

Yeah. I so should not have made eye contact.

There was a reason I taught tiny humans and avoided the bigger ones. And certainly avoided the ones who I was unrequitedly in love with for my entire high school career.

Why I came to this wedding was anyone's guess.

Why I came back to my hometown, which I hadn't set foot in for half a decade, could only be attributed to temporary insanity. There was nothing here for me in Amber.

This place held only personal demons and a family that made it their mission to emotionally distance themselves from me as much as humanely—or demonly—possible.

Maybe it was that romantic part of me that the events, the disasters of my life, had yet to kill. That part that still harbored a little hope for a slice of some sort of fairy tale in this cruel and ugly world.

That's why I came. So my friend could help bolster my hope in a way my books couldn't. Not even the Brontë sisters.

Lexie and Killian, they were perfect. And imperfect.

All the classics I'd poured over couldn't hold a candle to watching her walk down the aisle while Killian stared at her like there was nothing else on this planet that could make his heart beat.

Even in high school, he looked at her like that.

Everyone knew it. That they were meant to be. Destined.

Even I did when he broke her heart so she could take Unquiet Mind to the top of the world.

Didn't all the great love stories have obstacles? Didn't every single great couple have to go through almost unbearable amounts of pain in order to be together? Wasn't it the watermark of true love?

So I couldn't be so cruel as to say the day all of those obstacles disappeared to let marriage happen was a disaster.

For them, at least, it wasn't.

For me it was. Standing awkwardly in a dress that I'd bought because the mirrors at Macy's had lied and showed a svelte and slimming cut that smoothed over my curves. Now, in the sunlight, I was doing a great impression of a potato squeezed into silk. Sweating because I was nervous, and because I was in a biker compound that not only housed men who looked like they had a few bodies in their closets, but also who were hands down the most attractive people I'd ever seen.

Ditto with their wives.

Runway models, *Playboy* centerfolds, frigging actresses, all strutting around the dirty club like it was a five-star hotel.

Okay, they weren't, but they looked like that. Airbrushed and beautiful, all uniquely and utterly stunning. And nice. You expected women that beautiful to be evil. Like they'd made a deal with whoever created them that they'd insult their lessers, just for fun. But no, I didn't think there was a cruel perfectly structured bone in their bodies.

Even being a short distance from them highlighted just what an utter disaster I was. It didn't help that I was standing beside Emma. She was another beauty, albeit a little more unconventional. Her look certainly fit in with the biker/rock-star vibe the wedding had. She was wearing a black lace, skintight dress with ripped fishnets underneath and scuffed combat boots. Her hair was tumbled into a messy bun, the rings of last night's makeup on her eyes somehow managing to be better than any smoky eye I could attempt. Her trademark red lipstick was just the tiniest bit smudged, but she still looked like a cover girl. She fit right in with all the rest of the cover girls, otherwise known as the members' wives.

And me? I was the potato in the light pink dress, that in the mirrors of Macy's had implied made my pale skin look flawless and delicate. Now it brought out the pink splotches that emerged on my arms and chest when I got nervous.

I was distracted from most of that during the ceremony. It was as if time itself stood still; even the rough bikers looked like they were sucked into the magic of it all. Lexie's stepdad, who scared me more than fluorescent lighting, even smiled.

It was after the ceremony when the magic snapped away, replaced by the reality of a booming stereo, pumping music that grated to my ears, and the bitter smell of beer in the air as people toasted congratulations.

My breathing almost became nonexistent at that point, unsure of what to do with myself, how to stand, how to structure my face so it didn't look like I was going to pass out.

"Come on, let's find something stronger than beer but weaker than cocaine," Emma decided, snatching my splotchy arm in hers, emphasizing the difference between her iridescent and skinny biceps and my so not skinny nor iridescent ones.

I let myself be dragged through the crowd, thankful that I at least wasn't alone. I didn't want to educate her on the fact that I didn't drink, scared that this confident and loud girl whom I'd only met a handful of times might abandon me. She seemed nice; plus she was Lexie's best friend, and Lexie was one of my best friends, of which I didn't have many. Now she was a rock star who performed in sold-out arenas and graced the covers of every glossy magazine you could think of. But she was still the same. Even in high school, she was the most beautiful and interesting one in Amber, could've owned the school and settled herself on the popularity throne. But no. She didn't even blink at social hierarchy and became my friend, despite the obvious gaps in our social status. Even now, when they were actually real, not made up by whoever decided high school needed to be like a jungle, she acted like they didn't exist. Like she wasn't the bohemian, beautiful, famous rock star married to a sinfully delicious and scary outlaw biker and I wasn't the bookish, chubby, and unremarkable friend who, even now at twenty-three, couldn't say boo to said husband, nor his friends. Or her bandmates, one of whom I'd carried a candle for these last nine years.

One who was leaning on the bar that we were approaching.

I tried to pull my hand from Emma's grip. "You know what? I'm not really thirsty," I said, trying to keep the desperation from my voice.

Her grip didn't even loosen; even though she had waifish skinny arms, they were strong. Her laugh was throaty and rough and made Wyatt, who was leaning beside Sam, instantly turn.

"I didn't ask if you were *thirsty*," she replied, studiously ignoring Wyatt's gaze as she let go of my hand to propel half of her body on the bar, leaning across it to smile seductively at the attractive yet young man with a "Prospect" patch on his leather cut.

The rest of the men in the Sons of Templar MC were "full patch," with a huge image of a grim reaper riding a motorcycle stitched onto their leather vest. I didn't know much about them, but I knew the attractive dark-haired man called Cade was the president. Though he didn't look too menacing when he was cradling his baby daughter in his arms or smiling at his pretty wife.

"No one drinks spirits because they're *thirsty*." She regarded me, holding up a single finger with chipped red polish on the nail. "You either drink the hard stuff because you're sad"—she held up another finger—"mad"—third finger—"or sad *and* mad. Or scared." She paused. "Or bored. Or like in Russia or something and it's the only thing to keep the insides from freezing in frigid temperatures. Why the fuck anyone would want to live there is anyone's guess. Though, broody and mostly silent Eastern European men are tempting," she pondered. "I bet they'd be *wild* in the sack too." She winked, sinfully oblivious to the laser beams Wyatt had begun to stare into her tousled head at the mention of Eastern European men and their bedroom prowess.

Her dress, which was barely covering her ass as it was, rode up enough to give a show of just how many of her butts could fit into mine.

At least four. Into one of my cheeks.

Sam's eyes hadn't even registered me. They were fastened on the black lace panties in front of him.

I couldn't blame him. Yet I still tasted ash.

I really should've been used to it.

But apart from the shows, which I watched on my small TV in my small house, this was the first time I'd seen him since high school, and nothing had changed.

Well, *he* had changed. Not drastically, but he'd grown into a *man*. Even at seventeen he was a man-child, with a certain quality about him that no other boy possessed. He was unashamedly himself, dressing in all black more often than not, including his fingernails, and usually wearing enough silver to fell at least twelve vampires. Everything about his style, the way he spoke, laughed, it was something different. Above high school. Removed from the "cool" archetype, like Bob Dylan. He wasn't cool because he strived to be but because he strived *not* to be. Because he genuinely couldn't give a shit whether he fit into some kind of stereotype.

His muscles were impressive back then, enough so he always had at least two girls hanging off his sculpted biceps.

Now the forearms exposed by the expensive black shirt he had rolled up to his elbows were covered in tattoos, even his hands and knuckles. The fingernails were still inky black, and almost every finger had a silver ring on it. Though these weren't like the cheap ones from vintage stores in high school. No, these betrayed the fact that he made millions, had platinum records and was one of the most famous people alive.

A large hand smacked his inky hair, mussed to perfection in a man bun that had its own fan page.

"Ouch," he hissed, jumping from his position.

Wyatt glared. "Eyes up," he commanded, his voice tight.

Sam grinned at him knowingly.

"Gina," Emma called, making me rip my eyes away from

the men, who were now directing their gazes to me at the mention of my name. I was thankful to Emma for rescuing me, but at that moment I could've strangled her with her own hair for bringing the attention to me. I caught Sam's blue irises for a millisecond before yanking mine away to settle on Emma.

"What do you want?" she asked.

Sam.

To lose twenty-five pounds.

To gain some confidence that would let me strut around in a skintight lace dress and show my panties to a motorcycle club of Adonises and two rock stars.

To not be so damn ordinary.

So damn forgettable.

"Oh," I said, my voice thick and quiet. "Nothing. I'm fine."

She rolled her eyes. "You're not fine." Her eyes flickered up my body. "Well, in that sense, you totally are. But your hands are empty of beverages containing alcohol, so you aren't fine in that sense of the word. Vodka?"

I itched to rub my clammy hands on my dress but feared they would spread sweat stains on the pale fabric, bringing more attention to the garment and what it was trying to encase. "I don't drink," I said, my voice little more than a whisper as two sets of rock star eyes settled on me.

"Oh, okay." There was a pause. One where I was sure she'd declare me strange and sacrifice me to the bikers. "Tequila, then," she decided, turning back around. "Two margaritas please, barkeep," she requested, her voice throaty.

Sam's eyes focused on me, and yet again, I found myself trapped in his gaze.

"What do you mean you don't drink?" he asked, as if I'd declared I didn't imbibe oxygen.

I gulped and felt my face flame red, my chest itching with the telltale anxiety rash.

"I mean I don't drink," I replied, my voice somehow even, albeit smaller than a mouse.

He downed the chocolate-colored liquid in a glass that was a lot fancier than his surroundings and swiveled in his chair to give me his full attention. It became obvious that when he focused on you, his entire *being* was focused.

My knees quivered.

He opened his mouth, eyes still on me, perusing me and my dress lazily, hungrily.

No, wait. *Hungrily* couldn't have been the right word.

A man like him, a man who could have any woman in the world with a snap of his tattooed fingers, wouldn't look at *me* hungrily. Perhaps a little self-deprecating, but I'd moved past the whole body hate thing I had when I was a teenager.

Or at least I thought I had.

With his aura focused on me like the laser of a sniper's rifle, I was back to that girl, uncomfortable in her own skin. Not knowing how to inhabit her own body so instead inhabiting books where such self-reflection, self-acceptance, self-love could be shelved away with all the other realities, like the fact that I hadn't been kissed and I was sixteen years old. Like the fact that my only friend my age was a beautiful girl who happened to have just started a band with a boy I was in love with and therefore could only be my friend from a distance, because I could only love him from a distance.

Unrequited love was rather glamourized in books. Yes, we were told it was painful. The best authors showed the pain. But even then, even immersed in a book, you were witnessing it at a distance. A safe one at that.

There wasn't really a safe distance away from Sam at school, especially when I had English lit with him. And even when I wasn't around him, more often than not I was around a girl he'd screwed, was screwing or would be screwing in the future.

So I had to take what distance I could. For what self-preservation I could create.

Therefore, Lexie was still a friend, but couldn't be what I craved for her to be. So I had my other friends. The safer ones who Sam hadn't screwed or would ever screw, considering they had a few years on him. I didn't doubt he dated older women, but I did doubt he dated ones who resided in Mabel's, where their lunch came with a side of pharmaceuticals. Designed not for recreational use but to keep them alive.

I got to know them because that's where my grandmother used to live. Until her mind withered away and her body took a disturbing long amount of time to follow.

But it did.

Eventually.

And it broke my heart. She was pretty much all I had in the world. I didn't count the mother who only paid attention to me to tell me what new diet I should try, or the father who spent as little time as he could in the family home my mother had made so cold and angular, full of sharp edges, like her own body.

So when I lost her, *I* was lost. The ladies I'd come to know while reading to my grandmother had noticed.

"Now you see, my eyes aren't what they used to be. And I do love *The Bronze Horseman*. You were only halfway through. How about you come and finish it for me?" Hazel had asked me on the phone a week after we'd buried my grandmother.

She was right. Grandma died right when the siege of Leningrad had begun. I was going to finish it, even though I'd read it a thousand times, but I'd been dreading it. My body wouldn't physically let me leave a book unfinished, though. Much like I was sure a painter couldn't stare at a half-finished masterpiece. Just because I wasn't creating this one didn't mean the necessity wasn't there.

So I kept going. Survived high school. Survived loving the

boy whose gaze glazed over me in not an entirely unfriendly way, but because I wasn't enough of an anchor to keep it there.

Well, that's what I'd thought as an insecure teenager. As I grew into a woman, I learned some lessons the hard way. I learned how a man could not control your self-worth. Or rather he could, but only if you *let* him. Sam had controlled it, not out of cruelty but merely out of ignorance, out of youth, out of him being *him*. Already in high school, his life was fast just like the way he spoke, the way his hands smashed down on drums, echoing the loudness of his existence that had always been that way. Now everyone could hear. It was merely that I lived slow, quiet. Unseen. I was just a blur to him.

I had understood that when I experienced the other side of the coin. What happened when a man actively manipulated your relationship with yourself in order to manipulate everything else.

And how he'd called it love.

And I'd called bullshit.

Eventually.

But what doesn't kill you makes you stronger, right?

And it did.

Or at least I thought it had.

Until now when I had those eyes on me. And they were stationary. I wasn't the blur anymore.

A hypnotizing moment was broken, thankfully, before I could devolve back completely to the girl I thought I'd grown out of.

A cold glass was thrust in my hand, which closed around it out of habit. And having something corporeal, physical to grab on to was a welcome anchor to wrench me out of the fantasy that had me thinking that Sam Kennedy was looking at me in any capacity other than friendly recognition.

"Tequila," Emma declared, bumping my shoulder slightly

as she came to stand beside me.

I ripped my eyes away from Sam to glance at her. Her narrowed eyes had been focused on Wyatt, who was looking at her in a way my subconscious had tricked me into thinking Sam was looking at me.

With hunger.

Real hunger.

She somehow didn't melt into the slack-jawed mess that I did with the stare of a world-professed rock god focused on her.

"Let's go." She glanced around to a corner full of leather and muscles, guys who could kill with their sheer heartbreaking and badass beauty. Oh, and their guns, I was sure. "Over there," she decided, waving with her chipped fingernail.

My eyes flared at the suggestion. I had been treated with nothing but kindness since the beginning of this wedding, but then again, I'd done everything I could to make myself a part of the stained wallpaper. That was until Emma, who would never sink into any wallpaper on this world, had all but handcuffed herself to me. She was naturally in the spotlight. Not in the way famous people were, but just through a human quality that certain people had. The French called it je ne sais quoi. Americans called it awesomeness. The men around here would most likely call it hotness.

Wyatt let out a low growl at her suggestion, rocking forward slightly, as if he was intending on physically restraining her from going to the corner—where a man with piercing green eyes and a jagged scar decorating his handsome face was glancing at Emma with interest.

Then his green eyes met mine.

It turned out it wasn't just men I'd been in love with in high school who turned me slack-jawed.

So I held his gaze.

A small grin painted the side of his face, moving his scarred skin upward to somehow make him more attractive. He lifted his beer at me in a virtual kind of "cheers" motion.

I swallowed and somehow, or someone, lifted my own glass back at him before returning to the situation at hand. Rather Emma's hand, which was now firmly around my shoulders. I wondered if she put it there to use me as a human shield against the oncoming tattooed rocker.

Many girls would kill for that job.

Not me.

Luckily I didn't have to commence in that job. Sam, eyes on me, this time with less of that light humor and a little more hardness that hadn't been there before I met eyes with the green-eyed man, placed his own tattooed hand on Wyatt's expansive chest. The gesture itself stopped him, though I didn't doubt, if he wanted to, he could have plowed forward. The chest in question was wide, and the motion of Sam's hand hinted at the sculpted muscle underneath. The rest of him was the same. Even though he was wearing a dress shirt, it couldn't hide the shadow of his biceps and the width of his shoulders.

My eyes weren't focused on that, though. They traveled along the tattooed skin of Sam's sinewy forearm. The veins protruded against the ink, defining the line strongly while at the same time demonstrating that Wyatt wasn't the only one who'd filled out since high school. His bicep bulged, visible because he wasn't wearing a dress shirt, merely a tight black tee and leather pants that clung to every inch of his body. He could've been bronzed in that moment.

"Now, ladies, why would you want to go out for Nickelback when you've got Nirvana right here?" he asked, his voice fluid, easy, betraying none of that slight glint in his eyes. "I'm sure Wyatt and I can entertain you." His eyes went to Emma, then focused on me with such intensity I jolted imperceptibly like

I'd be shocked. "Thoroughly," he finished, slowly taking a sip of the liquid in his glass, eyes staying on me over the rim.

I swallowed heavily, unable to look away, barely able to breathe.

Had I slipped through a tear in the space-time continuum? Was Sam hitting on me?

Me?

The hand around my shoulder tightened. "We don't need to be entertained," Emma said, her husky voice teasing and somehow mocking. She wasn't addressing Sam, though. Her eyes were on Wyatt. "We need to be *satisfied*," she continued. "Nor do we need to be exposed to whatever cutting-edge STD you've contracted, or more likely *created*, Sammy," she said, eyes still on Wyatt. "You boys have a nice night now."

Before either of them could move, we did.

I let myself be moved because it took a second for my mind to catch up with my body, and it was nice being able to breathe better when my lungs weren't constricted under the weight of that confusing situation.

Now they were just being crushed by underwear designed to flatten all my curvy bits.

"Emma, I don't think I'm well suited to speaking to…." I trailed off as she navigated us through the party that was beginning to get more rambunctious.

I spied Lexie and Killian in a corner. His arm was firmly around her waist. Not too firmly, considering she was still recovering from a bullet wound from a crazed stalker, but I still reasoned his grip was tight enough that death would be the only thing that could have a hope of prying him away from her. And from what I'd seen throughout their years together in high school, and at the ceremony not hours before, the grim reaper might even have some trouble there. Considering he'd already tried to take Lexie from Killian.

And failed.

Sometimes even death wasn't strong enough to sever the ties of fate.

I jolted myself away from the happiness mixed with melancholy I had at seeing that. Because now we were close to the scarred man and his attractive friends.

The no going back kind of close.

"No, I know I'm not suited to speaking to these men," I said firmly, trying to stop our trajectory that would have us face-to-face with hot guys in two point five seconds.

Though she was small, Emma was strong. I guessed that had a lot to do with her determination to get away from Wyatt.

She kept us walking but glanced at me, then my glass. "Shut your perfectly formed lips. Or fasten them around that. Once you've had some tequila, you'll consider yourself well suited to talking to anyone." A mischievous twinkle filled her eye. "Or, in my case at least, hopefully not too much talking."

Then she winked.

Then we were in front of them.

I had two choices: drink the drink that she proclaimed would somehow have a magical effect over me and my social anxiety, or make somewhat of a scene and run out of here as fast as my wedged heels could take me.

I lifted the glass to my apparently well-formed lips.

Chapter Two

"Gina, right?" The voice trailed up the back of my neck, cutting through the ruckus of the music that seemed to vibrate through my body. My skin was slightly damp from the exertion of the dancing that I had abandoned in search of fresh air.

Little note: one does not find fresh air, even outside, when within a biker compound. Even the open air of the backyard boasted cigarette smoke, whiskey, beer, and now the delicious scent of man I could've identified by smell, even if the throaty voice hadn't accompanied it.

I turned slowly. Or quickly. The way the world blurred slightly as I did so made me think it was the latter.

But it seemed so much slower because, in stark detail, I could take in all that was Sam.

His leather pants, tucked into scuffed yet very expensive combat boots, molded over his strong thighs.

I even found some confidence to let my eyes linger on the sizeable bulge that left nothing to the imagination before they skimmed over his thick belt buckle and tight black muscle tee that had been underneath the shirt he'd worn for the ceremony.

I trailed over the ink on his muscled arms to look at his large tattooed hands covered in rings, his fingers boasting chipped black polish.

I kept my eyes there, at his hands, as opposed to his face.

Those hands had gotten him where he was today.

Not standing in front of me but in front of the world. Having it, and millions of women, worshipping at his feet.

His face, angular yet boyish and soft at the same time, was impressive. More than impressive. Totally sculpted, with all but a few strands of wayward hair pulled off it to fasten into a messy bun. Even his bun was famous. To be fair, it was the best man bun this side of Brock O'Hurn.

There were fan pages dedicated to it.

But it was his hands that fascinated me.

In school, I'd watch them tap on the weathered wooden desk in the English class we'd had together, playing imaginary drums. Even then it was obvious that he wouldn't be staying in Amber. That his life would never be still, he'd never be stationary.

"Babe?" His throaty voice snapped my eyes up to meet his.

I swallowed.

"You called me babe," I breathed.

Then, at his widened eyes, I slapped my hand over my mouth. "I didn't mean to say that out loud," I murmured through my fingers.

He grinned, crossing his arms over his chest and making his biceps bulge as he did so. "I'll gladly call you it again." He winked. "Preferably when we're horizontal. But it is Gina, right?"

His words were a burst of cold water, drowning whatever small adolescent heat that ignited from teenage me from his usage of the word "babe" directed at me.

He didn't even know my name.

We went to school together for five years, had two of the same classes, and *he didn't know even my name.*

I had been in love with him for 7 years, 364 days and 23 hours and he didn't even remember my name.

The hungry look from before wasn't because he was finally stationary to notice me, or somehow I'd sped up to get in step with him and he'd finally opened his eyes and seen me.

He had thought me a stranger. I guessed I'd changed a little since high school. Or a lot. My chocolate hair was now sprinkled with streaks of honey blonde, thanks to my hairdresser who shouldn't have been sequestered to a small-town salon but doing celebrities like Lexie's hair. I'd grown it longer and wore it in soft curls trailing down my back. She'd created bangs that swept sideways on my face, looking fashionable and bohemian.

My face hadn't changed much, still as round as it had been in high school, but I'd somewhat grown into the features that had always been a smidge too big for my face. That and I'd learned how to contour since I spent Saturday nights with a box of M&Ms and watched YouTube tutorials on how to apply makeup.

I had Jaclyn Hill to thank for my expertly applied smoky eye. One that wasn't weirdly warped by my glasses, since I got contacts.

Since I finally saved enough money and got my backyard landscaped into the beautiful sanctuary it was now, I spent a lot of time outside on my sun lounger, which meant my skin was kissed slightly honey—when it wasn't splotched with red, signifying my extreme anxiety. Like it was now.

I still carried the extra pounds I would always carry unless I decided to starve myself like I had tried to in college. That little diet had resulted in me fainting in the middle of a midterm and almost failing my favorite class. So instead of changing my body, I'd decided to learn to love it. And somehow, not because I was working to change it but because I was growing into the extra skin I'd always cursed, it become different. I looked different. Not the awkward girl with glasses and "puppy fat," but the girl who had the body of a *woman*. Sure, like everyone else,

I wanted to lose the jiggly bits, but I also wouldn't hate myself if I didn't. I dressed for my curves, embraced them.

Normally.

But today that little subconscious mind of mine must have been in the Macy's dressing room with me, warping the image of myself, letting the nerves of seeing him again chase away the common sense that would've had me buying a slimming and timeless little black dress that hugged in all the right places and finished a little above my knee.

No, I had to decide that my sun-kissed skin looked luminescent with the feminine pink, the bias cut tumbling over my curves in just the right places.

Silk!

I'd though *silk* would somehow slide effortlessly over those aforementioned jiggly bits. Even with my Bridget Jones underwear, I was sure the dimples in my thighs showed through the fabric.

And now I was standing in front of Sam, in this ridiculous dress, having the heartbreaking revelation that I'd been borderline obsessed with the idea that he'd have some kind of epiphany at this wedding. Where he'd have the "big bang," the monologue of our forgotten moments together, and magically fall in love with me after seeing me in my silk dress with my soft curls and my tanned skin and my expertly applied makeup.

Just like in a great romance book.

But no matter how hard I wished for the contrary, books were fantasy.

This was reality.

And in reality, he'd just plain forgotten me.

No, that was wrong. You had to *remember* someone to forget them.

If it was possible to somehow curl into myself and disappear, I would have. In response to that being physically impossible, I glanced around the crowded night air. If this were ever a time for that door to Narnia to appear, now would be the time. I'd even welcome Roland, the gunslinger, to rope me into whatever twisted adventure Stephen King had him on at this point. Flesh-eating lobstrosities would be preferable at this point in time.

Unfortunately neither appeared.

"Looking for someone?" Sam asked, his brow furrowing slightly and his tone becoming a fraction less playful.

Without thinking, I replied, "Roland." Tequila obviously inhibited my brain-to-mouth filter.

I had downed three in the hour I'd been talking to Jagger— that was seriously his name—and some other men from New Mexico. Emma had been right—it helped. Immensely. I had been enjoying a delightful vacation from inhibitions and self-awareness, and my body had felt light, my thoughts the same.

Until now. Now my thoughts were apt to sink my blush strappy heels into the ground.

Sam's furrowed brow turned into a full-on scowl and his eyes lost their playful twinkle. "Who's Roland?" he demanded. He didn't wait for me to answer. "Is he your boyfriend?"

I regarded him. The muscled, tattooed, heartbreakingly beautiful rock star who had a website for his hair. The man who graced the wallpapers of thousands, if not hundreds of thousands of phones across the world.

The man who was on last month's cover of *GQ*.

The man who used to be the boy I'd daydream about in English lit.

Who, if I was honest with myself, —and tequila was forcing that honesty—I'd harbored a small flame for in the darkest recesses of my mind to light up the small shelf I'd created to store my memories, my fantasies of him.

The man who starred in fantasies that I'd dreamed up on the flight here, in fact.

The man who didn't even remember my name.

I had two options here.

Tell this particular man that Roland was not my boyfriend but a fictional character in one of my top ten fantasy series of all time, authored by one of my top five authors of all time, that I'd lapsed into my own head where I imagined these characters were real, and that I did not in fact have a boyfriend, or even any prospects.

Or I could actually pretend I wasn't a giant weirdo spinster at twenty-three and clutch onto whatever dignity remained from this interaction.

"Yeah, he's my boyfriend," I said. "Roland's my boyfriend."

Sam's brows relaxed, as did the rest of his face, into that easy and lazy grin that was characteristic to him. That won the hearts and minds of thousands. He stepped forward, replacing the polluted night air with his own scent, a faintly sharp yet pleasing aftershave that smelled like cedar and something uniquely him.

He smelled like he looked, if that made sense.

We weren't touching but we didn't need to be. Not when someone had a presence like Sam. That was the beauty of it. You could be in the back row of a concert, thousands of sweaty gyrating bodies in front of you, and you'd still feel *it*, the magnetic electricity he possessed.

It hadn't been created by the rock star he became. It *made* him that rock star.

"It seems, Thumbelina, that your boy Roland is nowhere in sight. And I say *boy* because no man would leave a little beauty such as yourself alone in shark-filled waters." His eyes scanned my now-trembling body. "One of the best-looking, most talented and most satisfactory sharks is likely to eat you.

Right up," he murmured, his voice husky, thick with the erotic underdone.

I was lost for a moment. In the words. In the shock of the invitation.

Then I remembered.

"Gina, right?"

I straightened, stepping out of his immediate orbit, shaking myself of the thin film of his scent that seemed to have settled on my skin.

"I've seen *Jaws*," I retorted, my voice so icy I barely recognized it. "So I know how to avoid the sharks." I downed what was left in my glass. "You don't go in the water," I finished before turning on my heel.

I had planned on strutting victoriously away, but I was wearing heels and walking on soft grass, so I only succeeded in some strange kind of galumph where I had to wrench my foot out of the earth with each step. I was almost certain I looked like an ogre trudging back into the clubhouse, but I didn't care. It was dry land and I was getting the fuck out of the water.

Well, until I'd had three more tequilas.

Then I dove back in. Headfirst.

"We should have sex," I blurted.

Right to his face.

Without blushing or stuttering or crying or anything.

I decided I liked tequila.

It had given me the courage to strut—not trudge, since we were inside on carpet—over to Sam and utter those words confidently. Right in front of Noah, who choked on his drink, nearly spitting it all over his shirt.

I didn't pay attention to that. I paid attention to Sam.

Which was what I had been pretending not to do for the past hour, talking to bikers I normally wouldn't have said boo to, telling jokes I hadn't even realized I knew. And the whole time, like a brand, Sam's gaze burned into me. Every time I turned in his direction, he grinned, showing all his teeth. Once he'd even snapped them together in a biting motion.

And somehow, that ridiculous gesture had sent a spark of desire from my head to my... *there.*

And that spark had turned into a full-on inferno, one I decided I wasn't going to fight anymore.

One tequila decided I wasn't going to fight.

"We should definitely have sex," he replied with a wolfish grin, snatching my hand and pulling me toward the parking lot before I properly knew what had happened.

I decided I loved tequila, even if it did make the parking lot blur as we passed it by.

Then my blurring vision came to an abrupt stop as the man leading me by the hand did the same.

"I'm not usually one to take the moral high ground. Or go near it, in fact," Sam said. "But I do fear that you're a woman deserving of someone who at least vacations there," he continued. "So I feel vacation-bound to ask. What about Roland?"

"Who?" I blinked.

"Your boyfriend?"

Oh yeah, the fictional character I'd previously wished to save me from an embarrassing situation that happened four tequilas back.

"Roland's... not coming," I said carefully, only slurring my words slightly.

His eyes scanned me, and for a moment I was worried he saw through my lie. It's not like I was well versed in the art of deception. Then again, I wasn't well versed in the art of sexually propositioning the boy I'd been in love with who was now a man and a world-famous rock star.

"Stupid fucking Roland," he murmured.

Then, before I could give myself a mental high five for lying about my boyfriend being a fictional character, I wasn't doing anything.

Apart from being kissed by Sam.

Sam Kennedy.

Kissing me.

More accurately, Sam Kennedy kissing *the fuck* out of me.

All I could do was clutch his biceps and pray I didn't fall into a puddle at his feet—or worse, forget how to kiss.

It was over far too soon. He'd only been kissing me for, like, an eternity. Far too short.

His face was illuminated by the lights of the party thumping in the distance. In another universe, it seemed.

In this one, the one created by the big bang, Sam's eyes glowed and his mouth turned into a lazy grin.

His hand spanned my neck, the largeness of it, of him, making me feel small. Tiny. And not in the bad way.

"Yeah," he muttered, eyes on my swollen lips. "Stupid fucking Roland."

I found myself nodding.

Yeah, stupid fucking Roland. For not existing.

"You most likely shouldn't be driving."

Sam's head turned to regard me with what I could gather was a smile. Then he regarded the road we'd been traveling from the Son's compound back into town.

It was empty.

Amber was a small town and had little to no nightlife. And any sort of nightlife it had, we were driving away from it.

"Haven't taken away my license yet, babe," he replied dryly.

Babe.

It was the second. Yes, I was counting. I was collecting them, the moments. So I could put them on my shelves and store them and revisit this when the bad moment happened. Where reality would crash in and he would realize who I was and what I was.

Which was so not someone he would want to date.

His last girlfriend was a Victoria's Secret model.

The one before that had won an Academy Award.

Before those thoughts could take me down a road I didn't want to go on, his hand brought me back into the present.

More aptly, his hand on my leg.

His eyes stayed on the road, his other hand casually resting on the top of the steering wheel.

I glanced down at the hand on my thigh. It squeezed gently over the thin fabric. Like it was natural. Like he did it all the time.

Maybe he did do it all the time. With other girls. Not with me.

I swallowed.

Heavily.

Then tried not to breathe, scared any sort of movement would take his hand away. Then I thought about where it was. On my thigh. They were *much* larger than the matchsticks I was sure he was used to clutching, and having them flat on the car seat made them double in size.

Shit.

Was there a way to suck in your thigh?

I contorted the muscles the best I could, holding my breath as I did so. It didn't work apart from making me want to pass out.

Instead I worked to distract myself from the tattooed hand

burning a hole through the silk of my dress and igniting the throb between my legs.

"You shouldn't be driving," I continued, following my last train of thought before the hand on the leg incident. "Because you've been drinking."

I thought of the amber liquid he'd thrown back like water throughout the night. I knew for a fact that I could barely navigate my heels, let alone a motor vehicle. "And drinking and driving is dangerous and illegal. We could crash."

And then your hand wouldn't be on my leg, I thought sadly.

And then we wouldn't drive to wherever we were going and I wouldn't get to have sex with Sam. The thought of dying in a fiery heap on the side of the road in a town I'd escaped from five years before was only a fraction scarier than sex with Sam.

But sex with Sam was scary in a good way.

I think.

I caught my train of thought again. "Or get a ticket," I added.

He chuckled, and the sound filled the air of the car like music. It was throaty, rough and genuine. Easy. I wanted to find a way to put it in a bottle and drink it up.

I settled for placing it in a spot on my shelf.

"Thumbelina, I don't know if you know this, but I'm kind of a big deal," he quipped, quoting *Anchorman*. "And if Amber's finest does happen to pull over the hometown hero, America's bad boy and the best drummer this side of Travis Barker, I'm sure they'd look the other way."

He glanced at me and winked.

I rolled my eyes. "America's bad boy, and humble to boot," I muttered under my breath.

Not that there was any real weight to what he said. Not in the egotistical way, anyway. That was just Sam. It wasn't the fame that made his head that big; he'd already had trouble getting in the door in high school.

Though I reasoned it was more about deflecting attention away from the things he didn't want people to see about him—what he didn't want to see about himself—more than any sort of vanity.

With maybe a sprinkling of vanity.

The hand on my thigh squeezed again, harder that time, before it moved so his fingers grasped the fabric of my dress, bunching it so he could pull it up and expose the bare skin underneath.

I sucked in a breath.

"Secondly," he continued, his voice still easy, eyes still on the road as his hand settled on my flaming skin. "I'm an *excellent* drunk driver. The designated drunk driver of our little motley crew, which some call the most talented and attractive rock band on planet earth." His eyes twinkled. "Not only that but I stopped drinking the moment I saw the most beautiful girl in the room brush her silk against the leather of the bikers and look like a lamb in for the slaughter, eyes wide, not even noticing that every fucking wolf in the place wanted to gobble you all up," he murmured, voice husky and hand going higher.

Much higher.

I swallowed and then sucked in a ragged breath at the heat on my inner thigh. "Wolves," I stuttered. "I thought they were sharks. You're mixing metaphors," I pointed out, my words ridiculous at this current juncture as the lights of Amber twinkled outside while we drove through the deserted streets toward the ocean.

I didn't even have time to figure out where we were going. Or to be thankful he didn't expect to come back to my place. I was staying at my childhood home. For the first time in five years. It was not exactly the place I wanted to finally consummate the fantasy I'd nurtured for all of my troubled teenage years in that house.

"Not the best with words, babe. I'm better with my hands," he growled, his voice thick at the end as those very hands moved higher, well under my dress now.

I let out a sound that could be described as a moan and could also be explained as totally fucking mortifying.

I had enough tequila that I could pretend that hadn't happened, even as it was happening. So I latched onto another train of thought. "Plus, that's a lie," I accused as we headed down the little street where I knew Mia's boutique hotel was housed. "I. was watching—" I stopped myself from saying 'I was watching you all night,' a statement that would come off desperate. "I mean I caught a glimpse of you every now and then, and you were drinking," I fumbled.

He chuckled, the hand at my thigh pulsing slightly. "I said I wasn't *drunk,* not that I wasn't drinking. I'm not a monster, Thumbelina, unlike you, sucking down your tequilas," he teased.

The car stopped before we could carry on our conversation. We were in front of The Cottage. Lexie's mom, Mia, owned it now since the owners and Lexie's adopted grandparents had been murdered by Lexie's father. Who then proceeded to kidnap Mia after shooting Killian. Yeah, that happened. Mia was quickly rescued by her then biker boyfriend, now biker husband.

You couldn't make this stuff up.

Both Spencer woman had men who had and would always walk through fire for them. And I loved that. It wasn't common, nor even occasional, that kind of love, despite what books said. I was a dreamer, not an idiot. I knew Amber had reached its quota of love like that. It was a single grain of diamond chips on an entire beach.

Like lightning.

And it had struck two of the best people I knew.

Plus all those beautiful woman married to the bikers in the compound we'd left. I didn't know them well, but they were kind and welcoming and each of them had gone through their own versions of hell. They deserved that stuff that most people wouldn't even get a taste of, let alone the whole cake.

Leave it to me to make love metaphors something to do with food. That was the closest I'd get to true love—red velvet. Or chocolate with peanut butter frosting.

"You're staying here," I deduced as he turned the engine off. His hand was still on my thigh. It hadn't moved upward but it didn't seem to be going anywhere anytime soon.

Sam gave me his attention. Though tequila had muddled my mind, I got an inkling that I'd always had it, even when we were driving. Maybe before that. Even before I'd propositioned him. But this was him actively showing me that I had it.

"Sure am. We've rented the entire place out." I could just barely make out what I thought was a wink in the dim moonlight. "Keep us safe from all those pesky commoners."

"But your parents live two minutes away," I blurted, not thinking about what a dork I was for knowing where he lived and then broadcasting it.

It may have been a trick of the light, but it seemed all easy teasing left his face for the smallest of moments, for a slip in a second before his easygoing grin returned. "I became a world-famous and wealthy rock god precisely so I could do baller things like rent out entire hotels in my hometown and be sure that I'd never darken the door of my childhood home again." He winked again. "Plus, for what I've got planned, the walls are far too thin and my childhood bed is far too small."

My stomach did a dip. A big one. That inferno of arousal from his touch, from his proximity, his words, his *everything* was flickering throughout my entire body. I also felt like I could vomit too.

Not just because of the tequila. Not even a little bit because of the tequila.

This was *real*.

Before, when the car was in motion, I was able to think that maybe it might never stop. Maybe I'd ride with Sam's hand on my thigh and his easy conversation and intoxicating presence for the rest of forever, and that would be just fine.

But now that we were stationary, it was evident that movement was required. I looked down at my seat belt. I would need to unbuckle that. Then I would have to open the door, get onto my heels and hopefully not fall over, and then walk through those arches that were so beautiful in the sunlight but were now menacing, disquieting. Because I would cross over there and end up in a hotel room. With Sam. And a bed. And lights.

Oh God, sex meant I had to be naked. In front of Sam. With *lights*.

I tried not to hyperventilate.

Maybe if I just sat very, very, still, he'd forget I was there and I could melt into the seat. He'd get out of the car and I could make my escape.

I'd done it before. Not melted into a seat, but turned invisible. Well, not technically turned, since I'd started off invisible.

But I wasn't to him, for whatever reason. That became evident when his hand left my thigh, fluttering the fabric of my dress as it did so, and came up to my chin, lightly grasping it between his thumb and forefinger to gently move my gaze from the arch to the beautiful shadows of his face.

"There's no expectation here, Thumbelina," he said firmly. "No pressure. You don't feel comfortable, we can just eat the fourteen bags of peanut M&Ms I have stashed in my room safe and watch movies. I think there's a Twilight marathon on HBO, and I do love those sparkly fuckers," he remarked lightly, but the undertone of it was something more serious. Something that took my breath away yet again. Concern. Consideration. Some kind of sight or power that made him sense the unease and utter fear vibrating through me.

Maybe he could smell fear. Like a horse. Or was it a dog? Though he was not technically a dog, I and the rest of the world were aware of his revolving door of a bedroom, so he was, in fact, a *dawg*.

His thumb moved to stroke my flaming cheek with a gentleness that I didn't even know was possible.

"I don't expect anything, babe. May sound like a line— fuck, I've used it as a line. I'm pretty sure I *invented* it. But this, with you, it's different." He paused eyes steady on me. "Fuck, that sounds like another line." His hands tightened so he pulled me across the car, straining the lengths of my seat belt. "But it's not. I just like spending time with you. Being in your orbit. It's nice." He paused again, looking into my eyes as if he was searching for a word. "Calm," he said finally, his voice little more than a husky whisper.

I inspected it. His words. His eyes. The truth in them. Tequila made you speak the truth, but it also made you see it. It stripped you of all the lies you told yourself about what people thought of you. Sam wasn't lying.

But I didn't want that. It was the safe choice, to take him at his offer. The most sensible thing to do would be to get out of the car, walk the short distance home and spend yet another night in that room dreaming of Sam Kennedy.

But that was pretty much the definition of my life. Safe. Boring. A Master's in Education, minoring in Literature.

A house I'd purchased when the market was good, with a sensible interest rate on my mortgage. A savings account.

No. I wouldn't go back to my little sensible but cute house

in my small and incredibly forgettable town and torture myself with my cowardice. If anything, I wanted to be able to dine out on this night for years to come. Even if it was just one night of recklessness, I needed *something*. I didn't have an exciting or life-changing future ahead of me. I had a carefully planned and boring lifetime coming up.

"Problem is," I whispered, not breaking eye contact, "I don't want calm. In fact, I'd quite like chaos."

And then, before my brain could catch up, I unbuckled my seat belt in a smooth motion and crossed the short distance between our faces to kiss him.

Full.

On the mouth.

Tongue and everything.

That unclicking of the seat belt signified a lot of things. The beginning of the most incredible kiss of my life that promised the most incredible sex in my life, which would be followed the next morning by the most incredible pain I'd ever felt in my life.

Not that I knew the last part at the time. I didn't really know anything but the taste of Sam and the beauty of his tongue in my mouth.

A split second and our lips were apart.

"Just so you know, babe, this is it. Point of no return," he growled against my mouth, eyes seeming to glow in the moonlight. "You taste like fucking strawberries and drive me fucking crazing. I kiss you again, there's no going back. I'm taking you in there and I'm going to do things to you that will make you forget my name. That will make you forget your own name. I'm sayin' that because I can taste how much you want me. How much you *need* me. No safe words, just no and I'll stop. But I have a feeling there's not going to be any stopping for either of us once we get close to a horizontal surface. So here we are, at the crossroads. We leave everything behind here. Speak now or forever hold your chaos."

I blinked rapidly at him, unable to catch my breath, not unless his mouth was against mine. So I didn't say anything, just did as I'd done moments, hours before—grabbed him and kissed him. So I could breathe. And hold the chaos.

I had taken it. Control. Done something so un-Gina-like and kissed him. Sam.

I may have initiated the kiss, controlled its inception, but Sam stole it, owned it. Me. Everything.

And like Alice, I was down the rabbit hole. And it wasn't a Mad Hatter I was spending time with, but an arguably mad and criminally sexy drummer.

And like Alice, I would never be the same again.

Chapter Three

I didn't really remember getting into the room. Not that I was that drunk. Sam's kiss had somewhat of a sobering effect. Like a survival instinct, like my body was making sure I was able to fully and lucidly comprehend the magnitude of this moment.

I was sober, but not exactly vigilant when my mouth was attached to his.

Our kiss in the car seemed to have no end. He'd stopped it at some point, with stormy eyes and an aura that stifled the air in the car. There was silence as he'd opened my door, the salty ocean air doing little to dampen Sam's scent or bring about whatever sensibility I was known for.

Maybe that was because he kissed me for what seemed like the entire journey to his room.

Which was where we were now.

In his room.

Against the door in his room, more accurately.

He'd slammed me against it and circled both of my wrists with one of his hands, restraining them in his viselike grip before placing them above my head.

His other hand skimmed the silk of my dress, ghosting over my curves. His mouth worked against mine, relentless, brutal, beautiful. Whatever gentleness had existed in the car belonged to a different man entirely.

This wasn't the Sam who stroked my cheek and made jokes about *Twilight*. No, this was the Sam whose eyes were almost black with desire, who slammed me against a wall so hard my head cracked off it, not painfully but forcefully.

The Sam who was quickly making me forget my own name. Who was making sure I'd never forget his.

The light touch of his hand was gone when he found my breasts, kneading them roughly, exquisitely, tweaking my nipple so hard I cried out into his mouth.

He broke our kiss and grinned, but not with humor. It was like the Devil would before he collected your soul.

And I was going to give it willingly.

"I'm going to taste you. Every inch of you. And you're not going to move your fuckin' hands," he commanded.

I couldn't even if I wanted to. I was paralyzed the moment his mouth fastened over the thin fabric of my dress to suck on my nipple, graze it and send shockwaves through my entire body.

His hand snaked down my waist, slipping under my dress as it had in the car but this time with a destination, a purpose in mind. I welcomed it. I craved it. I feared I'd die without it.

Then, when his magic fingers almost reached the edge of my panties, I froze.

Completely and utterly.

He noticed it.

Immediately.

Like he was somehow in tune with my body, like that moment in the car.

Black eyes cleared and he locked his gaze with mine.

"You good, Thumbelina?" His voice was thick, muffled, but lucid. Concerned. "Did I hurt you?"

He straightened fully, gently grabbing my hands and pulling them down so he could make circles on my wrists with his thumb.

"No!" I said immediately and much louder than was necessary. "No, that was... lovely," I said on a softer tone.

His eyes gentled and he grinned lazily as his eyebrow rose.

"Lovely?" he repeated, moving forward to trace his fingertip along my collarbone.

I nodded rapidly. "Yes, I just have to... um...." I pointedly looked for a bathroom door. "Freshen up," I finished lamely.

Who even freshened up? That was shit from the movies; no one actually did it in real life, unless they had forgotten to shower or shave or something that day.

I hadn't.

Oh God, now he'd think I'd forgotten to shower or shave.

He was going to think I was hairy and smelly.

Good one, Gina. Way to ruin the moment.

Sam grinned lazily again, his face dawning with understanding. It wasn't a grin that made it seem like he was contemplating the fact that I had a feminine bikini line situation. He didn't step back—no, he stepped forward, so his entire body imprinted onto mine and he pressed his very obvious arousal against me.

I almost melted. Right there at his feet.

His mouth brushed against mine, not kissing me, just touching slightly as he spoke. "Okay, babe. But for the record, you're pretty fucking *fresh* already." He took an audible inhale that was so personal and erotic my knees quivered. "Smelling you alone makes me hard as a fuckin' rock," he declared.

Then, thankfully before I could do anything frightfully embarrassing like collapse at his feet, he stepped back, eyeing me like a wolf. He grabbed my hand and wordlessly led me into the giant suite.

I distractedly took in the king-size bed and the armchair, the simple white décor, the longue area opening onto a balcony where the waves crashed against the sand.

It was beautiful.

But I had other things on my mind right that second.

Sam stopped us in front of the bathroom and yanked me into his body in a motion that juxtaposed the slow and gentleness of before, which disrupted my sense of gravity entirely.

I definitely would've fallen to my feet if it weren't for Sam's arms around me. His lips crashed against mine for a quick but life-shattering kiss.

"Don't be long," he ordered. "I'll miss you too much."

The last words were teasing, light, jarring me with their contrast to the intensity of the kiss.

Then he stepped back.

And I didn't move.

Just stared at him.

At the tattoos snaking down his arms, covering every inch of his sinewy flesh, even his hands, knuckles, the insides of his fingers.

"Gina." He said my name softly and it hit me right in the stomach.

My head snapped up.

Sam was grinning. "Though I'm not hating you checking me out—like *at all*—I thought you had things to do. And if you keep looking at me like that much longer, I won't be able to control my motor functions. You'll be on that bed, naked, within the next ten seconds, whether you like it or not," he continued with darkness dancing in his eyes. "And I promise, you'll like it."

The words sobered me once more.

"Right," I whispered. "Yes."

He smiled at me once more, but not a Sam smile I was used to. One the world was used to. This was new. Different. It wasn't for the world. It was just for me. And not up for dissection right at that minute. So I gathered it up and carefully stored it away with everything else.

I darted into the bathroom, slamming the door and flattening myself against it.

I wasn't in there because I was having some kind of crisis about what I was doing, about the magnitude of all this—though that was coming at me like an impending tsunami. But I was only at the yellow warning zone right then. We wouldn't have a code red until after the fact. I was going to make sure of that.

Nor was I freaking out about the brightness of the lights in the hotel room and the fact that in order to have sex, I'd have to be naked.

In front of Sam. The muscled rock god who'd been shirtless in *GQ* not one month back.

No, it wasn't that exactly, though now that I focused on it, it made me slightly dizzy.

It was the process of getting undressed. He'd have to take my dress off, obviously. And what he'd find was a rather boring white bra with a sprinkling of lace on the sides, which wasn't ideal, though neither was it cause for concern. No, it was what almost met the bra.

My giant fricking panties, which had been compressing my internal organs all night.

The pain had been rather uncomfortable at first. Then there was tequila. Then there was Sam. He was like a physical version of Advil.

And Sam could not see these panties that could be mounted on a small sailboat.

No.

The prospect of him seeing the untoned and slightly jiggly belly underneath was scary but not mortifying. No, it was a woman's stomach. A woman who actually ate. Who adhered to the Marilyn Monroe shape as opposed to the women strutting down a runway so emaciated you could count their ribs.

I wasn't proud of it, but I wasn't ashamed either.

What I was ashamed of was that I'd gone to great lengths to hide that. And when Sam peeled it off and my stomach jumped at him, he would notice the whole false advertising thing. Sam did not need to see them.

So I was in somewhat of a dire situation.

First thing was to get the offending panties off.

I hooked my thumbs into the top of them and with a considerable effort peeled them down my body and stepped out of them. It took about five straight minutes.

They were *tight.*

I let out a full and unobstructed breath for the first time since I'd put the torture device on. I'd totally taken the full use of my lungs for granted.

I stared downward. And then panicked.

The panties weren't small or delicate, and I couldn't hide them anywhere.

Purse! I thought, having a lightbulb moment.

I looked around the bathroom. My purse wasn't there. What kind of self-respecting girl was I? Everyone brought their purse into the bathroom with them. It was girl law. It was half the reason why we lugged them around everywhere.

Not me.

Mine was on the floor at the door.

Where I'd dropped it the moment Sam had slammed me into it.

"Fuck," I muttered under my breath. I didn't exactly curse often, a habit I'd gotten into considering my job. I couldn't be swearing around little humans who had minds like sponges.

But this was definitely an "oh fuck" moment.

I bent down at the waist to snatch the panties off the floor, then whirled around to inspect the opulent bathroom.

There were two sinks in front of me, polished marble with a countertop full of hair products and all sorts of toiletries.

I shook my head, smiling.

Classic Sam.

Wayward pieces of silver were scattered on the marble, thrown haphazardly as if they weren't likely worth thousands of dollars.

I had one pair of diamond earrings my father, in a rare moment of parental generosity, had given me when I graduated college. They stayed safely in my jewelry box. I didn't even wear them. Not that I had any occasions for diamonds anyway.

Which was not my concern at that juncture. My concern was destroying or hiding the giant panties I had thought were a good idea at the time. Even in my fantasies I didn't think I'd find myself in any sort of situation where I'd be taking my dress off.

I continued my scan of the bathroom. There were no cupboards. There was a toilet and a huge walk-in shower, but nowhere to hide underwear the size of Texas.

I looked at the toilet. Then to the panties in my hand.

No, I couldn't flush them. They'd likely back up the entire plumbing to the town of Amber.

Just as I was about to give up hope, a gentle breeze kissed the clammy skin at the back of my neck.

I whirled around once more.

A window!

Salvation.

It was open enough to let the wind through. A small crack.

I rushed over to it and pushed it as far as it would go so I could look down. Luckily there weren't any balconies underneath, just piping and an inlet where the sand came right up to the building.

I would somehow make a plan to retrieve them in the morning; I didn't condone littering, and I didn't want them to find their way to the ocean and kill a small school of fish.

Before I could think too hard about it, I dropped them. They fluttered like a plastic bag in the wind before settling on the sand below.

Then without even so much as a glance in the mirror, I stepped over to the door and opened it.

I'd expected him to be lying on the bed in some sort of seductive position. Maybe naked. With some stupid grin on his face and a one-liner ready. I wouldn't have put it past him to have a rose clutched between his pearly whites.

What I didn't expect was to see his naked tattooed back—not expected but incredibly welcomed—his front facing the ocean that was blanketed in shadow. The white curtains flowed silently in the breeze, salty air lightly fragrancing the room.

If he heard the door open, he didn't let on.

It was unnerving, seeing him so deep in thought, seemingly lost in his own head. When you've only seen someone in the company of others, in the company of thousands, and on television screens and magazine covers, the weirdest thing you could witness is them being normal. Being unremarkable. Doing what we all do, contemplating life and everything and nothing at the same time. Having moments to themselves when you only considered their moments with everyone.

My earlier bravado disappeared with that observation. The fever storm of the kiss and the desire and darkness in his eyes had disappeared. Now came the realization that we were alone.

With each other.

I was *alone* with Sam Kennedy.

And I wasn't thinking that like the countless girls who had been in my situation would've thought that. Not the Sam Kennedy who was the drummer for Unquiet Mind, who'd been to the White House, who'd won Grammys, who consistently behaved badly in front of the cameras to make him rock's resident mischief maker. I didn't think about those labels or his bank accounts, his connections or his fame.

No, this was Sam Kennedy, who'd once lent me a pen in English lit and who'd told a stupid joke to cheer me up when he came across me crying after some idiot girls made comments about my weight.

I still remember that moment in the deserted halls like it was yesterday.

I hadn't even realized he was standing in front of me. Which before this moment I would've considered impossible. I had a Sam radar and knew where he was at all times. Because when I knew where he was, I could place myself as far away as our small high school afforded.

But not now.

I had been focusing on the ugly words Stacy, resident mean girl of Amber High, had treated me to. It wasn't like I didn't know it was all true, but it hurt nonetheless, hearing it out loud. Having someone else broadcast it.

I didn't notice him until he spoke, his head turned, watching the gaggle of Kate Spade–toting hyenas walk away.

"I have this theory that if you cut off all her hair, she'd look like a British man," he said, putting on a heavy California accent and excellently quoting Mean Girls.

It was so perfect, so meant for the moment and so unexpected that it made me remember the humor in the ridiculous situation. I giggled, wiping my eyes with the heels of my hands and rubbing my glasses with my shirt once that was done. When I put them on, he was in focus.

Sam.

The boy I'd been crushing on because he was so unashamedly different with his black-painted nails, his shiny long hair, his jewelry. And his attitude toward it all. His presence.

And he was talking to me.

Laughing with me.

He playfully shucked me on the shoulder. "Feel better now? Laughter is the best medicine, I hear." His nose screwed up slightly as he thought, and even he managed to make that hot as heck. "Though my mom's Valium is pretty good too." He winked.

I let out another giggle, not sure if he was serious. He kind of looked serious. And Sam Kennedy never followed any rules and was always getting into trouble. Which was why I hardly ever ran into him. I stayed away from trouble, and excitement, and fun.

Everything, really.

"Laughing is good. I'll save hard drugs for a real crisis. I won't credit a substance abuse problem to empty-headed girls," I said, surprising myself at my words and the quantity of them. I tried not to speak much. Well, that wasn't exactly the case. No one ever really talked to me much, so that resulted in me not speaking much. But I didn't exactly invite chats considering I walked around reading a book almost 100 percent of the time. Or maybe I walked around with my nose in a book because that made it feel better than walking around with nothing and realizing I was on my own. It was a real chicken and egg situation.

Whatever it was, I'd reached my unofficial quota of words for the day on Sam Kennedy. The Sam Kennedy. The coolest boy in school. And not a label made from the mishmash of supposed qualities forced upon us by pop culture that defined what was "cool." No, he subverted every one of those paradigms, and that was it. What gave him his edge. He was himself, without any outside influence.

Or it seemed that way from the outside, anyway. I knew from experience that what we saw on the outside could be calm and beautiful while an ugly and blackened storm raged on the inside.

But I didn't think that was the case. Maybe there was a storm, chaos, but it wasn't ugly. He was genuine.

It helped that he was also one of the hottest guys I'd seen up close.

Well, not counting Killian Decesare, but I was too scared to get too close to him. Not that he'd given me any reason to be, but I could taste it. His menace. He was beyond my comprehension.

Not Sam, though.

He smiled and laughed with me, and then his eyes turned serious, glancing at the backs of the girls who'd made a comment about my weight and glasses. Original. Why steer away from a great tradition of bullying girls because of their dress size? It wasn't like society had evolved.

Then again, high school was a different ecosystem entirely, which meant different rules applied. Or the same ones did and they just never changed.

"They're jealous," he murmured.

I let out an unladylike snort. "Yeah, jealous," I agreed sarcastically.

He frowned at me. "They are. Because they're so fucking unoriginal and plastic. They're cutouts of each other because it's easier than figuring out who the fuck they are. You, on the other hand, know exactly who you are. And that, my beautiful friend, scares the shit out of them. Do you know what scared animals do when they're cornered? They strike out with whatever they can. And it's nasty and ugly because they know they won't win. Not in the long run, at least." He winked at me. "You're an original. Own it."

And then he sauntered off. Just like that. Like he hadn't just blown my mind and made me fall completely utterly in love with him.

People might dispute that. That you can't fall in love in a moment, in a single conversation. But that was the thing. Love wasn't uniform, so there was no blueprint for how it was meant to go. No way it was meant to fit on you. So when you were a troubled teenage girl, with her mind half in books to escape real life and half to give her tools to navigate it, and you added a boy who shouldn't, by rights, even notice that girl but instead saw more than anyone could ever see in one glance? And said it with an unapologetic honesty that was somewhat of a unicorn in the jungle they called adolescence? It was love.

And the rest, as they say, is history.

It was the memory of that unapologetic honesty that gave me my courage. Before I could talk myself out of it, I crossed the room circled his body with my hands.

The taut ridges of his abs pulsed under my shaking hands as his crisp and intoxicating scent cut through the sea air.

He didn't move, just slightly sank back into my embrace.

It was the weirdest and most natural thing to be doing at that precise moment.

There is that cliché about moments and how you should acknowledge them because sometimes a moment can be your life. And that one, where neither of us spoke, where we somehow lingered in-between the people we were and who we wanted to be, in honest contentment, was life. Or a slice, a morsel of what I imagined the whole thing was all about.

What all those great authors and poets were all about.

And then it was gone.

Because something else rushed in.

Sam.

He moved, quickly so I was no longer embracing him, and then he was owning me. I didn't even realize we were on the bed until I felt the cool comforter against my skin.

My naked skin.

At some point during the journey between the balcony and the bed, Sam had divested me of my dress, or I had divested myself of it.

Whichever one it was, the feeling of his bare skin on mine while he kissed the sense out of me was beyond perfection.

Then he was gone—his body, his heat, everything. He pushed up, regarding my body with hungry eyes. And I didn't shrink away from the gaze like I expected I would. No, not when I could taste it. His appreciation, his desire. His simple gaze was anything but that. It made me feel beautiful. Perfect. Like all my imperfections added up to something.

And I'd forgot them all. My insecurities. My misgivings and my worry about how exciting I'd be in bed when I was competing with all the other girls that came before me. Because it was physically impossible to feel insecure when a man looked at you like that.

His eyes flared to midnight when they went lower.

All the way lower.

"No panties?" he rasped. "You saucy little minx. Holy fuck, if I'd known that earlier, I wouldn't have even gotten out of the car. Or the fucking parking lot," he growled.

I bit my lip, deciding to let him think I was adventurous enough and that my hips were smooth enough to wander around a wedding wearing no panties.

This was not exactly the time or place to discuss the truth.

"I'm tasting you. Now," Sam declared, voice thick.

And then I descended into something I called the Sam Haze. Or other people might like to call earth-shattering, mind-blowing, life-changing sex.

And it *was* life-changing.

For the better.

And then later for the worse.

Chapter Four

"Texas?" he repeated, as if the word itself, not just the location it represented, offended him personally. "Why in Hannah Montana's name would you want to live *there*?"

I blanched, feeling the need to defend my life and chosen home. "It's peaceful. Quiet."

I didn't know what time it was. Very late. Or very early, depending on how you looked at it. I was tucked into Sam's chest and he was playing with tendrils of my hair. We were both naked. Naturally.

And I didn't care. Not one bit. It was like he'd not only given me multiple orgasms, but everything I worried about, all of that stuff that stifled me from really *living*, had floated away in that moment regarding the sea.

I was still in that moment. Nothing else existed.

Apart from Sam, and me. And Sam asking me where I was living. And obviously not being impressed by my chosen location.

He scoffed. "Peace, if you hadn't noticed, is the reason for all wars. Or the pursuit of it. People who are chasing that little rabbit at the dog track, not realizing they're playing someone else's game. Until the race is over. Then it's too late." He eyed me. "It's too late because you're dead. End of the race equals end of life, babe," he clarified.

I screwed my nose up at him. "I get the metaphor, Sam."

"You may get the metaphor but do you get *it*?"

"What?"

"Life?"

I didn't move from his arms but lifted my head slightly to regard his expression, expecting a smile or twinkling eyes. But this was the other Sam. The naked Sam. Not just physically but emotionally. So I answered as the other Gina, who was also naked in more ways than one. "As much as anyone can. Not that I think anyone can truly 'get' it. I like solitude. It's hardly a death sentence."

My words came out light, meant as a joke, but they were not taken as one.

"That's exactly what it is," he replied solemnly. "Solitude is a prison for the lonely and the damned. Which are you?"

It shocked me. The insightful, almost philosophical statement. The words themselves, and the tone. More appropriately the change in the tone. From playful, almost empty words to somber ones that filled the room.

The shock from this combination caused a pause in my response, though through the course of the night, long pauses seemed to have become my norm. I had been retreating to my high school self, sucking in air and clutching silence like a shield. And back to myself with him, when that shield broke and tattered with his hateful words, yet still the silence remained. But this was different, though. Instead of being the weapon of an insecure girl or a battered woman, it seemed to be an instrument of a content one. Of one slightly confounded at the situation in which she found herself.

And moreover, Sam seemed content to give me my pauses. Like time was just another currency he had to throw around, another perk of being a rock star.

I blinked at him, my shyness urging me to break his gaze,

to find solace by curling away from the reflection of myself that I saw. I worried it would be like Medusa seeing her own reflection and that being her destruction.

But I found it.

Courage.

Or maybe he gave it to me.

That was a troubling thought.

One that would have to wait till later.

Even the rich could run out of currency.

"Which one is it, Thumbelina?" he asked softly, calling me the name I'd yet to ask the reason for.

"I don't think I'm damned," I said just as softly.

He searched my face. "Going to agree with you on that one. If you're damned, then there's not even a scrap of hope for people like me. Not that I want nor need hope." He paused. "So it's the second. Beautiful girl like you doesn't deserve to be lonely. Not that I want to bring him up at this precise moment, but I feel like it's needed. What about the boyfriend? Ronald?" His tone was teasing yet held an edge.

One that cut through my initial confusion. "Roland," I corrected.

"That's what I said," he huffed.

I smiled nervously. "I've got a confession to make," I told him, darting my eyes away as my shyness and uncertainty returned when confronted with my lie.

"This isn't your real hair?" he asked, tugging lightly on the strand he'd been toying with. "Well, your wig guy is a genius. You can't even tell."

I rolled my eyes and smiled nervously. "I'll pass on your compliments," I replied dryly. I sucked in a breath. "Roland isn't my boyfriend," I began.

His hand stopped moving. "What, is he your husband?" he asked, his voice cooled down to arctic as he yanked at my left, naked hand to inspect it for telltale jewelry.

I smiled nervously again. "No," I said quickly. "I'm not married to Roland." Then I laughed. "I, um, couldn't be married to him. Because he doesn't technically... exist," I said, my face flaming.

Sam was silent for a second, a long one that had me feeling sick and ready to burst out in hives. I cursed myself for my stupidity and for being such a nerd. An honest one at that. Why couldn't I have just carried on the lie? It wasn't like he truly would've found out. I wasn't like we were going to last longer than the sunrise, despite the idiotic hope I had been nursing. We had an expiration date. The chubby kindergarten teacher from Texas and the sexy-as-sin rock star who set the world on fire.

"Well, thank Buddha," he said finally.

In my surprise, I found the courage to meet his eyes. "What?"

"I'm glad he doesn't exist, because that means I'm not going to fuck up my hands smacking him around for not treating you right. Of course he doesn't exist. No man has this in his bed and lets it roam around to fucking parties—"

"Weddings," I corrected.

He waved his hand dismissively. "Wedding, party, same thing. Both have cake, booze, and horny chicks. And guys. So yeah, no man with two balls, two heads and one brain is going to let you walk around a fucking *grocery store* without him, let alone a party."

"So you're not mad?" I asked.

He raised his brows. "Why would I be mad?"

"Because I made up a fake boyfriend based on the gunslinger in one of my favorite Stephen King novels of all time," I blurted.

He stared at me for a beat, and then his chest vibrated

beneath me with the power of his laughter. He kept eye contact the whole time, and somehow it comforted me from being embarrassed. It wasn't a cruel laugh; he was technically laughing *at* me, but it still felt nice, intimate. Like a real couple on a Sunday morning, just living life and being happy together.

Natural.

"Why Stephen King?" he asked when he'd gained control of himself.

I frowned at him. "What do you mean?"

"I mean, if you're going to pick yourself a book boyfriend, then shouldn't you have gone with Nicholas Sparks or Nora Roberts? Not the guy who writes about killer clowns."

I screwed up my nose. "You read Nicholas Sparks?" I asked, teasing.

He screwed up his own nose. "Of course not!" he defended. "The movies are much better."

I giggled.

"Hence my question. Why didn't you go with Noah or Landon?"

I smiled and decided not to tease him mercilessly for knowing the names of the heroes of both *The Notebook* and *A Walk to Remember*.

I regarded him soberly before explaining, "Because if I wanted to magic someone into existence, it wouldn't be a run-of-the-mill man who is all hearts and flowers. I want someone from a forgotten age, from a different world," I said without thinking. "Also because Stephen King is an almighty god and if I relate to anything in my life, it's him."

He grinned, but it was the same one he had used before I went into the bathroom. Not exactly amused or cheeky, but something else. Something deeper. "If I'm not mistaken, the dude writes about killer dogs, killer cars, and creepy twins in hallways."

I nodded. "Among other things. But within the supernatural is the most poignant commentary of natural life I've ever read. It's like exploring the human condition through inhuman situations."

"But with cars that have minds of their own," Sam teased.

I hit his shoulder, which was like hitting a brick wall. I was pretty sure I did more damage to my hand than him. "Have you read any of his books?" I challenged.

"I have not. I'm a busy man, you know. I'm not sure if you've heard, but I'm kind of famous," he stage-whispered.

I rolled my eyes. "Fame isn't an excuse. You'll read it the same as anyone else. And just like everyone else, you'll get something different out of it. Maybe a lesson on not being so arrogant," I teased back.

He rolled me over and I let out a little squeal as he pinned me to the bed.

"Arrogant, huh?" he murmured, voice thick.

"Extremely," I whispered.

"Hmmm." He nuzzled my neck. "Well, I think I've got my work cut out for me if I'm to change your opinion of me," he said before he kissed me.

He did indeed have his work cut out for him. And come morning, he would've changed my opinion of him. Completely and utterly.

Just not in the way he intended.

"We should sleep at some point," I mumbled against Sam's skin.

We'd just finished round four, or was it five? I'd lost count of the amount of orgasms. My body felt like lead. But it also felt lighter than it ever had. Worshipped.

Sam grunted against my head. "Sleep is for sissies," he murmured.

I laughed. Truthfully, I didn't want to go to sleep. Because welcoming oblivion would mean this, whatever this little ripple in time and space was, would end. And the morning would change everything. In the darkness, there was just us and the soundtrack of the ocean, the response of our bodies. There was no other outside world.

The darkness had a way of doing that. Making everything infinite and also tiny at the same time.

So sleep was not looking like a preferable option.

"You know what you said before about solitude being for the lonely or the damned?" I asked after a compatible silence.

"Yeah."

"Well, if that's what you think about solitude, then wouldn't you say the same theory applies to the opposite?" I asked.

He lifted his head slightly. "What do you mean, babe?"

"I mean those who isolate themselves are one of the two, according to you. So I am going to argue that those who surround themselves with people are in the same situation. Being around people all the time, relentlessly, it's kind of like being constantly alone," I said.

I'd been chewing over that thought ever since he'd asked me his question. Because it didn't come from a vacuum. It came from experience, as most things did.

"You talking about me, Thumbelina?" he asked, moving me in his arms so he could make eye contact. His irises were still dark with residual desire, sparkling in the moonlight, pensive as he regarded me.

"Yes," I admitted, deciding not to dance around the question. I was sure naked honesty was something he was rarely ever presented with. "Peace and chaos are sisters, after all. I would say that the extremity of being known by no one might be the same as being known by everyone. No man is an island, Sam."

He grinned. "True. But this man can buy one, and that's technically the same thing."

His comment was classic Sam, deflecting the truth with humor. But he wasn't convincing even himself at that moment, so I waited.

"You know what it's like to be loved by millions of people?" he asked, his eyes dancing with a childish glint. Perhaps if my soul hadn't been as broken as it was, my heart as jaded and scarred, I would've seen that glint and only that. Appreciated the package on the outside.

But it had and I did, so I saw more.

I considered his question, holding his eyes with a courage I didn't know I possessed.

"Lonely. I would say it's incredibly lonely to be loved by millions of people," I said decisively.

He flinched. Not in pain, like my words had caused a physical blow, but in surprise, and if I wasn't mistaken, appreciation and respect.

He blinked once, twice, before the mirage of intensity disappeared from his face and his lazy smile returned.

But now that I'd seen it, I knew he wasn't just a rock star—he was an actor too.

"Babe, you're telling me you think that having the whole world obsessed with you is *lonely*?" he asked.

I blinked back at him. "I would say it's most likely the loneliest feeling in the world," I replied. "Because love can do one of two things, depending on the kind. And the kind millions have for you? It's empty. And selfish. Because they want to take from you, from the person they imagine you to be. They don't care who you *are*, only what you *represent*. They care about the cardboard cutout of you. And not being loved at all is almost as bad as being loved for the idea of you. For the mold. Not for what you are. An original." I ended the last part on a whisper, as some kind of warped test in a practice of emotional self-flagellation. Alluding to that moment that meant so much to me all those years before to see if it clicked with him, if he held those memories of me anywhere.

His face didn't betray much but the careful and intense perusal of my own. And my words. His eyes flickered with something for less than a moment, and then it, whatever it was, was gone.

I pretended not to feel hurt and disappointed. But I wasn't as good an actor as Sam was. Even his Academy Award–winning girlfriend wasn't.

He let out a long sigh, yanking my body upward so he could find purchase on my mouth. And he didn't stop kissing me. Not until we'd exhausted our bodies so that we drifted into oblivion without much choice in the matter. My last thought was of the test. And whether his response noted a pass or a fail.

Inconclusive.

Or maybe that was just wishful thinking in the infinite darkness.

Everything looked different in the soft morning light. In the movies, it illuminated the slender and tanned body of a woman tangled in the sheets with her lover. Her hair splayed artfully over the pillow, glistening in the sunshine like flecks of gold. The fabric of the bedding covering nothing but the bare minimum, the man she was tangled up with covering the rest. The man himself muscled and with ruffled hair, a five o'clock shadow, a presence that gravitated beyond the screen while he clutched the woman tightly, for he knew that he couldn't let such a creature go.

Creatures were exactly what they were.

Unicorns.

Because the soft light of day didn't exist. Nor did unicorns, much to my disappointment. No, it was only the cold light of day.

Which was what I was currently enjoying.

I was half in fantasy, half clutched by the claws of reality. The fantasy being that I was, in fact, tangled up with the afore-mentioned man. The man with tattoos, stark against the crisp white sheet. Exploding life from beyond the fabric, from his naked skin. Even still clutched by the sandman, he radiated it. Movement. Every inch of his body was covered in it. Both of his muscled arms. A huge angel playing a drum set spanning across his broad chest, snaking down his six-pack. His neck was circled with the intricate wings of the angel, script threading delicately through the feathers. I didn't have the time I craved to make out all of it, but I did read one line.

'Come as you are, as you were, as I want you to be, as a friend, as a friend, as an old enemy.'

It struck a chord of recognition within me and at the same time touched a part of me that usually only a great book could do. I shelved it and regained my hungry consumption of the naked and sleeping Sam.

His face didn't need ink or art because it *was* art. Not sharp or carved from marble like so many novels liked to describe the ultimate man as. He did have a strong jaw, but the rest of him was soft edges. Subtleties. Ironic, since Sam was the op-posite of subtle. And that's what it added up to. The slightly tanned skin, the shadow of stubble glistening in the light. Long black lashes. Brows that were perfect, not too busy but enough to frame his masculine face. Midnight hair flopped across one of his eyes, having escaped from its famed bun. I liked it messy and wild; it was more… Sam. Unlike the oh-so-famous bun—an unpopular opinion, I was sure.

Heck, it was probably insured for five million dollars.

Everything, on its own maybe, was subtle. But put together, placed in perfectly imperfect harmony, it was Sam. And that was from an outsider's perspective.

He was hot, sexy, iconic—whatever the masses called him these days.

But when you knew more, when you *saw more*, you couldn't define him by that.

He was beautiful. Simple as that.

And as complicated as that.

And then there was me. I wasn't beautiful. There were times, when I had a great makeup day and my hair decided to cooperate, that I felt it. In that temporary fleeting way that lasted as long as a long-wear lipstick. I never felt ugly.

Just ordinary.

And I was okay with it. At peace.

Until I woke up with a tattooed rock god next to me and wanted to crawl into my own skin and not come out until I'd morphed into some sort of butterfly, or at the very least a Victoria's Secret model.

My skin didn't glisten in the sunshine. It looked soft and dimply next to the tight and defined inked muscle mass beside me. The sinewy forearm thrown over my jiggly belly taunting me with its lack of body fat. I was sure my hair was mussed into a wild tangle that *was not* sexy bed hair, probably erring more on the side of deranged mental patient. I hadn't taken my makeup off last night, so most of my mascara was likely painting my cheeks, channeling Alice Cooper and not pulling it off nearly as well.

Sam's eyelashes, the ones I'd been admiring as well as coveting, fluttered. I froze as he blinked once, twice. I felt like a total creep, lying there watching him wake up, but I couldn't help it. I even grasped the soft, pale skin on my arm to give it a small pinch to make sure I hadn't just overdosed on tequila and was really drooling and unconscious on the dirty sofa in the Sons of Templar clubhouse. The small lance of pain told me that wasn't the case.

So I just kept watching Sam wake up.

He regarded me lazily at first, smiling wide in an honest and beautiful type of way. Like he somehow didn't notice the dimples, the pale skin, the bird nest that was likely my hair and my no doubt horrendous morning breath, which was why I was breathing though my nose.

There were a lot of times a person could lie. I learned that the hard way, like people learn most things. People lied about feelings, about love, happiness, unhappiness—about *everything* to gain power. Control. Because they were troubled and scarred from whatever the world had done to them to make them need that. Or because those people were just douchebags.

But once you could recognize the lies and liars, it made it easier to spot the truth. And first thing when someone woke up, before their brain could catch up, that was the truth.

It was one of the first signifiers of before, with *him*. One I'd missed for a long while, one that may have saved me a lot of time and heartbreak. But then again it was the hard way that I'd needed to learn after all.

But I did recognize the hard, cold and indifferent looks eventually.

So Sam's expression shocked me—in a good way. There was nothing cold or hard or indifferent about the soft, affectionate, almost reverent look Sam was treating me to.

And it felt like that.

A treat. One that was even better than a Reese's Peanut Butter Cup while I was PMS-ing.

And then, much like that Reese's Peanut Butter Cup, it was gone quicker than I imagined or wanted, and I could only taste the memory of the sweetness on my tongue.

It was a strange kind of backward dance with my past. Simon would start with that calculating sociopathic glare, then quickly transition to the affectionate and loving mask, which I eventually ripped off. With Sam, he started off with that genuine warmth, but then I almost got frostbite from the rapid cooling and hardening of his expression.

I swallowed, trying to convince myself I was imagining it, though somehow convincing myself this couldn't be good because all I was used to was bad. When that's all you knew, that's what you came to expect. It's easy to convince yourself of the worst, so much so that you can manifest it. Expecting good is harder than fitting into the skinny jeans you brought when you thought you'd drop a dress size just to realize the opposite.

So I decided to expect good.

Instead of flinching away from the stare, which was my first instinct, I willed myself to remember the last twelve hours and the utter magnificence in their normalcy and their extraordinariness.

"Hey," I whispered, my voice like my face: naked, open.

He explored my face in a way that punctured every bit of my exposed skin, both emotional and physical. I had the urge to glance in a mirror to see if the pinpricks from the iciness of that stare drew blood.

"Mornin', sweetheart," he murmured. His voice was husky. Sexy. But it was wrong.

Very wrong.

It was empty. Unfamiliar. Polite but detached.

The Sam of last night may have seemed like a stranger at times, especially when he'd forbidden me from coming for what felt like an eternity, when his eyes hard turned so black that midnight had a rival. When he pushed my body to the edges of pleasure and pain. But underneath it, somewhere, was still Sam. *My* Sam. The teenager. The man. The rock star.

But this was a complete and utter stranger. And worse, that's how he was treating me. Like I was someone he'd dragged in from the random masses without even bothering to learn my name, let alone where I was from or what genre of books I liked to read.

He effortlessly rolled off the bed in a motion that deposited me roughly onto the soft mattress, still warm from his body even though I expected it to be glacial.

By the time I pushed myself back up onto my elbows to stare at him and hope that I was imagining this, the bathroom door was closing.

I stared at it. Listened to the shower running and the gentle humming of a song I didn't recognize.

It was nice.

For a second.

Then I remembered the truth that even his husky humming couldn't mask.

Yanking the sheet up to cover my exposed body, I inspected those seconds, the ones between the mask. What had changed in those seconds? I hadn't said anything, hadn't done anything. Everything about me had stayed the same. Despite that, those logical conclusions, my vulnerable brain told me it was me. That I was somehow responsible for it. Or more accurately, my imperfections. That split second of blame, of self-hatred or self-awareness, was familiar in such a way that I wanted to crawl out of my own skin to escape it. But as quickly as it came, I banished it. I had spent enough time blaming the actions of selfish males on my own shortcomings. Such blame had caused a lot of wounds to an already fragile sense of self-worth.

But I knew I needed to save myself. Repair myself. Because

in a lot of the great romance novels, men were the saviors of a woman's life. But in reality, they were more often than not the cause of their destruction.

That's what love was, in the crux of it. Destruction. We all wanted to be in love. Until we were. And then the only thing worse than being in love with someone was the thought of losing that someone.

So I learned—again, the hard way.

That time, no matter how much it hurt, no matter how much my natural instincts told me to crawl into a ball and cry and ask myself why I wasn't good enough, pretty enough, funny enough, thin enough—just *enough*—I fought against that. I would *not* put this on my shoulders.

Anger blossomed from the hurt that had begun to grow. In situations such as this, anger was the safest thing to promote. It protected against hurt.

For a time, at least.

I glared at the door when the shower turned off. Whatever happened in the bed where I thought all of my dreams had come true, it wasn't on me.

But because I was a romantic at heart and I still harbored a sliver of hope, I waited. With my arms crossed protectively over the sheet covering my breasts, I waited. For him to come out with the familiar softening features and tell me he was a bear in the morning, then jump on the bed and make sweet, sweet love to me.

But dreams were free.

Reality was infinitely more expensive.

And painful.

Sam emerged from the bathroom, towel slung dangerously low on his waist, exposing the V that the whole world had seen many times, since he wasn't afraid of exposing the goods. In real life, it was all the more droolworthy, especially with droplets of water trickling down the taut ridges of his inked abs.

His hair was wet too, falling around his shoulders, dripping more water onto his defined pecs. I could've snapped a picture of him with my phone right at that moment and it would've been a perfect *Rolling Stone* cover. Though he'd already done one of those. His tongue had been sticking out from between his crossed drumsticks, his eyes dancing with mischief.

These eyes were empty.

I blinked at him as he glanced at me, dismissed me, and went to the exploded Louis Vuitton tote in the corner.

It would've been funny under different circumstances. The me from last night would've teased him relentlessly for his overpriced and idiotic accessory. But that would've only worked on the Sam from last night.

This was not him.

I swallowed roughly. Found some courage. "Uh, Sam?" I said quietly.

"Yeah, darlin'?" he said without turning.

That hit me in a way an endearment wasn't meant to. Like it was used for mass production, for the girls whose names he didn't remember in the morning.

"Are you... is, uh, everything okay?" I asked, sitting up, feeling more than a little vulnerable naked as he slipped on a pair of ripped jeans, going commando.

He turned around, shirtless, the top button of the jeans undone enough to see the darkness of his hair. Trimmed neatly but still there.

"Sure, everything is righteous," he said, voice light. His eyes roamed over me again, a flicker of something appearing before it left too fast to grab. Which was probably good. I didn't need false hope.

It was like arsenic in those moments.

Of which, unfortunately, I'd experienced many. I'd just never expected it from Sam. From any of the Sams I knew. Even the ones who didn't know me. I would never have entertained the idea that Sam would treat *anyone* like this.

That wasn't him.

Or at least that's what I'd thought.

"You need me to call you a taxi?" he asked, padding over to the other side of his bed, snatching the black phone off it, focusing on scrolling through with his inked thumb.

"A taxi?" I repeated.

He nodded, not looking up. "Yeah, sweetheart. To get you to your car."

"My car," I said slowly. That time it wasn't a question. That time my voice wasn't small and confused and hurt. That time my voice did its best to match the chill in his tone.

He glanced up. "Yeah, well I've got things to do, and I'm sure you do too. Last night was…." That glimmer came back, then left quicker than before. "Fun. But I'm sure you know the deal, Georgia."

Georgia.

He didn't even remember my name.

That cut a lot deeper than last night had.

A lot deeper. Exposing a part of me that I didn't even really know I had.

A part of me that had courage. Or fury. Like chaos and peace, I understood fury and courage to be sisters, or at the very least cousins. Whichever one it was, it let me yank the white sheets back, still smelling of our lovemaking, to expose my dimpled, naked and pale body to the world—and more precisely Sam—without the embarrassment I would've usually been crippled with.

Without a glance at him, I stomped over to the door where my dress lay crumpled, already a skeleton of the night before.

"Yeah, I know the deal," I snapped, snatching the dress off the floor and yanking it over my head. The fabric protested slightly and I was pretty sure I ripped it, but I kept going, hoping the rip wouldn't expose anything important, or embarrassing.

I whirled around to where he was watching me, his phone forgotten. "The *deal* is you're an asshole." I snatched my purse off the ground too, haphazardly grabbing the rogue items that had spilled out of it. "Just because you hit drums with sticks, have some shiny trophies and a few more zeros at the end of your bank account than I do doesn't give you carte blanche to act like this." I waved my hand up and down his sculpted body in disgust. "To throw away who you were before and treat people like dirt. You're still Sam Kennedy from high school, who was nice to everyone and wore silver that turned his fingers green. I'm sure not many people see you like that anymore, including yourself. But *I did*." I grabbed one shoe while searching for the other, finally locating it before having to pry it from underneath the space between the minibar and the floor. "*Did* being the operative word. Now I'll think of you how you're longing to be treated. Like a rock star. Just another one in the crowd. You were original before. Now you're just like everybody else. Plastic and unoriginal. Congratu-fucking-lations. You've made it, Sammy."

On that note, I turned around and fumbled with the lock on the door, pretending my clumsiness wasn't hampering me storming off, then slammed it behind me when I finally got it open.

I didn't let myself cry until much later.

Until I was at home in my adopted town amongst my things, my shelves, and was safe.

Until Sam was thousands of miles away, most likely not thinking of me.

Most likely in the process of forgetting me. Because now

he could truly forget me since he had something to forget. Not that it was important enough for him to do so. I was sure, now that I'd seen what he'd turned into, that scenes like that were just another normal Sunday morning for him.

And I only gave myself a certain number of tears. Then I did what I always did with these memories—I shelved them away to that lonely corner of my mind. But that time I made sure to clear off all the other ones that I'd nurtured up until that morning.

Chapter Five

Sam

One Month Later

Tap, tap, tap, tap.

"So we're going to tentatively plan all of our Europe dates. Killian's head of security, obviously. He's already made it *very* clear that he gets to sign off on every venue. But we've got the first five in the clear."

Tap, tap, tap, tap.

"*Lonely. I would say it's incredibly lonely to be loved by millions of people…. I would say it's most likely the loneliest feeling in the world.*"

The feel of her skin. Of being inside her. Like coming home. All of the music inside of his head, all of the chaos, emptied the moment he locked eyes with her. Her lips, tasting of strawberry. The flushing of her face when he called her "babe." Fuck, the honesty of her face in front of him. Stripped of all intentions, of all pursuits. Not wanting anything but him. The real him. Not the adorned version, the shiny, fucked-up Ken Doll. Not the Sam used for mass production. No, the stripped-down version. The one no one saw. Not even the band. Not even the mirror.

And somehow he'd shown her, shown himself. And then realized what he'd done when he showed that. Then he fucked it up even more than he thought imaginable. Fucked up as bad as he ever had in his life—and he once took home two washed-up child stars who were strung out on meth.

He was the king of fucked-up shit. Usually it was funny. Made for a great story, great headline, great memory.

But this one haunted his steps. The impact of his sticks on his set. Every damn day. Every fucking hour.

His hands itched for something to take the edge off, the craving for that more intense than he'd had in a long while.

The craving for her touch couldn't be recreated by any drug. Battling both was his own personal hell.

Not even the good kind. Kurt Cobain was nowhere to be seen.

Tap, tap, tap, tap.

"We've got the set list. I need you to organize who you've got coming. Which groupies are on which rotation…"

Her face. Fuck, her face when he pretended he forgot her name. Fuck. That was imprinted on his fucking soul. She was stripped bare to him too. Not just in that moment but every fucking moment before that. That's why he'd called her Thumbelina, because she was so delicate, so breakable.

Not weak. No, he saw it in her eyes, the strength that only experience of pain could produce. But not jaded, not ruined by it. Not guarding herself with a mask that everyone seemed to wear. And that's why she was that little beautiful girl. One of a kind. And if he wasn't careful, she'd be crushed in the palm of some asshole's hand.

That, beyond the obvious fact that she was a fucking knock-out, was why he'd made it his mission to take her home. At the beginning, it wasn't to fuck her. He'd wanted to do that the moment he laid eyes on her, of course, but he'd decided he wouldn't. This wasn't a girl you just fucked and politely put in a town car in the morning with a memory to take into her golden years.

This was a girl you held the fuck on to. With both hands. That you took home to your parents. That you made a home with. Had some sort of ending with.

Sam didn't do endings. Happy or otherwise. He was all about the journey, the ride, not the destination. The destination, being stationary, was death.

But that had changed after he watched her. After he watched her throw her head back, laughing at what that fuck Jagger said. Laughed. Like music. Music that exploded through the room in a way Kurt Cobain shouting about life, love, and death just couldn't do.

And he watched that, and the way he saw the other fucking bikers watching, and he had to stop himself from doing something that would most likely get him shot. Or at the very least punched in the face.

He wasn't afraid of a punch to his face; it wasn't his moneymaker. His hands were. And even then, at that moment, he'd have crushed them both against the hard jaws of the biker who was standing way too fucking close to the sun. His sun.

Bullets too. He'd take them.

But it was Lexie's wedding. She'd had enough of bullets.

That thought had set his blood cold. Distracted him of thoughts of her for just a moment.

The memory of his best friend dying right in front of him. The man who considered her his sun dying right in front of him as his sun went out.

The time in the hospital when a part of him died too. When he was faced with it. The reaper. The very real fucking prospect of death. The terrifying reality of it happening. Not to him. He wasn't afraid of that. He wouldn't be here to give a fuck about that. But to someone else who he cared about.

That had been the scariest moment of his life.

And he'd do anything and everything to make sure he wasn't

put in that position again.

Which meant not making a home with anyone but his music and his family. The crowds he played for were bright enough to warm earth ten times over. His earth, at least.

Or so he thought. Until that fucking laugh.

Until that fucking flushed face and electric eyes taking over his vision and her naked proposition.

Even now, the memory of it made his dick hard.

Though it went soft pretty fucking quickly when he remembered what he'd done that morning.

The morning after.

You were original before. Now you're just like everybody else. Plastic and unoriginal. Congratu-fucking-lations. You've made it, Sammy."

Tap, tap, tap, tap.

"Sam! For fuck's sake, will you stop with that incessant tapping?" Mark snapped.

Sam's attention was thankfully diverted from the replay reel of that morning to the present moment. To the room in the towers of their recording company where Wyatt, Noah, Mark, Jenna and some other suits he hadn't bothered remembering the names of were organizing the world tour they were setting off for in a month.

Lexie had been cleared to fly, and although Sam was itching for the oblivion of the crowd to swallow him up, for the music to replace his thoughts, for the drums to drown out the echoes of her words, of his own, he was not happy about going on the tour when Lexie had only just recovered. And yes, the madman who had stalked her, kidnapped her and almost killed her was dead, but the idea of him was still alive. Sure, they were rock gods, but they weren't immortal.

Only music was immortal.

The people who made it were a lot more breakable.

Lexie was the heart of the body that was Unquiet Mind. And—even he could admit it—the brains too. And the beauty. All of it, really.

The rest of them, they were just fucking decoration. She could take over the world on her own. But she didn't want to. She never would. None of them would ever go the way of Guns N' Roses. He was sure Axl, Slash, Duff, Steven and Izzy had thought the same in the glory days, when the money was bountiful, the fans loving and the novelty far from wearing off. But there was something in him, a certainty that he knew he would be playing in Unquiet Mind until he was old and gray. Well after the crowds had moved on to the newer, younger version of him. And his family would be beside him.

Since they were family, Lexie was the little sister they all adored and they eventually gave whatever she wanted to.

And she wanted to tour.

So they were touring.

Sam looked at all the eyes focused on him, his smile already in place. He was an expert at not betraying the battle in his mind to the masses. Even to his family. *Especially* to his family. Because if you couldn't hide your true self from your family, who could you hide it from?

He glanced down at his hands, which had been, of their own volition, tapping his drumsticks against the table, giving the chaos of his thoughts a rhythm of its own.

Everything had a rhythm.

Even chaos.

Especially chaos.

"What?" he played dumb. It was what all the most intelligent people did. "You can't try to scold me when I piss you off. You're the one who insisted I be here. You know what I bring to the table." He played a short Guns N' Roses solo—it was only apt—and then held his drumsticks up with a grin. "In addition to good looks, insurmountable talent, sheer sex appeal, and obviously a smile that even Julia Roberts can't beat, I bring the boredom in face of organization. You didn't give me crayons." He pouted, then held up his sticks. "I had to entertain myself. Which I would rather being doing with the Russian model I've got on speed dial," he lied. "Why do you need me here when we pay you all disgusting amounts of money to do the boring stuff so I can do the fun stuff? The fun stuff that actually seems to *pay all your bills.*"

Wyatt shook his head. Noah grinned.

The suits shifted in their seats.

Mark did nothing but stare at him blankly. Dude had his emotions locked down tight. It was necessary to be a shark, he guessed. Mark was the band's manager, so he was an actual shark; he spent his days biting shit, drawing blood, organizing the band.

"You need to be here because you're part of this band," Mark said dryly. "You need to know what's going on when you go on your world tour. Especially considering you've got an interview coming up in a couple of hours. It would be good for the band to actually know stuff that helps promote the tour that pays for all the *fun stuff.*"

Sam rolled his eyes. "I know plenty of stuff," he replied, standing. Sitting there ignoring all of this talk was not good for his state of mind. He needed a stage or, failing that, a bar.

It just so happened that he had an excellent bar at his house.

"You don't worry your graying head over how I'm going to handle the press." He winked at his publicist. "That's what we pay Jenna for."

Then he left, hoping copious amounts of alcohol might help him escape from those pesky fucking emotions. Those pesky and fucking painful thoughts of her, wondering what she was doing, who she was with.

But, as he knew far too well, hope didn't really exist.

Chapter Six

Gina
One Year Later

"Conrad, where did you get that?" I asked, inspecting the purplish blossom marring the boy's porcelain four-year-old skin. It was just above his elbow, in the fleshy part of his bicep, spanning the size of a hand.

An adult hand.

I didn't let it show in my voice how much that upset me. I had my "teacher voice" firmly in place, though my hands shook a little.

He glanced away from the picture he was scribbling away at to regard his arm. His eyes glazed over it in surprise, as if he'd forgotten it was there. That was the thing with kids—they got hurt easily, most of them screaming bloody murder when it happened, but moments later it was forgotten.

Adults were not the same.

No matter how much I wished it.

If that were the case, I wouldn't still be stinging from something that happened a year ago.

"Oh, I... fell," he said uncertainly, the lie rolling off his tongue bringing an unnatural taste to the air.

Kids barely knew how to lie. Really lie. Not little fibs about how they did, *really truly* brush their teeth before bed or how they weren't even a bit tired. But those weren't lies in the actual sense of the word. The real ones didn't spring from an innocent mind. They weren't instinctual. It was because of the adults in their life who tainted their truth and made lies necessary.

I frowned, a thick heat of anger blossoming in my stomach. Also a profound sadness of the horrors in this world, one of the worst ones staring me right in the face. Tears pricked at the corners of my eyes before I got myself together and remembered my responsibility to the children in my care. My knees cracked slightly as I bent down to the small table where Conrad and some other children were drawing.

The closer I got to the little man, the more my anger built into an inferno. Conrad had messy blond hair, which was never brushed but always seemed to fall like he'd styled it to be a member of a boy band. Four-year-olds weren't obsessed with appearances like us. Sure they loved to play dress-up, but it wasn't for anyone but themselves. They were trying on different images, personas, to see which fit.

That was one of the many reasons I loved teaching kindergarten. Their minds were like a vast garden of possibilities, yet to be poisoned by the pollution of this world's ideologies.

They just *were*. And they believed in everything, until someone or something proved them wrong.

And the fact that this wasn't the first bruise Conrad had come in with, saying he "fell," made it all worse. Any kind of deliberate injury to a child is the most despicable act, but continued abuse of a being who knows nothing but happiness and possibilities is beyond low.

Conrad was the most sensitive of all my students. He was always the one consoling his fellow classmates the minute someone got upset over whatever it was four-year-olds got upset over. In other words, everything. He always asked me about my weekend and worried about the fact that I was a "lonely spinster," obviously a little gem he'd picked up from parents.

Along with a nasty bruise.

I lightly traced the baby skin with my finger, making sure my touch was as light as possible. "Does that hurt, Conrad?" I asked.

He shrugged. "Not so much."

That was another thing that troubled me, him dismissing the pain like an adult spraining their wrist when they'd broken their arm before. It's the "meh, I've had worse" attitude. The "worst" a four-year-old boy should've had was some skinned knees from a playground fall.

Not this.

Not targeted violence.

"You know you can talk to me about anything right, Conrad?" I said softly, watching him work on his picture. "You won't ever get in trouble, I promise. And I'll do everything I can to make it better. To make it go away."

His little fingers slackened their grip on the crayon and he stopped coloring for a moment.

I held my breath.

Then, decision made, he continued to color. "I know, Miss Gina. But I just fell. It was my fault. Daddy says I'm krusty."

I gritted my teeth. "Klutzy?" I offered, correcting him.

He nodded very seriously, then made great efforts to concentrate on his drawing of a monster truck. I took that as my cue. I put my hands on my thighs to push myself up and regard the little blond head.

And then I made a promise to myself that I'd do whatever it took to make sure that little child would never have worse than that bruise.

It was a week later that there came a result from the call I placed to Child Protective Services the day I'd seen the bruise on Conrad's arm.

The result came as a knock at my door late on a Saturday afternoon.

Or, more accurately, a pounding.

I'd just finished my cleaning ritual, which I did every Saturday—I was all about routines—so I was treating myself to a cup of sweet tea and enjoying the last of the rays before the sun disappeared.

I was currently spending time with the magician Kvothe, lost in the fantasy, so the pounding of the door back here on earth made me jump enough for the book to tumble from my hands.

I reasoned that the pounding was for logic, not for anything nefarious. I mustn't have been able to hear a regular knock out on the patio, and the caller had seen my little Beetle in the driveway and knew I was home. They obviously wanted something.

Most people who move away from stifling small towns where everyone knows your business seek refuge in equally stifling but joyfully anonymous cities where they can melt into the crowd and establish themselves as a hip urban dweller.

It had been established that I was not exactly a "follow the pack" type of girl. So, after college, I'd chosen something at random on the map, googled images of the small but picturesque town of Hampton Springs, just an hour outside of Dallas. I applied for a job at the one place they'd had an opening, a kindergarten. I was qualified to teach secondary school students and had planned this gig to be temporary until a slot at the high school or middle school opened up, but it turned out that I loved working with little children. The thought of working with older ones didn't entice me as much anymore, though I did still hold a dream of being an English teacher and being able to discuss my passion every day. Even though high school students of today weren't exactly passionate about Anna Karenina or Tolstoy. Not the average one, anyway.

Everyone knew almost everyone in Hampton Springs. Which meant it didn't cross my mind that the pounding at the door could have nefarious or violent undertones.

I did get the violent undertones from the fist that landed in my face the moment I opened the door.

I had never been subjected to violence before. Despite my home life being less than ideal, to say the least, my parents gave me not so much as a smacked bottom.

Punishments implied some sort of caring on either of their parts. Some sort of active participation in their roles in my life.

But no such thing happened. And instead of running wild like most kids with unlimited slack would do, I made sure I was well behaved. Did my chores, excelled in school, never broke curfew. In fact, I never had a curfew to break. A curfew implied having somewhere to go, which I did not.

So I spent a lot of time at home when I couldn't be with my grandmother. When she died, I spent time buried in a book, mostly on my own. And while a lot of that was emotionally painful, it had nothing on a right hook to the eye.

I wasn't expecting it when I opened the door—who would be? My shock and surprise meant I hadn't found a strong base before the strike, and I therefore ended up cracking my head on the hardwood floor with the force of the blow. Spots exploded in the front of my eyes.

"Bitch!" a strong voice slurred at me.

I rolled onto my back, trying to scoot my booty backward, away from Wayne, Conrad's father.

I recognized his large form and his voice, even though it was obscured by his obvious drunkenness.

His boot in my ribs hampered my motions to crawl back into my house in search of escape or a phone. The pain in my eye remained and more blossomed in my midsection, winding me. I tried to cry out, but it was just motions of my mouth as my lungs struggled to suck in air.

Because I was rendered stationary, Wayne could step into the doorway I was half lying in and grab me by the hair to yank me up to his face. I let out a soundless scream as my scalp erupted in white-hot pain.

His eyes were bloodshot, unfocused, his stubbled cheeks patchy with hair growth, broken capillaries scattered about his face.

"You think you've got a fuckin' right to put your prissy nose in my fuckin' business? Take my *fuckin' son* away from me? You're going to be so sorry you did that," he promised. "You don't have no cop boyfriend to protect you now." He grinned wickedly. Evilly. "In fact, he's most likely to sympathize with me now that he knows what a cunt you are."

I managed to glare at him through the pain, the insults and the ugly words. The glare was fueled by the memory of a small arm bruised by a much larger one. "Oh no, I'll *never* be sorry for what I did," I wheezed. "Every time you hurt me, it cements what a coward you are and makes sure you'll *never* see your son again. I'll make it my mission to ensure that," I gave him a promise of my own.

My words penetrated through his drunken haze and sobered him. But not in a way that invited reason. Men who abused their children had something missing in their brains.

Reason didn't exist, only hateful anger. Violence. Ugliness. So I knew he was going to unleash more of that on me.

I was scared. Terrified, actually. But I was telling the truth—nothing that could happen right now would make me regret my decision. Because the terror and pain I was feeling was what a four-year-old boy had been feeling up until then. Wayne had found someone his own size to pick on, and though I wished it wasn't me, wished it wasn't anyone, I was glad that at least it wasn't Conrad.

That didn't mean I was going to lie down and let a cowardly, sick man hurt me like he thought he had the right to.

No way in hell would I do that.

So just as he reared his hand backward to strike me again, I lifted my knee awkwardly to make contact with his balls. It wasn't near as hard as I would've liked, or what he deserved, but it did the trick.

He cried out in pain, stumbling back and letting me go in the process. My head hit the hard wood of my floor again, painfully and hard. So hard I saw black spots in front of my eyes instead of the white ones of before. I looked around them, gritting my teeth and using my anger and fear to push me upward. I acted on sheer survival instinct, running not into the safety of my house but around Wayne's groaning and writhing body and onto my front lawn.

I was intending to run across the street to my closest neighbors, who just happened to be some of my best friends.

My only friends.

Garth wasn't a big man, but he didn't need to be big. He just needed to be someone a bully wouldn't pick on. One he wouldn't perceive as weaker. My destination seemed an age away, even though my street was small and compact and if I'd had a good arm I could've thrown a stone and hit their front door.

I didn't need to do that. Nor did I need to cross the street and seek solace and protection.

Because those who swore to protect and serve screeched up to the curb right in front of me.

I sighed in relief at the flashing lights and what they represented.

Safety.

Well, that was before the government-issued boot hit the grass I was about to collapse onto.

Safety from the man who'd punched me might be offered here, but not much of it.

Simon had never offered that.

Even though it wasn't a pounding at my door and the ink hadn't even dried on my restraining order, I definitely paused before turning the handle. My newly purchased pepper spray was hidden in my left hand, finger on the trigger.

I mentally reminded myself to get a peephole installed. Or research some sort of security option. Surely in the days of smartphones and drones I could have a more sophisticated way of identifying my callers than a peephole.

Though the technology no doubt existed, my means of purchasing it might not.

Whatever disposable income I had left after bills and savings, I put toward books or little pieces for my house. To create a home. And there wasn't usually that much left over in the first place. Kindergarten teachers in small towns weren't exactly making the big bucks.

I reasoned the chances of me getting punched again in broad daylight on a Wednesday afternoon were relatively low. Especially with Wayne still residing in the lockup we had just outside of town. Hence me opening the door.

I also yearned for a little human contact, despite the black-and-blue bruise spanning my temple and underside of my right eye, showing me just how ugly human contact would be. I wasn't allowed at work because my appearance might "scare the children" in addition to the whole "child's father physically attacked me" scenario. I was put on paid leave until I healed.

Physically I wouldn't take long. The bruises looked particularly nasty now, but they would fade. I knew the emotional ones would take longer. Not just from the beating, but having to deal with Simon when I'd been fragile and scared afterward. Wayne was a buddy of his; that said enough about him. He said he'd turned up because of a text Wayne had sent about me, which made him worried for my safety.

He'd never been worried for my safety before, even when we were together. It was laughable, his superficial concern. I was happy to make my statement quickly and then retreat into my little sanctuary, pretending I wouldn't have to testify or deal with Simon.

My stomach turned slightly at the prospect of Simon being on the other side of the door. That would've been about on par to a fist to the face.

Though it wasn't a fist to the face, I was greeted with a whole lot of angry male when I opened the door.

Precisely the last male in the entire world I expected to be darkening my doorstep.

"What the fuck?" Sam hissed, his entire face turning into a mask of fury as he spotted my own. Not that the bruises were easy to miss. They'd come out terrible. And I did admit they kind of scared me, so I hated to think what they'd do to my little class. Which was why I hadn't put up much of an argument when my boss had firmly suggested I take the week off.

"What are you doing here?" I demanded, blinking rapidly

to make sure Sam on my doorstep wasn't some kind of mirage caused by a delayed concussion.

The doctor had warned me about that. Not a rock star who I'd slept with and then had my heart broken by appearing on my doorstep after a year, the delayed concussion. Pria, my neighbor and friend, had stayed with me the first night and dutifully woke me up every hour to make sure I hadn't lapsed into a coma as a result of an overlooked brain injury.

Not that I needed waking up since I wasn't really sleeping. Hadn't for well on a week.

I came to the conclusion that Sam was not a coma-induced apparition considering he stepped forward, close to me. Close enough for me to feel the heat of his body, inhale his scent and realize that yes, he was really there.

"What the fuck happened to your fucking face?" he demanded, not answering my question. I didn't even know if he'd heard me, or realized I'd spoken. His arm twitched as if he had the urge to lift it and inspect my injury with the gentle touch I knew he had command of.

The shelves rattled.

No. I wasn't allowed to think of that.

"Never mind that," I dismissed, not wanting to go into that whole nightmare in front of Sam. "Why are you here?" I asked coldly. "And how did you find out where I lived?" Now that the surprise was fading, I could hold on to the anger that seeing him brought on.

I found myself presented with yet another one of Sam's many faces. I'd be a liar if I said I hadn't thought of them in the months since that horrible morning. If I'd said that I hadn't dusted off some of those memories and put them back on the shelf, despite all logic and reason.

Since I wasn't a liar—most of the time, at least—I found myself comparing this current face to all the others I'd seen on

Sam. Like the one that horrible morning. This one was hard, carved from granite, but it wasn't cold. No, you could fry a proverbial egg on the heat of his fury. And concern, if I recognized it correctly.

But I didn't have the energy to analyze the subtleties of all the small expressions making up this version of Sam.

I was tired. Tired from dealing with statements, of being in pain, of staring my ex in the face and having to grit my teeth through his false concern that was mingled with undermined comments.

"Why didn't you come to me instead of involving outside organizations? I would've spoken to Wayne. I could've taken care of it. Instead, you decided to put yourself in this situation. Really, Gina," he sighed, shaking his head.

Yeah, he was a cop. And an asshole. Blaming me for getting a kid out of an abusive situation, getting myself into one and putting one of his best drinking buddies behind bars. Though I was sure he'd find a way to get him out.

I worried about that too. Amongst other things.

I was even more tired from dealing with the nice comments that came from my friends the moment they found out what happened. Which was approximately two minutes after Simon had rocked up in his patrol car. Pria and Garth had come out on their front porch at the commotion. I was sure they were more than a little surprised to see that I was the cause, considering in the two years I'd lived there I hadn't caused any commotion—of the violent variety or otherwise.

Then came Pria's insistence that she be with me throughout the whole ordeal, her husband standing sentinel with a grim expression that made me think he somehow blamed himself. Which, even though it was totally ridiculous, was the mark of a caring man.

It had been almost a week since "the incident" and I'd only

just gotten rid of Pria. Not that I didn't appreciate her hovering and concern, but I needed to decompress. Or more accurately compress myself into another world and cocoon myself away from this one.

What I needed didn't factor into the universe's plans, it seemed. Or Sam's.

He appeared to have lost whatever battle he was waging with his left hand as he stepped forward, right into my space, and lightly cupped my injured cheek, eyes glued to the bruise.

"Who. The. Fuck. Did. This?" he gritted out, every word its own sentence. Its own zip code.

I stepped back, the second time in a week I'd had to escape from an angry male on my doorstep. Though I knew this particular one wasn't likely to punch me in the face.

He was able to do much worse than that.

If I let him.

I entertained the idea of punching *him* in the face. He definitely deserved it. But I reasoned I'd probably just break my hand, and I really didn't need another injury.

His jaw hardened at my retreat and his eyes glittered with fury. Thankfully, he didn't try to advance on me. He seemed the same as before. People didn't normally add up to the image you'd built of them in your head. You usually remember them taller, with more muscles, more commanding in presence. Just *more*.

But not Sam.

Imagination, even the likes of mine, was a poor reproduction of the real thing. His hair was messily thrown up into a bun, longer than the last time I saw him. The shades that had been covering his face were abruptly pushed up the second I'd opened the door. He was wearing all black, as usual, a tight black tee decorated with silver chains hanging from different lengths around his neck. The slogan was slightly obscured but still readable, a line drawing of a head with horns with "Bad Samaritan" written in childlike writing underneath. It was tucked behind a thick silver belt buckle on tight, ripped black jeans. They were tucked into scuffed black Doc Martins. On anyone else, such an outfit would look ridiculous. Much like Johnny Depp as Jack Sparrow. He was the only person in the world who could pull of such a persona.

It was out of place in my quiet suburbia street in the middle of nowhere. As was the sleek black convertible parked in my driveway.

The latest Corvette, if I wasn't mistaken.

Sam was anything but inconspicuous.

I crossed my arms, forgetting my one cracked rib. I tried in vain to hide the wince but Sam caught it. He seemed to be making it his mission to imprint me onto his mind.

That time he stepped forward.

"Lift your shirt," he commanded roughly.

"Not even if you took me to dinner first," I shot back, surprising even myself at the venom in my tone. My decision to let my anger go and be Zen had flown out the window the moment Sam came into my orbit and the pain came back. The best salve for pain was anger.

In that situation, at least.

He narrowed his eyes at me. "Either you do it or I do it for you." There was no erotic teasing in his tone, just grim determination.

I eyed him. "You'd force yourself into my home, then put your hands on me and forcefully undress me?" I said calmly. "I've had more than enough of *that* for one week. So I'll respectfully decline your offer that you so kindly packaged as a command."

His entire form stilled. Like he somehow had control over the air around him, even that seemed to hit pause. Like the way it went quiet in the eye of a storm.

Eerie.

Dangerous beyond belief.

"Forcefully undress you?" he choked out, the words apparently physically painful for him to say. Even through the shroud of my fury, they were painful for me to hear. "Did someone—"

"No," I cut him off briskly and simply. Even though I wished petty things on Sam, like someone—maybe me in about ten minutes—would back into his car, I wasn't about to let him think I'd been raped in order to exact some kind of fucked-up revenge on him.

"No. It wasn't like that," I said firmly.

Though I didn't know what it exactly was *like*. Without warning, a replay of that whiskey-drenched breath and those red-speckled cheeks assaulted me. And that time I didn't escape, nor did my ex-boyfriend come and save the day. No, I was dragged farther into my house and was rendered helpless and brutalized....

I snapped my mind from that scenario with a swift intake of breath. Until now, I'd been rather good at compartmentalizing the event, the reason for my stiff midsection and black-and-blue face. I'd buried the reality of it almost as deep as I'd buried Sam. It was as if his appearance had rattled those shelves loose and thrust them upon me.

Whatever it was, it winded me. More than the one cracked rib.

Sam noticed.

I recovered. Or at least tried to. On the surface. I was in the company of a celebrity after all, and appearances meant everything. What wasn't shown didn't exist in the world of the superstar. Which was what Sam was to me now. He wasn't Sam anymore. Not since that morning.

"The man who so kindly tried to give me a free and rather

painful nose job was here on a different sort of business than…
that," I continued. I was ashamed to hear my voice quiver. "He
was here on account of his four-year-old son being taken off
him as a result of a call I made. His four-year-old son who I
teach. His four-year-old son who he, until a week ago, had
been physically abusing."

Sam flinched—actually *flinched*—at my words.

I ignored it. "So he was coming over here to have a discussion with me the only way a man like him knows how to
discuss such things—with violence. It is, after all, the commu-
nicative tool of the evil, unintelligent or emotionally crippled."
I glanced down at his clenched fist pointedly.

Sam tilted his head and regarded me for a while. A long
while. In a way that I knew he was no longer transfixed by my
outward wounds but more interested in the ones underneath.
Beneath my words.

But that couldn't have been right. This Sam didn't see beneath. Or if he did he disregarded it. I knew that now.

"Well I don't think of myself as unintelligent," he said finally. "In fact, I have my SAT scores framed in my bedroom.
Above average. True story." He winked. And that time I saw
through it. The image he was using to gloss over whatever it
was that had been on his face moments before, whatever it was
that he'd seen on mine. "Despite my self-proclaimed ability to
out-science Stephen Hawking, I'll totally call off the grudge
match with him in order to wear the badge of unintelligence I
need in order to pummel the living shit out of the man who did
this to my—" He paused abruptly, his voice thick. "Who did
this to *you*. So if you'd be so kind as to give me his address and
last known location, I'll take my freshly unintelligent—and
might I say perfectly sculpted—ass out of here and do Batman's
job for him."

I stared at him in shock.

He clearly mistook it for confusion. "Serving justice. That's Batman's job," he clarified. "But since the fucker got all famous, he got an ego and started slacking. And if it's one thing I don't have, other than herpes, it's an ego."

It was a strange thing, to hear the familiar nonsense coming out of Sam's mouth like he was tripping acid, but watching the way he held every inch of his chiseled body taut and still. Like marble. How the previously soft and pleasant edge to his words dripped with a darkness that wasn't there before.

Or it had been and it hadn't had a chance to see the sunshine until now.

"You're joking," I said finally.

He crossed his arms. "I never joke about Batman," he countered. "Or herpes."

I blinked at him, then stepped forward to grasp the corner of my door, intending on closing it on him and making my intention known to him as I did so.

"Well this little trip down the rabbit hole has been most unpleasant," I lied. Some fucked-up part of me had savored every moment of the exchange, of his scent, of him. Even with everything that happened. Luckily, she wasn't in control. "If you don't mind, I've got things to do. And it's a *long* drive back to LA." I nodded to the car, mostly to reinforce my point but also to avoid eye contact. Or almost wholly to avoid eye contact. It was only the absence of it that made it possible for me to keep my icy and detached done. "It's even longer to Gotham City, if you wanted to pop into the Batcave and give Batman a stern talking to. Or party with him. I hear he gets all the pretty empty-headed damsels, so I'm sure there'd be a stray or two scuttling around for you," I clipped. I found my courage and met his glassy eyes. "Because here in Hampton Springs, there's not an empty head to be seen. On your side of the conversation, at least. And there sure as heck isn't a damsel. I may not look like it, but I can take care of myself just fine, and I will protect myself. Which is precisely what I'm doing."

I tried to close the door on him but a tattooed hand flat on the wood, plus a Doc Martin at the bottom, hampered such an effort.

"All appearances to the contrary, I do believe there is a little stock in what you're saying," he murmured. "A whole lot. You sure can take care of yourself. And it looks like you aren't too keen on having me do that for you." His eyes darkened. "For now, at least."

"Forever," I clarified. And lied.

Sam's eyes flickered, but he otherwise didn't acknowledge my words. "So if you don't want nor need me to take care of you at this immediate juncture, I'll take care of everything else around you. More precisely the man who is going to be drinking his meal through a straw for the next five to eight weeks and will no longer be able to have children," he gritted. "So, Thumbelina, *give me his fucking address.*" His command was rough, animalistic.

The sheer volume of emotion in the words, in his body, in his eyes almost gave me pause. Almost had me doing the insane and not only opening the door to him but giving him what he requested.

Almost.

"No," I said, the single word a physical chore to yank from my lips. "I'm not going to do that just because you command it. For whatever fucked-up reason you think you need it. Whatever reason you're here. Just because you can get whatever you want in your little bubble doesn't mean you can get it everywhere else. With me. You're just another jerk from high school to me." I eyed the foot at the door. "One who is not only harassing me but forcing his way into my home. Which, as I mentioned earlier, is something I've already ticked off the list for my week. Preferably my lifetime. So kindly get your hand off my door and your person out of my doorframe, get into that ridiculously showy car and drive. I don't care where you go. As long as it's away from me, I'll be happy."

The lies rolled off my tongue easier the more I told. So well I could almost convince myself that I was telling the truth. That I didn't want Sam there. That I didn't need him there. That even his sheer imprint on the memory of the place where I'd been assaulted didn't somehow exorcise the ghost of those memories.

Almost.

I was never a good liar. Not until I had to be. Now I was all right. but still a long way away from being able to lie to myself.

Sam seemed to buy it. Or at least he saw he'd met his match in a scared, scorned and scarred woman.

He dropped his hand. Moved his boot. Stepped back.

"This isn't over," he promised, reaching out to the air close to my cheek, not making contact but hovering, seeming to ask for permission.

I stepped out of his reach. "Oh yes it is."

Then I slammed the door in his face.

Chapter Seven

Sam

"Yo, Mark, my business trip has taken longer than expected," Sam said between strikes.

The thump of flesh against flesh echoed into the phone and sent a grim sense of satisfaction through Sam's boiling blood.

As did the moan of pain.

But it wasn't enough.

The image of her porcelain skin marred with the purplish evidence of violence that she should've never even *witnessed*, let alone tasted. That would remain on her soul long after the bruises disappeared.

Sam knew that. Had seen it happen to his best friend. He watched her heal physically. Watched her bounce back with remarkable speed and come back to rock sold-out arenas, to smile as if she'd known nothing but love and light all her life. Or that's what it was on the surface.

But the surface didn't mean shit.

Not to Sam. That image crap was what kept him in flashy shit he didn't need. He only truly needed the music. And the single characteristic of the music was its honesty. Its inability to be anything but surface. Even the worst song on the planet had to come from somewhere, somewhere beyond, somewhere beneath. The greats, they knew it; that's why they were great, after all.

Kurt Cobain once said, "Thank you for the tragedy, I need it for my art." And that fucker hit the nail right on the head. Ultimately the nail in his coffin, but that's what music was. Someone's tragedy, be it beautiful and extraordinary or ugly and pitch-black, that's what was woven into the music. That's what the music was born out of. Pockets of someone's soul that they never let see the surface. Somehow it had gotten warped, twisted that the industry itself represented the exact opposite of what it was built on.

The image.

The surface.

But he saw through that shit. He *lived* through that shit. As did the rest of his family. Even Lexie, the most honest of them all. *Especially* Lexie. She shone the brightest, and therefore her shadows were the darkest. First in the four years that propelled them into the fame that was fueled, created, by her bone-shattering heartbreak. Her tragedy was the band's success, the big bang for Unquiet Mind.

And then when her man came back to her, repaired what he'd broken so savagely without Sam breaking his face, even when everything fell into place, she was knocked again. Almost off the face of the earth. She saw the ugliest of humanity, and her skin saw the physical manifestations of violence. But when they disappeared, it was her soul that kept the scars.

Despite her having a man who would and had taken a bullet for her, who gave her the utter devotion that every great love song tried to capture, despite the light in her life that was now like a supernova, her shadows remained.

And Sam had the sinking feeling they always would.

He reared his fist back, barely noticing the pain in his hand as it smashed against bone.

His girl, the bruised one on that doorstop, would have those shadows. In eyes that didn't deserve any.

Why the fuck was it always the ones who deserved the best life had to offer who always saw the worst of it?

"You don't have business. That's what I'm here for," his manager informed him. Then paused. "Fuck, Sam, have you holed up with a girl again?" Mark snapped.

Which didn't even make sense. Sam had never, not once, traveled in a plane and then a car for a girl. Granted, it was a private jet and a kick-ass car, but still, he hadn't needed to exert effort before. But they'd finally gotten back from their world tour last week. When they'd been moving, amongst the chaos, Sam could deal. With the constant thoughts of her. He'd worn the memories of that night away to almost nothingness due to the amount of times he'd replayed them in his mind.

And it was when he got home, got back to the life he'd once considered so fucking epic, that he realized he couldn't just have memories.

He needed her.

There was another thud against flesh and a cry of pain. He wasn't as vocal now, closer to unconsciousness than he deserved. Putting his hand on a woman and a *child*? The fucker deserved to be chained up on Mount Olympus and have crows eat his liver for all eternity like that dude Prometheus.

"Are you calling me in the middle of sex, Sam?" Mark demanded. "We've spoken about this." His brisk tone bordered on parental reproach, which Sam had never experienced with his actual parents. You had to care to scold. Mark's concern might have been mostly toward his paycheck and Sam's part in it, but it was something.

Sam jostled the phone as he dropped the prone body of the asshole onto the ground of his filthy apartment, disgusted that the coward barely stayed conscious for a beating a child could've taken.

Sam tasted bile with the thought that a child had taken a beating in this very stench-filled hovel.

He made a mental note to ensure the kid was with good people and would be set up with a college fund or whatever else people needed to bring up kids.

He barely registered his bleeding knuckles. "No, of course not, Mark," he said, his voice light. "You know I'd never make you participate in a threesome over the phone. I'd invite you to one in person, like the gentleman I am." His tone, easy and joking, came natural to him on most occasions, but now he had to work for it. Not because of the violence he'd just unleashed on a half-comatose man. No, he didn't give two fucks about that. He'd smiled through the whole fucking thing. No, it was because he couldn't get the image of Gina's bruised skin from the front of his mind.

Couldn't store it away with all the other fucked-up shit he pushed into the junk drawer of his mind for later inspection. Or never.

The replay of her speaking about what happened, her convincing him she wasn't raped and that sheer look of animalistic fear that clutched her the moment she realized she *could have* been was playing in his mind. Eyes open or closed, it was there.

"Well, why the fuck are you telling me that you're going to be away from LA longer than you'd planned?" Mark demanded. "And just to inform you, you didn't plan on being gone *at all.* You stood up a prominent actress for dinner and texted me saying you were on a "quest of the loins" and left me to clean up the fallout with her fucking publicist. Who is going to put you on her permanent shit list for this," he said.

Sam wiped the blood from his hands on his jeans, spitting on the body of the man splayed at his feet. Another stain on the discolored wife beater he was wearing, his beer gut sticking out of it like a hair-covered boil.

He laughed as he turned to escape the smell before it seeped into his favorite boots. "Not possible. I'm a media darling, she's a media whore. I'll never be on her shit list. I'll never be on anyone's. Haven't you heard? I'm Sam fucking Kennedy."

He shoved his sunglasses over his face at the glaring sun, smiling at the woman passing him, laden with grocery bags. She gaped at him, doing a double take.

She obviously recognized him—who didn't these days? He didn't exactly go to great lengths to make himself inconspicuous, nor did nearly shouting "I'm Sam fucking Kennedy" help. If fuckstick in there decided to press charges, then it wasn't exactly brain surgery to figure out who did it.

But fuckstick wasn't a brain surgeon, so Sam guessed he wouldn't be going to the cops. He didn't care either way. He was sure Jenna, his publicist, would have something to say about it, though she always had something to say about something.

Not that it would exactly damage his image, since he'd established himself as the bad boy of the group. But that was just an image. More surface.

"Jesus," Mark muttered into the phone as Sam blew the woman a kiss and sauntered down the open-air walkway of the crappy two-story walk-up.

"No, *Sam*, remember? I just said that, Mark. Have you been checked for early onset Alzheimer's? They say those with high-stress jobs are more at risk."

"Well I'm speaking to the source of 90 percent of my job-related stress," he snapped.

Sam descended the stairs. "And 90 percent of your gross annual income," he countered. "So even if I do drive you nutty enough to need medical intervention, you'll be able to afford the best. Silver linings, my friend."

"Sam, for a second, can you be serious? We've got an album to record, appearances, photo shoots." Mark listed them off as he was known to do.

"Boo," Sam called into the phone as he got into his car. "I need a vacation. I've got shit to do. You'll handle it, I'm sure. 'Cause that's your job. Got things to do, people to wow with my fists. Toodles."

"Sam, don't you hang up—"

He hung up before Mark could finish his sentence.

The low hum of the car vibrated his balls slightly and gently reminded him how fucking blue they were.

That had been his first intention coming down here to bum-fuck teen-pregnancy, Bud-Light country. To search for what Austin Powers had lost in *The Spy Who Shagged Me*—his mojo.

Since that fucking night at Lexie's wedding. Since that night that might be classified as one of the best of his life, surpassing even when he played on the hallowed ground of The Fillmore in San Francisco. He was haunted by the stupid decision he'd made because he was a fucking coward.

Pushing her away because of his own fucked-up junk drawer that rattled when she was around. Because she didn't hide anything. And the thing with people who didn't hide anything about themselves, they promoted the same action from yourself when you were around them. And Sam didn't need that. To feel that fucked-up yearning for slow mornings, slow sex, whispered nothings at 3:00 a.m. instead of partying it up at the latest club opening with the latest it girl on his arm.

There was a reason why he chose those girls. They were temporal. Always moving. Appearing. Disappearing. Empty enough so he saw nothing in them. So, more importantly, they didn't see anything in him. Not that they tried; they were mostly leeches, sucking off his fame or status. The thing with Gina was she didn't see the surface, didn't take anything from him. She gave.

To the man who had it all, she gave everything.

And that scared the shit out of him.

So he did what he thought was the best: cut it off before it could grow. Like a weed, like a limb with gangrene. He was the limb and weed in this situation.

Because she wasn't right for his life. She was quiet and honest and innocent. His world would eat her up. Destroy all that was good about her. And her world would do the same to him. But it would destroy all that was bad.

And he couldn't take that.

Without the bad, he didn't know what the fuck he was. And he didn't want to know. Because he was a fucking coward.

So he was cruel and broke a girl who wasn't meant to be broken.

And his dick had paid the price for his head's fuck-up. He had been on a world fucking tour. Of *the world*. Which meant a girl—a thousand girls—literally in every port. Of every nationality. With every type of accent, piercing, tattoo, kink you could think of.

And nothing.

A Danish chick took him to a sex club in Amsterdam and it was like his johnson was watching *Antiques Roadshow* instead of a woman getting plowed while the Dane sucked on his neck. And tried to rouse a response between his legs.

Nothing.

He'd thought this was a myth. Cock fright. That's what he had. In the face of something real, something actually fucking permanent, his cock had been scared off everything else. Ruined for it all.

He hadn't gotten it with Killian and the rest of those motorcycle fuckers, the way they doted over their women, like no other bitch existed. Sure they were knockouts and seriously amazing babes, but the world had billions of women to choose from. *Billions.* Sam considered it to be bad manners and an insult the big guy upstairs to not sample at least half of them. Why chain yourself to one when you can have two chained up naked to your bed and fifty more on speed dial?

A beautiful girl with eyes almost violet who wore a pink dress and saw someone all the stage lights in the world couldn't illuminate. That's why.

She may have said that he couldn't get everything he wanted, but in his life in the fast lane, that had proved to be untrue thus far. In the slower lane, her lane, it seemed she was right. Which meant he just had to get *her* to want *him*—or at least admit it.

And forgive him.

She couldn't lie for shit, so he saw it behind her crudely designed mask. She wanted him.

The forgiveness thing was another story. He'd worry about that later.

First, he had to go all Batman on this shit.

He glanced down at his phone to dial another number.

"Yo, Keltan, what's the ETA to get a commando down to Hampton Springs?"

Even Batman had to get some hired help. He was a busy man. Plus, he was rich; delegating was just good business. What else was Robin for?

Gina

"Dude, look out your fucking window, like *yesterday*," Pria ordered into the phone as soon as I answered, not even saying hello.

"Is the Reynolds boy mowing the lawns in his boxer shorts again?" I asked. "You know that's totally inappropriate, Pria. He's a *child*," I scolded, already making my way over to my little bay window jutting onto my front yard.

Not that the Reynolds boy held too much appeal to me now. Now I had the memory of Sam's ripped and defined body imprinted onto my memory. Had the ghost of the hardness of his muscles on my fingertips and in… *other* places.

"He's legal," she hissed in protest. "But no, this is better than that. Like *way* better. Are they filming some kind of Thor movie on our street or something? I thought they were meant to, like, alert us if they were doing that. Though my outrage would be quelled slightly if Thor came in for… tea."

I rolled my eyes. "Dude, you're married."

"I'm aware. Garth's standing right here," she replied. "Say hi, Garth."

"Hi, Gina," he called dutifully into the phone.

I couldn't help the giggle that erupted from my throat, the first since that day. One that was silenced immediately when I got to the window and saw exactly what was going on in the street.

"Holy Hemsworth," she exclaimed. "The hot guys are *walking up your path*. To your door." She said this as if I couldn't see this with my own two eyes. See two men carrying large hard-topped suitcases in their hands. They were both wearing jeans, tight tees, and dark sunglasses, looking like they were, in fact, filming a movie.

"What do you think is in the suitcases?" Pria whispered. "Are they assassins? Strippers? Why would you order strippers and not invite me?" she whined, in front of her husband, who I imagined to be smiling good-naturedly, as was his way.

Not much perturbed Garth. Pria definitely wore the pants in that relationship, and he gave them to her happily, like he'd give her the world if she so asked. She didn't use her power over him for evil. Only at that time of the month when she needed the good donuts from two towns over.

I watched them travel up my front walk and shrank back slightly when a sunglassed head flickered in my direction.

"Um, because you're married," I reminded her, forgetting for a moment to correct her that I had not ordered strippers for just me. Even I wasn't that pathetic.

"Um, I'm married, not dead," she snapped. "So they *are* strippers"

"You've known me for two years, Pria," I said. "I teach your kid. You know me. Therefore, you know they are not strippers."

"So, that means they're assassins," she concluded.

I sighed and then jumped slightly as the door vibrated with the power of the knock.

"Yet again, Pria, you know me. My boring life. Therefore, you know I don't do anything exciting enough to warrant assassins."

"Wayne," she offered, a small darkness seeping into her cheerful tone.

The small twinge in my ribs as I moved to the door reminded me of Wayne. Not that I forgot him. The bags under my eyes were not just bruises; they were delayed wounds from the beating. Living alone was all well and good until darkness came. And for someone who'd read thousands of books and had a considerable imagination, the darkness meant thousands of possibilities. Almost all of them bad. But they were fears that weren't properly actualized and would contribute to only a few restless nights. Now that they were actualized, I'd all but abandoned the charade of sleeping, for every time I tucked myself into bed I heard a noise that made me certain he was coming back.

"Wayne's not smart enough, connected enough or cashed

up enough to hire assassins. Especially ones who look like that."

"True. Who do you think hired them?" she asked, not willing to abandon her assassins theory. She was a housewife after all, with only a slightly more exciting life than mine. She needed to get her thrills from somewhere.

My hand was on the doorknob. "No one, considering no self-respecting assassin would perform a hit in broad daylight in the view of a nosy housewife," I teased.

"Well maybe they're assassins with no self-respect," she quipped. "And I'm not a housewife. I'm more than just a patriarchal label. My job is by my own choice, namely I don't like working."

I couldn't help but grin wide as I opened the door to two of the hottest men… well, ever. I would've had a more drastic reaction had I not been subjected to every single male in the Sons of Templar MC and all three male members of Unquiet Mind. One in particular had been on this doorstep yesterday, and I'd spent the last twenty-four hours trying not to think about that. Wonder why he was here, wonder if I had made a mistake scaring him off, taunting myself with it all.

Because of my practice with guys too hot to be human, I was able to greet them without gaping or drooling or anything.

Mental high five for Gina.

"Hi, um, I know it's the height of rudeness to greet a caller while speaking on the phone," I said, my iPhone still at my ear.

"Holy shit, you're talking to the assassins! What do they smell like?" Pria demanded. "I bet they wear expensive cologne. The type that doesn't even have a name, just a number, and costs $500 dollars a bottle."

"Don't ask her what they smell like," I heard Garth demand in the background. "Tell her to do a bird call if she needs saving."

"Gina doesn't know a bird call," she snapped. "Who knows

a bird call? And it's not like you could save her from two seasoned assassins," Pria scoffed. "I love you to death honey, but… no."

"I could totally take them on if my wife's or my wife's friends' lives depended—"

Throughout this spat I was listening and looking. As were my visitors. At me.

Each of the men had looked the same as they'd come up the walk, but upon closer inspection they were incredibly different. Both were built like brick shithouses, but that's where the similarities stopped. The one closest to me, the one who was grinning with the squarest jaw and whitest teeth I'd ever seen, was blond with Scandinavian-type features, the smile contrasting the hard edges of this face. His skin had a sun-kissed tan, and defined muscles strained out of his tee shirt.

The other was not smiling. His face was blank, but that didn't mean it wasn't striking. He had dark features. The same bulky muscle mass as the other, but a menace and a danger seemed to seep from his very skin.

He unnerved me, the quiet malice of him. Though the smile of the other one didn't mean he wasn't capable of something dangerous. Alligators smiled before they killed you, after all.

"Yes, sorry, terribly rude," I continued, speaking to both the men after realizing I'd left them in a long silence while listening to my friends bicker over the phone. "I just have to re-assure my friends, who happen to live right across the road." I nodded and two sets of sunglasses glanced over to the small but well-maintained townhouse with the greenest grass on the street. It was Garth's pride and joy.

The curtains in what I knew was their dining room moved quickly as I spoke.

"Don't bring us down with you," Pria hissed. "Now they

know we're witnesses. Say your goodbyes to the grass, honey," she said to Garth.

I grinned and the sunglasses focused on me once more. "Anyway, these friends have decided you're killers for hire or something, and I can't hang up until they've been assured otherwise," I explained.

There was a long pause and my cheeks flamed slightly at the attention of both men. Okay, my cheeks flamed a lot more than slightly, but I was proud that I hadn't burst into some kind of inferno, which wouldn't be an overreaction to the hotness in front of me.

The smiling one grinned wider. "No, not assassins, babe," he said with a wink.

"Though that's exactly what an assassin would say," the other one grunted.

I couldn't tell if it was a really dry joke or an observation of someone who had intimate knowledge of assassins' protocol.

"Okaaay, well that sounds like a no," I said. "So that's going to sound like a goodbye for you, Pria. Go and do something. Anything. Finish the last episode of *Game of Thrones*. I'll call you after the non-assassins leave. But no spoilers or I will cut you," I warned.

I hung up before I could no doubt get a protest.

"Sorry," I apologized once more with a still-flaming face.

"No problem," the blond Viking said. "That was cute as all fuck."

I frowned at him while still smiling. He can't have meant *me* cute. "Umm, yeah," I said uncertainly, deciding to abandon that little comment. "So, how can I help you? Are you lost?"

"Never get lost, babe. I've got an *excellent* sense of direction. It's never steered me wrong before, and it doesn't look to be doing that today either."

My smile dimmed. Was this hotter-than-Hades guy *flirting*

with me?

No, he couldn't be.

Luckily his grim-faced friend injected. "We're here to install your security system," he told me.

"My security system?" I repeated.

He nodded once. "You move aside, let us in, we install it, we leave."

"Or we could stay for a beer. Or go out for one. Or a milkshake. A taco?" the blond one interjected.

The grim one looked like he was about to step forward, which would give me no other choice but to let him into my house. Now, I wanted two hot guys in my house as much as the next girl. But not while I was sporting a nasty black eye, hadn't slept in days, hadn't washed my hair in days and didn't have a lick of makeup on, let alone deodorant.

Plus I didn't like letting people into my house. I avoided strangers coming in at all costs. Even when I actually needed people to come in and fix things, I either tried to fix it myself via YouTube or learned to adjust to the freezer beeping nonstop every time I opened it. At first I thought it might be a good deterrent to eating frozen Twix bars at 2:00 a.m.

It was not.

My house was my sanctuary, built and decorated over the years I'd lived here. Most of the walls in the living room were taken up by bookshelves, surrounding a huge comfy sofa covered in pillows of differing sizes and patterns, and snuggly throws for the times when I fell asleep reading.

Which I did often. Hence me splurging a lot on the sofa.

And since I wanted my house to be a sanctuary, I didn't let many people in. Kind of the defeated the purpose of the whole sanctuary idea.

So I put my hand up to make sure Mr. Grim didn't get any ideas.

"There's been a mistake, I didn't order a security system."

"You Gina?" he asked.

I nodded, unnerved that he knew my name.

Strange men on your doorstep with large suitcases who knew your name were bad, no matter how hot they were.

Just because someone was physically attractive on the outside didn't mean they weren't warped and rotten on the inside.

I knew that well. Too well.

My stomach dipped with unease as my heart slammed painfully against my injured rib.

"Maybe you didn't order security but someone did. On behalf of you." His hand went to his pocket. I braced for a gun, but instead he presented me with a small square business card.

Greenstone Security was typed in sleek block letters with names, numbers and an intricate curved logo.

I pursed my lips. "I don't need security," I clipped shortly.

His eyes went to my bruised skin and they flickered slightly with anger. "That communicates something to the contrary."

I swallowed. "This was an isolated incident that has been resolved," I argued.

"Man comes to a woman's home and assaults her, that's not an isolated issue," he replied. "In fact, it's a precursor to a plethora of other issues. Especially since the asshole in question is out on bail."

My blood ran cold.

Bail. I hadn't been in contact with anyone from the sheriff's office after my initial statement, which I'd selfishly been glad about because that meant I didn't have to communicate with Simon. Even after two years, he still had the ability to affect me. Make me uncomfortable in my own skin. Make me question everything about myself. The way I walked, sipped my coffee, styled my hair. Stupid things, things you did without thinking.

Until someone you loved with all your heart said you were doing them wrong.

Then, of course, you obsess over doing it right. *Being* right.

I'd been enjoying feeling right in my own skin, no matter how bruised or jumpy it was at that moment. I'd just assumed the sheriff had remanded him, considering he was being investigated for child abuse and he drove over to a kindergarten teacher's house, forcefully entered it and then beat the shit out of her. I thought that would be the "do not pass go, do not collect $200" situation.

It seemed not.

"You didn't know," he said—or more accurately accused.

I shook my head.

"Stupid fuckin' hick towns and fuckin' hick cops," he muttered under his breath. Then he focused on me. "So yes, I would say the man who forcibly entered your home and assaulted you walking around, or limping around, gives you renewed motivation to let us install a security system that will hopefully stop him from entering your house and hurting you again. And if he doesn't, it will make sure that he doesn't have enough time to kill you before the cops get there if he's smart or stupid enough to bypass one of the best security systems in the county."

"Stupid," I whispered, still dwelling on the "killing" portion of his casual statement and completely skipping over the "limping" part for the time being, "would be the correct answer in that hypothetical." I snapped my head up, not moving to let them in the door. "And though it would take some doing—heavy drinking to kill an infinite amount of brain cells, for example—I'm not as stupid as Wayne Harken. Therefore, I'm not going to let two strange men into my home. Who are here to install a security company *I didn't order.*"

I glanced down at the business card and read the LA part again, then snapped my head back up. "You guys are from LA."

The Viking nodded. "Yes ma'am."

"Long way from home," I mused, my blood boiling as I connected the dots between yesterday's visitor and today's.

He nodded once again, that time not saying anything, but I saw the shadow of a grin begin at the edge of his attractive mouth.

"And what would two security professionals from a rather prominent firm in the City of Angels be doing in the town of alcoholic child beaters?" I asked through gritted teeth.

The stern one shrugged. "Got a call. Owed someone a favor. Here we are."

"You're here, a four-hour flight and another hour drive away from the city in which you reside as a *favor* to someone?" I clarified.

Another nod.

"And this person wouldn't happen to be a drummer with too many tattoos, and an ego the size of the gosh-darned state we're currently in?" I snapped.

Menacing guy grinned. Actually *grinned.* "Did you just say 'gosh-darned'?" he teased.

I didn't answer, mostly because the roar of an engine took my attention.

"Yes, she did just say 'gosh-darned,'" Viking muttered.

The car's engine echoed through our sleepy street like the throaty roar of a giant through a silent cave.

Our street was full of mostly middle-class families, rounding to the dead end where my house was the second to last before the forest spirited the road away.

I didn't know all my neighbors because I was… well, me. The only reason I was good friends with Pria because she was, well, her. In other words, crazy.

In a good way, because she accepted my quiet nature and need for solitude.

Not many people got it.

Lexie.

Sam.

The Sam who was currently tearing through the silence and solitude I'd created, not only with the rumble of his engine but with his everything. I knew it was him because everyone on this street drove midrange SUVs or minivans. I had a convertible Beetle.

I knew engines. And the rumble of 500 HP. And the sound of the engine was familiar to what had roared off yesterday. It seemed he had kept his promise of "this" not being over.

I hated that it made a little part of me happy.

Luckily the rest of me was still hurt enough to be furious.

I crossed my arms and glared at the car's tinted windows as it parked behind the sleek SUV belonging to the commandos.

"Sam is in for it," Viking muttered, grinning.

Menace's eyes went up and down my body in a glance that had my cheeks reddening with the sheer maleness of it.

"Yes he is," he agreed. "Lucky fucker."

I decided to ignore this weird behavior. Maybe the flight from LA had been longer than I thought if they considered me in my sweatpants, bruised, with greasy hair and at least an extra pound from all the stress eating as anything to direct such male gazes toward.

As if he didn't have three—or most likely five, counting Pria's and Garth's—pairs of eyes on him, Sam lazily and leisurely folded himself out of his car, running his hand up on his head to fasten his hair into a sloppy bun.

Despite being spitting-tacks mad, I felt that gesture, most annoyingly, between my legs.

He grinned wickedly, as if, from across the lawn, he could sense my reaction.

I glared at him.

"Yeah, lucky fuckin' Sam," Viking muttered.

"Heath, how's it hanging?" Sam slapped the menacing one on the shoulder before glancing between all the eyes on him. "Guys, I know, I'm famous and am an intoxicating presence, but don't we have work to do?" He glanced to the suitcases the men were holding, then to me. "You know, other than chatting up my girl? I'm the only one who gets to do that. I mean, you could try, but then I'd have to punch you and I'd hate to cause a scene." He paused. "Oh wait, I love causing a scene. Just not that sort of one."

"I'm not your girl," I snapped immediately, increasing my glare tenfold.

He put his hand to his Ray-Bans, lowering them enough so I could see him wink, then he turned his attention to Heath.

"We haven't started because the lady of the house hasn't let us in since she didn't know anything about this security system," Heath said dryly, but with a grin.

"Well of course she didn't know. It was a surprise." He turned to me once more and held his muscled arms skyward. "Surprise!" he yelled.

"No," I said.

He frowned. "'No' is not an appropriate response to surprises. Girls usually scream, or cry, or at the very least smile. A kiss with a lot of tongue is my request. Don't worry, PDA doesn't bother me."

"You think you're cute but you're not," I gritted out.

He pouted. "Well thanks. That little insult is going to shatter my vulnerable self-esteem and it'll take *years* with a therapist to build it back up," he said, feigning hurt.

I gritted my teeth. "Well, go and begin your sessions. Now. And take your action men with you. I'm sure you'll need protection from all your fans. You know, the ones who *don't live here*," I snapped.

"They're not going anywhere. Except inside where they can set up the security system they traveled very far to install." His tone was still light and joking but it was firmer.

I glared at him. "*I* didn't ask them to travel. *You* did. I hope you reimburse them generously for the fuel and effort it took to get here and deal with you. And that you tip them handsomely because seriously, dealing with you is worth at least 40 percent. And that's if you're a stingy tipper."

"I'm a great tipper, babe," he assured me. "Look, here's one. Step aside, let the guys in the house and let them install the system before things get ugly. Or fun. Or attractive."

I stared at him. "They already have. Gotten ugly," I clarified. "And no. I don't need a security system. I need—"

I let out a strangled scream when he cut me off by stepping forward and effortlessly yet very carefully lifting me on my uninjured side. He pulled me out of the doorway, not stopping until we were on my front lawn.

"Put me down!" I yelled. Mostly because I was angry that he'd just moved me bodily to get his own way, and also because I was embarrassed about how heavy I no doubt was.

Sam wasn't small. At all. He was all muscle.

But I wasn't small either. And I was not all muscle. I was all Pop-Tarts. Or Twinkies.

"Do I have to?" he whined, sounding like a kid.

"Put me down. You're hurting me," I lied.

As I predicted, the statement had my feet immediately but softly placed on the slightly damp grass. Unfortunately, Sam's hands remained lightly on my hips as his eyes ran over me in concern. "Fuck, I'm sorry, baby. I thought I was being gentle. Where are you hurt?" All trace of joking was gone from his voice, and it lingered with regret.

I almost felt guilty. Then I looked at the SUV on the curb.

"My ass," I said.

He blinked in confusion.

"Because I have this huge pain in it by the name of Sam Kennedy, and he won't seem to leave me the heck alone since he inexplicitly turned up on my doorstep after brutally dismissing me a year ago," I snapped. "So, if you're so concerned about my well-being, how about you rectify that pain by getting the heck off my lawn and *out of my life*?"

He rubbed at the small sprinkling of stubble on his jaw, eyes swimming with more regret the moment I'd mentioned him brutally dismissing me. But that was soon gone, replaced with light teasing.

"Well, of course I care about your ass's well-being," he said seriously, peering around so he could get a glimpse of the ass in question.

Every instinct told me to squirm away from the gaze but I held strong. Though I still flushed beetroot red.

He squinted. "It looks like perfection to the outsider's gaze, but I'd be happy to get a closer look at the area, see what I can do about that pain. You'll quickly see, once our clothes are off, that I don't specialize in pain but *pleasure*."

His words may have been teasing, but pure erotic promise coupled with pure erotic memory caused me to have a very serious reaction. But then I remembered what happened after that pure erotic memory.

"No, thanks. We tried that, remember? Sure, you're fine at pleasure, but nothing a battery-operated device can't reproduce. And it doesn't come with all the fucking headaches."

Sam grinned. "We can include this battery-operated device as well."

I blew out an audible breath in exasperation.

"Bite me," I hissed.

He grinned, and I hated how that exercise of facial muscles did things to me.

"I would, baby, because you look de-li-cious." The way it rolled off his tongue drenched the air with sex. "Doesn't mean you can't bite *me*, though." He started to cross the distance I'd put between us. "But," he murmured when he came close enough for me to smell the unquiet mixture of his expensive cologne with the scent of him—the ocean and cigarettes. No matter that we were inland and it was preposterous for him to carry the scent of the ocean around with him. "My lawyer says I have to stop doing it. It's getting expensive." He winked, then trailed a hand up my jaw.

I found my feet in quicksand, unable to move from his touch even though it spelled disaster.

So I stayed there for a whisper of a moment. Until I found my sense. Or my pain.

Then I jumped back, stumbling slightly but catching myself before I could do anything embarrassing like fall on my ass. I glared at him in an attempt to mask my reaction to him. "Yeah, I'm sure it does get expensive, what with all the girls on rotation. You buy all your other groupies a brand-new security system too? That's what I am, right? Your word, not mine."

Sam flinched, all sense of humor gone from his face. "Thumbelina, I—"

"You *nothing*," I cut him off despite being desperate to hear what he had to say. "I know you live in a different world now. I understand that, as much as a *lowly commoner* such as myself can, but that doesn't mean you can saunter in and play with people's lives like you play a fucking drum set. You turn up here, feigning outrage at my assault, running around buying me security systems, exacting violent retribution on my behalf?" I looked pointedly at his bruised knuckles, connecting the dots to the Viking's earlier statement about Wayne limping. "That's not how this works, Sam. Life. That's not how life works. You don't get to do that."

He stared at me. "Is there a set way that life works?" he asked quietly. A blueprint?" He didn't wait for my answer. "No, there isn't. That's the whole point of it. We're all just making it up and fucking it up along the way. I'll admit it, I fuck it up more than most. And I do it often. Never have I done it as bad as that morning in the hotel room. Middle of a fucking yard isn't where I'm going to lay out the whys of it, babe." His eyes flickered behind him to Pria and Garth's house, as if he could sense the eyes behind the net curtain. "Especially with an audience. I'm at home in front of an audience usually, but not with this. Not with you. So for now, I'll say the way life is working for me, at this current moment, is making my way up here to apologize. Explain. Grovel. I'm not going to lie and say my intentions were completely noble. I can't get your pussy out of my fucking head. Either of them," he muttered, the crude meaning of his words somehow not insulting me but making me feel hot and cold at the same time.

I cursed my responsive body that had never had this particular response. Ever. I failed to admit to myself that it was something special regarding Sam. I wouldn't.

"But that's not the half of it. And life happened, meaning when I come here, with an apology and a fuck of a lot of sex in mind, I'm presented with the evidence of someone hurting you. I couldn't have prevented that. Or maybe I could have, if I hadn't been such a flying prick a year ago. Life unfortunately doesn't deal in what-ifs or do-overs. So instead I've been doing whatever it is in my considerable power to make you feel safe again. Can't heal your body, babe. Much as I hate to admit it, I can't heal your mind either. That's on you. But I *can* take care of the rest. Me comin' here? It's not playing with you. It's me trying to...."

I cursed myself for watching it fall like silk, letting it hypnotize me as Sam continued speaking.

"Fuck, I don't know what I'm trying to do. Win you back? But that's assuming I had you in the first place. And I know I'm an arrogant motherfucker, but even *I'm* not that deluded. I know I had the chance to get you. Had you in my grasp. So I guess I'm not trying to win you back. I'm trying for a second chance?" He structured the sentence as a question, his face naked with hope. With a lot of other things. With everything there was that morning right after he woke up. Right before he put on that mask of indifference.

If I hadn't been well-versed in that mask, I might have relented. Melted. I was still tempted, of course, but once you'd seen someone's ability to shut off, turn their face into someone else, *be* someone else, you knew it would always be there. That mask. And it would come back.

I knew that. Despite how convincing Sam was.

And he wasn't done.

"I'm taking full responsibility for my actions here, babe. Honestly and completely apologizing." He sighed in exasperation, ripping the elastic out of his hair so he could run his fingers through it, as if he could find the words he was searching for there. "It's no secret that I'm not exactly *monogamous*," he said sheepishly.

I snorted in answer.

He was never photographed with the same woman twice, except Lexie. Every issue of every trashy magazine displayed at the supermarket had another tanned, emaciated and well-dressed woman hanging off his tattooed arm.

"Yeah," he agreed to my snort. "It's not something I was ashamed of. I was a fuckin' *kid* when we blew up, when all this shit started getting offered on a silver platter. Booze, money, women, drugs. I took everything on it, including the fucking platter, because I was wrapped up in it all. Because I was wrapped up in the music and what it gave me. And I had this warped idea that it was what I needed to do to keep up with the music. You ever met a rock star who stayed at home on his off nights, drank herbal tea and stayed loyal to his childhood sweetheart?" he asked. "No. They were rebels, outlaws of society who played out their lives on a stage, paid to do so like animals in a zoo. So we did what good animals and musicians do—we performed. And off the stage it didn't stop. Only I wasn't doing it for them, the masses. I was doing it for me. For the greats. So I could make the history books of rock 'n' roll. You can only be heard in the roar if you roar the loudest. Stay ahead of the pack by living the fastest. And avoid getting fucked up entirely by avoiding the big L. And I don't mean LSD. I *loved* that shit for a while."

I must have shown it on my face, my shock, because he held up his hand.

"Full disclosure, I'm sober now." He paused. "Mostly. If you don't count hard liquor. I'm not perfect. I'm a rock star, not an angel." He flashed me a grin. "And all that shit plays with my mind, babe. I like to let people think my head is empty and always has a dancing monkey playing drums on repeat running through it rather than anything of substance. And I *liked* it that way. I made sure everything around me was so loud that I didn't hear the shit inside my head. And it's fucked up and almost impossible, but that one night with you, I heard it all. Everything you said. And didn't say. And, babe, I used to think the slow and quiet was the grave. But it was paradise all along." He stepped forward. "And I woke up like that. Happy. In a way I couldn't recognize. Didn't want to recognize because it was connected to someone. You. And seeing you look at me and realizing what a fucking rigmarole it would all be, I took the easy way out. I was a coward, I'll admit that, but

I'm trying to make it up to you. Never tried harder. So why can't you just give me a fucking chance?"

I stared at him. Long and hard. Digested his words. "Because this"—I waved my hands between us—"would never work. You're the world-famous rock star who lives in the spotlight, thrives on it, on everyone knowing your name, knowing your life. I'm the plain and unremarkable kindergarten teacher whose own parents barely remember her name. I'm not made for the spotlight."

He surged forward. "Bull-fucking-shit," he hissed. "If I ever met someone more remarkable, it was in a dream or on an acid trip. You're remarkable, babe. No fuckin' way you're forgettable. I wouldn't forget you. I can't. It's physiologically impossible. It's why I'm fucking here. You've cast some sort of spell on me."

I laughed. It was bitter. Ugly. And I didn't like the way it hung in the air. "But I am," I whispered. "And you did. Forget me, that is. You recognize me from high school, right?"

Something flickered in his eyes, finally. Far too late.

I laughed again. "Yeah, right," I muttered. I sucked in a long, painful breath that had nothing to do with my cracked rib. "You're right," I said flatly. Hope started to bloom into happiness on Sam's face. "Life doesn't deal in what-ifs. And mine doesn't deal in second chances."

And then I turned on my heel, though not toward the house. I knew I didn't have a chance of convincing three strong-willed males *not* to install a security system when I'd been the victim of an assault.

Victim.

I hated that that's what I was.

But hating it didn't change it. And despite the principle of the entire thing rubbing me like nails on a chalkboard, I wasn't going to let my pride influence my physical safety.

I was looking out for my emotional safety when I crossed the road in the direction of Pria and Garth's house.

And I pretended I didn't feel Sam's stare the entire time.

And I also pretended one solitary tear didn't trickle out of my bruised eye and down my cheekbone.

Chapter Eight

"N o. Fucking. Way," Garth spluttered after a long and considerable silence following my story.

I looked at him in surprise. Garth did not say such things in such tones—ever.

Then I looked to Pria, expecting her to be gaping at her husband in much the same shock as I was. But her expression mirrored his instead.

She kept her eyes on me and jerked her thumb toward Garth. "What he said."

I had just finished my entire Sam story.

Despite the pair of them being two of my closest friends, I had neglected to tell them anything about that night with Sam before now. In fact, I hadn't even told them I knew him. Once the story of Lexie's kidnapping and near death came out, so did where she came from. Before that, strangely, the band's origins and connection to an outlaw, recently reformed motorcycle club had gone unreported. I reasoned that the aforementioned motorcycle club had a lot to do with that.

But it became impossible even for some of the most notorious badasses this side of *Sons of Anarchy* to keep under wraps. That meant everyone and their sister sold stories about their connection to the band. Countless girls from high school touted themselves as old girlfriends. People used their historical connection to Sam and the rest of the band as some sort of social currency.

I did not.

Even if I was somehow the kind of person who did that, I wasn't about to broadcast the fact that I'd been obsessed with Sam before it was socially acceptable to be that.

It had kind of become inescapable when Pria snatched me by the front of my shirt, dragged me inside and slammed me against the wall in her foyer, demanding why in the fuck Sam from Unquiet Mind was eye-fucking the shit out of me and then arguing with me on the lawn. Then she asked me where I would like to be committed since I must've been batshit insane to walk away from Sam fucking Kennedy.

You never would've known Pria came from an incredibly conservative Indian family. Very traditional. I'd met them. Her mother was kind but quiet, her father friendly but incredibly stern.

So how they'd raised a daughter who swore like a sailor and married someone her parents did not technically approve of was anyone's guess.

Well, they hadn't technically approved at the start, or for a long while after, but they loved their daughter and were good people who wanted to see her happy.

So they accepted the Texas-born, utterly and completely American Garth. Though it was hard not to. His smile was infectious, his heart almost as big as the state he hailed from.

So I'd told them both the sordid story, hence them gaping at me now.

"B-but you're Gina," Pria said finally.

I sipped the wine that she'd uncharacteristically offered me. She accepted the fact that I didn't drink often, though she openly grumbled about me making her drink alone. But she'd offered the full glass, knowing, as friends did, that I needed it.

And I did.

"Yes, I am Gina," I agreed.

"You don't drink, don't party. Don't date after that cockface ruined you for everyone else. And not in the good way." She glared at that. She'd seen Simon for what he was from the start and had tried to tell me. But I hadn't listened. And because she was a good friend, she supported me anyway. Then picked up the pieces afterward. Then very seriously researched hitmen until she grumbled about having to send her three-year-old to college.

"You read books and teach babies and you're *quiet*," she continued.

"All of this is true." I nodded.

"So you can't possibly be sleeping with a rock star," she surmised.

Garth, who'd been quiet in his corner, chimed in. "It's always the quiet ones." He winked at his wife, who scowled at him.

"I know I'm not—"

"No, this is not because I don't think you're beautiful. You know I hate that shit you spout about you not being a fucking knockout. That's not it." She bulged her eyes at me to reinforce her point. "It's just... you're Gina."

"The quiet ones," her husband repeated.

I regarded both of them. "Let's get one thing straight. I'm not sleeping with him. I *slept* with him. Once, singular." I paused. "Or one night, more aptly."

Pria grinned wickedly at me with the underlying point of such a statement.

I didn't wait for her to interject something dirty or demand specifics. "It will not be happening again. He was here...." I trailed off, trying to wade through everything he said.

He was here for another chance.

For lots of sex.

For me.

"He's here because he's insane," I lied. "Who knows why. Maybe he's screwed his way around LA already. But whatever the reason, he got here, saw my face, for some insane reason felt responsible for it and has insisted on buying me a security system. Once my novelty or excitement or whatever wears off, he'll be gone," I said firmly. Convincing them, convincing myself. Because if I did that before he actually did leave, then maybe it would hurt a heck of a lot less.

Pria regarded me soberly, even though she was on her third glass of wine. I was only halfway through my second and was feeling slightly silly.

Though I did have the tolerance of a toddler.

"Honey," she said. "Even from a window across the street, I can see that man is not here for a screw or because you're some kind of novelty. You're so much more than that. You're just the only one who can't see that. It's broken my heart for years, and I've tried to show you that you're so much more than what he made you believe you are. Maybe this one is finally going to make you believe it. Because he sure as heck does. And, honey, you were wearing sweatpants, had greasy hair and no make-up on and he watched you like you were strutting down a red carpet dripping in diamonds. That's some *shit* right there. You better believe it."

She was so serious, more serious than I'd ever seen her, that I almost believed her.

Almost. Then I focused on the wine in her hand and the loving husband at her side.

She was in the perfect place to believe in fantasies.

I, however, was not.

Chapter Nine

"You sure you're okay, Gina?" Robyn asked, inspecting my expertly concealed face for the shadows of bruises that still lingered.

"I'm sure. I need to get back to work, Robyn. The kids need me."

The bigger truth was that I needed the kids. For once, the solitude my home offered, that my books created, did not satisfy me. In fact, it did the opposite. It drove me crazy, the quiet of it all.

Ever since Sam left, if I was honest. Since I drove him off, convincing myself it was for the best. Convincing him it was the only thing he could do.

So I'd called my boss and pretty much begged to come back to work.

Robyn was an okay boss. She could be a bit of a pain sometimes, not because she was a bad person but because she owned a kindergarten, was in charge of all the kids under her care, had two children of her own and a husband who didn't do anything to help.

I'd met him at a BBQ Robyn had hosted last summer. I didn't like him. Or the way he spoke to Robyn. It was familiar, and not in a good way. I hadn't stayed long that day. Because Simon had turned up. It was a small town, so his attendance wasn't a surprise, nor was his friendship with Bill, Robyn's husband. But his appearance rattled me. At that point, it had only been six months since the breakup. The glue holding me together had barely dried, and it was vulnerable to breaking all over again with his mere presence.

"Is Conrad back?" I continued.

Robyn nodded. "He is. I don't know for how long. His mother's relatives have come into town. I've met them and they seem to have been oblivious to the situation their grandson was in. They look like good people."

I frowned. Everyone looked like good people. Until they weren't.

Heck, half the town still idolized Simon, thought I was insane for letting him go. He'd been born and bred there, star of the football team, helped around town before it had become his job.

It was only behind closed doors that he showed himself. And even if I was the kind of person to tell everyone what an asshole he really was, which I wasn't, there was no true evidence to lay out.

That's where he was a genius.

"Is he holding up okay?" I asked, putting my focus back where it should have been, on Conrad.

"As well as I can see. He's resilient little guy."

"Yeah, he is," I agreed.

"Gina, what happened… it was horrible. If you ever want to talk about it—"

"I don't," I said, my voice coming out harsher than I'd intended. "I just want to get back to work, if that's okay with you."

Robyn regarded me. "Of course. The kids have missed you."

I relaxed when it became apparent she wasn't going to press for more.

Everyone pressed for more.

People I never usually talked to. People who didn't even like me. The incident was the talk of the town. And since Wayne was friends with Simon, he was influencing opinion in his favor.

I was not popular.

But then again, I didn't want popularity from people who would make excuses for a man who beat children and people who tried to help those children.

I just needed to focus on the things that mattered. Right now, it was getting back to my normal and pretending there was not a rock star somewhere in town, lying in wait to lay waste to my heart.

Though it had already been established that I was terrible actor.

~

I left the small building that the kindergarten was housed in, exhausted. I'd come back to work in search of noise, of the comfort that came with spending time with my favorite little humans. And I'd gotten it. All the noise. All the questions asking where I'd gone, what I was doing, who I was with. And then the hyper energy that they were all expending due to the excitement of having me back.

Midway through the day, I'd taken Conrad aside to try to talk to him, to make sure he was okay. He'd smiled wide at me and told me his grandma made the best cookies ever, and his grandfather had the best hugs and always had toffees in his pockets.

I hoped that meant he was happy. That these were good people. That they would nurture that little boy the best they could to try to repair whatever scars had been put there. There was no removing them. My degree in infant development told me that. Years one to five were some of the most formative in a child's life. Yes, it was true that most people couldn't recall those years with great detail, but that was because most people were lucky enough to have a relatively happy childhood. People who remembered were the ones who went on to have problems in their adult lives. Those who were unlucky remembered all of the bad and almost none of the good. And even if they didn't consciously remember, the crimes done to them in infancy presented into adulthood, affecting development.

And that only saddened me deeply. I prayed Conrad would have a new loving environment that nurtured him a way he hadn't been with his father.

I was so deep in thought that I didn't notice the presence in the parking lot until he spoke.

"What's up, gorgeous?"

My head snapped up and my eyes locked on familiar sunglasses. A familiar man bun. Familiar tattoos.

A familiar *Sam*.

Immediately my body relaxed with the noise I'd been searching for since his car had roared off a week ago, the husky cadence of his voice settling my mind. As much as I hated to admit it to myself.

Though I made sure not to show it on my face.

"What are you doing here? Why haven't you left?" I demanded, stopping and jostling the folders in my arms.

Teaching kindergarteners wasn't just playing with them and teaching them ABCs. I had to write development reports, progress stats, and research on the newest techniques for formative years.

He pushed off the car he was leaning on. It wasn't the same black one he'd been driving last week. This one was red. Blood red. And had a familiar horse on the front of it.

Of course.

If it didn't *demand* attention, was it even Sam?

I wouldn't expect anything less.

And I appreciated it almost as hungrily as I appreciated the man leaning against it.

The man who had been gone for two days and I'd convinced myself was gone forever.

"You know me, I love hanging out in the parking lot of kindergartens." He grinned. "Though I think I might have made a few parents nervous. And this time not with my good looks and fame. Turns out a guy hanging out in a parking lot not picking up a kid can be defined as 'creepy.' Even an attractive famous one. They seemed to calm down a little when I told them I was waiting for my *girlfriend*, who is of age. I went through great pains to convince them of that."

Without asking, he took the folders out of my hands with ease.

I glared at him. "I'm not your girlfriend," I snapped.

"Not *yet*," he agreed. "But in the future, you will be. So technically, here in the present, you are. Time is a construct, so what happens in the future already exists in the present." He winked.

"Not now, not ever," I said. "Give me my folders back."

I tried to snatch them off him but he lithely moved out of my grasp, lifting them above his head and out of my reach.

"Nope. Not until you agree to let me take you out for dinner."

"What are you, twelve?" I hissed.

"No, though I do know I have great skin for my age. I'm old enough to drink, fuck, and take a beautiful woman out for a steak dinner."

"I'm vegetarian," I informed him with a grin.

"Perfect, so am I," he said without missing a beat.

I narrowed my eyes. "You're lying."

He shrugged. "You'll just have to come to dinner with me to find out."

I stared at him, hating he was wearing me down so easily. The promise I'd made to myself was quickly shattering with his easy grin that had more behind it than it seemed.

As if my thought magicked it into existence, the glint of seriousness that sparkled beyond his smile took over completely. "Cards on the table, babe? I want you. Not in a way I've ever wanted anyone else. Not because I can't have you or whatever you've dreamed up in your head, but because I like spending time with you. I like that you don't talk a lot but when you do, you say something worth hearing. I like that you seem to be as quiet as a mouse with everyone but me, and I like that little fire you get behind your eyes when you're pissed off with me. Though I more than like it. I'd also like to see if I can conjure some other looks from you too, not just irritation or impatience. See if I can get back those glances I was treated to before I fucked up." He paused. "But, if after dinner with me, you still decide you don't want to explore this, and you know this isn't something, I'll leave you alone. I swear it. On my signed Nirvana record." He stepped forward, the folders he was holding brushing my bare arms. Though that wasn't what was giving them goose bumps.

"I know you said you didn't give second chances, and I sure as shit don't deserve one. But I'm willing to get down on my knees and grovel, even if this dirty parking lot will ruin my favorite pair of jeans." He glanced down, then back up. "Just dinner. No strings. Just some tofu and spinach and more of your fabulous company."

Despite all my better judgment, despite the knowledge of the fact that it was most certainly not just dinner with no strings, I found myself nodding.

"On one condition," I relented.

He beamed. "Anything."

"I get to drive the car."

"You do realize I'm quite attached to living and breathing?" Sam said, clutching the "oh shit" handle in the car as I roared around a corner.

The wheels stuck to the road and cornered smoothly, the purr of the engine humming like a kitten.

"This was your plan all along. You never intended on going to dinner with me. You're going to kill me in a fiery crash," he exclaimed, panic creeping into his tone as I flattened my foot.

I'd taken the long way into town, one that circled the woods and went out into the wilderness. It was an old road that no one ever used since they put the highway in to bypass the town. It was mainly for teenagers causing trouble on the weekend or the handful of people who lived in the isolated cottages peppered through the forest land.

The bypass had made it so there were a lot of hard times on the mom-and-pop stores, as way-through travelers were their bread and butter.

But the town was slowly growing again, new developments and low house prices bringing families in from the city.

"Calm down," I muttered.

"I am calm!" he half screamed. "The Dalai fucking Lama couldn't reproduce my zen right now."

I grinned.

If there was one thing my father taught me how to do, it was drive. Like really *drive*. His one financial vice that he refused to let my mother control was the high-speed sports cars he circulated on a yearly basis.

Mom called them his midlife crisis.

I called them his escape to sanity.

I didn't blame him, looking for an escape from my mother. They weren't his only one. I'd known that as I grew older. But they were the only one where he let me escape with him too.

"Now the key to driving excellently is acknowledging the possibility that you could crash. No matter how much of a good driver you are, there're always going to be bad drivers on the road. Defensive driving is what you need to master before you can attempt offensive driving," Dad told me with a grin. "And in the car, you don't have to be shy or worry about talking to people, like I know you do. In the driver seat, there's nothing to worry about but crashing. And even though that may seem something rather scary, it's peanuts compared to everything else life has to throw at you."

I was surprised at this insight from the father, who I thought was rather oblivious to the fact that he had a daughter, let alone her idiosyncrasies.

I flattened my foot on the last straight before we would hit town and I would have to obey the traffic laws.

"In racing, they talk about something called 'the line,'" Dad said as we sat on an abandoned highway just outside of Amber. A developer had gone broke and it just lay here, desolate, ending in a dirt road going nowhere.

"The line is basically just that cars go faster in a straight line." He grinned at me, nodding to the stretch of landscape before us. "In other words, flatten that foot."

Sam cursed audibly, but it was soon lost over the roar of the engine and the euphoria of flying through the open night. I'd never driven a car this fast before. It literally felt like a plane takeoff, the motion and speed pushing me back into the seat. I breathed into it, let my instincts take over.

Then, too soon, we were approaching the beginning of town. I touched the brakes slowly, knowing the dangers of hitting them hard at a high speed. I did it just in time to pass through town in what seemed like a blur, to me at least. I yearned to continue the speed, the one that had me almost certainly in the realm of losing my license, but I wasn't exactly well liked by town law enforcement, regardless that I didn't have as much as a parking ticket against my name.

What I had against my name was an officer named Simon.

So I slowed and maneuvered through the town I usually dreaded venturing into. I was dreading it tenfold now.

I glanced over at Sam as I parked outside one of my favorite restaurants. Not that there were many to choose from. Especially ones that offered a half-decent vegetarian selection. Not that I went out enough to really have a favorite. Simon just never took me here, so there was *that* going for it.

Sam was staring at me. Intensely. In a way that reproduced the vibration of the engine under my seat despite the fact that I'd turned the engine off.

"Uh, Sam—" I began.

But then I was cut off by him unbuckling my seat belt and literally dragging me across the seat of the small interior of the car to plaster my mouth to his.

Driving fast was like a drug to me. In order to drive, my father had taught me to follow my intuition, not to overthink anything and just *go*. I was still in that mindset, still riding that wave. So I didn't overthink the way I instantly melted into the kiss, the way I enthusiastically participated in it.

He yanked at my hair roughly, beautifully. There was nothing tender or soulful about the way he kissed me. It was brutal, like his life depended on it. Like he was a man presented with a buffet after dancing with starvation.

Or maybe that's just what it felt like for me, considering I hadn't been kissed since that night.

And I hadn't been kissed like that ever.

He pulled back and I let him, reluctantly. Somewhere in my mind, I realized we were in a flashy car that literally screamed "look at me" on the main street of a town that was always looking for new gossip. The chubby kindergarten teacher who had just been beaten up by one of her student's fathers making out with a rock star in his hundred-thousand-dollar car could be classified as "gossip."

Could be *sold* as gossip.

That thought filled me with icy dread.

"Where in the fuck did you learn to drive like that?" he rasped.

I was unable to wrench myself back to my side of the car. The proximity to him, his touch, the soft warmth of his breath against my face was just too enticing. Even with all of my previous logical thoughts whirling through my mind.

"My dad," I whispered. "It was kind of our thing. Open roads and empty minds."

His eyes flashed with something. Something that didn't disappear quickly, like the rest of his flashes. It was like he kept it there purposefully, in order to communicate to me that this moment meant something to him.

I just had to figure out what it actually meant.

"You're the most interesting person I've ever met," he said.

I laughed, leaning back, and he reluctantly let me go. "Now I know you're lying. You're a rock star who travels the world. I'm a kindergarten teacher who rarely leaves the house past 8:00 p.m. I'm likely the most boring person you've ever met," I informed him.

He frowned. "Not what you do that makes you interesting, babe. It's who you are."

And then, laying that on me, his face returned back to his

easy smile. "Now let's eat some *delicious* vegetarian food."

I couldn't help but smile back at him at the way he said it.

"Yeah, let's," I agreed.

The effect of him had been apparent and immediate the second we entered the restaurant. I didn't come here often but it was a small town, so everyone knew me and I knew most of the people scattered around the booths. It was only just after 5:00 p.m., but that was the busiest time for this place. Families and old people dined early, and they boasted about three-quarters of the population here in Hampton Springs.

The hostess, Adrienne, gasped when we walked through the double doors.

Gasped. Audibly.

As was characteristic of small-town eateries, people glanced at the door when someone new came in. People fit into two categories in small towns, or even in the big cities, or just life in general: people you wanted to talk to, or people you wanted to avoid. And that was the sport when you were out for dinner, figuring out how to avoid the people coming in the door, or waving them over for a chat to escape the monotonous dinner with a spouse you hated or children you resented.

It started with murmurs, people elbowing their tablemates and staring at Sam.

Gaping, more accurately.

"Holy fuck, is that Sam Kennedy?"

"With that kindergarten teacher, what's her name? Jasmine?"

My face flamed, and the pleasant feeling of before dissipated in two point five seconds. Sam was oblivious to the attention, probably because this wasn't an uncommon occurrence.

In fact, I was sure it was a common occurrence. We were a culture that worshipped at the altar of celebrity, so this was a god in person for most of these people.

Even if you hated their music, their movies or their political stance, the proximity of celebrities made you forget your own opinion and just be star struck.

Sam was used to having people look at him. I was not. It would've been okay if they were just looking at Sam, but that's not how it worked.

He had grasped my hand naturally when we'd gotten out of the car. I hadn't protested because it felt… right. Easy.

Now it was the harbinger of the sinking feeling rapidly approaching as people glimpsed at our intertwined hands.

I was now an attachment to Sam, and therefore up for inspection. I already knew I'd be found lacking, that people would be questioning what the heck Sam was doing with me.

I was questioning what the heck he was doing with me.

I tried to yank my hand out of his grasp, but Sam's grip tightened in response.

"Your finest booth, please," Sam requested. "Private, if possible," he added with a wink.

"Yo-you're Sam Kennedy," Adrienne breathed.

"That's what they keep telling me." He grinned. "And I'm a very *hungry* Sam Kennedy."

She gaped at him for a second more and then snatched two menus from the hostess booth, extending her hand. "Please follow me. I'll give you the best table in the house."

Sam gave her a grin and a nod in thanks. "Appreciate it," he murmured, following her.

That meant I was also following her, since Sam was making sure it was physically impossible for me to detach myself from him without causing a scene. Or *more* of a scene.

I didn't know if Adrienne designed it that way, but "the

best table in the house" led us right past every other table in the house. It was as if she was treating the other diners to a moving zoo exhibition—"watch Sam Kennedy walk through your dinner, then discuss what he's doing with the plain girl whose name we've just gone and forgotten."

I idly wondered if she'd get more tips for orchestrating the spectacle.

"Here we are," she said, holding out her hand like before, as if she was presenting us with our solid gold table overlooking Mount Everest.

Sam, the charmer that he was, treated it as such, grinning widely.

"Thank you"—he looked down at her name tag—"Adrienne."

She beamed at him, as if he hadn't read her name from a blatantly readable tag but plucked it out of his head.

He didn't notice, too busy focusing back on me to lay a chaste but very effing public kiss on my head. "This good, baby?" he murmured against my forehead.

I yanked away and sat down in the chair, wishing in the year that had passed that I'd managed to figure out how to fully dissolve into one. Since I hadn't, I had to settle for scooting as far over to the edge of the wall as I could.

Adrienne had given us the "most private" booth in the place. Pity the restaurant was well lit and open plan, with most of the tables scattered around the middle of the room. Ours was way in the back, slightly obscured by a pole and some fake trees, but we were still on display for pretty much the whole room that seemed to contain the entire town—with the exception of Simon, thankfully.

To my utter mortification, Sam didn't sit across from me in the booth. He scooted in next to me. Right next to me.

These booths were designed for four people to sit comfortably, I was sure. But Sam was tall, his limbs long and bulky with muscle. He took up a lot of space. I was not tall, but I was wide. Therefore, I also took up a lot of space.

"Sam," I hissed under my breath. "People usually sit *across* from each other when there are only two."

I tried to make my voice as quiet and forceful as possible, since Adrienne was still standing there staring, as was the rest of the room. Some were trying to do it covertly, over their menus, but most were just flat out gaping.

Sam fastened his hand on my thigh and grinned, oblivious to the audience, looking at me like we were the only two people in the room. Which would've been sweet if we actually were the only two people in the room. "So?" he said.

"So sit on the other side of the booth," I snapped.

Instead of frowning in the face of my snippy order, his grin widened. "Why would I want to be so far away from you? Here, I get to touch you whenever I want." He squeezed my thigh. "Kiss you whenever I want." He laid a small kiss on my nose. "And just be close to you."

I did not melt at his words and actions, no matter how sweet they were. Sam may have been able to melt the spectators away in his mind but I couldn't.

"Everyone's watching," I told him under my breath.

He didn't even glance away from me. "So? Let the fuckers watch. Every single one of them, guys *and* girls, can be jealous of my date for the whole night. And if I'm sitting all the way over there"—he nodded to the other side of the booth—"I won't be able to cock-punch anyone who comes up to try and talk to you." He smiled, then directed his attention to Adrienne, who still hadn't moved. She was clutching the menus, somewhat frozen in her place. Sam glanced at them, then waved his hand. "Oh, we won't need those," he said.

I frowned. I didn't think it was possible for my entire body to stiffen more, but it did with what he said. Simon ordered for me. Every single time we were out together. At first I'd gritted through it, because I thought it was because he knew food better than I did and it was his way of showing affection, of taking care of me.

I was also very deluded.

As with all the rest of the changes, the food orders became a weapon he could use against my self-esteem. We'd be out with his friends and their wives, or just his friends—Wayne was there on a multitude of occasions—and he'd order me a garden salad, no dressing, with grilled chicken. Nothing else. Most people got appetizers, desserts, while I just picked at my salad with a flaming face and tears in my eyes.

I'd been too upset to call him on it the first few times. But then it got too much, too mortifying, so I'd stood up for myself.

Or tried to.

"You know I'm doing what's best for you, Genie," he said, tone dripping with a sweetness so sickly I felt nauseas despite my empty stomach. "Did you see all of the other women out tonight? What they ate? It was much the same as yours. And you look much different than them," he said diplomatically.

He didn't need to come straight out and say it. We'd been out for dinner with his college buddies and their wives, who were all in town for a wedding. The women were nice, friendly. And all size six and under with tanned and toned skin. None of them had made me feel bad that I was not a size six, nor was I tan. They didn't need to, of course. Simon did that enough for the whole table.

"I didn't want you to be embarrassed when you ordered some veggie burger with a big side of fries and they didn't." He laid a patronizing kiss on my head. "I'm just looking out for my girl."

I wished I could say that was the beginning of the end.

It wasn't.

I put up with that crap for seven more months. And I'd cursed myself for doing that. But regret did nothing to the past. It could ensure that it didn't repeat itself, however.

Hence me glaring at Sam and opening my mouth to rip him a new one, no longer caring about the audience.

"We'll have one of everything that doesn't contain meat," he said. Then he turned to me. "Wait, what's your favorite dish?" he asked.

I blinked at him. "The veggie stack with a side of grits," I said automatically, immediately forgetting the Simon past when presented with the Sam future.

He looked back to Adrienne. "So we'll have *two* of those, one of everything else."

She gaped at him, that time in something else other than star-struck amazement, though there was a lot of that sprinkled in too. "You do know that our menu is rather… large," she said.

He nodded. "I'm in Texas, and I would be disappointed if that wasn't the case." I watched him wink. "I'm a Libra, we stink at making decisions. I'm not going to be buried behind a menu, stressing over tofu or veggie burger, wasting time that could be spent talking to this lady. You see?"

Adrienne gave me a once-over, as if she'd only just realized I was there. Her expression told me, as a woman who was well-versed in such looks, that she indeed did not see. But she beamed at Sam.

"Of course," she chirped. "To drink?"

He glanced at me. "I know you don't like the hard stuff, so you a tea or soda girl?"

Once again, I blinked in confusion, no doubt giving Sam and everyone in the room the impression that I was suffering a series of strokes. As before, I answered on autopilot. "Um, tea. Iced. Sweet." I said them all, like we weren't in Texas, where all tea was served sweeter than sweet and colder than Simon's heart.

He nodded. "Two teas. Thank you so much."

And then, having served her purpose, Adrienne was dismissed. It wasn't cruel, but it was purposeful.

Sam gave me his entire attention, and I did my best Adrienne impression, gaping at him.

At some point she wandered away.

"I can't believe you did that," I spluttered.

He stroked my hand absently. "What? Ordered a tea that didn't have Long Island in front of it?" he asked. "Me neither. I will say it's a first for me. Such things are normally necessary when eating in a fish bowl."

That was the first inclination that he noticed the situation, and his slightly chilly tone told me he didn't bathe or revel in it like he made everyone believe.

The hand that was stroking now grasped mine. "But you don't drink. And not only would it be incredibly rude for me to suck down drinks while you sip tea, despite my monster tolerance, but I want to be stone-cold sober for this night. No mind-altering substances. You've already got me turned all kinds of upside down." Another squeeze. "And I like it, babe. But I want to talk to you. To *know* you. Just be with you. Maybe pretend we're on a date and I hadn't majorly fucked anything up?" he asked hopefully.

I wished it was that easy. More than I wished to magically lose twenty pounds or not crave chocolate-covered... anything.

Watching his face, which was filled with childlike hope and manly determination, I thought maybe, just perhaps it could be that easy.

"Ordering everything on the menu was a little excessive," I said with a small grin.

He grinned too. And it wasn't small. It was wide and

triumphant. "And two of your favorite dish," he added, as if I would've forgotten.

"Yeah, excessive," I repeated.

"Life is meant to be lived in excess, babe. Or else it's not even fun."

I stared at him. Then did the only thing I could do at that moment. The only logical thing I could. I leaned forward and kissed him, pretending we were just us and the past, future, and multitude of eyes on us didn't exist.

Chapter Ten

"That was… nice," I said, perhaps the biggest under-statement this side of Watergate.

Sam raised his brow. "Nice? Despite that being an utterly and horrific description of the magnificence of my company… and yours too"—he winked—"you sound surprised. Did you not think I would offer titillating conversation? I read too, you know."

I smiled. "Oh, the conversation was well titillating—though for everything I didn't expect, fun being one of them, titillating was a given," I teased, underplaying just exactly how titillating it was. I thanked the lord that I was in my work clothes, a thick camisole and light sweater that obscured how hard my nipples were trying to protrude from their confines.

And they weren't doing so out of some fancy, expensive and sexy lace number. No, comfortable and practical cotton. I only needed them for support, not for exhibition.

Though I'd learned the lesson about my Bridget Jones underwear. The sucking-in mechanism was not without the mortification factor. Plus the damage to my internal organs. Pria and I had had a bonfire in my backyard on which we roasted them and Garth's favorite tee shirt, which she despised and had snatched out of the laundry pile.

"That's marriage, Gina," she'd said when I raised a brow at her throwing the shirt onto the fire with a hysterical grin. The

polyester in it fed the flames. "Marriage is pretending you don't hate their fashion sense, their cooking, and their parents until you think of a way to get rid of them."

I gaped at the way the fire illuminated her eyes, bringing a mania to them that only flames could produce. Hellfire and all that.

"Holy crap, are you going to—" I glanced around my empty backyard and whispered, "get rid of Garth's parents?"

She laughed, the mania gone from her eyes. Well, not completely gone—she was still Pria. "Gosh no. I wouldn't go to that much effort. Even though I could totally get away with it." *She winked.* "But they're old, so nature will do my job for me soon enough."

"So we've established my ability to titillate," Sam said, bringing me back into the present, which, until now, had been worth totally and utterly living in. Now it was time to remember the past and think of the future—specifically what would happen in the future if I didn't stop this right now.

Sam's eyes darkened, the darkness of the night seeming to seep into them. "Well, in the conversational arena, anyway. We've haven't even scratched the... other arenas." His voice remained light, like it had all night, but it roughened, and the scent of sex sifted through the air. Or the promise of it. The memory of it.

Memory.

It was a slap in the emotional face.

I stiffened, and Sam, being as perceptive as he was, would've noticed had he not launched into the second part of his statement.

"But you didn't expect to have fun with me? *Me*? Sam Kennedy, who legally got his middle name changed to Fun last year."

"Really?" Curiosity salved my emotional burn. Most

people said that and you automatically knew they were joking for dramatic effect. Sam didn't just joke for dramatic effect. He lived his life for dramatic effect, so I wouldn't put it past him to do such a thing.

He grinned. "No, I actually got it changed to Eagle, but the principle is the same. Any dude who changes his middle name to Eagle just because is obviously fun. Oh, and the guy who, every year, hosts the most kickass Cannes yacht party that pond has ever seen. So I think my fun credibility has been solidified." He paused. "And my sex appeal, by *People*, *GQ*, and *Rolling Stone*, just in case you were wondering." He winked.

I rolled my eyes. I may not have been immune to the Sam I'd had dinner with, who'd shouted at me for trying to go dutch on the bill and who looked at me in a way that melted the world away. But I *was* immune to Sam Kennedy, the rock star, the one everyone got to see and experience. The one who melted everyone else because they didn't know him any better. Didn't *want* to know him any better.

He frowned at my eye roll, then decided to continue his tirade because he was… well, Sam.

"My badass street cred is obviously way up there. Just standing next to Killian is like a testosterone shot. Not that I need that." Another wink.

Another eye roll.

"But I don't need that moody biker Ken doll. In case you hadn't heard, I apprehended a murderer and—"

The slice he ripped out of his sentence was so abrupt it cut through the air.

The silence as his brain caught up with his mouth. He had been so busy being Sam that he tried to outrun emotional wounds that, by the looks of his tortured eyes, hadn't healed.

Then again, it had only been just over a year since he and Wyatt stopped Lexie's stalker from murdering her, despite having already shot her. And then they had to witness her dying. Actually *dying* in front of them while the paramedics worked on her.

They brought her back, obviously. But she'd flatlined twice. Once while she was in Killian's arms, then again at the hospital.

That left a mark.

A big one. Especially when the band was something more than a bunch of pretty people who played good music and got paid a lot for it.

They were a family.

Each of them brought their fragmented families into the fold and, like a jigsaw puzzle, had created one that had stronger ties than blood.

Not that anyone but Wyatt and Lexie had a semblance of a family. I didn't know much, but I knew Noah's and Sam's parents were worse than mine. A lot worse. Which was why what they had, what they created when they were teenagers, was so special.

I witnessed it in high school, and even from the outskirts, I felt the warmth of it. And that residual warmth, plus my books and my ability to propel myself out of my circumstances, gave me the tools, the strength to get through high school without freezing solid at the lack of warmth in my own family.

My outlier status was self-imposed. In the blink of eye, Lexie and everyone would have welcomed me in. Lexie tried.

She still did. Which was the reason for the invite to the infamous wedding.

But I couldn't be in that family.

Not when I was in love with one of the key members.

Who would never love me back.

Who would never see me.

Even now, I couldn't believe this was anything more than temporary. I wouldn't. I knew better. Sam was a good guy, despite getting in his own way a lot of the time, but we were worlds away from each other. He'd realize that soon. I needed to remember that, no matter how permanent his touch, his glances, his presence felt, this was temporary.

And the pain of that, the need for emotional survival, trumped my need for emotional warmth.

The chill from Sam was palpable as I extracted myself from my own head in order to do the same for him.

"Sam," I said softly.

My voice, perhaps the absolute softness of it, counteracting the harshness of his thoughts, jerked him out of his stupor.

His eyes, just a little too bright, focused back on me and not the ghosts of the past. "Anyway, that's history," he said cheerfully. "So, these amazing qualities profoundly exist in the man before you and you didn't think you were going to have *fun*?" he asked in disgust.

I regarded him, considered pressing him on the Lexie subject, inviting him to talk about it. Despite his bravado, Sam had demons. Large ones. It was usually the people who smiled the widest, laughed the hardest who had the biggest reasons to break down. He needed someone to break him down so he wouldn't implode.

But then those memories reminded me.

Someone.

That someone wasn't me.

Despite this strange behavior of late, the sentiment stayed true.

"It was not all of your qualities, including incredible modesty, that made me question the funness of the evening, but rather the prospect of being a goldfish inside of a bowl. The bowl being our table. And everyone being the people tapping against the glass. I know it's second nature to you by now, Sam, but I'm not used to being looked at. People don't look at me.

And that's fine. Nice. I don't do well in the spotlight. I'm not made for it, nor do I desire it. You are born to it. Whether or not you had found a drum set and a stage, you would've found it. Me? No. So I was dubious, among other reasons"—I gave him, and the elephant in the room, a pointed look—"about being suddenly visible when I've always been comfortable in my invisibility."

He was silent for a moment. Most likely looking for another smart quip.

He leaned forward, grasping my neck lightly. Not like before when he'd yanked me over for a brutal kiss. No, this was tender, for the contact rather than a larger purpose.

"No, babe. You've got that wrong. So wrong. It's not that people don't notice you. They notice you." His eyes scanned over me. Even as the disappearing light made it harder for me to see them, the fire down my body showed me their journey. "People notice me because I'm Sam Kennedy. The drummer of that band who once got in a fist fight with Ozzy Osborne in front of a Bed, Bath and Beyond." He paused and grinned, but it was full of melancholy. "And sure, if I wasn't that Sam, I'd like to think my devilish good looks and je ne sais quoi would get me looked at just for that. Just me. But life isn't about what-ifs and could've-beens. It's what is. So *I am* Sam Kennedy. I do play the drums. I have my stage and my spotlight, and that's why they look. And it's because of our society and the way it's structured around the spotlight that they make sure they're *seen* looking. Not because of who I am specifically, but who I am to *them*. What looking at me, talking to me, taking photos of me eating my burger will do for them. And their path and outlook on life. Or their status in this fucked-up social totem pole."

He paused, the bitter expression and words to match not seeming right on his face but at the same time they did. Because they were honest. It wasn't the script about living for the fans and loving the fans and living an excellent life. It was the truth that I suspected he hadn't shared with anyone. Even himself. Especially himself.

He regarded me watching him. "It's a shitty thing to say about the masses who legitimately keep me in the lifestyle to which I'm accustomed and should have been born to, but they're leeches. All of them. They look to take something from me. And sometimes that's not bad. Hell, sometimes it's the only fuckin' thing that keeps me sane when those twatrockets with cameras are chasing me about the place, getting all my wrong angles. It's the knowledge of a kid who used to live in Amber and had a shitty home life and was searching for an identity. Something to take from life. The meaning of it. The point. Whatever the fuck you're meant to get from blood." Again, the darkness from outside seeped into his eyes, that time not fueling his dark desire but feeding the demons. Not the ones who'd made an appearance earlier. Those were young, toddlers really. These were old, ancient in the scheme of Sam's life span, and much deeper, much more ingrained in him.

"So I took. And I took from Cobain, Hendrix, Vicious, the list goes on. And fuck if that isn't the reason I'm here today." His hand, which was still lightly at my neck, tightened. "And I mean here, Gina, *right here*. In this car, with you, in the middle of some fucking travesty of a town in a fucking travesty of a state. But the whole twisted and wonderful journey, the ride that had been fast and relentless and fucking great, it's slowed down. And I'm happy as fuck about that."

His words were like poetry plucked from some book, some hero's monologue about fate and everything in his life happening to take him to his girl. It filled me with a pleasant warmth. But it didn't sink into my bones. Because nothing took me to him. There was no journey that put me here with him. I was already there. I had already been there. I was always there. And that was the bitter, rotten, twisted pill that tainted his words.

He furrowed his brows, and at first I thought he'd read it in my eyes, all of those tumultuous emotions.

"I kind of went off my point there a little," he said with a grin. "Not that I mind. But back to looking. More precisely people looking at you and you having the fucked-up thought that somehow people weren't looking at you. That they didn't notice. Trust me, babe, they've noticed. But you don't see it because they're not taking shit from you, sucking it out. They're reveling."

I blinked at his words, trying to keep my hands inside the emotional roller coaster he was in control of.

He leaned forward so his breath was hot on my neck. "And, babe, it's not gone over my excellently styled head that I was one of those fuckers still taking from others, trying to build up who I was instead of looking at you and seeing what I see now," he murmured.

I swam the depths of his eyes, tasted his words for a long moment. Listed every specific detail of the moment for preservation, for later. For whenever this blew up in my face and these moments would be all I'd have left. And I'd be self-deprecating and visit them. Seldom, perhaps, but I would.

And because I was self-deprecating, I asked the next question.

"And what do you see now?" My voice was less than a whisper.

He stared at me. Actually at me. *Saw* me.

And I realized maybe I was blind to him seeing me all along. That I was just another one in the masses, taking from him what I thought I saw. What I wanted to see. What I needed.

"Everything," he said simply, his voice so rough I was surprised it didn't graze the very air it caressed.

And then he kissed me. Not brutal and needful. Not

taking. Slow. Patient. Tender. Giving. Giving me the moment that I hadn't even realized I needed. You know, that moment every girl, no matter how much she denies it, has when she gets kissed.

Really kissed.

Like in those Nicholas Sparks movies, or in any romance ever written. Kissed like no one really got kissed in real life. Like the man attached to your lips couldn't breathe without you.

Something created to give us humans something to dream about, to think of fondly, that something so perfect and right and simple existed somewhere. Not anywhere in the real world, but somewhere.

But it did exist.

Right here outside my ordinary house in my ordinary town in Sam's bright red Ferrari.

And then it didn't. Moments only existed for short times. That was the very definition of a moment.

And the cold air was a sharp taste of another moment.

One that lasted significantly longer.

Called reality.

Sam went back to his side of the car, clutching the steering wheel tightly. His entire body tight, juxtaposing the softness of seconds ago.

"I need to go," he gritted out.

"Okay," I whispered, trying to hide the hurt in my voice. The confusion. I was now off the emotional roller coaster and was experiencing emotional whiplash. "Well, thanks for letting me pay for half of dinner, after a strong discussion. And for a… nice evening," I said, trying to bulk up my tragic tone with an equally tragic joke.

It hurt.

The rejection.

Second time around.

Third, if you counted high school.

But you couldn't really count that considering he didn't even know I existed, let alone that he was rejecting me.

He must have noticed it, the way my own body tried to curl in on itself, because his head snapped to me and he grabbed my hand before I could move it to open the door.

"I have to go," he repeated. "Because if I don't I'll do what every one of my instincts—two blue ones in particular—is screaming at me to do. Which is to take you into your adorable but ridiculous fucking house and fuck you against your front door first. Then drag your half-naked, flushed body into your bedroom and do depraved and fucking exquisite things to that equally fucking exquisite body. I'd do it on those cat sheets you had swinging on your washing line two days ago. And that's all night, babe. And the next morning, I'd wake you with my mouth, and then we'd be going sheet shopping because I wouldn't want an animal, flannel or otherwise, having to witness that again. And I will be doing it again," he promised.

My breathing quickened the second he started speaking, my entire body flushed at the images in my mind. I could feel them. His words. *Right there.*

"But not yet," he murmured, voice firm, as if he was trying to convince himself more than me. "Because I don't want to fuck it up like I did before. Because I know I did fuck it up before. More majorly than when U2 got stuck in that lemon. And I don't want to repeat the mistakes of that night after the wedding. That morning." He eyed me. "The mistake was not me sliding inside you, tasting you or talking till the sun went back down again, just in case you got my meaning wrong. My mistake was not seeing you. And then seeing too much. Not of you, that's never going to happen. Of myself. And because I was a fucking coward, or because I wasn't used to seeing, I was a prick. And I want your forgiveness. I want to earn it. I know you haven't given it." He glanced up at me. "But you wouldn't punish me like some other chick by torching my car, or selling the story of my crooked dick, or killing me on the way to dinner." He grinned. "Because you're nice. Kind. And most importantly, you're not like any other chick. None other. You're an original."

His eyes twinkled with something that looked like a memory. That made me lose my breath a little with the thought that he might remember that day in high school. The day I'd fallen in love with him, that maybe might have meant something to him too. But before I could grasp that twinkle, that hope within a hope, he continued.

"I'm not going to lie and say I'm not the Christopher Columbus of that certain brand of chicks. I was a stupid kid who liked to spend time with empty heads because they helped keep my own head empty. But you're not that. I'm in uncharted territory here, so I'm being careful. 'Cause last time I wasn't, I hurt you. And for as long as I live, I'm not gonna put that fuckin' look on your face again. Ever. And even if this shit doesn't work out, for whatever reason—life's always a good one—I'll still be here to kick the ever-loving shit out of whatever idiot guy gives you that look after me. Not that I'm planning on there being an after me."

There it was. He just said it. Like that. Laid out his forever. And if I hadn't misheard, his forever intentions.

After one technical date.

And despite the thoughts I'd had minutes ago about how temporal this all was, a part of me, a very large part, believed him.

"You can't say things like that," I choked out.

"Who says?"

I blinked. "I don't know, the laws of nature?" I grasped at

straws. "You can't know that yet. It's too soon. Much too soon. We haven't even.... We're not even...." I trailed off, not really knowing where to take that.

"Too soon? Babe, I've known you since you wore overalls and literally walked down the corridors of school with that beautiful face tucked in a book. Just because it took me longer to figure out that face buried in that book was *my* face, that doesn't mean it wasn't there all along. It's like backdate dating. I already know it's all mine, but I'm putting in the work because I want to. Because I need to."

Despite the utter beauty of the sentiment and the words, the stubborn, independent and scarred woman inside of me bristled. "Already know it's yours?" I repeated, my voice holding hints of warning.

He grinned. "Yeah, babe. And you know it too. You've known it longer than I have." He winked. "Though that's because we both know you're smarter than me. Much smarter."

I pursed my lips. "If I was smart, I wouldn't be sitting in this car right now."

He grinned, but there was something behind it, beneath it that told me he was entertaining the memory of that horrible morning after. Somehow, I saw the guilt and pain he carried around from that. Like I could read it in his tight and fictitious smile.

Which, of course, was ridiculous. But I saw it all the same.

The back of his hand trailed along the top of my cheekbone. The touch was barely even a touch, a whisper of his skin against mine. Despite that, I felt it everywhere.

"Whatever it is, smarts or stupid, fate or luck, I'm glad you're sitting in this car right now. That I get to earn back the right to be in your bed, in your life, in your *everywhere*." His eyes darkened. "Don't earn much these days, babe. Silver platters are so common they're like chipped Tupperware at this point. I know for a fact that what I'm working toward with you is going to be the most precious thing a man has ever possessed."

I blinked again at words that should not have been uttered at the end of a first date, yet made the air sweeter and lighter but heavier at the same time.

His touch was no longer gentle as he grasped my chin between his fingers.

"Now get in the house before I remember that I'm not the good guy I'm pretending to be," he growled.

And it was a growl that went right down to the base of my spine and then traveled between my legs.

I nodded, unbuckling my belt on autopilot, clutching the door and opening it an inch, the muggy night air rushing in, a welcoming escape that I both craved and dreaded.

Before I had the chance to properly move, to catch my breath in the solitude of my home, Sam clutched my wrist, yanking me backward so our eyes met.

"I'm telling you that I'm only pretending to be the good guy for the sake of honesty. I'm also telling you so you can prepare for when I'm not good. For when I get bad."

In theory, the sentence should've sounded ridiculous. And because Sam was saying it, it should've made me laugh. He was the perpetual joker, after all.

But there was no joke in his eyes. I could see it. The darkness the joker hid. The unhinged part that even Jared Leto in full getup couldn't replicate.

He squeezed my arm. "You get it, Thumbelina? Need you to get it now. To brace. Keep your hands inside the ride at all times, 'cause once I get going, there's no stopping me. And you won't want me to stop. Ever."

I just gaped at him. Like an idiot. I was probably even drooling. I couldn't exactly tell. My whole body felt numb. Apart from the place where he was holding me. All of my nerve endings were singing. Screaming. In a good way. In the best way.

"Babe? You get me?"

I nodded. Cleared my throat. "Yeah, I get you," I whispered.

He grinned wickedly. "Great. 'Cause I *know* you're not pretending to be good. You are good. Which means you're going to be the best at being bad."

And on that, after completely and utterly soaking my panties, his mouth inches away from mine, he leaned back and let me go.

It looked easy, effortless, the motion. But the way he held his body, the way he clasped his hands into fists the second he stopped touching me, told me different.

Told me he was exercising great willpower.

And that made it that much hotter.

I opened the door fully, unable to deal with all my emotions without spontaneously combusting.

"So, I'll, um, see you," I stammered lamely. Like the big dork I was.

To all of that, I said, *"I'll see you."*

Dork.

He grinned wickedly again. "Oh, babe, you'll see me," he promised. "And I'll see you. *I see you.*"

Chapter Eleven

"Hear you're with a rock star now," Simon said, leaning against my car door so I couldn't get in. I was laden with groceries after fielding all the inquiring stares that I was not used to while doing my Saturday shop. No one had actually found the courage or lack of manners to come right up and say anything to me, but the stares themselves were exhausting. I just wanted to get home to where I was safe and could eat four of the frozen Twixes I had in one of these bags.

It should've been the carrot sticks, considering the sheer amount of food I consumed last night, but whatever.

Of course Simon had heard I was with a rock star. I'd only just gone to dinner with Sam last night, so that was more than a sufficient amount of time for the rumor to fly around town. I should've counted myself lucky that it was only around town at this stage. It was only a matter of time before it was around… well, everywhere.

Still, I wasn't counting myself lucky at that point in my Saturday, when I was innocently running errands and found my asshole ex in my path. I glared up at him. "I'm not *with* a rock star," I snapped. "I've just got one stuck to my shadow."

Simon furrowed his brows slightly under the aviators I despised. His face was too small for them. They swallowed him up like he was some reality star hiding a hangover.

He wore them because he thought they made him look badass, like some cop from a movie. When really he looked like a manlier, paler Khloe Kardashian.

"So you're not dating him?" he clarified.

I narrowed my eyes at him and glared, something I hadn't had the courage to do ever before. Even when I finally broke up with him, I'd been as quiet as a mouse, my eyes glassy with unshed tears though not with actual sadness. I was so angry with him, though more importantly with myself for taking so long to do what I should've done the second he started hurting me. So I'd cried out of anger.

Now I couldn't believe I wasted a drop on him.

Hindsight was 20/20 in most scenarios. With exes, it was more so.

It was safe to say he hadn't exactly taken to the breakup well. He hadn't expected me to gather up enough courage or self-worth to do so. He'd harassed me for weeks afterward, after first making sure the whole town believed it was him who broke it off. Not that I gave a crap about what the town or his idiot buddies thought about our relationship finally ending. It took me threatening to take a restraining order out on him to get him to leave me alone.

He'd blanched with real fear at my real threat. Then his eyes changed and he scoffed. "Yeah, like anyone at the sheriff's office would believe someone like me would be harassing the chubby kindergarten teacher he's been throwing a pity fuck to for a year."

The parting shot had done what he'd intended it to do. It hurt. But my threat had done what I'd intended it to do, and he left me alone.

Until now.

"It's not really your business who I am or aren't dating," I informed him. "It stopped being so when *we stopped dating.*"

That time his brows furrowed in a look of disdain that was

oh so familiar. "Of course you're not dating the rock star," he said, ignoring everything I said, as was his way. His aviators went up and down my body in the way a farmer might look at a stud mare that wasn't as promised. "They date supermodels and actresses. You're not really cut from the same cloth, are you?" he asked pleasantly. "It's fine. You're *fine*. Just not extraordinary. Plus characters such as that always have photographers following you around, taking pictures at unflattering angles. Then the world can judge you for not saying no to dessert. You don't deserve that," he said, feigning a caring tone that I saw straight through. Even so, he knew where to hit me. Right in the insecurities I'd been wrestling with the entire day. Since the moment Sam's Ferrari had roared off last night, in fact.

Not that I let it show.

"Jesus," I muttered. "How did I ever date you? You are *such* an asshole. I'll just have to plead temporary insanity for the time that I thought you *deserved* me. You're a small man with a small mind and a nasty heart. Let's hope you find a woman who's the same. I hear the supermodels in LA are going through a drought, you know, considering Sam's spending time with someone not cut from the same cloth. Or able to wear the scraps of cloth they call clothing."

And on that note—because I knew Simon and knew he wouldn't let me get the last word, especially when he was bodily preventing me from getting into my car—I turned on my heel and stormed off.

Home wasn't far away. That was the good thing about small towns—nothing ever was. I'd get Pria to drop me off at my car later on tonight when it didn't have an asshole stuck to it.

About ten minutes and some seriously sore feet later, I was reminded of the bad things with small towns: running into the last person you want to see at the worst possible time.

Or the first person you wanted to see at the worst possible time.

I couldn't figure out which column the dark-haired man in the convertible fit into.

"Hey, hot stuff, want a ride?" the voice offered. "Also, would you like a lift home in my vehicle before that?"

I glared at him in answer, stomping over to the car and dumping my shopping bags in the back before depositing myself in the seat.

I wished I had enough willpower to be stubborn and tell him that I'd walk the mile and a half. But I didn't, because it was summer in Texas and I was unfit and not wearing footwear designed for such a walk.

"You are giving me a lift," I informed him, slamming the door and glaring at him. "*Nothing* else."

He regarded me. "Sure, yeah, that's fine. Just out of curiosity, what's got you walking in the middle of a day that is remarkably similar to the temperature in hell when you're wearing sexy but totally unpractical shoes? And what's got you in that particular mood that is nothing like the one I left you in last night?"

"No talking," I snapped.

The car purred underneath me, but even 550 HP and the man I was obsessed with sitting in the seat next to me did nothing to cheer me up.

I hated that I let Simon affect me, let him sow the seed of uncertainty within me about Sam. Though he didn't exactly sow it, since it was already there, had been the entire time. He just watered it so it grew too big to ignore.

"Alrighty then," Sam said cheerfully, pulling back onto the road.

I was sure Sam would be one of those people who sensed

when you needed complete silence and then continued to fill it anyway. His entire personality gave me that certainty.

But he was not. He gave me the silence I asked for, or rather demanded, the entire ride home. Which was a lot shorter than it would've been if I'd walked.

We pulled up to the curb, the short drive having done nothing to quell my anger. It had done a lot to feed my insecurities, however.

Sam turned the car off and I sat there, simmering, even forgetting the fact that my Twix bars were well and truly melted by now.

"So, can I talk now?" he asked, face tentative. "Or kill someone for you?"

I glared at him. "No, you can do neither. You can do me the great big favor of leaving me the heck alone," I snapped. "My life wasn't perfect or exciting or anything really before you came along, but it was *mine*."

Sam's easy and relaxed smile disappeared with my outburst, giving way to confusion. "I thought last night—"

I cut him off. "What? You take me to dinner *once* and I forget everything else? Everything being that you and I are never going to work."

He stared at me. "Stop trying to list all these reasons about us not working," he commanded. "How about you give us a chance to just work?"

I found myself losing it. The last stubborn strand of my frayed cord of sanity or patience or whatever it was snapped. *I* snapped.

"Why?" I screeched. "Why is it that you want me, Sam? Why is it that you've made it your mission to come down here and harass me until you get your way? Which would most likely be having your way with me and then you'd throw me away again, just like you did last time. Why?" I demanded.

"Because I can't get you out of my head," he replied simply. Too simply.

"No, not an answer," I snapped. "Why, Sam? Why can't you get me out of your head? What is it about me that has you so certain you need to turn your life upside down for me?" I yelled.

I was pushing. I knew I was pushing. For an answer I'd never get. And when I didn't get it, it would hurt. But I had the hope, that stupid one that had flared up as high school me whispered romantic reasonings in my ear.

"I don't fucking know!" he yelled back. "I don't fucking know, okay?"

I waited. For more, for something else. Something tangible. But nothing came.

Except a ringtone that shattered the extremely uncomfortable and painful silence between us.

I jumped slightly and Sam frowned at the center console. When he saw the name illuminating the screen, he picked it up.

"Babe, the last fucking thing I want to do right now is answer this phone, but I have to. I've kind of been neglecting shit in LA."

I glared at him, because that was much more productive than crying. "Feel free. In fact, please go all the way back to LA. I can't do this right now. I don't need this right now. Just give me some fricking space, okay?"

He must have caught on to something hysterical in my tone that made him grasp my sincerity because his face slackened in defeat. "Okay," he said. "But don't take me leaving as me not wanting you or that I'm giving up on you or whatever warped shit chicks believe when a man listens to what they keep saying they want even when it's really just some sort of test that a guy will fail either way. I want you. That's not changing any time soon. And I'm coming back." He yanked me across the car and kissed me before I or my anger could stop him.

But he let me go quickly enough for me to snatch my fury once more and stomp out of the car before I could do something insanely stupid like beg him to stay.

He didn't. Stay, that was.

And even though I'd convinced him, and myself, that that was exactly what I wanted, I hated every second of the week we were apart.

⁓

Sam

When Sam walked into a recording studio, he usually felt instantly at home. An itch in his bones automatically began the second he crossed the threshold, yearning for the music to flow through him. To create it, live it.

That time there was an itch, but not to be there. To be in a little cottage in the middle of nowhere. One that smelled like vanilla, was warmer than the Bahamas in the summer and was the only place he truly felt at home other than sitting at a drum set.

Just over a year ago, if someone had asked him to describe his Nirvana, he'd say bright lights, a screaming, writhing crowd and music. Fast. Loud.

Now his answer would differ.

It would greatly fucking differ.

"Dude!" Wyatt pounced on him the second he entered the room.

He was still wearing his sunglasses. Mostly because it was a nice signal for any people he ran into in the halls that he was not into speaking, and also to hide the huge fucking circles lingering under his eyes from lack of sleep.

He was used to lack of sleep. Fuck, he usually existed on Adderall, coffee, whiskey, pussy and great thoughts. He and Wyatt consistently partied for three weeks straight not two months ago.

He would've done that and still looked as fresh as a daisy.

But spending all night escaping yourself, living fast was a whole lot less exhausting than spending a night in bed unable to fucking escape the thoughts of *her*.

Of her bruised face.

His fists flexed with the thought of it. Not just because he needed to beat the shit out of that fucker once more, though he made a mental note to do so as soon as he got back to Hampton Springs. And he'd be going back.

It had felt wrong, driving away, getting on that plane, putting the distance between them she'd pleaded for.

Though that's why he'd done it. Not because of the string of threats and curse words Mark had shouted over the phone but that desperation on her face, for him to leave.

It had hurt. But he did it for her. He reasoned he'd cut off a limb for her if it made her just the littlest bit more comfortable.

He hoped it wouldn't come to that.

But he'd be back there, with her, in her as soon as he could. Sooner.

Not just so he could *fucking sleep*. So he could work to repair that look on Gina's face.

The memory of her begging him to leave stung.

If it hadn't meant letting the whole band down by missing this recording session, he never would've left in the first place.

He would let anyone and everyone else in the world down but these people. They were his family. His real one. Despite the death stares two-thirds of them were treating him to.

"Where the fuck have you been?" Wyatt demanded.

"We've been calling and texting. Bro, you haven't even posted a Snapchat story in like *days*. We would've legitimately thought you'd died if you hadn't send Lexie that video of you catching those M&Ms in your mouth."

Sam grinned, his eyes softening at the sight behind Wyatt, where Lexie was leaning against Killian, smiling at him knowingly.

He didn't like that look. The one that made it seem like just because she was held hostage by that motherfucker called love that she could recognize it him. Was it a cult or something?

Love. Fuck. Did he just *think* the word love? And immediately think of Gina while he was doing it.

Not that there was a second in the day when he wasn't thinking of her.

"You've got to admit, that was hil-ar-ious," he said breezily, the tone well practiced. "Are we going to rock or just stand here with our dicks in our hands?" He glanced at Lexie. "Obviously I know you don't have *your* dick in your hands." His eyes moved up to Killian. "You have his."

Lexie, used to his crude and what some had called immature verbiage, laughed.

Killian, also used to it, did Sam a solid by not killing him. The guy was super protective when it came to that chick. Hence him now being head of security and always attached to her if she wasn't on stage or he didn't have to be off on his Harley doing whatever outlaw motorcycle dudes did.

Sam liked to imagine they buried infidels to their heads in sand and left them in the desert for days to pay for a disrespectful comment against their wallet chains. He didn't actually ask Killian much because he didn't want his fantasy to be ruined.

He tried to move past Wyatt to his drum set, which didn't hold as much draw as Gina in her stupid fuckin' pj's, which were somehow hotter than any skinny supermodel in a scrap of lace.

Wyatt clutched his upper arm to stop his journey.

His pushed his glasses onto his head. "Bro, watch the moneymakers," he scolded.

Wyatt didn't let him go. "Where have you been? Seriously, bro."

Though he seemed pissed, there was concern in his tone too. The band was close. Closer than family, which wasn't hard in Sam's case at least. They barely went a day without speaking or seeing each other. Hell, Sam and Wyatt lived together. As had Noah and Lexie before she married Killian and got all domesticated and shit.

Well, she wasn't technically domesticated because she was the lead singer of their band, but whatever.

"I am Keyser Soze," Sam replied. "I have been everywhere, yet nowhere."

Wyatt narrowed his eyes, Lexie grinned and Killian glowered, most likely still stewing over the dick comment, or doing whatever badass bikers think about. Glocks, waterboarding, whatever.

Noah was quiet in the corner, as was characteristic. Sam was the most vocal of the group, despite Lexie being the lead singer, then Wyatt and Lexie, and then Noah. He'd been like that since they were kids. Someone had to take one for the team and swallow some words while the rest of them spat them out on a regular basis.

"Did you get a chick pregnant or something?" Wyatt asked seriously.

"No I did not grace some lucky woman with the incredible gift of my thoroughbred genes," Sam said, doing his best to ignore the way his dick hardened in his pants at the thought of Gina growing his baby.

He definitely did his best to ignore the warmth that settled somewhere in the vicinity of his chest at that thought too. The dick hardening was natural, but that other feeling was… not. He had always sworn to himself that he would *never* have children. No man to repeat the sins of his father, plus he was a selfish motherfucker. Kids required a lot of attention. And they were breakable as shit.

He knew that. Since he'd been broken as a kid. And no way would he open up the prospect of having the same thing happen to another kid.

He was about rock. Like Stephen Tyler, Mick Jagger and Bob Dylan, amongst others, he'd stop when he was dead. Even then, he planned on jamming it out with the greats downstairs.

"Jeez, can't a guy have some mystery?" he asked, shrugging out of Wyatt's grasp and sauntering over to his drum set.

Wyatt glared at him while he strung the strap of his bass over his shoulder. "Mystery?" he repeated. "You leaked *your own* sex tape. There's no such fuckin' thing as mystery with you."

Lexie giggled again and pulled out of her husband's embrace. Not before he kissed her tenderly on the head and whispered in her ear. Sam never got how he did that without looking like a total fucking hemorrhaging pussy. Killian made no secret of the fact that he adored and worshipped his wife since she'd taken him back. Granted, he'd come pretty fuckin' close to losing her, so it was only natural that he wanted to make sure she was real. But he was still totally pussy whipped. And still he somehow managed to keep his badass card.

Sam sat down, grasping his drumsticks. Usually, the moment he was in front of the kit, the sticks in his hand, he felt complete. Whole. It unnerved the fuck out of him that he realized that was no longer the case. Whole was when he had Gina's body writhing underneath him. When he was filling her to the hilt. When he was holding her fuckin' hand. Shit, he was pussy whipped too. And he'd only fucked her once. Okay, technically more than once, but it was one night one fucking year ago. How was that even possible?

"Okay, you got me. I got late admission to Hogwarts and I was learning how to turn annoying bassists into pigs," he snapped. "And now they're going to kick me out for revealing the secret to a *muggle*. Happy now?" He didn't wait for Wyatt's response before he put his headphones on to drown out the noise.

Problem was, even when they started playing, when the music was almost deafening, he still somehow heard Gina's small whispered voice over it all.

"You ready to talk about it now?" Noah asked, sipping his beer.

"About climate change? Yes, I do worry about the polar bears quite a lot," Sam replied, not sipping his whiskey. He drained it in one gulp. No matter how much of the shit he drank, he didn't seem to be able to get wasted. It was getting frustrating.

They were at his and Wyatt's place in Calabasas. Lexie was at the beach house with Killian. It technically belonged to all of them, having bought the place with the first real money they'd made, amongst other frivolous things. But unlike the other frivolous shit, that was a good purchase, one that lasted. It was theirs. Though Lexie did all the decorating and chick shit, they all owned it, made it into their sanctuary.

They'd all agreed to make it Lexie and Killian's marital home when they needed to be in LA and not in Amber, where Killian had built Lexie a kickass home by the sea. Sure, they had the means to buy something else, something bigger, flashier, whatever. But they didn't have the means to buy what was already in that house: love, memories, all that girly shit.

Sam twirled his glass between his fingers. Gina didn't exactly have the means to buy a mansion, he was pretty sure, despite her cute little car and her trendy-as-shit clothes. But she owned something that money couldn't buy.

Her own little sanctuary.

Even though he had barely spent enough time in it, hadn't even seen it all, including the bedroom, he knew it was his too.

She was his.

He made a mental note to get a realtor the next day so he could get out of his current pad. It was nice. Impressive. Huge. Expensive. None of that shit would impress Gina.

And no way did he want to bring her back to the same bed where he'd entertained countless girls, most of whom he barely even remembered.

He was thinking all of this while his two best friends regarded him as if he'd grown a third head.

Wyatt crossed his boots over his ankles, dangling his beer from the neck of the bottle between his thumb and forefinger. "Cut the shit, bro. Spill," he ordered. "You refused to go to a fucking *lingerie launch* tonight." He paused. "Fuck, are you dying or something?" he asked, half-serious.

Sam chuckled. "Yeah, you wish. Then you think you'd have a shot at the most attractive dude in the group. But that title would pass to Noah. You just don't have his bone structure." He winked at Noah, who shook his head.

They both stared at him, not saying anything. Just waiting. They knew how much Sam hated silence. Even with Grateful Dead playing in the background, that's what it was, silence. Music didn't count as noise when it was necessary to your existence. You didn't count oxygen as food, did you?

"Fuck's sake. What are we, chicks?" Sam snapped. "I just

didn't feel like going out, okay?"

Wyatt took a pull of his beer with a raised brow. "Yep, you're definitely dying," he surmised.

Sam huffed out a breath, scrolling through his phone, ignoring all the notifications from his Instagram account. He wouldn't admit it to himself, but he was looking for some kind of communication from Gina.

It had been ten hours.

Nothing.

"Fine, but when I tell you this, you're not allowed to scream or cry or ask for a fucking tampon, because even though you're acting like a chick, you're not one. Evidenced by the fact that I am not feeling any attraction toward you. And you'd make a striking woman, just FYI," Sam said.

Wyatt ignored him and waited.

"I've been in Texas," he began.

Even Noah, the master of the poker face, looked moderately surprised. "You hate Texas," he said with a frown. "You said the only thing you like about it is the girls in short shorts who are the most polite at giving blow jobs—your words, not mine."

"A girl lives there," Sam continued, glaring at Noah. He didn't remember saying that. He was sure it was true—it sounded like him—but it still pissed him off.

"*I knew it,*" Wyatt hissed. "It's happened. Hell has frozen over. You're going to have nowhere to go when you finally bite it."

Sam glared at him. "Eat shit." He drained his glass. "This girl, she's different. Hooked up with her the night of Lexie's wedding, fucked it up majorly the morning after. Hence me turning into whatever the male version of a nun is—"

"A monk, douchebrain," Wyatt cut in.

Sam flipped him the bird. "And battling the worst case of

blue balls this side of the sun," he continued. "So, on behalf of my treasured balls, I went to go fuck her out of my system."

"So romantic," Wyatt muttered.

Sam ignored him. "When I got there, all that shit went to the wayside. She opened the door…." He flinched at the memory of her bruised face. And the paralyzing thought of her getting hurt again. He wasn't there. And she could get hurt.

And it'd fuck him up.

More than he already was.

"Let me guess, she punched you in the face and the blue balls still remain?" Wyatt asked.

Sam glared at him. "No, the opposite, actually." He paused, hearing how that sounded outside his head. "Wait, I didn't punch her in the face," he said quickly. "Some other fucker did. Repeatedly. She was bruised as shit when I saw her."

The energy in the room immediately changed. It had been light with harmless ribbing, with amusement. Like a fire sucking the oxygen out of the room, Sam's words snuffed out all air of joking. Wyatt's grin left his face. Noah clenched his fists.

"Fuck, bro," Wyatt muttered, his words heavy with fury.

"You kill him?" Noah asked conversationally.

Sam shook his head. "Wanted to. But the only color I don't look good in is orange. Though I am researching the best options for killing someone and making it look like an accident. I'll give Killian a call after this."

Wyatt nodded. "Need another shovel to bury that hole, man, I'm there."

Sam nodded in thanks. "For now, he's behind bars. Had to pull some serious fuckin' strings to get him there, though. Idiot local force had him out on bail. After going to *my woman's home* and assaulting her. For reporting him for assaulting his kid," he seethed. It came natural, calling her his. That's what she was. Even if it was taking longer than he liked for her to admit it.

Longer than he liked was any longer than it took for him to realize it. He knew he was an impatient motherfucker. It hadn't been a problem for the past half a decade though, as he hadn't had to wait for anything. Even those rare seasonal peaches he loved. He got them flown in from whatever part of the world had a favorable climate at the time.

Gina was not something to be bought. She was something, someone to be earned.

Noah's body went rigid. Sam felt for him. Hard. He knew his brother's demons. Not all of them, not even half of them, but he knew his dad had used him as a punching bag until that punching bag grew biceps of his own. This shit was going to hit home for him.

It hit home for Sam, whose own father had been too drunk to actually hit him on the regular, but he'd tried, on occasion. He was usually too drunk to land a solid hit. Not that the hit needed to be solid for it to hurt.

"Kid's four," Sam continued, shaking himself free of his own demons.

"Motherfucker," Wyatt hissed.

"Yeah," Sam bit out.

"Where's the kid now?" Noah asked. His brother's tone was still calm, but his entire body shook. Just slightly.

Sam clenched his teeth. "With relatives. Mother's side. Already got Keltan to do a comprehensive background search on them, seem to be good people. On paper. Though it's pretty fuckin' easy to be good on paper. We've got eyes on the situation. Duke stayed down there watching both him and Gina until I can get back." He scratched at the back of his head. "Whole thing doesn't sit right with me. Got a bad feeling."

And he did. He didn't believe in psychics and all that shit, but despite that, he felt something in his bones. Dread.

Expectation. The similar bitter taste the air had when Lexie had been going through all her shit.

Wyatt's face changed. Realization dawned. "Wait, *Gina*?" he repeated. "Lexie's friend Gina? Gina, who we went to fuckin' high school with?"

Anger Sam didn't understand polluted his tone.

He frowned at Wyatt as he pushed from his chair in the direction of his whiskey bottle. Luckily he'd made sure it was within easy reach. "The very same. Though now she's *my woman*, Gina." He paused halfway toward the bottle. "Even if she won't admit it yet."

Wyatt stood and, in a gesture that shocked the shit out of Sam, yanked him out of reach of the whiskey bottle by his collar.

"What the fuck, man? This is custom!" he growled as Wyatt wrenched him up.

"Gina?" Wyatt yelled in his face. "All the girls in the planet you had to fuck over, and you fucked over *her*?"

Sam blinked at him, his own rage simmering. "What's with the Hulk act, bro? You got a thing for her? I'll tell you now, that *would not* end well," he warned.

Though he strictly knew that wasn't the truth. Wyatt had some fucked-up shit going on with Lexie's other friend, the little spitfire who'd punched Killian in the face last year—Emma. Logically, he knew that. But Sam didn't do very well with logic in a normal situation. With Gina, logic didn't fucking exist.

"What's not going to end well is you fucking with this girl," Wyatt hissed. "Jesus, Sam. Are you fucking insane?"

Sam glared at him. "Of course I am. But what the fuck does that have to do with Gina?"

"Do you even *remember* her in high school?" Wyatt demanded.

"Of course I do, despite how much cheap booze I drank,"

Sam snapped. It wasn't untrue. Though he wished he could un-remember most of it. A lot of it when he wasn't with his friends was a fucking shit show.

But Gina, yeah, he remembered her in high school. He'd noticed her.

Snatches of the girl caught his attention, in her quiet world. But he'd made it his mission to move fast so he didn't have to focus on anything too hard. He remembered appre-ciating her for her understated beauty, remembered thinking if his life was different he might have asked her out. As it was, even back then, he wasn't about to pollute a girl so obviously innocent. Plus, he'd been a selfish fuck, focused on escaping his own situation. He hadn't needed anchors. Some strange part of him had sensed back then that if he went near her, he would be chained to her.

Right now, that prospect made him feel warm and fucking fuzzy, filled him with whatever warped sense of joy his mind allowed him to feel.

Back then he had the emotional capacity of a teaspoon; therefore, even though he appreciated her, he sure as shit didn't deserve her. Fuck, he didn't deserve her now.

"You're so full of shit," Wyatt seethed.

Sam was starting to get pissed right the fuck off. "What are you talking about? Did you get into my Adderall or some-thing?" he demanded, yanking out of his grasp.

That was the second time today Wyatt had put his hands on him. The dude was obviously battling his own chick shit and rubbing it all over him and his fabulous wardrobe. Sam could barely handle his own shit; he did not need to take on Wyatt's.

"You have no clue, do you?" Wyatt asked.

"I have clues about anything and everything," he snapped.

"She's a sweet girl, Sam. She's not someone you fuck over." Wyatt regarded him levelly, reaching down to snatch his beer and drain it.

Sam narrowed his eyes. "I'm not planning on fucking her over," he gritted out.

Wyatt sighed. "You already fuckin' have." His anger deflated and he sank down back onto his seat.

"What are you talking about?" he demanded. He felt as if he was missing something. A big something, considering Wyatt's violent reaction to news he'd only just shared with them. Sam had been relatively certain his friends would be happy for him. Sure, Wyatt's chances of getting laid would likely be cut in half since he was losing the ultimate wingman, but he'd survive. And his chances of getting laid would likely even out since Sam didn't plan on touching another pair of fake tits attached to a fake bitch. Which exempted most of Hollywood. Most of the world, in fact. He only planned on touching one pair of tits for the foreseeable future, and they were not fake. Whatsoever. His dick twitched in his pants at the very thought of them in the palms of his hands. Of the way her nipples strained out of her shirt when he kissed her in the car.

He hadn't touched them, tasted them in a fuckin' year. It was past time.

Something dinged in his tit-filled mind. Maybe the reason Wyatt was so pissed was because he somehow knew about that horrific morning.

But he couldn't. Gina hadn't told anyone, not even Lexie. And he'd expected that for months. Chicks talked, especially about guys who treated them like shit.

Lexie hadn't attempted to kill him, so that was his reasoning that Gina hadn't told anyone. So Wyatt couldn't be mad over how he'd treated Gina that morning because he didn't know the specifics.

But he obviously knew something else.

Something Sam didn't. And he hated being out of the loop

at the best of times. This was the worst of times, considering it was about the woman he wanted to know anything and everything about.

Wyatt glanced to Noah, who like always was watching, observing. "You want to tell him?" he asked.

"Tell me what?" Sam demanded, feeling uneasy. And that had nothing to do with the half bottle of whiskey he'd downed.

Okay, it had a little to do with that.

The last time he'd eaten was all that vegetarian shit with Gina. And fuck if some of it was pretty darn good. But that was almost two days ago. He made a mental note to eat.

"Dude, the girl was totally in love with you in high school," Noah said bluntly, but not unkindly. "Not in a creepy pathetic way, but in a sad kind of way. Like she knew you'd never notice her. Despite her being beautiful, kind, and actually pretty fucking funny if you got her comfortable enough to speak to you." He paused. "And you were blissfully ignorant because you were too busy chasing empty heads and tight asses and making damn sure you didn't have anything that would chain you to Amber. *Everyone* knew. I think you even fuckin' did. Even if you are too stubborn to admit it to yourself. And now, seven years later, you're comin' back into her life because, what? She looked beautiful at Lexie's wedding, so you finally opened your eyes enough to see her and you fuck her?" He shook his head, a glimmer of frustration peeking through his blank expression. "Fuck, man, did you even acknowledge that you *knew* her in fuckin' high school?"

Sam flinched at the memory of him deliberately calling her by the wrong name. He'd already been kicking himself for that without knowing this shit. Now he wished he had a time machine so he could go back and kick Sam from a year ago firmly in the balls.

Then he'd go back to high school and make sure he saw

Gina. He didn't even fuckin' care if it fucked up some space-time continuum balance and chained him in Amber on minimum wage for the rest of his life.

Noah took his flinch and his silence as answer. "Yeah, you've most likely been so wrapped up in how she makes *you* feel that you didn't even stop to look at how *she* feels. We know you're not deliberately callous, that's not you. You're emotionally dense, not cruel. But fuck, man." He shook his head again.

It hit him deep to hear the disappointment in Noah's tone. He had disappointed his parents often throughout his childhood, for existing amongst other things. His father blamed him for having to get a job on a local construction crew when he knocked Sam's mom up at sixteen. He blamed him for the fact that it meant he lost any chance at a football scholarship and the fact that he began drinking to deal with that loss when he gained a son. He gained fifty pounds, went bald early and turned bitter and ugly. That disappointment hadn't bothered him once he realized what a piece of shit his father was. But disappointing someone you respected? That shit was worse than forgetting the lyrics to Metallica.

They bathed in a long silence.

"I fucked up," he said to the room. To himself.

Noah nodded.

"Big-time,'" he said.

"Big-time," Wyatt agreed.

"Fuck," he hissed.

There was another silence.

Sam regarded his friends. "Think she'll forgive me?" he asked hopefully.

"If she's suffered mild brain damage, maybe," Wyatt said dryly.

Sam growled at him. Actually growled like a fucking dog. Shit. He was totally turning into Killian.

And he didn't mind one fucking bit. As long as that meant he got the girl.

He stood up.

He was getting the fucking girl.

The slam of their front door made both Sam and Wyatt jump from their spots on their respective sofas.

Wyatt had tempted him with a *Walking Dead* marathon while Mark was getting his flights sorted.

The jet was in the shop for maintenance so they had to do commercial, which on short notice was proving to be not as quickly as Sam would've liked.

And Sam would've liked it to be last night, when he'd decided to get his ass back to his girl.

He did realize how much of douche he was turning into worrying about private jets. Past him would've totally ass-kicked present him. But he really didn't care about the jet, though it had been pretty fucking epic when they'd first gotten it.

That was when he treasured possessions because he didn't have anything else worth possessing.

Now he had her.

Fuck the jet.

But he was so wrapped up in his favorite show and the slam of the door that he momentarily forgot all of that.

"It's the zombies! They've come!" Sam yelled, gaping at the monster eating a human. "I knew it would come. Take him first." He shoved Wyatt at the figure storming into their living room.

The figure turned out to be much smaller than the zombie Sam was expecting. And prettier. And not dead. Though she was incredibly pissed off and looked like she might be able to commit murder. "Seriously, Sam?" she hissed, her pretty face flushed with anger.

He stopped using Wyatt as a human shield, but kept him close considering Lexie seemed mad. "It could happen, Lexie. Just because you've got a husband who's likely more badass with a crossbow than Daryl, you should still worry at least a little bit." He held his thumb and forefinger together so an inch of space separated them.

"Cut the shit, Sam," she clipped, and Sam's eyes widened.

Lexie didn't get angry often these days. She was all into yoga and Zen and shit, and she didn't usually have much to get angry about. Before, yes, when things were dark behind those eyes and her heart was so broken and shattered even an emotional cripple like Sam could see it, feel her pain. But not now. She was somehow healed and whole and brighter than before. Now there were no shadows in her eyes. And nothing to worry about. Especially not an apocalypse. She had a husband to do that and zombie killing for her.

So seeing her this pissed had him more shocked than an actual zombie storming through the door would have.

"What? I didn't scratch your Jeep, it was Wyatt." He immediately pointed at the gaping Wyatt.

"Gina!" she yelled. Yes, *yelled*. "Gina! It's not enough for Wyatt to be *fucking* with my best friend." Her laser beams attached themselves on Wyatt for a moment, the weight of her curse like lead in the room as she didn't use "fuck" as a comma like the rest of them did. "Yes, I know about that. And Emma is well able to castrate you herself, but that doesn't mean I won't if you break her heart." Her gaze whipped back to Sam as she stomped toward him on her platforms. "But *you*." She pointed at him.

He half expected a shock to come from the gesture, it was

that violent. Plus, someone who did that much yoga had to have connected to magical powers underpinning the universe. Otherwise, why else would they do it?

She was so far from Zen right then it was laughable. "Gina. She's sweet and innocent and not someone you fuck with," she hissed. "You leave her alone. You hear me? She's not another groupie. Some empty-headed whore who doesn't care how you treat her as long as she carves a notch in your bedpost. She's my friend. A person with feelings and a heart and not meant for the fucking *circus* you call a life. The girls you take to bed know what they're getting into, Sam, but Gina doesn't. She isn't like anyone else. And I will get Killian to kill you if you hurt her." She paused, putting her hands on her hips in the universal chick battle stance. "No, actually I don't need Killian for that one. He can just dispose of the body."

Sam stood up, his own anger brewing at his friend, the girl he considered his sister thinking so little of him. Anger was easier and more comfortable to grab onto than the hurt her lack of belief in him created. "I know she's not like anyone else," he yelled. "You think I don't recognize that shit? Why do you think I'm trying to do everything in my power to make sure I'm fucking worthy of her? You all are so fucking certain that she's not right for me, but you guys don't know shit about what's right for yourselves, let alone me."

He glared at Lexie, whose eyes widened at his outburst. "You spent *four fucking years* in your own wasteland because you were so certain that the man who loved you throughout the whole of high school, the man who took a fucking *bullet* for you, was breaking up with you because he, what? Popped your cherry and suddenly didn't love you anymore? That's the biggest load of horseshit ever. You were miserable for four years because you didn't know what was good for you. You were so quick to think the fucking worst of him, just like you're doing to me. Right now."

He fastened his eyes on Wyatt. "You. You're just as much a whore as me, though you'll never fuckin' admit it. Just because you remember their names and make them breakfast after doesn't make you any less of an asshole. Especially when you're playing your fuckin' cat-and-mouse game with Emma. You were both lying to yourselves for that shit."

He narrowed his eyes at the gaping woman who had lost most of her fire now. "Lexie, you've clued in, got the happy ever after, and congratu-fucking-lations for that." He clapped his hands. "But, Wyatt, you're still lying to yourself, and we all know Noah is lying to fucking all of us. I'm the only one trying to live his fucking truth right now. And she's my *fucking truth*. Okay? She's it. You don't have to understand it, but I'd appreciate it if you'd fucking accept it, because I've spent almost ten years accepting all of your bullshit and now it's time for you to get right with some of mine."

And on that, he turned on his heel and stormed out of the room. He really wanted to see what happened with Rick's team at the prison, but his little outburst didn't really accommodate that. And he was all for dramatic flair.

Right then he was thinking not about dramatic flair but about getting to his girl. Even if he had to fly fucking *coach* to get there.

Fuck, he'd do a Forrest Gump and run the entire way if that's what was required of him.

As long as he got to her, as long he *got* her, the rest of the shit didn't matter.

He pretended not to feel the naked fear of the prospect of not getting her.

He was Sam Kennedy, after all. He always got what he wanted.

Chapter Twelve

Gina

I was walking through the parking lot after a long Monday when my phone dinged. I thought it was Pria, with another scolding text telling me how fucking stupid I'd been for dismissing Sam fucking Kennedy and not even at least sending him across the street.

Safe to say she hadn't been happy about me pushing him away. Even though she got it.

As well as a woman with a husband who adored her and family who'd nurtured her for who she was could, at least.

"*You deserve to be happy, babe. I know you know that, in theory. But you're so scared that everyone is going to break what you worked so hard to fix that you're going to break it all by yourself," she'd said when I'd gone over for* Game of Thrones *night.* "And also, it's Sam fucking Kennedy," she added.

It wasn't Pria.

Unknown: Is it okay for me to come back yet?

Despite everything I'd convinced myself of, my heart leapt when I read the message. I knew exactly who it was. I dumped all my crap into the passenger seat of my car, staring at the phone, deciding what to say in response. Deciding whether I should respond *at all*.

Of course, Sam wasn't waiting for me to decide.

Unknown: Because I am back. So you need to make sure it's okay for me to be back within the next twenty minutes, because that's how long it's going to take for me to get to your place. Just landed in Dallas.
And even if you're not okay with me coming back, I'm coming anyway. I'm going to make it my mission to make you okay.
Unknown: Whatever it takes.
Unknown: Even a limb.

I frowned at the screen. And at the last part about the limb. Dallas was not twenty minutes away. It was an hour away. In good traffic.

My phone dinged again.

Unknown: I rented a really fast car. I'm not fucking around getting myself to you, Thumbelina.

Maybe it was stupid and illogical and totally irresponsible, but I thought about my father telling me to trust my instincts while I was on the road. He might not have been a fountain of fatherly advice, or fatherly *anything*, but I thought maybe I might just listen to him on that. So I followed my instincts.

Me: I've decided. It's okay. Just get yourself to me in one piece, please. All limbs attached. You're nowhere near as good of a driver as I am.

His response was immediate.

Unknown: Know that, babe. I'm nowhere near as good of a person as you are, let alone driver. But I'm gonna try and be really good at pretending until you beg me to be bad.

Even reading that made my panties dampen. And then I realized the reality of what he meant. And the hair removal, or lack thereof, situation downstairs. Plus the utterly boring and sensible underwear I was wearing.

I didn't waste time in getting in my car and racing home to attempt to prepare myself for Sam in twenty minutes.

Though even if I had twenty years I didn't think I'd actually be prepared.

I opened the door, expecting Sam. Since I was expecting Sam and still floating on frigging clouds from the fact that he was here, I was opening the door with an uncharacteristic and wide smile.

Which, as it turned out, was wasted on who was standing on my stoop.

The smile deflated like a balloon when I didn't see a rocker with a ripped pair of jeans and a ridiculous tee shirt. Instead, I was treated with an asshole in an expertly pressed uniform.

"What are you doing here?" I asked tightly, my entire body stiffening.

He flinched back a little, the megawatt and totally fake smile on his face flickering slightly when my greeting, or lack thereof, sank it.

I understood why. He was used to the weak woman he'd battered down like a chef tenderizing steak. Molded from my natural state so I suited his purposes. So he could chew me up and spit me out.

I was not that anymore.

I was far from that. I had repaired myself, re-inflated everything that he'd tried so hard to destroy.

But he hadn't exactly seen me at my best when he'd taken my statement a couple of weeks ago. I was sure he'd forgotten about the other day, written it off as one of my "moods," as he used to call my attempting to stand up for myself. Somehow structured my strength into me being a raging shrew.

So I stopped.

And before that day, I'd made an art out of avoiding him. And it *was* an art. Avoiding people you didn't want to see in a town as small as this was nearly impossible.

Nearly.

But for someone like me, who had enough motivation, like survival… well, they learned quick.

So before what I was now referring to as "the incident," I hadn't seen him since he'd given me a panic attack in Walgreens a year and a half ago. And he hadn't even spoken to me. He'd just gazed at me, eyes smug with the knowledge that even though he was technically out of my life, he still held dominion over my mind.

Then, he did.

But this was not then.

"That's not the greeting I was expecting, Genie," he said warmly, using the name that had come to make me feel physically sick. An outsider might even say his response held a hint of good-natured teasing.

An outsider I wasn't. I knew better.

"No, I'm sure it wasn't the greeting you were expecting," I agreed. "But it's the greeting you deserve." I paused. "No. The greeting you deserve was the one *your buddy* treated me to two weeks ago. But I don't have enough upper body strength, stupidity and evil in me for that, so I'm just working with what I've got."

That time his smile did more than flicker. It disappeared completely, giving way to a moment of ugly reality. The empty and calculating stare that had stripped me bare, stuck me like a needle a million times before.

It did smart a little, hitting me like emotional muscle memory. But I was strong enough to let it deflect off me.

"Are you threatening me, Genie?" he asked softly. "I'm a police officer, remember?" A threat of his own lingered beneath his words, his poisonous, all-American smile.

I smiled right back. I wasn't as practiced in a threatening showing of teeth designed to patronize or wound, but I think I did pretty well for a beginner. "Of course I remember. The uniform and general air of a douchebag on a power trip are incredibly hard to miss," I replied breezily.

I didn't know where all of this was coming from. Being a smartass was not part of the new, or the old, Gina; this was a new me entirely. Sam flickered into my mind, as he did more often now. If I was honest with myself, he was becoming my constant, everything else temporary.

That was dangerous.

But it was the immediate danger right in front of me that I needed to focus on.

And he *was* dangerous. I knew that before and I knew it now. What was wrong inside him could never be fixed. There would always be something off, like that smell in the refrigerator that no one seemed to find the source of. The only thing that would change would be that he'd rot more.

He was just as shocked as I was, and despite my own confusion at my current brashness, I was thoroughly enjoying his reaction. He wasn't used to being on the back foot. It suited him.

"What has gotten into you?" he asked, voice sharp. His

eyes ran over my body in a way that settled a cold chill over my exposed skin.

There was a lot of it. It was a muggy summer's day, so I was dressed in a halter sundress that showed a lot of cleavage and molded down my curves in a way that I would've been uncomfortable with before.

He surely wouldn't have let me wear it before. He never actually ordered me to wear things; even in my beaten-down state, I would've bristled at that, refused to be demeaned like that. No, it was more pointed and hurtful comments that hit right in the soft spot, the tender areas.

Backhanded suggestions, even a look, were all used against the unsure and insecure teenager that still lived inside of me. It was stark now, the difference between the way he looked at me and the way I should be looked at. The way I deserved to be looked at.

Sam's hungry gaze felt like the pleasing ray of sunshine on my skin with a delightful tickle of desire chasing after it.

Simon was cold and uncomfortable and it prickled at me. Every instinct inside me was telling me to slam and lock the door and hide away.

But I would not run or hide from him.

I'd been doing that for long enough. He did not deserve the satisfaction with a thought that he'd ruined me for life.

"You're different," he said finally, rubbing at his clean-shaven jaw with his naked and manicured hand.

I found myself comparing every part of him to Sam. Listing everything Sam had that he didn't. And there was a lot of that. Simon worked out every single day, only ate carbs on the weekends or drank them with his buddies. So he had sculpted muscles that weren't actually that impressive considering the effort he put into making them. Sam ate almost his entire body weight in dinner last night and hadn't once mentioned a workout. He was still bigger than Simon.

Simon's skin was tanned, not from any kind of outside work but from the tanning bed he visited once a week. He did not have a speck of ink, often telling me that tattoos were for criminals.

His blond hair was expertly styled and slicked to the side, like usual. It took him exactly forty-five minutes to get it like that. I'd witnessed Sam construct a world-famous bun in less than five seconds.

Every part of Simon that an outsider might consider attractive took work. A lot of it. Just like his illusion that he was a decent human being.

"Good spotting," I replied, folding my arms. "Now, did you come here for a reason? Or just to fuck up an otherwise pleasant morning?"

He flinched again. I didn't curse around him. Not that I cursed often in the first place. But once, when I'd stubbed my toe on the edge of the coffee table and let out a string of only vaguely offensive words, he'd looked at me in disgust and informed me that women who swore were ugly and trashy.

Hence watching my Ps and Qs around him.

I didn't flinch at his look or his stiffened shoulders.

I know he expected me to, now that he'd dropped the mask of pleasantness. In the past I'd done exactly that, flinched away at his cruel and vaguely threatening stare. I would not do that now, nor would I ever again.

His eyes changed then. Flared with something I didn't like. The way they did toward the end, when his touch repulsed me and he'd somehow sensed that. It had turned him on more.

And that's when it ended. That one horrible night when I'd realized the monster he truly was, learned the hardest way. Woke up the most brutal way. But at least I woke up. And at least it was before he could do anything that look in his eyes hinted he was capable of.

He stepped forward. "Yeah, you're different. I like it, Genie."

I resisted the urge to step back. Doing so would not only give him the satisfaction in the idea that he intimidated me, but it would bring him over the stoop and into my space. No way was I letting another asshole brute his way into my sanctuary and defile it just because he was stronger than me.

So I straightened my back and braced against the ugly feeling of him in my face, at his repulsive cologne that I was sure he bathed in.

"Step back," I ordered, voice even, meeting the erotic sickness in his eyes.

He didn't listen. In fact, it seemed like my voice worked to encourage him more. My repulsion made his eyes flare with excitement.

"See, I came here to see if I could persuade you to recant your statement—you know, for old time's sake," he murmured, hot breath on my face almost making me gag. "Wayne's bail fell through and he's back inside. He's a good guy, just misunderstood. Doesn't belong in prison."

The knowledge of him being back inside filled me with joy. "No, Simon, you blithering fucking misogynist, that's exactly where a man who beats his child belongs. Here's hoping they throw away the key."

Simon regarded me. "So not even for old time's sake?"

"Not even if you promised me you'd become a monk," I hissed.

I turned to stone as he trailed his hand along the exposed skin of my collarbone.

"That's okay. I'm thinking there are a lot of things we could do for old time's sake," he murmured, like he hadn't even heard the disgust in my voice, or seen it on my face.

I flinched. I couldn't help it that time. The thought of him any closer than he already was, of him touching me again, made me taste bile.

He grinned wickedly when he saw my reaction, and he somehow used it as a reason for him to keep going.

"The only way you're going to get close to me again is if you're sick enough to be into necrophilia," I hissed. "And with you, I wouldn't be surprised. In other words, over my cold, dead body would I ever even *entertain* the thought of letting you sweat all over me like a teenage boy again."

His eyes turned then. Ugly. Empty. Evil.

His grip tightened on my shoulder and I *knew* he was going to do something more. Since I'd tasted the way the air changed when someone violent and wretched was about to do something violent and wretched, I knew Simon was going to do something. *What*, I couldn't exactly imagine, but it was something that chilled my bones and made me taste naked fear.

I wouldn't let that paralyze me. I wouldn't become a victim once more. So I prepared myself to fight. Planned the exact spot where my knee would meet his balls and hopefully sterilize him.

"What the fuck is going on here?" a familiar and welcome voice clipped, the words dripping with fury.

Both Simon and I moved our heads at the interruption, and I used the distraction to step back into the safety of air that wasn't polluted by his presence.

Simon's jaw hardened at my retreat but he didn't move from his spot. Now he had an audience, and he didn't show his depravity in front of an audience. He had an image to uphold, after all, so he turned his mask in the direction of my hero.

My hero was not on a white steed but wearing all black, covered in tattoos and shoving his Wayfarers onto his tousled head to reveal a fiery glare directed at me.

Or more aptly, the man in front of me.

"Who are you?" Simon asked, his voice brisk, eyes going over Sam in a way they would when presented with a vagrant teenager who he was going to arrest for disrupting the peace.

Sam laughed. "You know who I am, Officer Assface. The question is who are you?" He smiled at him. "Or more precisely, who *the fuck* are you, and why are you touching my fucking girl?"

Sam's voice was pleasant. Joking even. But dripping with danger. An open threat that starkly juxtaposed the wide smile on his face.

I tried to hide the grin on my own face, which was impossible, despite the thread of anger that I felt at being labeled "his" like an object in a pissing contest when that very label had only been debated last night.

The secret part of me, the one not chained by third-wave feminism and logic, *liked* this statement. The whole warmness of the moment, minus the manly aggressive and almost suffocating testosterone, was comfortable. I felt safe, secure, protected. Here it was, my past and maybe kind of present, beside each other. Challenging each other. And I, insanely, felt safe mere moments after I was almost threatened by the man who'd fucked up my life for the year I was with him and the time after I was recovering from what he'd done.

Simon looked to Sam, disdain at home on his classically handsome face, turning it ugly and warped so his outsides matched his insides. He didn't say anything, but his entire body stiffened and his left eyebrow twitched the way it did when he was raging mad. I'd seen that a couple of times, when I'd really "acted out" or "embarrassed" him. That was the point when I honestly thought he might hit me. When I started to shake myself out of the little corner he'd backed me into.

Then Simon looked at me in disgust, accusing.

I felt rather than heard Sam step forward, the air around him turning thick like the humidity before a storm.

"No. You don't look at her," he snapped, all pleasant farce disappearing from his tone. "You look *at me*. First, you step the fuck back before I make the whole "assaulting a police officer" thing something I do in every state, like collecting shot glasses." His fist flinched. Visibly. "And I am a stickler for traditions. Test me," he challenged.

Despite the fact that Sam was literally telling a police officer he was intending on breaking the law, his tone dripped with an authority that a badge, a gun, and a uniform couldn't replicate. This wasn't something to be taught or learned or trained. This was something instinctual, something you were born with.

And like an animal in the wild recognizing the alpha, Simon stepped away from me. I didn't even think he realized he was doing it.

I let out the breath I'd been holding.

In the seconds that it took Simon to take his government-regulation boots out of my space and back onto my step, Sam somehow darted through the small space—a feat in itself since they weren't small men—and yanked me behind him, so my front pressed into his back. Just like that. Protecting me bodily, shielding me as if there was an imminent threat. The threat had passed imminence. Though I had a sick feeling Simon wouldn't be done with me after this. He was about image, after all, and Sam, someone who embodied everything he despised, had just torn his so carefully constructed image apart in less than five minutes.

That same part of me that had been pleased with Sam's statement of ownership before did a girly little dance. Luckily that part of me was not in control.

"Sam," I warned him.

"Shush, Thumbelina," he muttered.

My spine stiffened. Even my little alter ego stopped her girly dance to put her hand on her hip. "Uh, did you just shush me?" I asked, momentarily forgetting Simon even existed, let alone was standing a few feet away.

Simon was not used to being ignored, and he seemed to have recover from Sam besting him in whatever man contest had just happened. He cleared his throat, so my eyes and presumably Sam's—I could only see the back of his head from my current vantage point—went to his to see him rest a hand on the butt of his gun.

"I will remind the *both* of you that threatening an officer of the law is a crime," he said, voice ice. "And I don't want to have to arrest either of you."

Blatant lie. I could taste his need to exert whatever little power he had over Sam. And me. Though that wasn't a new thing. But my resistance to his previous tactics made him want to test new ones. I knew Simon well enough to realize that.

Sam, on the other hand, wasn't intimidated in the slightest by the small man in a big body with a firearm on his hip. Instead, he turned slightly so I could see his raised eyebrows and cheeky grin that were now directed at me. Not even a sliver of the menace he'd treated Simon to existed when he was focused on me.

"You threatened this douchebag with violence, Thumbelina?" he asked cheerfully.

My cheeks reddened. "Well, only kind of," I muttered.

He grinned wider, then leaned in for a rough closemouthed kiss. "So proud of my girl," he murmured against my mouth. His eyes lingered there, hungry, dark. And once more, I forgot the presence of the man who'd emotionally abused me for nigh on a year as my blood bubbled under my skin. In a good way.

I didn't know how, but Sam seemed to sense my body's

carnal response. He winked at me and yanked me into his side, so we both faced Simon, but so he was still slightly in front of me. Outwardly, he might have been causally regarding both Simon and his gun, dismissing them as a threat, but it seemed he wasn't taking any chances.

"Now that we've established that neither of us are afraid to give you the beatdown you most assuredly deserve," Sam addressed the red-faced Simon, "I go back to my original question. What the fuck are you doing here?" His voice went back to that fake cheer, injected with menace.

Simon regarded him for a long while, then our position with each other. Originally I had intended on shrinking away from Sam's casual embrace out of principle, because we weren't technically together. But Simon's eyebrow twitch had me staying right where I was. And the fact that I felt like it was natural, easy, to be tucked into Sam's muscles that seemed to welcome me like an old sofa. A very tattooed and toned sofa.

Simon did the eyebrow twitch again before relaxing his features into his business face. The one he used when speaking to criminals. "I'm following up on an incident that happened here two weeks ago," he said, his voice robotic.

Sam's body tightened. "Oh, you mean the assault that had Gina bruised and *fucking beaten*?" he asked through gritted teeth, cheerful tone a memory yet again. "The one where there has yet to be any real police work to be done on? You mean that one?"

He yanked me into him tighter, as if the gesture could erase evidence of the event in question, fade the bruises, both emotional and physical.

The warm feeling that began with his arrival spread everywhere. Which I would've told you was impossible in the presence of Simon. Even healed, being this close to him had settled that ugly chill over my entire body.

Sam was like my own personal emotional space heater, chasing away the chill.

Simon's expression didn't change but his hand tightened on his gun. I didn't think he'd actually shoot Sam or me—he wasn't that stupid—but I remembered the glint in his eyes back toward the end of our relationship and then in the seconds before Sam had arrived. That emptiness. He might not have been that stupid, but there was something missing inside him. Something that knew no stupidity or intelligence. Something that was just *wrong* and wanted to destroy.

Sam noticed it too, and he maneuvered me once more, so I was almost directly behind him.

"I assure you, *sir*, I'm doing everything in my power to keep Gina safe," Simon spat through gritted teeth.

I couldn't control the sardonic snort that left my throat at that statement. I did curse myself for it, though not because of Simon's reaction but because the sound was so *not cute*.

I decided to speak to cancel out the sound of the snort. "Yes, you're looking out for my *safety* by coming over here with the intention of persuading me to drop the charges against your buddy, then aggressively—not to mention highly inappropriately—propositioning me in the very place your friend punched me in the face," I snapped, my anger doing the talking, the part of me that was so *done* with Simon's shit and him controlling my life. Whether it be Sam's presence giving me the strength or my own repaired self-worth, I didn't know, but whatever it was actually made me forget Sam was there. Not completely, considering I was plastered to his body, and forgetting Sam was physically impossible. Rather I forgot Sam's anger and protective persona were also there.

And the reaction was immediate and drastic.

Every molecule of the air seemed to pause with my words, Sam's jaw turning granite.

If looks could kill, then Simon would be little more than a flaming pile of ash staining my front walk.

"Get in the house, Thumbelina," Sam commanded softly.

I clutched his arm, realizing my mistake in prodding the angry rock star, albeit accidentally.

The angry *unarmed* rock star. One who, despite my contestation at the technical label of our relationship, I was rather fond of and didn't like the idea of getting shot.

Or arrested. Though he'd been arrested plenty. But not shot.

He *would not* get shot because of me.

"Sam," I protested, my own voice soft. I had the intention of backpedaling, downplaying what I'd just said, trying to yank him bodily away from this powder keg of a situation.

His eyes snapped to me, silencing me, rooting me to the spot with the ferocity behind them. Even though it wasn't directed toward me, it worked.

"Gina. Get. In. The. Fucking. House."

I used to be a woman who got ordered around. Daily. I was not that anymore. I prided myself on that fact. But, like Simon, I moved as somewhat of a survival instinct. I didn't even really know what I was doing until I found myself in my living room, dazed, blinking at my surroundings for a long while, trying to figure out what the heck just happened.

The sound of my front door slamming shut was what jerked me out of my stupor.

I waited with lead in my stomach for a gunshot. I half expected it. And I just stayed like that, frozen in the middle of my room, listening. Not doing anything productive. Not calling anyone, not running back outside with a garden hose to spray them both. Nothing. Just stood there like a good little woman, doing as she was told while the men took care of things. That was what men did, after all.

And in my stupor, I got mad.

Really mad.

So by the time the door closed, quietly that time, I was pacing and ready to spit tacks.

I didn't even readily appreciate Sam strutting through my archway not bleeding from a bullet wound. I was too far gone for that.

"What *the fuck* was that?" I demanded—or, more accurately, yelled.

I didn't know what Sam's intention was walking in here, didn't know what he expected from me, but it certainly wasn't that. He made that apparent by literally stopping in his tracks at my shout, face going from glassy anger to bewildered shock.

I didn't give him time to yell back or confuse me with tender compliments or promises. I didn't give him time to utter anything. "You think you have a right to strut up my front walk, being all sexy and aggressive and order me around like your pet fucking dog?" I hissed. The moment the sentence came out of my mouth, I realized my mistake. I pointed at him accusingly; he was the one who was causing this, after all, even my verbal missteps. That's what my furious brain told me anyway. "No, not the sexy part. I didn't mean to say that part. Forget I said that," I ordered.

The shadow of a grin at the corner of his mouth had me seeing red.

"This isn't funny!" I all but screeched. "I've *don*e the being ordered around part of a relationship, even though that's not what we have. That's not even what I had before, despite me deluding myself. With the very man you had your pissing party with, no less. For almost a year, I played that ridiculous game. Let him tell me how to do everything down to how to drive my damn car, wear my damn hair, and choose my fucking words." I shook my head rapidly so my hair fell out of its messy bun. "You think I'm gonna go round two with you just because you're famous, better in bed and a *hell* of a lot better looking? Uh-uh. No, buddy. I won't do that for anyone. I won't *be* that for anybody. So if that's what you're expecting from the quiet chubby girl you knew in high school, who you're having your pre midlife crisis with or whatever, you turn that fabulous car around and go right back to your fabulous life. Because that *ain't happenin'*."

My tirade, which had not been at all planned, ended abruptly on that note. My chest was rising and falling rapidly with the exertion of spewing out all that anger, the kind I never let out. I'd never used that many curse words in one sentence before.

I'd only vaguely registered Sam's expressions during the aforementioned tirade, but now I was replaying them in my mind like a newsreel. He'd gone from shocked, right back to furious around the bit of me talking about Simon ordering me around, then to something much more complicated, then to his current expression. Which was none of them. None of anything, actually. It was blank, like he'd used up all his facial muscles listening to me.

His eyes were the only thing that burned.

"You done?" he asked quietly. Almost in that same chilling tone he'd used on Simon. Almost. This didn't have that violent menace embedded in it.

This had something else.

I crossed my arms and decided not to speak.

He watched the gesture. "Yeah, you're done," he said.

I expected him to launch into his own tirade. Instead he crossed the distance between us in a scary amount of time and, without me really knowing what was happening, he was kissing me.

Kissing the breath, life, and sense out of me.

His hands tangled in my hair, yanking the knots out, pulling at it just enough to be both painful and pleasurable at the same time.

Then they were gone from my hair and were *everywhere.*

I thought it was utterly stupid when I read about those kisses that took every thought and sense of time and place out of a person. As make-believe as dragons and vampires.

I'd thought that authors used creative license to make us fall in love with their heroes that much more because they could manipulate time and space through their sheer force of feeling for the heroine.

I'd thought that.

Until now.

Because by the time Sam had finished with me, I couldn't have told you who the president was, let alone how much time had passed.

He seemed to sense my lack of connection with the world because he stayed silent, hands at my hips, watching me as lucidity returned.

"There is a lot wrong with everything you just said," he rasped when I was back in touch with reality. "There was a fuck of a lot more wrong with what that was out there." He jerked his head toward the front door. "So much so that I had to kiss you to remind me what was *right* in this fucking world where women like you get treated like that, brutalized and made to believe by some asshole that they're *chubby.*" He spat the word like it tasted bad.

"Sam—"

"Nuh-uh, I'm speaking now. You've had your turn, and it was as hot as it was fucking disturbing. And you know it was hot because that's not a drumstick in my pocket." His eyes darkened, and I registered the hardness below his waist pressing into the soft skin of my stomach. "But for once, my slightly smaller head is not doing the thinking and acting, and that means I'm talking about that shit. Because I'm not letting it sit between us. Rot in my brain. In either of our brains. So you're going to be quiet now and listen good."

I did as I was told and kept quiet for a multitude of reasons, mainly because out of all the expressions and versions of Sam I'd encountered, I'd never seen this one.

He watched me, understood that despite everything I'd just yelled, I was listening to his order. "Good girl. Now let's start at the end and we'll go back to the beginning." He was still holding me and wasn't giving any inkling that he was going to let me go throughout whatever he was going to say. Not that I particularly wanted him to let me go. Plus I worried about my knees' capacity to hold my body up at this juncture.

"You are *not* my midlife crisis," he said firmly, eyes not leaving mine. "The concept of you being anything but a fucking port in the storm of my life is laughable. I know that I haven't given you many reasons to believe that I'm here for genuine, albeit selfish reasons, especially since my fuckin' lifestyle certainly doesn't foster much faith in that assumption, but I promise you that. You know that good guy I was pretending to be last night? Well, this is where he leaves the building. He only had a visitor's pass, after all. My intentions were not noble coming here originally, to make up for the fucking abysmal way I treated you after Lexie's wedding."

He shuddered at that. Actually shuddered.

"If I were a good guy, I would've realized, known that I cut you. Even being the bad guy I was, I fuckin' saw that, babe. But the good guy would've known that you would've healed. Because you're you. You're so strong. Even as I was doing all that reprehensible shit, I saw that. So the good guy would've done his penance for that shit, regretted it for the rest of his life, but let you live yours. Far away from him." He squeezed me, then kissed my nose gently, his breath hot on my face. "I'm not too far away from the truth, am I, Thumbelina?" he whispered.

I figured it was somewhat of a rhetorical question, so I didn't answer.

"I came here because I haven't been right since that morning and I couldn't deal with it anymore. Without even knowing that's what I was doing because I was so wrapped up in my own shit, I came here to cut all your shit open again and I didn't even properly realize the depth of those wounds. Didn't realize the fucking treasure that I'd tarnished until you opened that door and I finally opened my fuckin' eyes."

He stared at me, held me so tight that I worried if he let me go I might just float away. "But I'm here for you, babe. I'm also here for me, I'm ashamed to admit it. Because for a year, I've been off center. My life that used to bring me so much fucking joy seems so empty it's a goddamn joke. So I'll say it, that I wasn't here for noble reasons. I was here to fix whatever I broke when I hurt you. Whatever I broke in myself." He paused, shaking his head in what I thought I recognized as shame. "Then I saw you, saw the bruises, felt them in my fuckin' core. Then I talked to you. Spent time with you. Watched you drive like a maniac, watched you eat dinner with me, wanting to shrink into your seat and somehow bloom like a fucking sunflower at the same time."

He pulled me closer, which was barely even possible since every part of our bodies was touching, but he managed it. "Then I tasted your lips and felt your body against mine." His eyes darkened, but not in the good way. "Then I saw that asshole close to you, heard you spew that fucking shit about yourself and what he did to you. Now my less-than-noble intentions have gone out the window and for once, I don't give a fuck about myself. I want to make sure you're safe. That you never have a mark on that beautiful body again, unless I put it there and you *ask* me to put it there."

Although I'd never been into that kind of thing, my stomach dipped at the mere suggestion of that, my knees, which had begun to right themselves, weakening.

Sam saw that, and the "not drumstick" pressing against me pulsed. Or maybe I imagined it did, because he kept speaking.

"You'll never have to deal with Officer Douche again," he continued. "I'll make sure of that, along with everything else. I'll make sure you never refer to yourself as anything other than fucking beautiful, which is what you fucking are. And most importantly, I'll make sure you're fucking *mine*."

Everything he said was a lot to take in, even for someone like me who absorbed information a lot more easily than she offered it up. I knew I liked some of it, a lot of it. I knew some of it, a lot of it, scared me. And I didn't like the parts of it that implied I couldn't do basic things like taking care of myself.

I opened my mouth to speak. Words I hadn't planned or chosen, but to say *something*.

Sam held his finger up to my lips, eyes midnight. "No, babe. No more words now. We've met our fuckin' quota for the day. Remember I said I'm no longer the good guy I was pretending to be?" He lifted me before I had a chance to realize what he was doing, let alone answer his question, which I think was his intention. Out of shock, I let out an embarrassing little shriek.

He ignored it and began walking in the direction of my bedroom, as if he scented it, like a bloodhound. "Done being a good guy, Thumbelina. So now I'm gonna fuck you so bad you'll forget good is even what you wanted."

Chapter Thirteen

My heart was loud. Deafening. I vaguely worried about the possibility of some sort of incident.

Like a heart attack.

Not only was my body so not used to *that* kind of physical exertion, the kind it has just been engaged in for about five orgasms—I wasn't sure how to measure it in conventional time—but in no way, shape or form was my mind even vaguely prepared for everything that had just happened. It had happened once, or technically more than once, that night a year ago. But I'd had the help of tequila to distract me from my lack of cardiovascular fitness and the fact that I was having sex with Sam.

Well, *during*, I hadn't thought much beyond our bodies. The same was true this time. I thought a lot *before* and I was thinking a lot *after*. But *during* was blissed silence, where there was just the two of us, our bodies, and the rest of the bullshit ceased to exist. Like the eye of some epic and destructive storm, there was stillness that was somehow wholly natural and unnatural.

Not now, though. We were out of the eye and firmly in the middle of the storm. The storm that was inside of my body, laying waste to it. I was filled with a lot of doubt and worry. That he'd hear my rapid breathing and then notice that I was having a heart attack because I'd skipped cardio every day for the last ten years. That he'd not only notice that from my breathing but from the untoned skin of my belly where his sculpted arm was resting. That he'd notice the dimples on my thighs whenever I had to get up.

That he'd notice that we were *so* not suited and he'd been in a *Shallow Hal*-type situation, and he'd run for the hills when I came into true and real focus.

So I was thinking about that and all of my other undesirable body parts when he looked at me.

My breath hitched the moment I'd finally gotten it back. His eyes were full, intense, ready for something to rival even the storm inside my mind.

This is it. This is where he realizes that he's not in bed with a Victoria's Secret model and that horrible foreign version of Sam comes back and breaks my heart all over again.

I cursed myself for being so stupid and began to plan all of the fried food and chocolate I'd be buying as Band-Aids for this particular bullet wound.

"What kind of food do you have in your refrigerator?" he asked, voice husky and almost as breathless as me.

That made me feel slightly better about my situation. If someone as fit as Sam was feeling a little winded, it made my breathing a little less embarrassing.

Then I realized what he said. I blinked. Once. Twice. Just to make sure I heard him right. I couldn't have heard him right, the look on his face far too serious for such a casual and incredibly odd statement. Sam said odd things all the time, but usually they had some sort of connection to the conversation at hand. I must've imagined it, my mind protecting me from whatever he'd actually said.

"What?"

He went up on his elbow, resting his chin in his palm. The chocolate curtain of his hair fell in front of his face, making him look like he could be posing for a Calvin Klein commercial. No preparation or airbrushing necessary. Like Emma Stone said to Ryan Gosling in whatever movie that was: *"Dude, it's like you're photoshopped."*

I didn't channel Emma Stone at that moment because I didn't look like Emma Stone at that moment, or *any* moment.

I was splotchy and red-faced and covered in a thin sheen of sweat. Where Sam could sell fancy underwear on a billboard in Times Square, I was the "before" picture in those weight loss advertisements that played at two in the morning.

His face was still blank as he stared at me.

I braced.

"Well, after a cum like that, I either need a cigarette or a *big* bowl of pasta. And considering I don't smoke anymore, I'm gonna have to go with the pasta." He paused. "But we can always order in if you don't have any."

It took me a long moment to register what he just said, and that it was not a comment about my thighs or stomach or extra jiggly bits at the bottom of my arms. Or about the fact that I could not, or would not ever be getting a pair of angel wings. Or about my lack of resemblance to Emma Stone. So when it did register, I didn't plan my reaction. As everything was with Sam, what I did next was instinctual, uncontrollable.

I laughed.

And it was not a little attractive and feminine giggle. It was a real, side-splitting, tears running down your face and unattractive snorting kind of laugh. For a multitude of reasons, but namely because the statement was just so *Sam*. After everything that went down in the past few hours—days, really—and the way he'd made love to me mere moments ago, straight out of some romance novel or movie. Barely real. Then he went off script. The script that would've had him whispering sweet nothings to me, heartwarming words about my beauty, about the intensity of our coupling or how he'd never felt more at home when he was inside me, yada yada yada. That would've perfectly fit the romantic and storybook narrative.

And it might've just made me lose my mind. There was only so much of unreality a person could take. Even if it was beautiful unreality. *Especially* if it was beautiful unreality.

I was sure a lot of girls might have been annoyed or disappointed or *whatever* in such a statement. But for me, it was so perfectly imperfect, it carved us out of whatever cookie-cutter mold society had created for love and made me fall even harder for Sam.

The real Sam. Not the high school one I'd barely known, or the other one I'd constructed and nurtured the years after.

He smiled at me with a little uncertainty and a lot of self-consciousness, squeezing me enough to make me laugh harder.

Then he bit my neck. Hard. "What?" he snapped.

It was the faux ferocity in his voice that made me laugh harder, so stark in its difference to his real fury in my yard earlier in the day.

"It's not funny," he whined, so childlike and pouty it made me kiss his mouth, hard.

I hadn't done that, kissed him of my own volition, yet today. He'd done all of that so far. I didn't linger too long on that thought, just pulled back slightly so I could meet his eyes.

"It wasn't supposed to be that funny," he muttered.

"No, that's precisely why it was," I told him.

"I'm sorry, I didn't mean to ruin the moment or whatever. My brain-to-mouth filter is kind of nonexistent," he said, his voice still holding a thread of vulnerability that was almost unrecognizable when attached to someone so outwardly confident.

I grinned wide. "I know you have no filter. I've met you. And you didn't ruin a single thing," I said firmly. "You *made* the moment."

He searched my eyes, for a lie presumably. I let him. I was sure the big and mighty rock star wasn't used to feeling so self-conscious, especially when he was naked. I, on the other hand, was very used to it.

Once he'd taken his time to find the truth in my words, he rapidly moved us so he was pressing his entire body onto mine from atop me. He was grinning now, all traces of the uncertainty of before disappearing.

"Well, finally you find me hilarious, like the rest of the world," he growled. "Though it was precisely at the moment I wasn't actually meaning to be funny."

I grinned back. "That's why it was funny."

He let out another growl and nuzzled my neck delightfully. I squirmed against the sensation of his stubble scratching at my skin, and at the other sensation that traveled down to my very sensitive downstairs area. I had been sure he'd tired that part of me out for at least a week, but it seemed a handful of minutes was all I needed to recover and want more of Sam.

I reasoned I'd always want more.

Then I decided to shelve that thought, and the bone-chilling fear of what I was doing, away for another moment, one where I wasn't so happy and content.

Sam's face left my neck to regard me once more. "So is that a yes or a no on the pasta?" he asked seriously.

I giggled, that one much girlier and feminine than before. "That's a yes on the pasta," I replied.

"Perfection."

And it was. That moment. Him. Me, even. But perfection, just like fairy tales, didn't exist.

You could live in a fairy tale, for a time.

But then, like always, the story would end.

And reality would hit.

"Wow," Sam said through a mouthful of pasta.

The whole spectacle of him—Sam, walking around my house shirtless, wearing only jeans with the two top buttons undone and eating a bowl of fettuccine I'd whipped up—should've affected me in a multitude of ways.

It didn't, because of the current direction of his stare. The intensity of it.

He even abandoned the pasta, setting the bowl down on my coffee table.

He regarded my pride and joy, my sanity with a focused gaze that made me feel incredibly self-conscious about something that had never embarrassed me before. Well, only once before.

Though that was because I never let people in who I thought would *make* me feel embarrassed or ashamed of being me. I wouldn't let anyone make me ashamed of who I was.

It wasn't a mantra I lived by through a monk-like ability to see oneself and be strong enough to control my own self-worth, not let other people control it. It was from the broken pieces of my previously shattered self-worth that I built my current mantra.

Sam's eyes on my floor-to-ceiling bookshelf that took over a whole wall in my living room brought back a memory. An unpleasant one. Because that was always the way, wasn't it? The brain never let us have new experiences without haunting us with the old broken nightmare.

Which was why I was afraid to dream while I was awake. Why I trained myself not to. Against that terrible human instinct to hope. Despite all the proof to make us think the contrary, we did it. Hoped. We were stupid creatures, really. We just kept getting knocked down, and that stupid thing called hope made us get back up again.

Until one day we got back up and we were missing that one thing. And it made us emptier and made everything a little less vibrant and colorful, but at least we didn't get knocked back down again.

I was sure I had nothing left of that feeble emotion left.

But the memory hit me nonetheless. Knocked me down.

Simon regarded my wall for a long moment, then smiled at me. It was a smile that made me feel instantly and unexplainably sick. Because it seemed to me like a smile a child with a magnifying glass might have in front of a stream of ants in its path, the insects unaware of their imminent destruction.

Like the ants, I was too stupid to escape.

Because of that little hope I was nurturing that the way Simon was treating me lately was because of stress at work and his lack of downtime. That it was a result of his circumstances, not of his character.

That it was temporary, this sick feeling that traveled with me everywhere these days.

"You've read all those?" he asked, still smiling.

Still feeling that sick feeling, I nodded.

"Makes sense, then," he muttered.

"What does?" My voice came out as little more than a squeak and I had no more control over it than I did my heart, which was what had me trapped in that spot, in that relationship. That and hope.

"Why you're so naïve about life," he said simply, and cruelly. "You haven't really lived it, have you?" He shook his head in a way that was both patronizing and hurtful without even needing the accompanying words. But I was learning that about Simon, that he was all about the maximum amount of hurt. And in a way that was difficult to pinpoint, to explain, so if I did outwardly react or cry or get mad as I had in the past, I'd be hard-pressed

to provide concrete examples of how exactly he'd inflicted the hits.

It was the emotional version of a well-placed stomach punch, with enough force to take your breath away with the sheer amount of the pain it created but not hard enough to bruise, to provide evidence. In that moment, it was worse than that, because it wasn't even accompanied by violence. The proof of abuse. It wasn't the first time a sick and ugly part of me that I didn't even know I had craved violence, the hit I suspected he was capable of. Even then in the early days, I'd known that.

Because at least then I wouldn't feel so small and pathetic for getting so upset. I'd have a tangible reason.

"It's a good thing you've got me, Genie," he continued, staring at me with a smile that I'd soon come to despise. It wasn't the smile that had reeled me in with its welcoming and reverent happiness. No, this was completely and utterly something else.

"It is?" I squeaked, still managing enough strength to inject a weak amount of sarcasm into my tone.

He grinned. "You know it is. You aren't really equipped to deal with the real world, are you? You should count yourself lucky you caught my eye." He winked. "I'll take care of you." He kissed me firmly on the mouth and I kissed back.

Even though the contact made me feel a chill that I couldn't distinguish between being pleasant or unpleasant.

Even though the "I'll take care of you" sounded a lot more like a threat than a promise.

"Thumbelina?" The questioning and pleasing voice yanked me out of that horrible memory.

I snapped my head up, only now realizing it had lolled downward to my chest as I lost myself in my own thoughts. As if the sheer weight of them was dragging it down.

Sam's brows knitted together as he crossed the space between us to yank me into his bare skin.

My skin wasn't bare. I didn't have the six-pack that made

it rather pleasing to walk around the room shirtless while consuming a huge bowl of carbs, cheese and butter.

No, I'd put on a floaty caftan that I'd bought on extreme sale at the one and only trendy boutique we had in town. Meredith was the quirky owner who was somewhere in her forties, though you couldn't exactly tell where. She had that kind of "stop you in the street" ageless beauty that could've put her in her early thirties. I'd only known she was past that because of something she mentioned in passing about a disastrous fortieth. And her eyes. They were hardened and haunted with an age of suffering that retinols couldn't combat.

She always called me when stuff came on sale in my size. She knew my financial situation didn't accommodate me to buy at full price, and even if it did, she only had a small selection of items in "plus size." Though I had a sneaking feeling she ordered specific things that magically looked good on me and then magically went on sale.

She was a good person. Good to me, despite not really knowing me that well, or really at all. She was kind and acted like we were friends even though I continued to gently turn down her multiple offers of margarita night.

"Sorry," I said, blinking away the remnants of my bad decisions with Simon to bring my even worse decisions back into focus.

He grinned. "Daydreaming about me? You don't need to do that, baby. I'm right here," he joked.

I smiled, despite everything. "Something like that," I replied dryly.

"You read all those?" He nodded to my bookshelves.

I didn't have the space or the means to make myself the library I always dreamed of in my tiny cottage, so I made do.

With a lot of help from Garth, we managed to structure the shelves so they molded around my plush white sofa that was pushed against the same wall. All my books snaked around it, from the feet to far beyond the top.

Two mismatched armchairs cornered the sofa, framing it, with a coffee table in the middle and footstools at the end. Each sitting surface had a surplus of mismatched pillows and various throws, to invite someone—me, considering I was the only one who spent time in my house—to stay a while. I designed it to be my little sanctuary, scattered with candles, some scented, that I burned according to mood, and others that were there mainly for decoration. A slightly frayed but beautifully designed rug covered the whole area. That was a steal from a random antique shop in the middle of nowhere I'd stumbled onto on a road trip with Pria. Most things in here were like that. Unwanted, thrown away at garage sales and rummage racks, but somehow, all put together in my living room, they fit.

Maybe that was why I felt so comfortable here, around things that didn't really have a place, since most of the time that was how I felt too.

Sam's eyes on mine made me realize I'd lost myself in my own head again. Another reason why I didn't make too many friends—most people tended to think you were weird when you lapsed into sudden long, unexplained silences.

It was the select few who just accepted it. Pria talked through it, not minding that I didn't hear half of it. Lexie, the only other woman in my life close enough to call a girlfriend, smiled through those silences and lapsed into many herself.

That's how we'd connected, and stayed connected over the years, despite our lifestyles being vastly different from one another's. When you found someone who recognized, accepted, or understood something about yourself that you didn't even quite get, you held on to that person.

I was beginning to understand that Sam got it too. The loudest, most hyper rock star on earth got my need for stillness and silence, and moreover, stood in it with me.

I wanted to hold on to him more than anything.

"Yeah," I whispered. "I've read all of them." I failed to tell him I'd read most of them at least twice.

Even with the safety I felt being in his arms, the warmth of his eyes on mine and his unwavering, genuine smile that he used just for me, I braced for that emotional gut punch. I half expected it.

He kissed my head, gently and slowly, mind working as he did so. "This, them, they're your stage," he stated firmly, confusing me. Not just because the statement wasn't designed to hurt but because it didn't make sense.

I frowned up at him. "Say again?"

He regarded me. "For me, my place, my little slice of heaven I escape to, it's the stage. It's my drum set in front of me. The roaring crowd and the noise that shakes my bones and tells me I'm almost certainly going to go deaf before I'm fifty." He grinned, then nodded to my shelves again. "That's what this is for you. That's your haven."

There it was. The emotional gut punch. Only this one didn't hurt. No, it took my breath away for sure, but not in a bad way. He stood there, looking completely and utterly out of place in my home and in my life, and he *got it*. In a handful of moments without a single word, he'd bundled up my life and simply packaged it for me. Like it made complete sense. Like it was natural. Like *I* was natural, not some kind of antisocial weirdo.

I swallowed roughly. "You don't think I'm weird, or… naïve?" I asked, verbalizing my last thought and first worry.

He furrowed his brows, his hands flexing around me. "Why the fuck would I think you were weird?" he demanded. "And even if I did, why would you think being weird is a bad thing? Have you met me? I'm weird and awesome."

I looked downward, suddenly shy even though I'd been writhing naked underneath him not an hour ago. Sometimes it was a lot more daunting showing someone your emotional stretch marks than it was showing them your physical ones.

He didn't let me escape his gaze, his tattooed hand going to the bottom of my chin, tilting it so I looked up at him. And it was up. Despite being a little on the larger scale, I was short, petite. And Sam was not short. He'd been lanky since high school, and he hadn't grown since then. He'd just filled out. Like a lot. He dwarfed me, made me feel small, but in the good way. Not in the Simon way.

"Gina," he demanded. "Why would I think that?"

"Um, well, because it's what… *others* have alluded to in the past," I said quietly.

The warm and pleasing air in the room suddenly thinned, giving room for the rage that seeped out of Sam at my words. I didn't think he realized his grip on my chin tightened, bordering on painful. "Others being that officer of the law who I'm going to make sure files for unemployment in the near future?" he asked flatly.

"Sam, you can't do that," I protested.

He narrowed his eyes at me and smiled, though not in the same way as he had before. "Oh but I can, my little beauty. I can and I will."

"You're not—"

"We're not speaking about that right now. I've been meaning to have this conversation since I saw him on the doorstep, standing too close to you like he fucking belonged there. But the need to get inside you superseded poisoning our alone time by speaking of him. Now it's time to speak of him. I'm guessing you two used to date?" He gritted the words out like they were physically uncomfortable to say.

I chewed at my lip like I did when I was nervous. Apparently it released some kind of anti-stress chemical in some people. And since I engaged in little else to relieve stress, it had become a habit.

"Yeah, we used to date," I said, voice small.

"He hurt you," he seethed. It wasn't a question.

"How do you know that?" I asked, still on a whisper.

His anger melted away as he released the slightly violent grip on my chin to run a featherlight touch along my cheekbone. "You've got a bad poker face, Thumbelina. It's one of the many, *many* things I find cute as fuck about you. You show every single thing on your face. It's particularly pleasing when I'm fucking you because you show me exactly how much I'm affecting you. How utterly I'm satisfying you."

The air thickened with desire instead of anger for a moment with his words and the memory behind him.

My thighs pulsed. I knew I should've been embarrassed at being so expressive during sex—God knew I didn't need another thing to be self-conscious about in the bedroom—but I wasn't. It made me feel warmer and more comfortable in… whatever this was.

Sam's touch moved to the back of my neck, squeezing it roughly. "Don't like it so much when I see the fucking footprint, the shadow, the ghost of whatever he did to you on that beautiful face. You healed from it, that much is evident. Not that I'm surprised because I know you're strong. Plus, you threatened him with bodily violence. That's always a good sign that a chick's moved on from a guy." He winked but the gesture was weak. "But I can see the scars he left, babe. The way you keep bracing for me to say something, *do* something. Like a dog that's been beaten, you flinch even when someone's trying to adore you. It's not noticeable to the naked eye, but I'm hypersensitive when it comes to you. I am now, at least. That's why I'm so fucking angry at myself for treating you the way I did last year. Now I know why it cut as deep as it did. I'm questioning why you didn't shoot me on sight."

"Don't own a gun," I said, trying to lighten the mood that was threatening to crush me with its utter truth.

"Lucky I didn't bring mine with me. And knowledge of a firearm in the house might have made this afternoon go a *whole lot* differently," he muttered, sounding far too serious.

I gaped at him. "Who let you own a gun?" I asked in shock. Not that I didn't think Sam could actually handle himself with a gun, but he was a loose cannon without any kind of additional weapon.

He grinned but it didn't meet his eyes. "State of California. Well kind of," he said.

I raised a brow. "Kind of?"

He shrugged. "Not important," he decided. "What did he do to you? I swear to Kurt Cobain, if he put a hand on you…." His stormy expression spoke for him.

"He didn't," I told him quickly. "Not physically."

He glowered. "I do *not* like the sound of that."

I stared at him, deciding whether I was actually going to tell him. Admit everything. Not lie and gloss over it like I had with everyone but Pria. And even she didn't know it all.

Instead of contemplating and overthinking, I decided not to think. If this was real, if Sam actually wanted me, then he had to know me. Even the ugly parts.

I sucked in a long breath. "He tore me down, gently at first. Chiseling at my self-worth with the delicacy of a geologist exposing a new site. So I didn't even feel it at the beginning. That was the trick—distract me with something he pretended he was, until he'd taken enough of me away and exposed the nerve, at the same time exposing himself. By then I was too far gone to properly realize what he'd done. Or even if I did, I didn't have enough of me left to fight against it. At the start, I tried—oh did I try. But naturally I'm not much of a fighter, I'm more of a surrenderer. Easier and all that. But on some level, I must have realized how important the fight was. There was still some part of me left to see that. Then he took that away too. And I'm ashamed to admit I let him. I'm not going to put all the blame on myself and sink into self-hatred. I am annoyed at myself, and I recognize that I was in control. I also know it's because he's a sick and horrible son of a bitch that it even happened in the first place. And I hate him for it. I hated him for the last six months of our relationship. But hate and love are so darn connected and we don't even know it. So it was hate masquerading as love, I think. Or whatever."

I looked at Sam then, inspected the pain my words had etched on his face. The pain he was feeling on my behalf.

He cared about me. Really cared. Even blinded by the past and my insecurities, it was impossible not to see that now.

I decided it was time. Time to tell him the truth that I thought I'd been hiding so well from everyone. It would most likely drive him away and this time make sure he didn't come back, but I had to tell him. I couldn't breathe around it anymore.

"I was in love with you in high school," I blurted.

And there it was. I'd spewed it out and I couldn't take it back now. For better or for worse. I'd averted my eyes before I said it. I wasn't on a complete emotional kamikaze mission. Watching his reaction, or witnessing the rejection—or worse, pity in his eyes—after I admitted that would've floored me, so I looked at his forehead. Concentrated on it. Decided to commit it to memory.

Then, my spot picked, I continued before he could speak.

"You normally fall in love with the most unexpected person at a time that is most inopportune. You fall in love with the wrong person at the right time or the right person at the wrong time." I paused, still looking at his forehead. It wasn't smooth anymore; it was scrunched up with whatever expression my words had created on his beautiful face. "You were the latter. I fell in love with you when you didn't have the capacity to recognize love. To recognize me. You couldn't love me because *I* couldn't love me. I didn't know that as a confused and insecure teenager. I just knew what I learned from my friends. From Cathy and Heathcliff, Tatiana and Alexander. I knew love, real great love, was exquisite pain. And it was for you. Painful. And juvenile. And a little empty. Because I loved you from afar and didn't even give myself a chance to *know you*. For you to know me. Because I didn't know how. You don't find your one true love in high school. Unless you're Lexie and Killian."

I thought about the four years of absence between them. The empty girl she had been without him. The shattered and broken girl she was, presenting her heartbreak to the world in the form of chart-topping songs.

"And even then, that comes with a price. A heavy one." I sighed. "So yeah, it was wrong. I wasn't ready. To be loved. To properly love." I paused and he let me. Let me journey into my own head and rifle through my shelves to figure out what to say. How to say it. I hadn't ever spoken this much to anyone. I glanced back up at him, still focusing on his forehead. "And then there was the former. That was Simon. It was the 'right time.' I was comfortable in my skin. I had enough respect for myself to realize I wasn't going to change, or at least not immediately, and I learned to accept that and not be filled with that terrible sense of inadequacy I was plagued with in high school. I might not have been as extraordinary as the people I read, but I wasn't as invisible as I'd convinced myself I was. I was just ordinary and that's okay," I lied. Though it was only now that I realized it was a lie. Ordinary was okay when you lived an ordinary life, when you didn't know any better.

And here was Sam in my living room, educating me on

better. And I wished so hard that I was more than ordinary so I could figure out how to keep the past in his life. Be worthy of it.

"Not a word ever to be used in your proximity, babe," Sam growled, the first sound he'd made since I spoke. "Know it's story time, which means I need to shut the fuck up and listen. And trust me, I'm doing that. Listening even harder than I was when I heard Chris Cornell singing 'Thank You' live at the Esplanade. But I can't let that shit slide by without me telling you that. Even in high school you were magnificent. You weren't invisible. Everyone else was just blind. Including me."

His words were strong. Weighted. Considered. And they sank into every part of me, anchored him to me in a way that terrified me. Especially considering the direction of this particular conversation.

I didn't know what to say. What does one say to that? "You see me now," I whispered.

His eyes glittered. "Oh fuck yeah, I see you, babe. I don't see anyone else. No one else exists."

I sucked in a breath, bracing for returning the naked honesty he was giving me despite the danger of doing so. "For me either. This, us, it makes me realize what I felt for you in high school was empty. Surface. And what I felt for Simon, well, I don't even know how to put a label on that. When I met him, I was a strange combination of strong and vulnerable. I was strong because I'd come to terms with reality and the need to control my own. To get away from the town that held only ghosts and a family who cared about little but the surface. And to them, my surface was not satisfactory." I laughed coldly at the bitter memory of my goodbye. "They didn't even give me any sort of special farewell. Mom just said, 'I'll be in touch. Be well. Remember, carbs aren't worth the calories.' Like, who even says 'be well'?"

I shook my head to bring me back to my original story.

"Anyway, I was strong because I knew I wouldn't have to deal with that anymore. Any of it. And I was weak because there was this huge gaping hole inside me. Of hope, or whatever it was at the time. Like blood in the water, a shark circled the moment I came to town." I grinned at Sam at the memory of that certain analogy. "Simon was a police officer, attractive, older, self-assured and relentless in his pursuit of me. I politely declined his first few dates, but he was persistent. And sweet. He sent flowers, dropped coffee to me on my break, told me I was beautiful. So I relented. And he was sweet. Kind. And most importantly he *saw* me. So it distracted me. So I didn't see him. Nor did I see the subtle changes in myself that he orchestrated. He didn't like the music I listened to, so I found myself making sure all tracks were approved by him. He mentioned he didn't like long hair on women, so I cut it. He didn't like my friends, so I distanced myself from them all. Without even noticing I was doing it."

I shook my head at my own blind stupidity, thanking all that was holy that I had good friends and hair grew back. I focused again on the statue that was Sam. "And then he stopped being sweet. Just like that." I snapped my fingers, the sound echoing through my small living room. "And I couldn't put my finger on it. He didn't hit me, or tell me I was ugly and useless. It was always calculated. He'd find little ways, little comments to chip away at my self-esteem, or just stop talking to me for no reason, belittle me and ignore me in front of his friends.

"At the start, when I was still strong, I called him out on it, upset, hurt and confused more than anything. And because he was so practiced, so well versed in whatever manipulation you could call our relationship, he found a way to make it my fault. He wasn't talking to me because I'd said something hurtful, which I didn't remember. Or he'd say he doted on me in front of his friends and I should think myself lucky because some of the ways his buddies treated their wives was abysmal. That's what he said. That I was crazy. Making things up. Not seeing him for the amazing boyfriend he was.

"So I began to question myself. Because he was just *so sure*. So firm. Listing off every nice thing he'd done for me in a day and then challenging me to tell him how he was cruel. I began to believe him. Because I loved him. And it was much easier to believe lies from the person you loved, especially when the alternative was the realization that they never really loved you at all. And it got worse. The 'lucky' thing was brought up more. He was a trim, fit, handsome police officer. Every girl in town would've killed to be in my shoes. 'You should see the offers I get,' he'd tell me. And he'd do it in a way that he would allude that these offers were from someone better. Someone thinner. More successful. More suitable to be on his arm. Just *more*. So he made me less, until I was this unrecognizable shell that he used as his puppet, walking on eggshells, waiting for him to explode over the way I'd said something, done something."

I paused, embarrassed over the dramatic monologue I'd turned it into. I had gotten lost in that naked honesty and didn't realize I'd shared everything until it was out there, lingering in the air. I glanced at Sam's forehead again.

"I realize it's not a great tragedy, what he did to me. He didn't physically hurt me, or abuse me—"

I was cut off because Sam was no longer across the couch, carved out of marble, watching me, listening to me. He was in my face, his hands at my neck and forehead on mine. "It was a fuckin' tragedy, babe," he rasped, voice thick, eyes hard. "Simple and shattering fucking tragedy. That fuckstick was handed the most beautiful thing in this world to take care of and he crushed it in his hands. Don't know any worse tragedy. Because of the simplicity of it. All he had to do was take care of you, nurture the fuckin' unicorn he somehow found himself possessing. Instead he tried to cut that horn off because he was rotten to the core and wanted to ruin the special in you because he knew you were too fucking good for him. Thing is, I *know* you're too fucking good for me." His eyes searched my own, and I got lost in everything that was in them. And what wasn't. Not a trace of that pity or rejection I'd feared. It was like the universe was in those eyes. One a big bang created.

He was far from done. "But instead of bringing you down to try and counteract that, I'll spend the rest of my fuckin' days trying to measure up to that. Try and grow a fuckin' unicorn horn of my own. And I'll protect yours with my fucking life. You don't belittle how he made you feel because it wasn't outwardly shattering. The most tragic things in life are usually the most anticlimactic. Everyday type shit. I know that because the most fuckin' glorious things in life are the same. Like moments when I'm sittin' at a wedding and see a girl in a pink dress with flowers in her hair and she smiles at me. Might not have collapsed any buildings, Thumbelina, but it was a tremor that leveled everything in my universe. Broke my Richter scale. And every time you smile, it breaks all over again. And fuck if I'm going to make sure I live my life like that."

Then he was done. With words, at least.

Then he set to making slow, torturous love to me on the sofa. Then on the floor. So that all those words I'd released into the air were swallowed up to make room for the delicious scent of sex and Sam.

All but the first sentence I'd uttered.

The one about loving him.

That stayed.

And it didn't settle somewhere nice and warm.

No, it settled somewhere else. To grow, and cause havoc, later.

Chapter Fourteen

"This is *awesome*," Sam breathed, taking a box of Pop-Tarts off the shelf and throwing them at the cart in wonder.

I frowned as I looked down at the box in the cart, settling amongst all of the other foodstuffs Sam had haphazardly thrown in there, like a child whose mother had given him free rein.

I didn't believe in diets and always saw to it that I had sweets in the house, but even I didn't go that far. I doubted there was anything that hadn't been created in a warehouse in the entire cart.

Which was not good news for me. I had nonexistent willpower. As evidenced by my ass.

"They're Pop-Tarts, Sam," I said. "I'm sure they have them in LA. Though I'm sure they're gluten-free, fat-free, fun-free versions."

He chuckled and then advanced on me, yanking me into his arms and kissing me full. On the mouth. In the middle of a grocery store.

Granted, it was just before eight on a Monday, so just before closing time, which meant it was all but deserted, but still. There were some rouge shoppers lurking around the corner, ready to catch Sam and me in an embrace. Or worse, take a picture of it. I blanched at the thought of someone photographing me in my black jeans and tee. Though they were flattering, and I was wearing wedged heels that elongated my legs, they still showed... me.

"Did you just make a joke, Thumbelina?" he murmured against my mouth.

I forgot about feeling uncomfortable. The concept was rather laughable in Sam's arms. I was quickly swinging into normal with Sam. Him.

Which was insane. Not because of his fame or his money or his lifestyle.

Because he was Sam.

I was living the dream that even my teenage self couldn't imagine. Because this wasn't him, the man my teenage self dreamed up. Granted, I was far too innocent to dream up a man who liked to spank me in the bedroom and order me around. And far too innocent to imagine I'd like it.

To imagine I'd love it.

"I think I did indeed," I replied, grinning easily.

He grinned wickedly back. "I'm not amazed at the Pop-Tarts, though I do love them. I'm amazed at the grocery shopping part. And actually being able to shop. Usually it's a spectator sport for me. I don't even attempt it in LA, which sucks because I *love* grocery shopping." He paused, grinning. "That was when I used to do it alone, without a thousand cameras. Now I have no cameras and you. And I'm discovering, like everything else, that I love grocery shopping with you, especially when you make a funny. I'm rubbing off on you, it seems." He pressed his hard body into mine with an evil hunger twinkling in his pupils. My stomach dipped, even though we'd only just gotten out of bed and he'd only just gotten out of... me.

I was also sad at the reality that such a mundane experience in ordinary life couldn't exist in Sam's extraordinary one. Sure, it wasn't a tragedy by any stretch of the imagination, but it was yet another example of the two different universes we inhabited.

I swallowed heavily. "Sam, we're in a grocery store," I reminded him.

"I know," he agreed, not letting me go, or even looking around the aisle, which was still thankfully empty.

"They frown on this sort of behavior here," I continued.

He glimpsed around at the deserted aisle. "They?" He raised a brow. "Do you see them too?" he rasped in a faux horror movie whisper.

I rolled my eyes and giggled, then clarified my original meaning. "This." My eyes darted between us.

"I know this is a conservative town, babe, but I'm not naked, nor are you. And I kissed you with barely any tongue, so we're good." He yanked me so I rubbed against his body. "But we will not be if you distract me with your womanly wiles much longer," he growled.

I giggled. "My womanly wiles?" I repeated. "I'm not sure I have those. And even if I did, I don't think asking you about Pop-Tarts counts."

A shadow went over his playful expression. Not completely, but it tarnished it slightly. "You are not to do that," he ordered. "I know you haven't heard it enough so you don't think it's true, but you've looked in the mirror enough so you should at least have an inkling." His hands ghosted over my hips, grazing my rib cage and moving inward so they brushed my nipples, which hardened immediately despite our public location. Or maybe because of it. I was learning about all sorts of things I didn't know my conservative self was into.

Or maybe I was just into Sam.

"You are beautiful," he murmured, his hand moving down my back to grasp my sizeable behind. "And womanly. Perfect, in fact. So much so, you could be talking about broccoli, which is much less sexy than Pop-Tarts, and you'd still be distracting me with your womanly wiles. You *breathe* and you fuckin' do it, Gina."

I blinked at him, and his words, which were floating around me, persuading me to invite them in to replace years of belief in the opposite.

But it wasn't that easy. And movement out of the corner of my eye had the moment broken.

I couldn't decide whether I was happy or upset over that fact.

"Sam, there's someone coming," I whispered, pulling—or trying to—out of his arms.

He had a firm grip on me. "Yeah, and not the person I want to be, and not in the way I want them to be," he muttered, his voice rough.

He squeezed me once more with a playful glint in his eye, then let me go. "This isn't over," he informed me. Then he glanced to the woman pushing her cart. She smiled at me.

I put my focus on her. "Meredith," I greeted, once I'd blinked away my sex haze. "Hey."

"Hey, Gina," she said warmly. "You seem to have the same idea I do. Shopping in Hampton Springs' version of the dead of night to avoid the masses." She winked.

Then she looked to Sam, her eyes betraying nothing but perhaps the smallest glint of recognition, her smile remaining as she looked between us. His hands were still twined around mine, as if he was loath to give up all physical contact.

It felt nice. More than nice that anyone would feel that strongly about me.

But Sam?

It was "melt in a puddle at his Doc Martins" kind of nice.

"Destroy me" kind of nice.

Since I was slack-jawed and in my own head, Meredith

kicked in to do the humaning thing I simply hadn't mastered in my twenty-five years.

She extended her hand. "I'm Meredith," she said to Sam. "Friend of Gina's."

He beamed, letting my hands go, but only to yank me into his side with one arm and extend the other to Meredith. "Sam. More than friend of Gina's." He winked at her.

Her eyes glowed. She took him in, took us in. And I didn't feel uncomfortable under the probing gaze. It was warm and appreciative. Not looking at the rock star and the girl who so didn't measure up, but looking at the girl and the guy and just being happy for this. For us.

Sam's head turned to me in shock, then back to Meredith. "And you're here to witness a rather pivotal moment," he told her. "This is the *very first time* that Gina has not disputed being mine in front of an audience."

I rolled my eyes even as I realized the truth in that statement. It both terrified and comforted me.

Meredith grinned wider. "I'm honored," she played along with Sam's insanity.

Sam looked around the aisles. "We should celebrate with cake. Or a fine bottle of champagne."

Meredith nodded. "All celebrations need cake. Aisle four, I think. But I'm sorry to tell you that the finest bottle of champagne this joint offers is twenty dollars, and I think it's made in Poughkeepsie," she deadpanned.

"Haven't you heard? Poughkeepsie is where the finest champagne is made. France comes in a poor second," Sam said seriously.

I shook my head, sensing this could go on for a long time if I didn't do something about it. "As important and riveting as this conversation is, the store is closing soon, and I'm sure you've got better things to do than entertain Sam," I told Meredith.

Sam nodded. "And we've got cake to procure. Aisle four, you say?"

Meredith giggled, nodding. I shook my head again.

She reached forward, squeezing my hand, face sobering slightly. "I'm happy for you, Gina," she murmured. "You deserve this."

It was such a simple statement filled with such a genuine sentiment that it caught me for a second.

Luckily she didn't expect me to respond. She glanced up to Sam, letting my hand go. "If you hurt her, I'll break both your hands, despite what a crime to rock 'n' roll it would be."

Sam beamed. "I wouldn't expect anything less. I'm glad Gina has such good friends. It's the best ones who threaten to maim new boyfriends."

Meredith chuckled in agreement. "And that threat is not empty, my friend. It was nice to meet you." She looked to me. "You are not escaping margarita night this time. It seems we have a lot to talk about."

And before I could protest, her heels clicked across the floor as she walked away.

I watched her with a warmth spreading through my bones at the realization that I hadn't isolated myself as much as I thought I had, and that Sam was beginning to show me that.

He squeezed me as his lips touched my head. "Aisle four?" he asked.

The smile spread on my face, unbidden by my mind, by logical thought. It was something much different, much bigger than my head controlling my facial muscles.

It was him. But whatever followed him around, the energy he spread just by being.

"Still crazy after all these years," I commented, still smiling.

His eyes twinkled with a smile of his own, but also something else. Something deeper. "Paul Simon? I'm impressed,

Thumbelina," he murmured. "This is turning out to be an excellent night. I'm quite certain I'm going to live in it forever."

So then there was cake.

And I didn't even think about the calories.

We more than worked them off later.

One Week Later

"Sam, you've got to let me go," I ordered, aiming for the stern tone I reserved for my students. Though it was hard to sound stern or even attempt to considering I was having trouble with the brain-to-mouth part of speaking. Sam had taken care of turning my brain to a post-orgasm mush.

Thoroughly.

Twice.

And it wasn't even 9:00 a.m.

"No, I shall never let you go," he declared, yanking my naked body to plaster against his so all hope I had of getting out of bed was squashed by his substantial strength.

It was crazy, how quickly I'd lost all form of self-consciousness about being naked in front of him. Even a woman with all the self-esteem in the world would feel uncomfortable next to the sculpted and tattooed god who was currently naked.

In my bed.

And had been for almost a week now.

This was a dance we'd been doing for that almost week. Him yanking me back to him, pleading with me not to leave for the thing I had to do to survive.

Even though that was quickly becoming *him*.

What he did when I was working was anyone's guess. He had his Louis Vuitton tote bag exploded in the corner of my room and my life and hadn't said anything about going any-where. Not that I wanted him to. I liked coming home to him pouncing on me at the door. Liked lying in bed with him, watching stupid sitcoms between lovemaking. Enjoyed see-ing his things scattered around my room, and a guitar resting against the sofa in my living room.

I'd asked about it, considering he played drums.

His face had gone slightly closed off before he shrugged. "Can't exactly fit a drum set in here." His eyes had gone around my small and comfortable living room.

It had hit me, that statement. I kept forgetting his was the rich and famous version of Sam Kennedy. It was kind of a big thing to forget. But he didn't act like that. He just acted like… Sam. With more expensive jewelry and obnoxious luggage.

That moment, though, I remembered. He was the Sam who sold out arenas around the world, whose albums went platinum, who graced the cover of many magazines and who went to the Grammys every year. Who had a yacht in Cannes, which he threw epic parties on, apparently.

And I was Gina, who earned just enough to pay for her mortgage, feed herself, keep herself clothed and shod and in a constant supply of books and knickknacks.

Just.

That Sam and this Gina lived in different houses. I was sure he had mansions scattered around the globe and my tiny, slightly rundown if lovingly decorated home was more than a little lacking to him.

He somehow snatched all that uncertainty from my mind as he snatched my body into his arms.

"Whatever you're overthinking about that statement, don't," he ordered. "This place is perfect. Beyond that. It has everything I need, which I'm holding in my arms. Home."

His eyes had gone faraway and strange then, and he'd

sucked in a breath that was similar to the one I'd used to give me the courage to pour out my heart to him the week before.

"From the start, I didn't have a home that existed within four walls and a roof," he said, eyes on mine. "It was one of those crappy Walkmans, you know the ones that took a cassette tape and should be fossilized and in the graveyard with record players and CDs? The graveyard being my library, of course. I never let music die." He grinned, the expression at odds with the sad flavor to his words. "It was bright yellow, and I had one tape in it for about two months. It was Stone Temple Pilots' *Purple*. I think Mom and Dad got it for me because it was another way to get me out of their way, make me invisible."

He laughed. I didn't like the sound it. It wasn't a sound of happiness. It was drenched in bitterness.

"If only they could see me now, see their little plan backfired." He paused. "I guess they can see me now, if they so wished. Along with a billion other people. But they don't. Unless they want cash, of course." He shook his head, as if he could shake away the pain of such memories. "Anyway, I played that fucking tape so much, I think I burned the music right off it. And because I didn't get enough money to buy them new, I'd troll secondhand stores for new ones. Or new old ones." His eyes twinkled. "One man's trash is another man's treasure, right? Or one man's treasure he was too fucking stupid to recognize finds its way to one who does. One who appreciates it for what it is and isn't fucking stupid enough to let it go. Ever."

The way he looked at me when he said that had me thinking he wasn't just talking about the tape deck.

"Those vintage stores gave me the impeccable sense of style you see before you, because it wasn't enough for me to just listen to the music. I had to embody it. Become it. Put on the trappings of the rock star. So that was my home for a very long while. A shitty tape deck, some scuffed Doc Martins, an old Rolling Stones tee and crappy jewelry that turned my fingers green." He grinned at me, holding up his sparkling bejeweled hands. "Still have the tee and the Docs, just upgraded on the hardware." He smirked. "Anyway, back to story time with Sam. One of my garage sale tape expeditions found me a pair of drumsticks. No kit, mind you, just two chipped and faded wooden sticks. They could've been kindling, but in my eyes, they were the sparkling rings amongst all the coal. My treasure."

His eyes flared with mischief and something else. Something deeper. Something I wanted to dive into and live in. Drown in.

"My precious," he rasped in an excellent Gollum impression. Only Sam could do such things in the middle of exposing his heart. "I couldn't explain the pull, but having them in my hands just felt *right*. Corny, maybe, or just a kid looking for something to hold on to when he'd never had anything to grasp in his life. Whatever it was, those one-cent sticks began a fucking legend. I'm not too humble to say it." He winked.

I got it then. I'd always gotten it before, that his humor was his defense mechanism, but I really got it now, when I was immersed in his story and in his past that I guessed he hadn't shared with many. It seemed like it was the first time he'd even shared it with himself. He said things like that, talked himself up, not because he was trying to convince me or the world of his greatness. No, both the world and I were already very well-educated on that. He was trying to convince himself. I thought I, a former and current chubby girl with self-esteem issues and an emotionally abusive ex-boyfriend, had a long way to go with self-love when no one really told her she was beautiful. But it was he, the magnificent and handsome and talented man before me, who needed it the most. When you had everyone telling you how great you were, it seemed like it was worse than no one saying it.

I snatched his hand and squeezed it, bringing it up to my mouth to first lay my lips on the cold silver of his rings and then onto the warm skin of his fingers.

They jerked in response, and his eyes flared like he understood the reason for my gesture, saw it all, the thoughts I'd just had and the silent support I was trying to share through my touch.

It was then that the man with so much to say said it all without even opening his mouth. And he heard everything I was trying to say.

The silence lasted an age and yet only a sliver of a moment before his eyes regained cohesion with his physical space and jumped out of my emotional space.

"So I got a paper route, mowed lawns, cleaned gutters and emptied my Dad's pockets when he'd passed out on the sofa." He jumped back into his story with gusto. Almost too much. Eyes too bright, like he was trying to compensate for the darkness of the thoughts his words brought. "I squirreled it all away for the crappiest drum set you've ever seen. Practiced whenever I could, which was usually when my dad was working, which was rare, and passed out, which was often." His eyes flickered with a horror that, even fleeting, cut through a carnal part of me.

"Told Wyatt and Noah, who decided we'd be rock stars. They got instruments of their own and boom! We began." He paused. "No. We really began when we heard Lexie singing Pearl Jam in the empty concert hall at school six years ago. That's the *we*, though. The beast. Unquiet Mind. We were *made*. But me? Music made me. Constructed me from all the collected, earned and stolen notes and I just followed. My home was a drum kit, then the stage, the excellent hair, the girls. All the trappings."

He played with my fingers in his, as if he was creating

notes, right there with our intertwined hands. "They didn't last, though. Like the high of the coke that I was so fond of for luckily just a moment, it wore off. All of it. And sometimes, if I looked too hard, the background of my life, my home, it'd whistle in the breeze and I'd see the thinness of it all like a background of a cheap Hollywood movie. It was all two-dimensional. Surface but no substance.

"Which was why I didn't look too close. Why I made sure to move fast enough so I couldn't look close enough. But then there was a point where I didn't have any other choice but to look. Because I found that real home, substance, in stark fucking 3D. And that's home. You. First, it was sinking into you." His eyes went hard and soft at the same time, and a small but intense smile licked at the corner of his mouth. "And forgive me for my crassness, but I convinced myself that it was just good pussy. Even when I knew better. I was still moving fast, you see. But then I slowed down. I woke up with your lazy eyes and naked happiness and I saw it. Home. Which is more than just your fucking pussy, babe. It's holding your fucking hand. Watching you dance like an idiot and butcher Bob Dylan when you think I'm not watching." He leaned forward. "And I'm always watching, just so you know. "This." He held his hands to my shelves, my cozy little room, and then yanked me to him to lay a kiss on my head, then my nose and my mouth. "It's all home," he murmured.

I didn't know what to say to all of that. Well, I did. But I wasn't going to blurt out "I love you" when he'd only been really, truly in my life for a week. He said a lot of intense things, the very last sentence being one of those, but I still sensed it wasn't time.

"We can make room for a drum set," I found myself whispering instead.

He laughed, yanking me into his embrace as he did. "No,

babe. Don't need one. Not when I've got you." His hands traced circles on my back, then started to tap. "But my hands get twitchy if I don't make at least a little music. I know it's hard to believe, but I get even more nutty if I don't get my hands on an instrument."

I regarded him, his hands and the guitar. "I didn't know you played," I said, deciding to focus on the guitar portion of the conversation while I digested the rest.

I'm sure it would take me about the same amount of time as it would that gum I swallowed last week.

He shrugged. "I sure don't play as well as Lexie, or Wyatt." He narrowed his eyes. "And I will deny, under torture, ever uttering that if you feel inclined to repeat that to him," he warned.

I grinned and made the motion of zipping my lips.

He grinned back. "I just hit the drums. Lexie writes the best songs, sings them even better."

I gaped at him. "You write them too?"

His eyes moved sideways, not meeting mine, as if he was embarrassed or something.

But that couldn't have been it. Sam didn't get embarrassed. Ever. Even when he should.

"Like I said, not as good as Lexie. Scribbles, really. Gibberish," he dismissed.

I frowned at him, then stroked at his own furrowed brow. "I doubt that," I said softly. "I'd like to hear something sometime, if you wanted."

He stared at me as if he was looking for ridicule in my eyes. "Yeah, maybe. Sometime."

He had yet to play in front of me. Though I knew he had been playing because the guitar was in different spots by the time I got home.

I didn't press, though. I saw it was something to him, and he wasn't comfortable with it. He needed time. I was one who could understand that. And even though I worried that time was one thing we didn't have, I gave it to him.

I worried about that because of how utterly perfect the last week had been. How enthusiastically happy I'd been. How easy, natural, mind-shattering everything was with Sam.

And I knew a life like that was temporary. It didn't last forever. Nothing did.

He had a life to get back to, after all. I was waiting for it to hit—reality. For the hordes to descend on our sleepy little town once word got out that Sam was here.

The media followed him everywhere. He was a guaranteed story. So I'd been beyond surprised that someone hadn't tipped them off about the whereabouts of one of the most famous people in the world.

That tip would've been worth a lot. And this wasn't exactly a cashed-up town. I knew my friends would never sell me out, all two of them—three, counting Garth. But I couldn't say much for the rest of them.

In fact, I would've bet my little lump of savings that Simon would've been the one to sell the story out of spite. But everything had been quiet. We didn't turn on the television, didn't peek at any social media. We were switched off from that world. Just living in our own.

And when I'd asked Sam about the absence of that other world knocking at our doors, he'd shrugged. "Maybe another Kardashian got divorced," he said. "Or that Korean guy set off some nukes. I'm not *always* big news."

That was a lie and I knew it. But I wasn't ready for the ugly truth just yet.

The loud screaming truth. I was rather enjoying the quiet truth. And surprisingly, Sam was enjoying my quiet life too.

He came to game night with Pria and Garth. And once both of them had gotten their jaws off the floor and stopped acting like psychos—well, Garth stopped, at least—it was a fun night. Sam slipped into stride easily with us. He acted like playing monopoly with me and my married friends was more exciting than whatever parties he usually went to on a Friday night.

Though he was not a good loser, muttering about the game being rigged when Pria and I had won.

He also seemed content with my usual lazy Sunday, though I was sure he usually went to some boozy Sunday brunch at some trendy rooftop café, or whatever it was that famous and fabulous people did on their weekends. Not that weekends had any meaning to such people, but I knew Sam worked. He'd been touring for a year and had played hundreds of shows, and played the part of Sam Kennedy for that year too. It must've been exhausting.

And I didn't miss his numerous phone calls, text messages, and notifications, all of which he ignored.

He mentioned something about being in the middle of recording an album, but when I expressed my worry about keeping him from his work, he dismissed me. When I tried to press him on it, he made sure to distract me. Thoroughly and utterly.

He seemed at home in my little cottage, my head on his chest as I read and he just sat there, stationary, nothing in his hands apart from me, looking and feeling completely at ease.

We were both in our underwear. I'd first fought against this dress code, yanking long dresses over my head whenever we ventured out of the bedroom. He'd yanked them right off and then swatted tenderly at the hands that tried to cover myself.

"No, you are not to hide yourself from me," he demanded, bending down to kiss my navel. It took every ounce of willpower not to shrink away, not to run from the room in fact. Every man should know that even the most fit women didn't like having their stomach touched. Or maybe the most fit women did. I didn't know since I'd never been a fit woman.

But his touch was so reverent, so loving, that I melted into it as his mouth traveled to my hips, marked with the blemishes of a thankfully small amount of stretch marks, but they were there. His lips brushed right over them.

"I know it's not as easy as me saying it and making you believe it," he murmured. "But you're beautiful. I've seen a lot of women. And not a single one of them can hold a lighter, let alone a fucking candle to you," he growled.

So I let myself wear my underwear around him. And as long as I didn't catch my reflection in the mirror, we were good.

"I like this," he muttered.

I glanced up from my book to his face. "What? The multitude of chins I'm currently treating you to at this angle?"

He scowled at me. "Shut that beautiful mouth if you're going to keep saying insane things like that." His fingers went to trail over my lips. "No, this. Just sitting here. With you. Watching you read. Just doing nothing."

I pushed myself up from my spot, as it wasn't exactly a favorable position to have a conversation in.

"It's Hygge," I said, placing my bookmark on my page and closing my book, setting it down with small grin.

He frowned in confusion. "Isn't that a children's diaper brand?"

I full-on grinned that time. "No, it's a way of life. A Danish one. It's slowing down, appreciating the small comforts. A warm fire, a good book, a hot cup of tea. It's seeing all that simplicity and recognizing it. Bathing in it and nothing else. Just letting it sit. Sink into your soul."

I'd started off confidently, lightly, explaining the concept to him. The one I thought I understood so well. But as I said the words, curled up in him, tasting them in the air, I watched the way his face changed and his smile disappeared, replaced with something so profound that I could barely even look at it without squinting. Like the sun or something.

That's what Sam was stripped down, his mask for the masses off: the sun. And I got why he wore the mask, because he'd blind the whole world if he let them see something like that. The homogenous mass couldn't understand that.

But for me, the one lucky enough to be in his arms for however long, I'd gladly go blind.

"Not good at slow, babe," he murmured softly. "Or at least I wasn't. Now I get it. Stopping. Not to smell the flowers." He inhaled deeply. "But this. This fucking moment where we're doing nothing but it's fucking everything. I thought it needed to be loud and big and fucking chaotic to feel things in your soul, but that didn't even touch the surface."

The week had been full of moments like that. Ones that were too perfect to even exist, in a week that was too fantastical to even exist.

But it did.

And I was in the present, and it wasn't a Sunday morning but a Tuesday, which meant a school day. Which meant leaving Sam. "I have to work, Sam," I told him against the warm and hard pecs I was nuzzling into.

He squeezed me tighter. "Can I come, at least?"

I giggled. "No, you cannot come. You'll be a distraction, among other things. And you'll most likely teach toddlers words that their parents would not thank me for. Words I probably don't even know."

He gasped in mock shock, yanking me up to lie half on his body. "I do great with children. They love me," he said proudly.

I giggled again. "I'm sure they do. But you still can't come."

He pouted.

I stayed strong.

He sighed long and hard as he did every morning.

"Fine, if you insist," he grumbled.

"I don't, my employer does," I corrected him, kissing his head and regretfully pushing up to get myself dressed.

I still held my breath a little turning my naked back to him, my dimpled ass in full view.

Even the most perfect of weeks, the most perfect of men, couldn't combat or erase what a lifetime of insecurity had created. What decidedly imperfect men had inflicted.

And even the most perfect of weeks had to end. With the imperfect man deciding it was his chance to destroy some more.

Chapter Fifteen

"Where's your mortar and pestle?" Sam demanded through the phone.

I dumped the wooden blocks that I'd gathered from my classroom and placed them in the bin where I kept them.

"I don't have one," I replied, straightening, one hand on the small of my back.

It was a long day. Longer than I would've liked since I'd had to stay late and finish paperwork I'd been neglecting, then tidy up the classroom.

It was after seven and the sky was beginning to darken outside, casting the room in shadow.

"What do you mean you don't have a mortar and pestle?" Sam gasped in shock.

"I mean I don't have many things to mortar and pestle, Sam." I smiled as I walked to my desk to retrieve my bag.

I wasn't exactly a chef. I usually had Lean Cuisines or a pint of that new three-hundred-calorie ice cream for dinner. Not that I told him that.

"It's a travesty," he muttered.

"Why do you need a mortar and pestle?" I asked, suspicious.

"I'm cooking," he declared.

I stopped at my desk. "But I haven't replaced the batteries

on my smoke detector."

We ordered in most nights we were together, or I cooked something simple, like the pasta he adored. We didn't put too much effort into dishes that would take too long, Sam making it very clear that we had better things to do than cook.

He scoffed. "Very funny. Do you take your show on the road?"

"Every August through November," I deadpanned.

"I'll mark it on my calendar." His throaty chuckle warmed my bones. "Do you like Italian?"

It was my turn to chuckle. "Have you seen my ass? Yes, I like Italian."

"I have seen your ass. And I plan on creating a cult around its worship where severe punishment is given to anyone who alludes to it being anything but fucking fantastic," he clipped. "Anyone includes you. And the sexual form of punishment is *exclusive* to you."

The warmth from his chuckle turned into a wildfire throughout my body. "Well—" I planned on listing some other qualities about my ass I didn't like, as I had learned that I rather loved his form of punishment.

But a shadow at my door stopped me in my verbal tracks. And my physical ones, since the shadow was not cast by the disappearing light but by a disheveled and manic-looking Simon standing in the doorway.

"Don't leave me hanging, Thumbelina," Sam said, unaware of why I'd stopped so abruptly. "I need to plan your punishment, and I know you're not done yet. I know my little good girl loves being bad."

"Sam—" I whispered.

"Is that him?" Simon demanded, interrupting me.

I froze at his voice. At the look in his eyes. At the fact that he was not expertly groomed. His hair was messy, greasy looking, dark circles lingered under his eyes, and his jaw was darkened with stubble I didn't think I'd ever seen.

Sam sensed it in my voice, the fear that chilled me just as desire had set me aflame.

"What?" he growled in my ear, instantly alert. "Are you okay?"

"It's rude to talk on the phone in the presence of someone else," Simon snapped, advancing into my room.

I skirted the desk so I could put it between us.

"Gina," Sam said urgently. "I'll be there in two minutes. Fuck, why didn't I bring my fuckin' gun?" he muttered to himself. "I'm buying you a gun."

"I'm, uh… I think it's okay. My ex has just decided to make a rather inappropriate visit to my classroom," I said, eyes on Simon as he continued to stalk toward me. And that's what it was. His empty eyes stayed glued to me, dripping with menace. "Despite not wanting to be a damsel in distress, I think I will request your presence, Sam."

I made sure to speak loudly, purposefully, making sure not to let my voice shake with fear.

"I'm coming for you, babe. Just stay on the—"

Simon decided to stop his measured approach and use the fact that I had nothing but a blackboard behind me to snatch my phone and throw it behind him. It clattered to the floor.

"I hate when I have to tell you things twice," he seethed. "You *know* I hate that."

He clutched my upper arms, shaking me roughly. But I didn't cry out.

I met his eyes. "Let go of me, Simon. You're the police officer here, so I'm sure you're aware of what counts as physical assault." I tried to keep a reasonable tone in my voice and not give in to the hysteria that was quickly growing.

He laughed. "I'm well aware," he spat, sudden fury leaching

into his previously empty tone. He yanked me forward, so close I could almost taste the booze on his breath.

Images of Wayne's rancid breath and his brutality rushed into my mind.

I began to shake.

"What? You and your pathetic buddy play out of the same hideous misogynistic book? I'll tell you now, this is the end of your job," I threatened, my own anger exploding into my tone. It helped me to not be paralyzed by fear.

"What fucking job?" he hissed. "Your vagrant boyfriend already took care of that."

The statement confused me somewhat, but I didn't have time to contemplate it.

Simon turned us quickly, roughly, and my hip slammed into the edge of my desk. I bit my lip hard in an attempt not to cry out in pain. The metallic tang of blood filled my mouth.

"What? That hurt?" Simon scoffed. "I would think there's *more* than enough padding there to soften the blow."

He squeezed my hip cruelly and painfully.

"What are you giving him, eh?" he asked, leaning forward so his breath was hot on the side of my face.

I flinched away the best I could, the back of the desk hampering any kind of escape. And the way Simon had tangled his legs in mine made it impossible for me to lift my leg and sterilize him with my knee as I so yearned to do.

"You fuckin' him dirty?" he asked, pinching my nipple. "'Cause you didn't do shit with me. If I knew you liked dirty, I wouldn't have let you break up with me. You save that for the rich ones?"

I struggled. Hard. As soon as it became apparent that he didn't just want to scare me, that he had an intention, a depraved one that would follow through on that sick look the night we'd broken up.

Simon's eyes brightened, a telltale hardness against my throbbing hip telling me my struggles were exciting him in the most sickening of ways.

"Get off me now, Simon," I demanded. "Before you do something you can't take back."

He glared at me, hand going from my nipple to the center of my chest. "Oh, I intend on taking something."

He started to push me backward with one hand as the other yanked at the skirt of my maxi dress.

I struggled more then, a lot more. He was stronger than me, that much was apparent, but that didn't mean I was going to let him *rape* me.

Terror made me strong too.

I managed to yank my leg free, making contact with his shin. It was a lot lower than my preferred target, but he grunted in pain regardless, slackening his grip slightly so I could get the space I needed to yank myself from his grasp and away from the desk.

Strong and comprehensive pain erupted in my scalp as he snatched my ponytail, yanking me backward.

He and Wayne really do work out of the same playbook, I thought distractedly.

My back roughly impacted with his front, his breath hot on my ear, his arousal jabbing into my back.

I did my best not to throw up.

"The more you fight, the more I know you want it," he murmured.

"You are fucking delusional," I hissed through the pain.

Simon still had purchase on my hair and gave it another painful yank. "You know how much I *hate* women who swear," he warned.

"And you know how much I hate assholes who attack and try to rape their ex-girlfriends," I screamed. I lifted my foot, bringing it down as hard as I could onto his boot.

It didn't do much, considering I was wearing flat sandals. It would've been a lot more successful if I'd been wearing heels, but that wasn't the appropriate footwear when you were running around after toddlers all day.

Though it wasn't as forceful as I wanted, and the motion sent a lance of pain from the base of my foot up my ankle, it made him let go of my hair and give me another chance at escape. I'd made it about two paces when a figure filled the doorway I'd been aiming for.

My entire body, pulsing from adrenaline and fear, relaxed.

Sam froze for one second. Less than that. Then he charged forward, yanking me by the hips forcefully but somehow not painfully. Well, it wouldn't have been painful if I hadn't already been injured there. But he didn't know that.

When I was safely deposited behind him, Sam advanced on Simon.

"What are you going to do, pretty boy?" Simon sneered, though his eyes flared with fear.

Sam didn't say a word. Not one word. He usually had them for any situation, but not this one. He just stalked forward, fury flickering behind him like a cape, advancing on the retreating Simon.

Simon knew, just like that day on my doorstep, that he was in front of the stronger predator. And now Sam was going to prove it.

And he did.

And it was terrifying.

Perhaps the most terrifying part was the grim satisfaction I got from every thump of flesh against flesh, every grunt of pain coming from Simon's body until no sound came when he lost consciousness.

The sound of nothingness rang in my ears for the longest

of moments, until the world rushed back in.

"Stop struggling," I demanded sharply, yanking Sam's hands back into my own.

"You shouldn't be the one taking care of me," he clipped as I carefully dabbed at his bleeding knuckles.

"*I'm* not the one bleeding," I argued, wiping at the evidence of the night. "You're lucky you didn't break anything," I muttered to myself. "Simon's head is hard since it's full of rocks instead of brains. I never would've forgiven myself if you'd broken your hand on it and couldn't play."

The thought made me shudder. Weirdly, it made me shudder more than the memory of almost being raped tonight. But that's because I was purposefully focusing on every part of the night *but* that. I sensed that if I didn't, my throat might close up and I'd have trouble breathing.

So I focused on the task at hand.

Sam's hands.

Sam's bleeding hands.

He sucked in a breath. Not at the hydrogen peroxide making contact with his exposed skin. No, I'd been doing that for a while and he hadn't so much as grimaced. It was at my words. "*You* would never forgive *yourself*?" he repeated.

I nodded. "I'm the reason why you're even here, neglecting your album, and I almost could've stopped the situation from even being created."

Sam yanked his hands from mine, and that time I couldn't snatch them back since they were fastened around my neck. Not firmly, of course. Sam had been constantly touching me throughout the entire evening. Throughout all the statements, the interviews, the paramedic check he'd demanded they do—twice. That was despite me being fine apart from a throbbing scalp and a bruised hip. I had yet to show him that though. I'd swallowed a couple of Advil that were doing the job, dulling the niggling pain.

His touch throughout the night had been constant but light. Barely there type of light. Before, Sam had always been firm, bordering on painful. But now he touched me as if I was full of cracks, as if he expected me to shatter at his feet.

"You need to listen. Now," he growled. "This isn't your fault. Evil fucking actions from evil fucking minds are no fault of the pure and good ones they attempt to defile. None at all. You're not to spew any sort of shit implying you're somehow *inconveniencing* my life. Because that's just bullshit," he seethed. "Even if my hands did break, they would've healed. I would've fuckin' snapped them myself if it meant you didn't have to live a second of this night. But you did. And you'll have to live it again and again in your mind." His eyes were black. "I hate that for you, baby."

His voice was soft, defeated toward the end. It broke me down more than anything else that happened tonight could have.

"I'm okay, Sam," I said firmly. "I'm okay. I stopped him from getting to me a long time ago. He didn't know that, until he saw it. And it was his weak mind that couldn't handle it when he saw he didn't break me. That he couldn't break me again. Not like before. So he tried to do it another way." I stroked his face. "He couldn't do that either. Because of you."

Sam flinched, eyes roaming over me as if to catalogue my face, as if he was sure there was a bruise or bump or bleeding wound he'd missed in the chaos.

"Sam," I demanded, sucking in a breath. "I need you."

His gaze met mine. "You've got me, Thumbelina," he whispered.

I pressed my body forward so it touched every inch of his. "No, Sam. I *need* you. I need you to erase every single bit of tonight. I just need... you."

He immediately stepped back. "No, baby. You're hurt," he protested gently.

I didn't go to him, just stood there in the middle of the living room shaking my head. "No, I'm not. I was, before. When I gave him the power to hurt me. He doesn't have that anymore. Not now that I'm stronger. Not now that I have you." I whispered the last part.

But he heard it. I knew he heard it.

He stared at me and I resisted the urge to squirm. You'd think after everything we'd been through, I'd have some coping mechanism for his stare. Maybe gotten used to it.

But you didn't get used to Sam Kennedy staring at you.

Not because he was Sam Kennedy the rock star, famed and known throughout the globe.

No, it was because he was *Sam*. And he looked at me like time had stopped. Like everything stopped the moment our eyes met. Like the way every single woman on the planet wished someone, anyone, would look at them. Most of us wouldn't admit that, that the simple thing we all wanted was to be adored, looked at like that. For me, it was somewhat more precious, because to see someone you loved look at you under normal circumstances was good, great, amazing. But it was something entirely different when you'd watched someone you love look at you with a cold and cruel emptiness designed to hurt you. When you'd watched someone take everything you gave them and crumple it up in their hands just for their own sick satisfaction, or so they could control you. You forgot that there were actually people in the world who would take that power to destroy you and use it. Not to destroy, not even to create, but to repair whatever had been broken so deeply, so utterly that you'd been convinced it would never be repaired.

"What?" I asked, unable to stand that look of adoration and reverence. It was almost as hard to exist under as Simon's hate-filled look of contempt.

Funny how we let ourselves feel more comfortable under a stare designed to hurt us than one we convince ourselves we don't deserve.

He stepped forward, not so he was pressed against me like before but so he could stroke my cheek. "Someone who was treated the way you were, the way no one in this fucking world should be treated" —his hand moved down my neck, ghosting over the tee shirt I was wearing, his tee shirt—"they should be jaded. They should be locked down so tight that no one could ever get in there. Ever."

His eyes darkened as he pushed the tee up, sliding his fingers downward so they slipped into my panties and then into *me*.

"But I'm in there," he rasped at the same time I let out a strangled moan. He rubbed his cheek against the side of my face so his stubble scratched against my smooth skin, creating delightful friction.

His fingers moved in a smooth rhythm. "And I don't just mean here," he continued, kissing up my neck, massaging my insides to make his point. "I mean everywhere. Even before I knew that shit, I considered myself fucking lucky because I know you had every right to stay locked the fuck down after everything I put you through. But you let me in. And I'd thought it was a marvel before. But now…." He shifted so he could watch me react to the way his fingers moved inside me.

I was having trouble breathing, let alone concentrating on his words, but I managed as he stoked the fire within me.

"Why, baby? How?" he whispered.

My breath hitched and I made a little sound of

disappointment when he stopped moving in order to elicit a response.

He smiled wickedly at me.

"Be-because," I stuttered. "I had two choices. I could've done that. Become emotional cardboard and hated the world and everything it told you about life and love because it was all a load of bullshit. I was like that, for a little while." I paused, shifting so I could get the friction I needed. Sam's other hand fastened on my uninjured hip, pressing down enough so I couldn't move the way I wanted.

"This is cruel," I whined.

"Sometimes cruel is good, Thumbelina," he whispered. "Gonna teach you that, erase all manner of memories relating to that. To him." He kissed my nose. "Now…." He nodded to prompt me.

I glared at him, but it fizzled out fairly quickly. It was rather hard to glare at someone you loved, especially when his deft fingers held you on the precipice of orgasm.

And when he was just so darn pretty.

"I realized that would be letting him win. Letting him control beyond what was one of the worst years of my life, in retrospect," I said, my voice rough. "He would not only be controlling my future but my past, when I had faith in the world, even when I had a shitty pair of parents who should've trampled my romantic notions. They didn't. I may have had my head buried in books, in another world, saw things, wished for things that didn't exist. And he made me feel stupid and ignorant for that belief for a while. But then I realized that was *his* sad view. He was cursed to live in this wretched world for the rest of his life. Maybe the way he saw it, the way he made me see it, was the truth. Who knows. But if it was, if it is, I'm happy in my own world. If I'm going to let someone create worlds for me, it's going to be Martin, Tolkien, Rowling. Not a fucking douchebag with a rotten heart." The words tumbled out of me quickly because then maybe I wouldn't feel so vulnerable saying them. I was also intending on rushing them so I could get back to the fun part of this exchange.

Sam just looked at me after I'd spoken with somewhat of the same expression as before, except there was more to it.

"I love you, Gina," he said simply. "*Fuck*, do I love you."

Of all the things for him to say to me in that moment, that was the last thing I expected.

The words, the three I never, ever thought I'd hear out of Sam's mouth—in real life, at least—struck me dumb. Actually dumb. I forgot how to speak.

"Now you're gonna say it's too soon or I don't know you well enough or whatever to convince yourself that it's not the truth. But it is."

He began to move his finger once more and I sucked in a rough breath.

"And I'll prove it to you tonight. And for every night after that."

He did.

For that night, at least.

There were a lot of complicated and painful ones after that.

Chapter Sixteen

Two Days Later

"Hey, Robyn. I promise I'm leaving the house in two," I answered her call as I hopped into my shoe. "I know we've got a meeting today to go over everything I've missed and to plan—"

"Um, yeah, Gina, that's why I'm calling," Robyn interrupted. "I don't think you should come in. In fact, I think we're going to have to close today."

I paused mid-hop, phone to my ear. "What are you talking about?"

"So I'm guessing they haven't found out where you live yet. That's good," she muttered.

My stomach dropped. "*Who* hasn't found out where I live?"

"The media. They've pretty much taken over the parking lot. I just called the sheriff's office to see if they could get rid of them, but I'm thinking they might not have the manpower to do that."

Yeah, they were down one police officer, since he'd been fired for attacking me two days ago.

"The media?" I repeated.

My eyes met Sam. He was shirtless in the doorway, his jaw hard and a phone to his ear. For once, I didn't appreciate his abs, the way the ink slinked effortlessly over them. Or I didn't appreciate it for as long as I would have.

"Yeah, I think she knows, brother," he muttered to whoever was on the line.

"I guess they found out where you work," Robyn said. There was a long pause. "I'm sorry, Gina," she said. "You're a great teacher, a great employee, a great person, but I can't have men with cameras hanging out in the parking lot. Parents won't stand for that. You can come back when it dies down, but for now, I think you need to take a vacation." Another pause. "I'm sorry, Gina, I really am. This isn't right, but I've got a responsibility to the kids, to my place."

Her words sank in and my heart beat around my ears. "Yeah, Robyn, I understand," I said meekly, my stomach churning with the cold pill of reality.

"You have two weeks' paid vacation on the books, since you haven't taken as much as a sick day in the two years you've worked here. I'll put you down for that. And who knows? Hopefully in two weeks we'll be back to normal."

I thought about the circus that followed Sam. Remembered all of the girlfriends who were harassed well after they broke up.

The pill settled.

Reality.

It was finally here.

"Thanks, Robyn."

"No problem, honey. Keep in touch."

"Robyn?" I asked before she hung up.

"Yeah, Gina?"

I sucked in a breath, thinking of my kids and one in particular. "Take care of Conrad, won't you?" I blinked through the tears that threatened the edges of my vision.

There was a long sigh. "Of course."

I lowered the phone almost at the same time Sam lowered his.

We stared at each other for a long beat.

"Thumbelina, I'm so fuckin' sorry," he began, his voice as tortured as his face.

He sounded it. He meant it. I knew.

And I knew the score, meddling with this. With him. I wasn't an idiot; I knew this had to come sometime. But I had been so deep in denial, so deep in Sam, so busy trying to figure out all the other disasters that kept popping up around me that I'd forgotten. Or made myself believe we were safe here in this boring little town in my boring little sanctuary.

"That was Robyn, my boss," I told him. "Reporters are in the parking lot of the kindergarten. She has to close for the day."

His face darkened. "Fuck," he hissed. "Babe, I'll take care of it. Mark and Jenna are doing everything they can to take care of it as we speak. I'll fix it. I promise."

Again, his words were sincere, strong.

"She told me not to come back," I continued.

Sam froze, halfway through rapidly tapping at the screen on his phone. "What? She fired you? She can't do that," he declared hotly. "I'll have a lawyer—"

"She didn't fire me," I interrupted. "Not yet, at least. But if, or more likely *when* she does, she has every right to. And I won't put up any argument. These are kids, Sam. *Kids*. They're innocent. I won't subject them to any of this. I'm the adult. I put myself in this situation."

I hadn't intended on being so cold, but I was pissed off. Not at Sam. A lot at myself, but at the world in general for making it so fucking hard to be happy.

"We'll figure it out," he promised.

I wished we could. More than anything I wished that. But

there had to be a time to face this.

No time like the present.

"I can't *work,* Sam," I said quietly. "Do you understand that? My boss doesn't want me there because of all the reporters I've dragged there. Because they're accosting the parents of the *babies* I teach," I continued, my voice still tight and low. I was stretching it like a rubber band, getting close to its snapping point.

He waved his silver-covered hand at me dismissively. "It'll die down, babe."

I glared at him, filled with the sudden and strong desire to wring his beautiful neck. "What if it doesn't?" I bit out.

He leaned forward against the doorjamb, grinning.

Grinning.

I was surprised steam didn't come out of my ears.

"Then it doesn't," he said simply, shrugging. "And you go somewhere that isn't a town at the ass end of nowhere. Maybe somewhere that starts with my and ends with house." He winked.

Winked!

The rubber band snapped.

"Are you fucking *insane?*" I screeched. "I know you're nutty, but this is off the fucking reservation. "You think since I'm in love with you that, what? That means the fucking dissolution of my livelihood and my job isn't going to matter? That I'll happily pack up my home, the one I built for myself, *by* myself, because I'm getting run out of town by assholes with cameras? I know you consider the world to spin on its axis at your pleasure, but this world"—I twirled my finger around the room—"does not."

I expected Sam to stand, to change expressions, to explode right back. He didn't. He just stood there looking at me. Speculating. Like he was trying to analyze me. It was disquieting, such a focused stare, even in the midst of my fury.

"I'm not gonna pretend that I'm not a little bit happy about these leeches with cameras attached to their necks finally doing something for me that wasn't orchestrated by my publicist," he said. "I'm gonna say I fucking hate taking you out of the home. The one you built. The one you *created*. The one that feels like mine already." His eyes flared. "I'm not asking you to give it up forever, but babe, you've got not one but two assholes who have put their hands on you in the immediate vicinity. One is locked up. The other is not." His face went dark. Midnight, much as it had when he'd been yelling at lawyers on the phone yesterday when they'd informed him Simon had yet to be locked up.

If you were going to attack someone and try to get away with it, it paid to be a cop.

"If nothing else, getting you half a country away from him, from the proximity of that, is reason enough to sedate you and take you forcefully if necessary."

I didn't like the way there didn't seem to be a joke in his tone.

Nor did I like the way he was beginning to make sense.

"Here, they can walk right up on your lawn," he continued, throwing his arm in the direction of the window. The lawn was thankfully empty. At that stage. I didn't expect it to stay that way for long.

Sam read my mind. "And they're gonna find out where you live. And quick. And, babe, I fuckin' *hate* that. Your man is meant to make you safe, not be the reason your safe place becomes a prison. A spectacle. I'm a fuckin' spectacle, and I despise that. Can't fuckin' believe I used to love it. I wish we could live here, anonymous and alone forever, but we can't. That's not reality. I've got responsibilities back in LA—"

"I've got responsibilities too, Sam," I snapped. "What, because I'm not earning millions, because everyone in the world doesn't blindly worship me, mine aren't important?"

He flinched as my words hit home, and I felt no satisfaction in that. "No, babe. You're important. Every facet of your life is important. It's worth ten of mine. That's what's fucked up about all of this. What you've built, what you've made is worth infinitely more than whatever I've stacked up. I want to regret yanking you into this, but that would mean I didn't have you in my life. I can't imagine that, Gina. I fuckin' can't. And it's not fair, and it's selfish as all shit, and if they didn't already know maybe I would just leave you for your own good. But they do already know, and I'm not leaving you. Plus, you're so ready to make this into a curse. Haven't you thought it might be a blessing?"

"And how, Sam, is me being taken away from a job and life I love a blessing?" I snapped.

He regarded me. "You really love it, Gina? This life? And don't you dare misunderstand me and think that I've said that because I find it lacking or because I find *you* lacking. You know that's not the fucking truth. I'm saying it because you are not designed to hide away here. To waste away here."

I stared at him. "What? I'm wasting away because I'm not fucking playing a part in front of thousands, Sam? Because I'm not a fucking spectacle?"

I stomped over to my coffee table, kicking off my shoe so I wasn't limping like an idiot. It hit my glass door with a whack but luckily didn't break anything. Although at that moment, I did feel like smashing something.

But I couldn't afford it to be my door since I was now seriously looking at unemployment.

Sam's gaze darted from the rogue shoe to me. "What's wrong with it? The limelight? You've been hiding here in the dark with your stories and your quiet, and you're wasted. Your beauty. Your everything. It's not made to be lived without witnesses. It may have its downfalls, but a life where the world gets to see you, and more importantly you get to see the world, that's a life. Not this. What's that stupid fucking quote?" He paused. "'A reader lives a thousand lives' or some shit? Well, a thousand lives are all well in good, but you only get one. And that's yours. You can live a thousand lives being someone else, but that's never going to measure up to the one being *you*. Because that scale is always going to be feathers and fucking diamonds, baby. Little hint, you're the diamond. And diamonds are made to shine."

I stared at him. At the words that had become corporeal. Flavored the air with their poetry. Poetry that wasn't labored from a long-dead artist, immortalized on weathered papers in a dusty book. No, this was poetry living, breathing, electrifying the air.

I picked up my weathered copy of *The Handmaid's Tale* that I was rereading for the hundredth time. I didn't know what to say, to explain to him what I felt. Who I was. So I let Offred say it for me.

"*We were the people who were not in the papers. We lived in the blank white spaces at the edges of print. It gave us more freedom. We lived in the gap between stories.*"

When I'd finished reading, I looked up at him. "I know you think I don't live my own life enough. That I use these"—I held up the book—"as excuses not to live it." I paused, chewing my lip. "And maybe, in some ways, you're right. But you're also wrong. I don't use them to stop me from living. Sometimes I use them to understand this thing called life." I glanced down. "You were born for the spotlight, Sam. That was the truth from the moment I first met you. Before you picked up drumsticks, before you painted your nails black, wore more jewelry than my mom, before you did all that to set yourself apart from the crowd, you were already there, standing in a place where only a few can stand. Where few were born to stand. To make stories, to help people understand their own. To become something bigger than themselves. Because you were always bigger than yourself. It didn't take long for you to realize it." I gave him a small smile. "You're not exactly humble," I teased. "But it's because that's who you are. You live in stark color in the middle of it all." I looked down. "Maybe not the best book to draw life lessons from, or perhaps the best. But I can't explain beyond the obvious,"

He kept silent, marble, so to fill the horrible silence that accompanied my honesty, I continued to speak. "You said it, this"—I shook the book at him—"is my stage. This is my haven. And now, what, you're trying to take it away from me because it's all too quiet for you now? Because life with me is too slow?"

I said it with anger but it came from a place of fear, as most things said in anger did.

He stared at me and the book, then advanced.

He threw the book out of my hands so hard it smacked against the wall and clattered to the floor.

"This is your fucking problem," he roared, advancing on me.

I scuttled to the couch in retreat, all my affirmations about remaining strong obliterated in the face of pure male fury.

It hit somewhere deep when someone so easygoing and so relaxed unleashed it all. The dragon. The one you knew was there, the one that had to be there, because no one looked like that, smiled like that, was happy like that without a dragon inside.

The only way someone was truly happy like that on the outside was because they were hiding something truly ugly on the inside.

I should know.

My stuff was ugly, and I wasn't even as happy as Sam.

The happier the person, the worse the demons. That was my theory anyway. And it was being proved right as the dragon breathed fire.

Sam took no notice of my fear. Dragons didn't mind mice, did they? "Instead of living, you read about other people doing it. Clue in, babe—they aren't real." He waved his muscled and tensed arm at my bookshelves. At my treasures. At my thousand lives I would never live and my thousand friends I would never meet. The thousand people I would never be. "None of that fucking shit is real." His eyes glowed as they fastened on me, the mouth of the dragon threatening to swallow me up.

As if I hadn't already been swallowed when I was fourteen years old.

"We are," he murmured. "Real."

I stopped, not because I wanted to, but because some idiot had put a wall in my path, hampering my escape.

I blinked rapidly, like the little mouse I was. "You're scaring me," I whispered.

His eyes darkened, the glow gone, his arms coming to either side of me, boxing me in as his palms flattened on the wall. "Good. That's part of it. Life. Being scared. 'Cause life— *real* life, not the shit in the pages of a book—it's fuckin' scary, babe. It's unpredictable, it's uncontrollable, and you only get to do it once."

In a puff of smoke, all of the fury left his frame as one of his hands, lighter than a feather, came to my face and tucked my hair behind my ear. "I'm here to make sure you do it right. That *I* do it right."

His words, the way he ripped apart my life to show me the bare bones of it, to show me what I'd been denying all along, they hit me somewhere. It deflated all that fury I'd been sure would carry me through to my forties. It didn't suit me, anyway, that anger. It felt wrong in my skin. So I went with something harder to channel—my truth.

"I can't, Sam. I don't know how," I whispered. "I shelve them all." Trailing my hands across the spines, I glanced up at him, in his extraordinary brilliance, standing in my ordinary living room. The image was so painful, so conclusive of just how much we didn't fit, would never fit, that I looked away. "My feelings. My hurt. Dreams that will never happen. Places I'll never go. Pounds I'll never lose." I stopped when I came to the edge of them, rather unsure of what to do. So I just kept speaking, words tumbling out of me in a heap. "They were neatly stacked away, ordered, manageable. Until you." I glanced up again, finding my courage. His eyes were glittering, muscled arms tense, hands that were covered in silver balled into fists. Yet his face was blank. He was silent. Still.

It unnerved me. He was never still. Never.

For someone who lived in solitude, quiet, it was uncomfortable. Unbearable.

So I filled it.

"But you, all of that out there." I gestured to the window. "The world that came rushing in like a tornado, it broke them. All of them. And now they don't have order, no place, so they fly through my mind. I need them back in their places." My voice was moving up and down, shaking with the tears I refused to shed. "I need my shelves back, Sam. I need them or I don't know who I'll be without them. I need them back because I need my life back. What I had before you."

"I'll give you anything but that. Everything, in fact. And in case you haven't heard, I'm a rich and famous rock star, so I have a lot."

I frowned. "I don't want any of it."

He smiled, but it wasn't like the others. It was sad, full of vulnerability and empty of that confidence and bravado that had seemed so real until this moment shattered it.

"I know. It's why I love you so much. One of the many, many reasons. You don't want anything from me. Problem is I want *everything* from you. You want your life back? I didn't even know what living was until I looked at you. I mean really *looked* at you. You want to know who you are? You're mine. And I didn't know who I was either. Until I figured it out. Until you figured it out for me. I'm yours. This shit is complicated. Life gets like that, and I know mine's more fucked up than most. But can you give fucked-up a try? For me?" He waggled his brows. "You might even like it."

Yeah, that was the problem. I'd like it too much.

"Okay," I whispered. "I'll give fucked-up a go."

It was like the moment I invited chaos into my life, it decided to come knocking. Literally.

I'd been packing my bags and trying to figure out how I went insane enough to let Sam talk me into leaving Hampton Springs and going to LA with him for an undetermined amount of time. LA, where I wouldn't be able to escape the spotlight and be invisible as I had been all my life, considering I was dating the most visible man in the world.

Maybe I'd agreed because he was right. About it all. How I hid away and convinced myself I was okay with living through the pages of a book, reading about great experiences instead of having them.

And Hampton Springs didn't really offer much for me right then, the forced vacation excluded. There was still the whole Wayne thing, for one. It may have been sorted with him behind bars and me somehow not having to testify, thanks to whatever strings Sam's scary lawyers had pulled, but it was still there, in town memory.

Small towns were like elephants—they never forgot.

And then there was the whole Simon thing. Sam had taken care of that too, first by pulling whatever strings he had to get him on unpaid suspension—he hadn't technically lost his job when he'd attacked me. But he had now, thanks to that. Getting him locked up was still a little complicated considering Simon was the town's golden boy, even after an attempted rape, it seemed. Plus, he was well liked amongst his coworkers—don't ask me how—and they were all keen to look out for their own, much to Sam's disgust.

I wasn't exactly happy about it either, but Simon didn't have a chance at being a cop again, so there was that. People like him didn't deserve to be anywhere near positions of power. I already felt sorry for his future girlfriend.

Mulling that over while I was packing my bags, I was considering the truth in Sam's words and why I'd been so violently against leaving a town that hadn't exactly been kind to me.

I guessed, until then, I hadn't had anywhere else to go.

The knocking at the door jerked me out of my stupor. I glanced down at my entire wardrobe strewn across the floor. What did I take with me to LA when I was going to be hanging out with his famous and fabulous friends who would most likely be wearing Chanel's latest fall line?

The best I could do was Target's latest fall line.

"I'll get it!" Sam yelled from the living room.

He was very forceful about me not opening the front door anymore, considering my track record. Not that it was my fault.

But I let him because I liked the simple domestic bliss of such a gesture. Whether it be a deluded domestic bliss or not.

I was expecting it to be the reporters, finally finding my house. I braced for it.

But I didn't hear the door slam, nor any angry shouts from Sam, so I was curious. I put down my toiletries and headed for the living room.

Crowded in my very small living room were all the members of Unquiet Mind.

Even though I was sleeping with one of the members and had seen the rest at the wedding last year, not to mention went to high school with all of them, it was still a little—or a lot—disquieting to see them all.

In my living room.

Plus Killian.

He didn't need to be famous to be disquieting. He just needed to be... *him.*

"Gina!" Lexie squealed, detaching herself from her husband's side to rush over and yank me into her arms.

I hugged her back out of reflex, though I hadn't expected such an enthusiastic greeting.

"I can't believe this," she exclaimed, letting me go and darting her eyes between Sam and me. "This is *so fucking awesome.*" She paused, frowning. "Well, not the 'you getting attacked... twice' part of this. That is so *not* fucking awesome."

The room thickened with all sorts of male fury when she uttered those words.

"Not fucking awesome. At all," Sam seethed.

"It's okay. I'm fine," I reassured Lexie. And Sam.

Mainly Sam.

"Fine means the opposite of fine," Sam snapped at me.

"At this juncture, it means exactly what the dictionary defines it as, me being fine," I snapped back.

"And the dictionary defines it as a woman's way of saying the apocalypse is imminent," Sam retorted.

I huffed out a frustrated breath and rolled my eyes. "Whatever."

"There's another one!" he exclaimed. "Brace positions, everyone. Fine *and* whatever used in the same vicinity means that we are *fucked*. And not in the good way."

Lexie grinned. In fact she, and everyone else in the room—including *Killian*—had been grinning since Sam and I started bickering.

"We're not fucked, bro," Wyatt said. "*You're* fucked. In the best way."

Sam flipped him the bird. "You didn't actually say what all of you were doing here. I know you missed me and I'm the glue that holds this family together, but I've got a *life*." He looked pointedly at me. "Couldn't you survive without me for another four hours? I told you we were on the way."

Wyatt punched his arm. "We decided we'd pick you up. Figured you might need some extra muscle when we heard the vultures had descended."

Sam screwed up his nose in faux confusion. "Well, that explains why Killian's here, not you."

Wyatt punched him again, and the thud of flesh against flesh told me it was hard that time.

Sam didn't even flinch.

Lexie continued to grin at me. "I'm so glad to have another girl in the family. Sometimes I worry I might choke on all the testosterone," she stage-whispered. "And don't worry, you'll love LA. We're going to be there for a while recording the album so we can hang out all the time! Plus Emma's flying in from Prague tonight, so we can do girls' night."

"No girls' night," Killian and Sam growled almost in unison.

Lexie rolled her eyes. "Once. Killian. *Once* I get kidnapped. That does not mean it's going to happen every time."

I could taste Killian's glare. "Not fuckin' funny, babe," he snapped.

"No girls' night," Sam repeated.

Lexie winked. "Don't worry, we'll wear them down." She

stepped back on her wedged heels. "Have you packed? I'll help."

Then, like she'd been here a million times before, she strutted down my hallway in the direction of my bedroom, to help me finish packing, presumably.

Wyatt winked at me. "Welcome to the family, darlin'. There's no getting out now."

Noah didn't say anything, he rarely did, but he smiled at me.

I sensed Wyatt was right.

I couldn't decide whether that was an incredibly good thing or an incredibly bad thing.

I did know it was off-the-charts terrifying.

Sam's words echoed in my mind.

"That's part of it. Life. Being scared…. It's fuckin' scary, babe. It's unpredictable, it's uncontrollable, and you only get to do it once."

So I decided not to focus on whether this part of life was good or bad. I decided to just *live* it.

I didn't really have much of a choice anyway.

The stewardess was barely finished pouring the clear liquid into his glass before he tipped it up and drained it in one easy swallow. He slammed the glass down on the table in front of him, not letting it go as one would expect, instead clutching it tighter, his knuckles whitening with the intensity of his grip.

I stared at Sam, a grin tickling the corner of my mouth. "Oh my God, you're afraid of flying."

I got why people were afraid of flying. I didn't do it often, but when turbulence got a little too rough and lasted a little too long, I got scared too. But that was because I was flying in coach, being jostled against some sweaty guy with body odor who thought he was being sly when snatching glances down my shirt. That put a person on edge to begin with.

We were not in coach.

We were in a *private jet*.

Yeah, people actually flew in private jets.

Well, maybe not people. But world-famous rock stars did. In jets with impeccably dressed and impeccably polite stewardesses. With leather seats and a full bar and bedroom at the far end. And a sofa on which Mark, Sam's manager who I'd met and spoken to between phone calls, was rapidly typing away on his laptop.

I was too busy being awed by the sheer luxury of it all to remember we were even on a plane, let alone be afraid of flying. Then again, I was sure that was the norm for him.

For all of them.

I tried not to let the huge gaping chasm in our socioeconomic statuses get to me.

I focused on Sam.

He scowled at me. "I'm not afraid of flying," he snapped.

"Yes he is," both Wyatt and Noah said in unison, as if this was a practiced routine.

I grinned at both of them across the aisle.

Sam directed his scowl their way, that one deeper and a lot more hostile than the one he had treated me to. "I'm not afraid of *flying*," he repeated. "I'm afraid of *crashing*. Any rational human being would have a healthy dose of fear being in a metal box thirty thousand feet in the air at the mercy of a fucking computer. Pilots don't even fly these things anymore, you know." He raised his brows. "The machines will turn against us at some point. I'm just being logical."

Wyatt smirked. "Yeah, I guess any rational or logical person might be afraid of flying if they thought about it too hard," he agreed. "Which is why it baffles me that *you're* afraid, since you're neither rational nor logical, and you never think too hard on anything."

Sam flipped him the bird.

I let out the snort I'd been holding in. And as with such things when you're holding them in, it exploded through the pressurized cabin, turning into full-on giggles I couldn't control. Perhaps it was because I'd had a lot to smile about in the middle of this big mess that I currently called my life, but I hadn't had a lot to laugh about. Or I hadn't let myself laugh. Because an outward gesture of happiness, one that went beyond a smile, was just taunting fate, drawing attention to this crazy situation. I was scared some benevolent force would realize how out of place I was here in this craziness and wrench me away from it to balance the universe or whatever.

And for someone who treasured solitude and quiet, I would have to be dragged away from this crowded and busy life kicking and screaming.

When you're thirty thousand feet in the air, your chances of plummeting to your death are always there, but it's still peaceful knowing you're in a metal box, shut away from all the bullshit below.

Instead of flipping me the bird as he had with Wyatt, which I half expected Sam to do in his current state, his glower dissipated with the echoes of my giggles. Instead, the moment his eyes touched mine, then lowered down to my mouth, his entire body softened like he'd had a shot of muscle relaxant dosed with Valium.

I stopped giggling and tried to subtly wipe my lips. The way he was staring at me had me scared I had something on my face, like I'd drooled or something while I was laughing uncontrollably.

Of course I'd be the one who drooled while I was in a private jet with my hot-as-shit rock star boyfriend and his hot-as-shit band.

Classic Gina.

"What?" I asked uncertainly, glancing toward Wyatt and Noah for a second. Though they weren't looking at me, thankfully, inspecting Sam's change in demeanor with interest instead.

He smiled lazily, setting his glass down to grab my hands.

His were dry and warm and comforting with their callused palms and tattooed fingers. My small, untattooed and uncallused fingers looked both out of place and completely natural in his grasp. The cool metal of his rings rubbed against my palms.

"Thumbelina, though you've got a beautiful smile, I'll get into one of these death traps every day of the week if that's what it takes to get you laughing on the regular. I'm used to making people laugh. I'm a hilarious guy." He shrugged with a sly grin that didn't reach his eyes. "But you, you smile plenty, and it's plenty beautiful, but it's that *laugh* I'm feeling in my dick." He paused, leaning in as if he needed privacy for the next thing he needed to say, though he'd near shouted the 'dick' part of his sentence. "And my heart. My fuckin' soul," he murmured, his breath hot on my face. "See, people are so quick to give me shit: their attention, their shallow fucking adoration, their smiles, their panties, their laughs. But you don't give any of that unless you mean it. Unless it's real. And it's like diamonds. But ones I can't wear or purchase. Priceless, all of it. Rarest shit I've ever held in my hands. And you don't give it to me because of who I am on stage or on camera. Because of who Sam Kennedy is. It's because of who *I* am. Who I was. And that's something no amount of money, of Grammys, or platinum records can buy."

I blinked at him. Once. Twice. Three times. Each time my vision grew steadily blurrier as tears obscured my vision. His gaze didn't waver. Neither did his grip. He stared at me while I got my emotions under control, like he had all the time in the world just to stare, like we weren't just the only people on this plane, but in the whole darn world.

I managed to get myself together and not cry like I felt like doing. Because I knew if I let myself, like my laugh, my tears would explode out of control and it would not be as cute as the laugh seemed to be. My laugh was even worse than Kim Kardashian's. I had a lot of reasons to smile and laugh lately, but I had a heck of a lot to cry about too. That was the way of the universe, I guessed; you couldn't be extraordinarily happy if you didn't also have the capacity to be extraordinarily sad.

It was a matter of choice between the two. I got that now. You picked one and you lived with it. That's what I saw in Sam. He didn't smile and laugh easily because his life was cushy and easy. No, he did it because he'd experienced the terrible ugliness life could give, and he chose to be like this.

That was one of the reasons I was done for.

That and the gaze that was searing my soul. I may not have been inked, but tattoos of his ownership of me covered my entire body.

"I don't recall giving you my panties," I croaked finally, deciding that talking about that forever love stuff might not be appropriate for the small space we were occupying.

He grinned, yanking me into his body for a rough close-mouthed kiss. He pulled back only slightly so I could see his wink. "Ownership is nine-tenths of the law," he teased.

"I'm pretty sure that's not right," I argued.

"You complaining?" he asked against my mouth.

"No, I'm not complaining at all."

"Good, and I'm here to make sure it stays that way."

"Dude, she's dating you. If she doesn't complain about you in the near future, you've gotta check her pulse," Wyatt cut in.

I kind of forgot we were in a small confined space where

everyone could hear every word. My cheeks flushed.

"I know you've always been jealous of me, and now you've got a reason to be immensely more so, but you don't look good in green, bro," Sam retorted. "Oh, and that reminds me. Find somewhere else to stay. Me and Gina are taking over the Batcave until my new place is ready, and I can't have you being you and ruining the romance."

"Fuckin' hell," Wyatt muttered.

"There's always Emma's place," Sam offered with a glint in his eye.

The air in the cabin changed once more.

Then I realized Sam was not the only member of Unquiet Mind with girl troubles.

Though I did hope that I stopped making trouble for Sam.

But hope didn't exist.

It was easy to forget that in the happy moments.

But they didn't last forever in this cruel and ugly world.

And I'd be reminded of that very soon.

Chapter Seventeen

"Okay, here it is," Sam said, something lingering in his tone that hadn't been there when he'd shown me the rest of the house.

Though calling his sprawling estate a house was a slight understatement.

I walked into the room and was stunned silent for a little bit. Okay, a lotta bit.

Not that I hadn't been stunned during the entire tour of the mansion that Sam shared with Wyatt in a gated community in Calabasas.

You could fit *six* of my houses into theirs.

About four more in their sprawling backyard, complete with a basketball court.

It was sprawling, spanning over three levels. It had a pool, a gym, and a fricking cinema. Plus a bowling alley.

A bowling alley.

"Seriously?" I'd asked when Sam walked led me into the narrow room.

He shrugged. "We never even use it. I was a dumb kid, thought it'd be cool." He grinned. "I was totally right."

It was that, the classic Sam humor, that stopped me from being incredibly overwhelmed and running back to the safety of my little home. Even then it was tempting. To say it was beyond intimidating being presented with this amount of sheer wealth was an understatement.

Despite my mother's aspirations, I'd never wanted this. Riches or fancy sofas or bearskin rugs—and Sam actually had one of those. I just wanted what I had. Well, maybe a little more of that. And somewhere a little more out of the way. By a lake perhaps, with a huge library spanning half the house overlooking a beautiful vista.

But not what Sam had.

Not marble floors and twelve hundred bathrooms and a collection of cars. It was a lot.

A *lot*.

It winded me. It didn't make me question who Sam was. He didn't define himself by what he had. In fact, he had all this stuff to distract him from having to define himself, but still, I didn't know how I'd fit into… this.

Plus, the place screamed "bachelor pad." It might have not been littered with empty pizza boxes and beer bottles— it was spotless, I assumed cleaned by an army of people who were paid to do so—it was decorated in masculine grays and blacks, with a lot of weird-looking art and expensive-looking electronics and not much else. There were framed album covers on the walls, framed magazine covers, and pictures of the four of them scattered on a few surfaces, but that was it. Despite the muggy California air, it was cold. It wasn't a home. It was a place where they entertained girls, or passed out after partying too much.

But the room we were in now was different.

Much different. It wasn't cold or impersonal or for anyone but Sam.

"This is the one place in the house where no one is allowed," he said, his voice barely above a whisper.

"Sam," I breathed, my eyes devouring the floor-to-ceiling shelves. Filled not with books but with records. The room was large. Cavernous, really. Every inch of it decorated with music memorabilia.

With Sam.

The walls were covered haphazardly with framed album covers, golden records, photos. The floor was littered with signed guitars resting on stands, a couple of drum sets and a big record player in the middle. It should've been chaotic, but somehow it wasn't. Somehow the room leaked serenity. Quiet. It was made to be loud, but it worked in the opposite direction.

"See, you've got a little library. Your escape. Your shelves," he said, clutching my hips so he could yank me back into his chest. "These are mine." His breath tickled my ears and he pressed a soft kiss to my lobe. "This is where I put it all." He squeezed me a second longer, taking an inhale of my hair.

Such a gesture should've made me uncomfortable and mentally calculate when my last shower was to determine whether my hair smelled like strawberries or sweat. It didn't. It was natural, like everything else with Sam was becoming. It was scary. How I felt less self-aware, less self-conscious. It was danger.

But I didn't let myself think such thoughts as Sam kissed my head and then let me go so he could approach the shelves, the heels of his boots clicking on the hardwood floors.

He yanked a slim sleeve out of place, seemingly at random. His tattooed hands ran over the cover, reverently glancing up at me as he did so. "This got me through the beginnings of this monster called fame. When I was living harder than I was now. Drinking too much whiskey, doing too much coke… just doing too much period. It reminded me what all this shit was about."

Though I yearned to stare at Sam, to do something else other than hear the pain in his voice, I looked at what was in his hands. It was thin, but the way he held it betrayed the true weight of it. The image was a pure white brick wall, black script scribbled over the front: *Pink Floyd – The Wall.*

He paused, sliding it back into its place before he strolled down farther and reached up to grab another.

I watched the fabric of his shirt ride up as he did so, exposing the inked and defined muscles of his back.

It took me a second to focus back on him, on the way he looked at the newest record in his hand. He stared at it much longer than the other one, his eyes faraway, demons dancing in them.

He glanced up at me and I flinched, thinking the glimmering in his eyes must've been a trick of the light. It had to be. Because the tears I thought I saw were blinked out of existence in the next second.

He cleared his throat. "This one I nearly played till it melted," he said, voice raspy. "I locked myself in here for hours, just with this and a bottle of Jameson. Or four." He didn't break his gaze from mine. "When I thought I was going to lose my best friend. I was still covered in blood from watching her die in front of me. I couldn't do anything. I didn't know what to do. How to act. How to be. So I let these guys tell me. Or at least distract me from the pain it took to keep inhaling and exhaling."

The pain in his voice was so real, so fresh, I could taste it. It stabbed through me like I could feel it.

I kept forgetting that Sam felt so deep because he spent so much time trying to convince everyone he was shallow.

I didn't want to look at his face, see the utter pain I knew would be there. So I looked down at the cover: two townhouses side by side, identical and taken in black and white.

"Led Zeppelin," he whispered. "*In My Time of Dying,* to be more specific." He put the record back and then came to stand in front of me, tilting my chin up so I could see his face. "It used to be all of this to get me through, help me cope with this crazy little thing called life. Now I'm staring at it. What's gonna get me through."

I stared at him for a long time, and then it suddenly didn't matter. All of those metaphorical mountains I knew I didn't have the skill or the emotion to climb all collapsed. Melted into the sea.

"The thing that's getting me through, that's you, just in case you didn't get that," Sam clarified after I'd lapsed into silence for too long.

There it was. Another imperfect moment within a perfect one, making everything exactly how it should be.

I smiled and leaned in to kiss him long and hard. "Yeah, I get it," I whispered.

And I did. I finally did.

Until I didn't.

I heard the crash. It was hard not to. People back in Hampton Springs would've heard it. I was sure if we hadn't been in such a sprawling, expansive and therefore very well-built mansion, the walls might've shaken.

Though it might have been in my head. The entire landscape of my mind had been continuously tremoring the moment I saw it. Read it.

Sam's fury, responsible for the crash, which I now realized was the slamming of the front door, entered the room.

I referred to it as being separate to him, because it was.

What rippled around him was more than emotion.

I saw it everywhere.

Tasted it.

You heard thunder and that was the warning for an

oncoming storm.

The crash of the door slamming and then subsequently smashing was the thunder.

Sam was the storm.

The expression on his face couldn't be explained. Like that magnificent but terrifying splash of lightning across the sky, words couldn't define it, constrain it. It could only be *felt*.

If I hadn't seen him put on the ripped tank top that exposed the sides of his tattooed ribs and equally ripped black denim jeans that very morning, I might not have recognized him. The sheer fury on his face had contorted his beautiful features that much.

I'd always toyed with the idea that under his surface, way down deep, in the highest peak of the lowest dungeon, lurked his Balrog—monster, for those who didn't read *Lord of the Rings*.

That was usually the way with the happiest of people, and forgive the *Hulk* reference, but you wouldn't want to see him when he was angry.

And Sam was angry.

Nothing like I've ever seen from him before.

He was little more than a blur as he stomped across the room, snatching the magazine out of my hands when he reached me.

Maybe he only seemed to blur because he was moving, liquid quicksilver, and I was frozen. Solid.

And had been that way for some time.

Since I'd walked past the magazines at the drugstore and seen the cover.

And the caption.

And the look on everyone's faces in the Walgreens the second my eyes made contact with the offending material.

Why did I buy it?

Why didn't I just slink away back to the haven that Sam offered and not let myself touch, let alone purchase this... *thing*?

Because I was human. And humans were good at many things.

Extraordinary people wrote books, songs, cured diseases, discovered planets. But there was a universal quality we humans all had, even when we didn't want to admit it. We all did things we knew would hurt us. Whether it was drugs, eating a whole tub of ice cream when you're lactose intolerant and sad, or the ultimate—loving someone.

All guaranteed pain. Our triggers and soft spots and tolerances might differ, but we were all masochists deep down.

Deep down, on the highest peak of the lowest dungeon, we all craved it.

Pain.

Pain made us feel alive, didn't it?

"You are not to look at this. Ever. Fucking. Again," Sam growled.

Actually *growled*.

He was not like the rest of the men in the strange little world of beautiful outlaws and cavemen who had found love and let it swallow them whole. He wasn't monotone and didn't speak in grunts, nor did he order me around or tell me what to wear, what to do. He knew what that meant to me. And that wasn't him. He was wild, and he loved me that way.

He was still alpha. Especially in the bedroom, where I let him order me around however much he liked.

But in real life, he was alpha-*lite*.

This was not lite.

I blinked at him, silent and still frozen.

His midnight eyes caught mine in their snare as he reached into his pocket with the hand that wasn't clutching the magazine. While holding my gaze, he retrieved whatever his hand had been searching for.

It was only when the reflection of the flames lit up his irises that I realized what he was doing.

Lighting the magazine on fire.

I could only watch in horror as the flames licked at the image on the cover.

The one of me.

From behind.

Straight on.

In the dress I thought I'd looked so beautiful in. That Sam had ripped off me and then demanded I buy four more like it. Or more specifically told me he was buying me four more like it.

I made a mental note to borrow Sam's lighter and burn each and every one sitting in the closet, tags still on.

"Rock god takes Shamu out for a feeding."

That was the headline.

What grabbed you.

Apart from my gigantic ass next to Sam's sculpted and beautiful body, of course.

There were more pictures inside. A whole lot more.

And an accompanying story, of course.

It was all flames now. Of course, just that *one* was in flames. There were *millions* of others not being turned to ash. Ones being sold. Read.

I cringed. Almost let that thought cripple me.

Then I focused on the flames once more.

"Sam!" I yelled, the fire making me momentarily forget about the millions of people leering and laughing at my expense. "You're going to burn yourself."

His eyes stayed glued to mine, the flames climbing fast toward his lithe and tattooed hands.

His livelihood. His life. Everything he was.

"Already burned, babe," he clipped.

He held my eyes for a beat more, as if he was challenging the one thing in life that wouldn't blink back—fire. Or maybe he didn't even notice the inferno in his hands, because the one in his eyes had already consumed him. And me.

Then it must have got to him. Sense. Or more likely pain.

We all liked pain, whether we admitted it or not, but we also had a teeny sliver of self-preservation, which was why Sam strode calmly over to the sink and dropped his burning magazine into it.

The flames hissed in protest as water from the faucet rained down on them.

Fire didn't technically emit sound, but while the flames were alive, everything had seemed so loud. Deafening.

Now, without them to focus on, everything was quiet. Well, apart from the headline that screamed at me, even from the ashes.

Sam's chest rose and fell in exaggerated movements, as if he'd run a marathon. Or like it sometimes did after he'd finished giving me the best orgasms of my life.

Usually even the memory of such orgasms had my stomach flipping, desire running through my body like a physical thing.

But not now. For once, even Sam couldn't chase it away.

"Sam Kennedy is off the market, according to inside sources. And the one to catch this prize fish, or more aptly eat it, is an unknown woman. This publication is yet to know anything about her (we're going to be changing that) but we do know she doesn't say no to dessert. Who knew Kennedy—who has a slew of Victoria's Secret models and actresses in his wake—is secretly a chubby chaser? We didn't. But this size zero is out to buy some Twinkies."

Sam hadn't burned it quickly enough. Not nearly. I read the words. Consumed them. Like my Twinkies, obviously. He hadn't stopped me from reading the entire article, not catching me until the fourth read-through. I could recite it by heart if I so desired.

I didn't desire.

But that ugly little voice that I thought I'd quieted years ago taunted me with those words. They were on a repeat reel, like *Friends* had been since before I could remember. As soon as it was over, it started all over again, no pause, no break. I barely knew what it was like before that.

I'd been watching them, the words, play over in my mind, so I hadn't seen Sam circle the kitchen island and come to stand in front of me.

His hands at my neck commanded my attention.

The memories of him didn't work to quiet the voice, but his hands did. Almost.

I glimpsed his face.

Angry, obviously. Furious. But also tortured. Guilty. As if it was somehow his fault that I'd had eating issues since I was twelve and would always be, as Bridget Jones said, 'just a little bit fat.' As if he'd taken the photo from an angle no woman had been photographed in, then sent it to a place wherever such hateful things are printed and wrote it himself. As if everything was on his shoulders.

"Baby, I want you to listen to me. I *need* you to listen to me," he demanded, his grip flexing on my neck as he spoke. "You need to listen real good. Not because I'm only going to say this once, because I'm not. I'm going to say this every damn day, twelve hundred times a day for the rest of forever if that's what it takes. But I want you to listen hard right now. To the truth. Not my truth—*the* truth. The one that trash has defiled and distorted for a quick fucking buck and fifteen seconds of attention. And I know these flimsy, empty fucking lies some-how become heavier and toxic and poison the truth when you're staring at them. When they're staring at you. But I'm not going to let that poison take. I can't. I can't have the most beautiful and pure thing on this planet tainted because of me. Because I put her in my world. I will not let that happen."

His chest was still rising and falling rapidly, as if the intensity of his emotions was triggering a cardiovascular response.

"That"—he jerked his head violently to the smoking sink—"isn't truth. Fuck, it's so far from the truth it'd be funny if it didn't hurt so fucking much. You are beautiful." His hands moved from my neck to trace down the sides of my body. Slowly. Reverently. Purposefully.

The memory of his touch may not have created flames of my own inside my body, but the actuality of it did.

Though the poison was still there. Taking. Sinking in.

"This world, babe, it's all about surface shit. About the appearance of beauty. So that's why, when presented with the real thing, the rarest of all things in this world—you—it has to crush it. Destroy it. Because you show the world for what it is, Thumbelina. You rip down the two-dimensional background. You show them how fucking pathetic their existence is." He paused. "You showed me how pathetic mine was. How empty. And I'm going to make everyone who hurt you sorry. I promise." He kissed me long and hard on the mouth.

Then he was gone.

Presumably to exact vengeance.

Pity it was in vain.

Sam

Sam was still reeling. Pulsing. On fucking fire as he stormed through his manager's offices.

Cindy, or Carrie, or some-fucking-thing or another stood as he approached her desk.

He didn't miss the way her eyes lit up as she took him in. He'd always known he lit up an empty head, known that when he'd made the huge fucking mistake of sleeping with her. It was a weak moment.

Jack was involved. And Daniels.

So yeah, he'd known it then, and when he'd seen her poking a hole in the fucking condom for round two.

But with Gina, when he saw the way her whole fucking *being* illuminated when she looked at him, it showed him this was bullshit.

She took down the fucking background so he could see all this shit for the *production* that it was.

"Sam, he's in a meeting but if you want, I can—"

He held up his hand, not even giving the bitch a glance. "No, succubus, I am talking to him. Now."

And with that, he was done giving her the most valuable thing he had. His attention.

The door rattled on its hinges as he swung it open with enough force to detach it from the frame, had it not been specially reinforced to suit the fickle emotions of the talent.

It wasn't the first time Sam had done such a thing before. Or the fourth.

But it was the first time his anger had rattled through him like a fucking earthquake. He was even scaring himself a little. *But being scared is good*, he reminded himself.

Mark's eyes flickered to the door casually, not perturbed by Sam's entrance. The woman sitting across from him was obviously a lot less versed in such things, so she jumped visibly, eyes going to Sam, first wide in probable shock and then in recognition.

"I want to sue them. Kill them. Burn their offices to the

fucking ground," he gritted out, pacing the room, picking things up on shelves and then putting them back down just so he could have something to do with his hands. "Or preferably all three." He stopped his fidgeting and folded his arms to still the twitching of his hands.

They were always twitching. Usually it was with a need to play, have drumsticks in them. Have music pulsing through them. More recently, it was to have Gina in his arms.

Right then, it was to punch someone.

Anyone.

More specifically the anyones who were responsible for the absolute emptiness in his woman's eyes. It was there. Defeat. All she had been through, survived, somehow retaining beautiful innocent naivety—and it was this world did that to her.

His fucking world.

Him.

It was his fault when he got down to the crux of it.

But he couldn't very well punch himself in the face, so those fuckers would have to fucking do.

Mark hadn't altered his facial expression, merely rotated slightly on his chair.

"Sam, perhaps we can talk about murder and arson later. Without witnesses," he said mildly, eyes on the woman in front of his desk.

Sam glowered at him. "I do not do *later*," he said. "I'm about instant gratification... in all things. Revenge specifically in this moment. So, excuse me for being rude, darlin', but you're gonna have to reschedule." He directed his statement to the woman, whose eyes were darting between him and Mark, as if she was watching a tennis match that she didn't buy a ticket to and was now expecting a rouge ball to hit her in the face at some point.

She hastily stood, unsteady on her heels.

"Ye-yeah, sure, that's fine. Fine," she stuttered. Her eyes darted to Mark, who stood too. "I'll call your assistant to organize a more"—she glanced at Sam—"convenient time."

And then she scattered. She didn't run, but it sure was close to it.

The door closed quietly behind her as she pulled it shut so carefully, like she considered it to be China.

"Well, she scares easy," Sam said mildly. "Back to me."

He stomped forward to twirl the chair she had just been sitting in around and sat backward on it, resting his elbows on the back and glaring at Mark, who wasn't glaring but had that same twitch in his eye he had when Sam accidentally on purpose leaked his sex tape.

It was his best performance pre-Gina. It would've been cruel not to share it with the world. Plus, it wasn't like the chick was completely unwilling. She had been the one to try and blackmail him with it in the first place.

Instead of paying her the six figures she'd demanded, he'd released it.

Bitches didn't trick him.

She should've thanked him anyway. She was on some idiotic reality TV show now, making money to inflate her tits, lips and ass.

And her ego, not that that needed any inflation.

"You can't just burst into meetings like that, Sam," Mark said patiently, like he was addressing a frustrating child—which was his default tone with Sam.

"Haven't you heard? I'm famous, so I can do what the fuck I want," Sam snapped. And for once, it wasn't with the empty humor he usually such statements in. No, his words were full of fucking fury, just like his entire body had been the moment he'd laid eyes on that fucking *travesty* of a cover. "Have you seen it?" he clipped.

Mark's eyes went stormy. His body tightened slightly. Fucker had an amazing poker face—he'd cleaned Sam out of thousands over the years, not counting his percentage—so this reaction was drastic for his cool-as-a-cucumber manager. He nodded once. "Yeah, I've seen it. I'm working on it. Jenna's working on it."

Sam stood quickly, the force of it pushing his chair from its position to slam into Mark's desk and then fall on its side. He didn't take any notice.

"If you were working on it, the article never would've been fucking published in the first place!" he roared.

"You know we can't control this, Sam," Mark said quietly. Calmly. "We've been here before with all of you. You specifically, thousands of times with thousands of other girls."

"She isn't other girls," he hissed through his teeth. "She is *the girl*. The fucking girl you only get one shot at. And me, the lucky fuck that I am, somehow got three of them. *Three shots*. You don't get any more in baseball, and I don't get any more in life. With her. She's once-in-a-lifetime type stuff, and she's precious and good and pure, and this world is shitting all over that."

The words spewed out of him in a river of emotion.

"Sam, we can't do—"

"I don't want to hear *can't*," he said. "I want to get the addresses of the people who wrote the article, the photographer who took the photo and the editor who okayed the story," he demanded, his voice adopting the calm quality that Mark's had. That was because he was forming a plan.

A fucking great one.

"Sam, I'm not giving you those. You're adding more fire to this thing. You need to—"

"I *need* the addresses," Sam interrupted him.

Mark folded his arms. "I'm not giving them to you." Again,

his tone was that of a parent dealing with a petulant and stubborn child.

And, in a way, Sam was a petulant and stubborn child.

He smiled, nodding at Mark, then saluting him. "Okay, boss."

Then he turned on his Converse and walked out.

He fished his phone out of his pocket, eyes not even touching the space the succubus inhabited.

He put it to his ear after putting on speed dial two.

"Keltan? Hey, it's Sam. Need a favor, bro."

There was a pause, and Sam swore he heard a *fucking grin* over the phone. Not a happy one, but this hardass Kiwi motherfucker's version of it.

"Addresses for everyone responsible for fucking with your girl?" his accented voice asked. "Yeah, I'll get them for you within the hour. Need backup?"

Sam grinned wider. "Nah, bro. I've got it."

His next call was to Noah and Wyatt.

A petulant and stubborn child he may have been. But one with a lot of money, good friends, and two fists he was not afraid of using.

Three of the four people he sought out were male. He was happy about that. Even if she was a reptile who made her living off lies and manipulation, Sam would never put his hands on a female.

Ever.

The bitch had made him wish that he was a lot less of a decent human being, though. Just for a second. But then he remembered what he was going home to. The sweet.

So he stopped wishing he was fucked enough to lay his

hand on a woman, no matter how much of a cunt she was.

She had the fucking gall to *hit on him*. And insult Gina. Again. To his fucking face.

Yeah, her career was over.

"Why couldn't she have been a dude?" Wyatt groaned as they'd pulled away from her condo.

Sam rubbed his knuckles. "Or why couldn't we have had Emma here? We *know* that little spitfire can throw a punch. And chicks can punch chicks. It's like the law. Plus, you would've finally had yourself a remedy for those blue balls. Win, win, win," he'd said.

Wyatt's eyes had narrowed and he'd told Sam to go fuck himself.

"No, that's not what I'm doing. See, I got my shit together and got my woman. You're the one who's fucking himself currently. Both literally and figuratively."

That had earned him a punch in the shoulder.

"Good, warm up for the next asshole. This one's a dude, thankfully."

They hadn't killed him, as Sam had been very tempted to do.

"It'd be a publicity nightmare, dude," Wyatt muttered as he'd held the swine by his polyester shirt collar.

Sam regarded the bleeding rodent. "Yeah, plus I'm too pretty for prison," he said back.

Sam didn't consider himself a particularly violent person. He wasn't particularly jealous either. And he thought the two of those went hand in hand. Jealousy was insecurity, at the end of the day, and no one would accuse Sam of being insecure. Plus, he never cared enough about a chick to get jealous. Many had tried over the years. Never worked.

The only time he'd gotten violent over a girl was when his best friend was dying in front of him and he'd shot the man responsible for terrorizing and kidnapping her.

That had tasted good. Revenge. Better than any drug.

But the comedown was worse too. Especially with the reality of the blood on his hands not changing the fact that Lexie *died*.

Luckily she came back from the dead—not zombiefied or vampified, just Lexie.

Though he thought they all came back a little different after that. Colder. There was a part of him that knew he could and would kill someone who hurt his family.

And he wouldn't lose a wink of sleep.

Now that feeling returned tenfold with Gina. It all started when she opened that door, her beautiful face bruised and tarnished. And he hadn't even actualized how much she meant to him then.

But it grew when he met Officer Dickface, saw the way he looked at her.

It grew even more when he found out what Officer Dickface did to her.

There was a pocket of him in that constant state of preparation for that violence. The one he'd just unleashed. The one he'd always unleash to protect his.

He pulled up to the house, with bloody knuckles and a stained shirt, and he knew it would always live within him.

And he didn't mind at all. As long as he kept being able to go home to sweet.

To her.

He had one destination when he got to the house.

And he flinched harder than any of the fuckers had with his hits when he saw her face.

"Hey," she said quietly.

She spoke quietly most of the time. Little more than a whisper. Except when she was pissed off. Which she was, with him, a lot. Then she was loud. He liked both, but her murmured words, her gentle tone, hardened his dick. Every fucking time.

Not this time.

Because it wasn't her gentle, quiet whisper, full of everything he loved. Like her eyes, this was empty. Maybe not completely, but missing something important. Something pivotal. Something that had been there when he'd left her naked and flushed in bed that morning. But something that wasn't when he'd walked into the house hours ago and seen her with that garbage in her hands.

"Baby—" He took her head in his hands gently, intending on saying… he didn't even know what. Something, fucking anything to put it back. What had been taken by people as deep as a fucking puddle.

She cut him off when her wide eyes took in his hands. She snatched them from the sides of her head, the nothingness receding a little as she inspected them.

"Sam," she whispered, trailing her peaches-and-cream fingers over his bloodied, swollen and inked hands. She snapped her head up, eyes narrowing slightly, with a little more life than had been there before. "What did you do?" she demanded.

Sam left his hands there. Even though he wanted to snatch them away, make sure no more ugly tainted her pretty, he liked the gentle touch and the way her hands trailed over the bruised skin.

"Tripped," he said easily, not taking his eyes off her.

She narrowed her eyes more, hands squeezing his in warning.

He sighed. "So someone else tripped," he said. "Into my fist. Dumb fuck kept going and going. Didn't learn his lesson after falling just once." He shrugged.

She dropped his hands rapidly, folding them across her chest.

It was the motion itself that had Sam's eyes directed to his second favorite spot. The first being her eyes, which was unusual for him in itself. He was a tits man all the way. Tits, ass, hair, face were what he noticed about a girl. In that order. But with Gina, it was her eyes. So big and fucking beautiful, like Bambi had somehow wandered out of those fictional woods and into the cruel world that did a lot worse than have a hunter shoot its mother.

They trapped him for the longest moment.

And that was in high school. Though it had taken him a decade to admit that.

He'd been trapped in them ever since, whether he'd known it or not.

But he also looked at her breasts. Often. And the style she had, the one he loved, the way she wore her clothes and did it in a way that seemed to make it different than anyone else, than even Lexie, accentuated the big and round and beautiful breasts that God gave her.

His eyes had gone to those breasts for a start. But then he realized what she was wearing.

A sweatshirt. Big. Huge enough to swallow all of her beautiful curves. When he'd come in, he'd been too busy making a beeline for her that he hadn't even noticed she'd tucked her knees and legs into it, like she was making a cocoon. She had been sitting on the sofa, contemplating the vista with an intensity that, even on reflection, scared him.

He frowned. "What are you wearing?"

She flinched when he spoke. Actually *flinched*. And the look on her face when he'd uttered those words punctured him so deep he wished there was a way for him to swallow them right back up.

But they had already hit. He didn't know what or how, but it was deep.

When he opened his mouth to say something, though no idea what, she beat him to it again.

"That's not what's important," she clipped, the hurt receding as her face settled into an expression so empty it shook him.

To the core.

He'd seen a senator do blow off a stripper's ass after said senator had paid him two hundred grand to play a drum solo that lasted three minutes.

He didn't shake easy.

But that did it.

"What's important is we get some ice for your hands and you tell me what happened," she said tersely, in a voice much like Mark had used. A voice Sam guessed she reserved for her little students. Not often, mind you, as Gina was the teacher every child loved and adored and wanted to be their mother.

She got up and he was so fucking awed by her, even in that ridiculous sweater, with her hair pulled into a sloppy bun and not a lick of makeup on her beautiful face, that it took him a second to catch up with her as she padded toward the kitchen in the direction of the refrigerator. For ice, he assumed.

His hands had stopped throbbing the minute he'd seen her face, replaced with a much deeper and more profound pain. For it's that way when you're feeling someone else's. Witnessing it when there's nothing you can do. Not enough people in the world to punch to take it all away.

He snatched her by the hips, yanking her back into his chest so her warmth radiated through all the coldness he'd unleashed with violence.

He burrowed his face into her neck.

"Not so fast, buddy," he murmured, sucking in the scent of coconut and vanilla that was imprinted on her hair.

Her natural reaction when he'd touched her was to sink

into his embrace, curl into him. That had become habit once they'd gotten over the bullshit of before. Even if they were arguing or if she was pissed, the minute he touched her, everything melted away. They fit. And the mind couldn't fuck with that.

Or at least that was what he'd thought.

"I'm getting ice for your swollen hand, *buddy*," she said, her voice flat. She'd stiffened, turned to stone much like her tone had. "So if you'll kindly let me go…."

Sam squeezed her harder, laying his mouth on her neck, slowly tasting the buttery coconut of her skin. She shivered at his touch, and Sam's dick jerked to attention.

He knew she felt that too because she shivered again, sighing audibly.

"No, afraid that's not possible. I don't plan on letting you go… well, ever. And for the next few hours or so, I'm going to make sure it's physically impossible. And then the next hundred years after that, of course."

Without waiting for her to respond, to let her brain catch up to her body, he bent down to sweep her feet from the floor and carry her bridal-style.

She let out a surprised little squeak, and it was the cutest fucking thing Sam had ever heard. He'd thought his dick already stood full mast, but he was wrong, that little sound inflating it that much more.

"Sam," she breathed, her eyes lazy as if she tasted his intentions. "What are you doing?"

He grinned at her, repositioning her slightly so he could walk up the stairs. "Oh, you'll find out very fucking soon."

She wriggled against him, something flickering in her eyes. "I'm too heavy, put me down," she whispered.

A blade of anger shot through Sam and his hands jerked slightly. "Babe, been carrying the world on my shoulders for twenty-six years. When I met you, that weight was gone. Trust me, you're not fucking heavy," he rasped. Then, with coordination even he was proud of, he laid a kiss on her while he ascended the last stair.

Then he prayed he had enough in him to take all the shit she'd lifted off his, that he'd unwittingly put on her own, and burn it to the fucking ground. To find a way to show her what she looked like through his eyes.

Chapter Eighteen

Gina

I let him peel the hoodie off me once he'd put me down.

This was after he carried me up his stairs.

Three flights of them.

And he wasn't even breathing heavily.

I knew that was a testament to his strength and fitness and not my lack of heaviness, despite what he said.

I had hard, photographic evidence to the contrary. And photos didn't lie.

His eyes roved over me in the tight cami and boy shorts I'd yanked the hoodie over top of. I wished I was wearing a ski suit, regardless of the fire, the desire that was all over his face.

"Turn around," he ordered, voice thick.

He'd deposited me not on the bed, as his dark eyes and his previous intention had led me to believe, but on my feet at the end of it.

Because he had magic sex wizard powers, his voice and the erotic command behind it had me forgetting about everything else but obeying.

When I turned around, I understood why he hadn't put me on the bed.

I tried to turn, to shrink away, Sam's body and firm hands

stopped me.

"Sam," I protested, looking anywhere but the reflection the floor-to-ceiling mirror in front of me was presenting me with.

"No," he growled. "I need you to look. To *see*. Not the lies that you've been telling yourself for too long. What bitter and ugly people have been telling you. You need to see yourself for what you are."

"I see myself, Sam," I gritted, focusing on the mirror. But not my reflection, on Sam's eyes.

"No you fuckin' don't," he growled. "*Look*," he demanded.

His hands went to the bottom of my cami, purposefully, slowly, showing his intention. His worship.

My entire body was stiff as he peeled it upward, exposing my bare skin.

"Watch," he ordered again.

The cami fluttered to the floor and I was standing there in my black cotton bra and black cotton boy shorts.

Sam's muscled arms contrasted the undefined skin of my stomach. He trailed his finger along it. I watched, even though I was still replaying those words in my mind, I was also letting another part of me respond to Sam's touch, letting it loosen my emotional muscles.

"Feel," he demanded. He kissed my neck. "Feel what you do to me."

He pressed himself against me and the hardness of his arousal did so too. "Ever since I saw you, once I stopped being blind to my own bullshit, this was my reaction. Before I knew how fuckin' beautiful you were on the inside, I was awed by how beautiful you were on the outside."

He kissed along my shoulder, hand going to my bra strap and pushing it down. Then he did the same on the other side.

"There is not one thing that I would change about you. Not one thing." He paused as his hands trailed up my back and then unfastened my bra so it tumbled to the ground with my cami, my hardened nipples exposed to the air. To Sam's hungry gaze.

My breasts were immediately covered with two tattooed hands, kneading them. "Most beautiful fuckin' tits I've ever seen," he rasped in my ear. My entire body shivered with need. "Ever tasted."

I sucked in a ragged breath as he trailed his lips up the side of my neck, grazing my skin with his teeth. And I watched him do so. Watched him worship me.

His eyes met mine in the mirror, wicked with desire.

The cold air bit at my nipples once more as his hands left them and went downward.

I watched their journey, felt it, my body humming with expectation.

He watched his own hands as they hooked into the top of my panties and rolled them down.

His lips left my neck as he lowered himself.

I should've felt self-conscious when his lips met my bare cheeks, when the lights were exposing every sin, every bite, every imperfection. But I was too far gone for that.

Before I knew it, I was stepping out of my panties and Sam had left a trail of kisses down the backs of my legs and was now literally kneeling in front of me.

His eyes ate me up, right there. I'd never been more exposed, naked, both physically and emotionally, to anyone. Ever.

"Most beautiful fuckin' pussy I've ever seen," he mumbled, voice thick, almost unrecognizable. His fingers trailed the insides of my thighs, danced atop the sensitive skin, but missed the important places.

It was torture.

Exquisite torture.

He leaned forward, not hesitating, not pausing, and then

he was *there*. Right there, kissing the most important place with practiced expertise. I would've collapsed right then and there if he hadn't gripped my hip to help keep me up.

He gazed up at me in wonder.

In *wonder*.

There was no other way to describe it, the way he was looking at me.

"Sweetest fuckin' pussy I've ever tasted," he said.

His mouth wasn't even on me, but I almost came from that sentence alone.

Then his mouth was there again. Bringing me to the precipice. Right *there,* dangling on the edge of the most orgasm I'd ever had. Anyone had ever had.

Then he stopped and I almost screamed in frustration.

He grinned up at me, eyes wild.

Then he was up, kissing me, my taste intermingling with his own.

"No, babe, you're gonna come around my dick. You're gonna come watching this. Watching us. Watching the beauty."

He'd yanked his shirt off at some point, so when he went behind me, his bare skin brushed against mine.

He flattened his palm on my lower back, putting gentle pressure on it to bend me forward.

"Brace yourself on the glass," he ordered.

I did as I was told.

"Good girl," he hissed. "Now you watch. You watch every fuckin' second."

I heard the crackle of his zipper lower as he freed himself, his eyes never leaving mine in the mirror.

Then he was inside.

I cried out, squeezing my eyes closed on reflex.

He stopped. "Watch," he growled.

My eyes opened immediately, taking in the cords in his

neck as he practiced extreme restraint in not moving.

The second my eyes met his, he moved.

And I watched.

And he was right.

It was beautiful. Magnificent.

And I forgot everything.

During.

Pity about the after.

"I've been looking everywhere for you. I swear I thought you ran away and joined the circus without me. And I was about to get so mad."

The voice, penetrating the velvet silence that goes with the inky blackness of the witching hour, shocked me into sloshing my thankfully lukewarm tea all over myself. The strangled scream that communicated my fright cemented my mortification. And it wasn't even a soft girly scream. No, one might go so far as to call it a grunt.

So while I was grunting and spilling tea and cursing myself for not screaming more attractively, the owner of the voice had traversed the shadowy landscape to come and stand right in front of me.

Like *right* in front of me.

I'd snuck out of bed, out of the grip of Sam's sleeping body, to come down to the living room, which offered floor-to-ceiling views of the twinkling beyond.

Now the twinkling beyond harbored no temptation.

Regardless of the dim moonlight casting him in shadow, I could see every inch of him. His tattoos, the silver glint of his jewelry, his washboard abs. I knew he was topless; one didn't need the gift of sight to know when a half-naked rock god was standing in front of them.

Girls sensed that kind of thing.

It was imprinted into our DNA.

That and the ability to sense the last Twinkie in the house on the first day of PMS.

The dead of night did an interesting thing to the human mind. Somehow that inky blanket of night, the silence that echoed throughout the stillness, it all created the environment in which to engage in self-reflection or self-inspection that wasn't possible in the light. Because monsters—hide-under-your-bed, eat-your-children type of monsters—resided in the night.

All those children's books got it half right. They did exist in the night, but not outward in a closet, or slinking in a window, or creeping out from under your bed. No, they exist inside your head, and that midnight chime is when we see them. And in that environment, inspecting your monsters, fighting them, having tea with them, another thing happens. You either feel incredibly lonely with only you and your demons, or you feel comforted that someone else and their own demons are battling the night too.

I had always been the former.

Even when I was with Simon. Which should've been my earliest warning sign, really. The worst thing isn't having no one in the night, it's someone who makes you feel more alone than you have before, even in your deepest moments of solitude.

Being alone is, by definition, a solitary endeavor, but one where ultimately another human serves as the catalyst. For you wouldn't recognize being alone if you didn't have someone to make you feel that way, whether they leave or make you stay with them, make you watch yourself disappear. That was alone. Someone who made you feel alone.

So yeah, I'd always been the former, the solo battler. Which was, at least in part, a reason for my love of books. Because not only did they distract me from my own demons, but they showed me how to fight them.

It's much easier, preferable even, to witness the heartbreak of others instead of facing your own. That's the ugliness of society. The best of us try to trick ourselves into thinking we're selfless and we *care* about suffering. The better of us might even do something about it.

Or try to.

But it's the worst of us, or maybe just the human in us, who admit it in that dark little place where the voices whisper and echo with unsaid words and unuttered rage.

Witnessing someone else's suffering is painful. It can be shattering.

But it's not as soul-destroying as looking in the mirror. And *really* looking. Beyond the nose that is just a little too small, the eyes that are a little too big. The extra pounds, the stretch marks, the dimpled skin.

Beyond all of that, it's the heartbreak.

Those of us who can, we heal it. But like a bone that wasn't set right, it's never the same. It aches in the cold, lonely hours where the barriers of the mind are lowered enough.

Those of us who can't heal, those of us who aren't just broken bones but scattered ash, we hide it.

And then most of us try to bury ourselves in other sadness. Like me with books. They took me on adventures, sure, made me think for a split second that magic could be real. Empowered me with strong female characters. Took me into a dream with love so impossibly perfect it could only ever live in the pages of a book.

But most importantly it showed me suffering. Presented me with other people's suffering. Not just the fictional characters I'd come to nurture and love like friends, but the person who sat and agonized over such words on paper.

Because no author conjures heartbreak out of nowhere. They can call up mystical dragons, witches, monsters of all the fantastical and supernatural varieties, merely from the made-up part of the brain.

But ones that write suffering, heartbreak so real you can almost taste the tears in your mind, that's not something even the most imaginative of minds can conjure.

Pain cannot be reproduced.

It had to be felt, reimagined, rewritten in all its ugly splendor for someone else to experience. Mostly it's a suffering so bad that you know the author had no choice but to externalize it should they go mad with only sharing it with themselves and the demons of the soul.

That's my ultimate escape.

My ultimate comfort.

Because knowing someone felt something so profoundly devastating, yet managed to finish the book, that makes me want to finish mine. And continue to hide my ashes.

I was so sick of hiding it.

So in the dead of the night, in the darkness, I decided to finally reveal it.

"I'm worried," I whispered, not looking at him, I couldn't, not then.

He settled in beside me, seeming to sense that it was not the time to touch me. "You're staring out into the nothingness in the middle of the night, baby. I'm getting that you're worried."

A long silence descended between us.

"A worry shared is a worry halved. Or doubled, depending on whether it's gonna make me worry too. Even if it does, I'd rather know," he said finally.

I smiled around my melancholy. "I'm worried that we

don't… fit. That I don't fit here, that I'm not cut out for the loud and fast life. You don't fit there either. In my little life. *I* didn't really even fit, but you certainly don't. You're not made for that."

I blurted it all out in a rush, still staring at the twinkling lights of the city.

Then Sam did touch me, turning me so those lights illuminated him just enough to see the expression on his face. He framed mine with his hands.

"I'm not here to fit neatly into your life, Gina," he said. "I don't do neat. I'm here to teach you that life isn't neat. Not the way I live it." His eyes danced with demons. "But getting messy is what life's all about. What *love's* all about."

"Is it?" I whispered.

"Yeah," he whispered back. "It is. There's the good kind and then there's the bad kind. I've had both. And the worst thing about the bad? It tricks you into thinking it's good," he uttered, his words the introduction to something the inky darkness had invited him to reveal. "Addiction is interesting," he said, smile still firmly on his face. But he wasn't smiling, not really. I'd come to be able to recognize that. That outside smile that he used to trick the world—and more importantly, himself—that he was okay.

I knew he wasn't. And I had a sinking feeling that I knew where this was going.

"Yeah, it's interesting. And great for publicity." He gave me a look.

"But only after you're dead, mind you. Most bands only really cemented themselves in the rock 'n' roll hall of fame when at least one of their members ODed, killed themselves, silenced the music in their own head. That's what drugs were, to me at least. But a kind of loud silence, you know? Not peaceful. Cocaine doesn't exactly give you *peace*." He laughed, shaking his head and rubbing at the stubble on his chin. "No, it speeds everything up. Makes it clearer and blurs it beyond recognition. And I don't know how it really grasped me in its hold, but it had to, at least one of us. Have you ever heard of a successful band without at least one drug addiction?" He shook his head again. "So I took one for the team, so to speak."

I blinked at him, shocked and saddened at the same time. Sure, he'd jokingly mentioned recreational drug use. And although that shocked the little bookish and naive me, I hadn't exactly been surprised, per se. He was right, that world came with a side of cocaine like mine came with a side of Earl Grey. So I'd accepted it. Didn't approve, or really even understand, but a foreign part of me kind of *got it*.

Everyone was just trying to get through life, fighting their own battles. Who was I to judge the weapons they used when they felt like they were backed into a corner?

Despite that, there was a little part of me that was disappointed. Not in Sam exactly, but this whole wretched world that was his dream and nightmare at the same time.

"But—"

He held up his hand to silence me, though not unkindly.

"Yeah, it wasn't published. Anywhere." He read my mind.

Because that's exactly what I'd been about to ask. Despite myself, over the years, I had bought those glossy trash magazines if Sam was on the front. Torturing myself with the stick-thin and beautiful models on his arms, the smiles on his face and the utter adoration of everyone who was close enough to be in his orbit.

Those images had hurt. A lot. But I didn't buy the magazines as a form of emotional self-harm. Well, not entirely, at least. I'd bought them so I could follow his success and watch him with a painful happiness. The kind of happiness I felt for Lexie, but a lot more complicated. I'd always known they'd all deserved to catapult out of their lives and go to something great. Because of their talent, obviously. But also because all of them, in their own way, needed it. Because their lives were not suited to anything else.

But talent and deserving something more than you were given doesn't guarantee that you get more. Usually it was exactly the opposite. The world liked to play with the people who deserved the smoothest roads by giving them more potholes than any asshole ever got.

Like Simon. His road had been as smooth as freshly laid asphalt.

But Sam's hadn't, by a long stretch.

So I'd reveled in life finally giving him smooth.

Or I'd reveled in the appearance of it. Apparently nothing was smooth beneath the surface.

He regarded me, cautiously, pensively, as if he were midway through an attempt to read my mind. Then he abandoned that endeavor to continue with his story. "Drug addictions may have been good for publicity after the fact, but Unquiet Mind has never been and never will be about publicity stunts. About broadcasting our skeletons and parading them out of our closets for a quick buck, a quicker fifteen minutes." He paused, a skip in his words signifying the interruption of his stream of consciousness with a memory. "Well, apart from the unavoidable." I knew he was talking about the stalker incident with Lexie. That was burned into public consciousness for sure; it shook up the world for a long while. And for a world with the memory of a goldfish, a long while was significant. But even for something like that, collective memory had a timestamp. The next tragedy, the next scandal was shiny and new.

Not for those in the inner circle. I knew that. Because even I, who existed in the shadows beyond that circle, still felt the chill from that memory.

"Sure, Wyatt and I were always in the rags for stupid shit," Sam continued, still watching me, smile now just another memory. Well maybe for the world, but not for me. I stored it away on my shelves for later inspection so I could recognize it next time.

"Parties, girls, fast cars, fights," he listed the qualities he and Wyatt were known for. "The odd international incident." He grinned again, mischievously. That one had a twinkle of authenticity in it. "But all of that was a performance. For the cameras, sure, maybe. Or maybe they just happened to be there while we were putting on a show for ourselves. Trying to trick ourselves that this was going to sustain us." He shook his head, then leaned forward to lightly trace circles over my skin.

The places he touched exploded in light and pleasing prickles of sensation.

"It didn't take long for that performance to become flimsy. Paper thin," he said, no longer looking at me but concentrating on his fingers journey around my skin. "I couldn't have that. I didn't need to see behind the curtain, so I looked for something to rebuild that shit. Or distract me. Or to make me move so fast I didn't recognize, didn't fucking care about what life I was living." He circled my hands with his and squeezed tightly.

Such a gesture was usually used to support the other person. But the way he did it, the expression on his face, made it apparent that he was clutching me for something. So he didn't drift away into whatever shark-filled waters he was currently wading in.

"So I did it for a while. Hid it for a longer while." He met my eyes then, trouble swimming in his. Strength too. And truth.

Tears prickled at the corners of my own.

"Then I couldn't hide." He shrugged. "Maybe it was on purpose. Drug addicts usually excel at that part. The act. The performance. Maybe that's why I became one. I was one all along, since I was a teenager. I'd perfected the performance, I just needed the drugs to compliment it." Another hand squeeze. "Whatever." He shrugged again. "I ain't no shrink. I hit drums with metal sticks. Whatever it was, Wyatt figured it out first. Tried to talk to me. I was in a world far too loud to listen. Lexie tried, but have you met that girl? When she's not singing, she's quiet as shit." He paused. "Well, unless she's yelling at her husband, and then she's loud. Brave too, because I wouldn't yell at that motherfucker. I actually enjoy my head being attached to my shoulders," he said, injecting comic relief into the moment, seeming to need the quick break from the harsh confession. "So that left Noe." His eyes swam with something. A memory. A dark one. One that hurt even to look at within the shadow of his eyes. They focused on me, clearing. "And he got through," he said simply, deciding to not treat me to the ugly details. I knew there was more to that particular story. Much more.

"I'm not gonna say it wasn't hard," he continued. "This isn't a fairy tale where it was goodbye cocaine and I was clean forever after."

Despite everything, the seriousness of the moment, I giggled. I couldn't help it. That was Sam's magic. He made you laugh in the face of tragedy. His own.

He grinned back at me.

That one was real.

"I relapsed. Couple of times. And when life gets a little too quiet, a little too much, I'm not gonna say I don't crave it." He paused. "Because addiction makes someone interesting, doesn't it? Somehow addicts and greats go hand in hand. That's what I told myself when I was in the middle of it. Cocaine addiction added to my character. It was creatively necessary." He grunted. "Yeah, I was a motherfucking idiot. That's not to say I'm not now, just a different kind. A more honest one."

He leaned forward, hands releasing mine so they could

frame either side of my face, forehead touching mine. "And this idiot needs to tell his girl his truth now. Because I get it. The quiet with you, the absolute silence that accommodates a lotta truth. All of it. I can't escape it when I look into your eyes." He kissed my nose. "And I don't want to. Ever. I don't crave anything that'll take that quiet, that truth away. I don't think I ever will. I'd have to be completely fucking certifiable if I did and I only vacation in insanity. I don't live in it." He paused again and something changed in his eyes, something so stark, so different than before that I almost got emotional whiplash.

And then physical when he let me go completely to lean back, his face blank.

"But you're used to it. Living your truth. Fuck, you're so much stronger than me, Thumbelina. You've lived it this whole time. Without escaping into cowardice like I did. So I get it if knowing that about me is it. The deal breaker. God knows I've dealt you enough of them."

I blinked at him, almost more surprised at what he was saying in that moment than the ones before. "So, let me get this straight," I said. "You think I'll want to end this." I waved my hands in the space that hadn't been there before, the space I despised. "Us. Because you had *one* weakness? Because life happened to you and you weren't some kind of emotional superhero?"

It was his turn to blink at me. Digest my words. He tapped his fingers on his knees, eyes never leaving mine. "Yeah, I guess that's exactly what I'm asking, Gina," he said quietly. Too quietly. He barely sounded like Sam with his voice full of that much vulnerability.

I shook my head. "Congratulations, Sam. You're human. I've got a secret—we all are. And you think I'm strong because I didn't find a substance to abuse to deal with my life? No, I didn't because I was too scared of my own shadow for a long time to even find the courage to do anything about… well, anything. You think you're weak because you escaped out of your own head? No. And I'm certainly not strong, because I didn't even make it out of my own, Sam. I gave burying your head in the sand a new meaning. I didn't live in the real world, which is why I didn't have a reason to escape. You said it yourself, I used all of this"—I shook the abandoned book in my lap that I'd intended to read—"as a reason not to live. We both went in opposite directions. You lived too much. I didn't live at all. And now here we are together," I ended the last part on a whisper. "That has to mean something. Both of us. Maybe you're here to make me live a little faster, and I'm here to slow you down just a little."

I sucked in an uncertain breath, my heart beating a thousand miles a minute with the preparation of what I was about to say. "Maybe we're just… meant to be. Us. You and me. So no, I'm not being an idiot either, Sam. My truth is sitting right in front of me. My truth is you. And for once, I don't want to escape it."

The words had barely come out of my mouth before Sam moved in a blur. And without completely knowing what was going on, I was underneath him on the sofa, his warmth pressing into every inch of me, one of his hands bracing on the edge of the sofa so he didn't give me his entire weight.

I thought he was going to speak, his eyes full of so much intensity that he needed to let it out with words.

But I should've known better. My man was all about actions rather than words.

Afterward, we were naked, lying in each other's arms, my skin flushed, heart thumping through my ribcage. We hadn't said a word since I'd spoken. Not one word.

They said actions speak louder. Whoever "they" were. I didn't know if they were right all the time, because sometimes words were needed. But at that point they weren't. The intense and silent and brutal love Sam and I made on that sofa was worth all of the words shut away in every single one of my favorite books.

I was lying there, trying not to burst into tears. Not because of the profound sadness I felt when I heard Sam's story. No, because I was so full and I was terrified. I didn't know a person could feel this much, could have something like this.

So as I was trying to steady my heart, my breaths, I didn't even notice Sam trailing lazy patterns on my jaw, watching me. Not until he spoke at least.

And that time the words spoke loud.

"No maybes, Thumbelina," he murmured.

I stared at him, confused, still a little love drunk. Yes, it was a thing, not a Hollywood concept. "What?"

"Us. No maybes. We are meant to be. You are meant to be mine. It was written somewhere, before either of us knew it. You're my truth. And unlike that shit you read about where some bloke saves some poor damsel and they create a love for the history books, your love saved me. You're my princess, babe. You're my fuckin' heroine."

Chapter Nineteen

"I don't *want* to go out," I whined.

Sam yanked a tee shirt over his head, covering up everything that I'd been perving at moments ago, which was enough of a reason to get pissed off. Abs like that should not have been covered. Though the tee molded over them perfectly.

"Yes you do. Because you're going out with *me*," he teased, pulling his hair into a bun. "And everyone else, of course. Plus crazy Emma is going to be there, so we'll get ringside seats to see what happens with her and Wyatt. Babe, we do not want to miss that."

I frowned as I slipped my heel on. My new heel.

Lexie and I had gone shopping today.

Some kind of exposure therapy, I guessed. The cameras were there. People stared. Yelled my name. Asked about Sam. I felt sick the entire time, even with my empty stomach, but I smiled through it. Pretended I was okay.

Lexie didn't believe me. Which was why she bought me the shoes.

I protested, despite their utter beauty. She was not buying me $700 shoes. I tried to tell her as much, very firmly. It hadn't worked.

"Babe. I know how crass this is to say, but I'll say it anyway. I can afford them. I can afford seven hundred pairs of them. Not

that I need seven hundred pairs—though my mother wouldn't agree with me there." She grinned. "In this life, in this world, sometimes you need to enjoy the spoils, whether you're a kindergarten teacher or a world-famous rock star." Her eyes twinkled. "Especially if you're on the world-famous rock star end of the spectrum. Because despite popular belief, there're a lot of downsides to this world." Her eyes went to the faint flashes of cameras beyond the store's tinted windows. "I hate that you've tasted that already. Know you feel like you're gonna swallow it whole and it's going to kill you from the inside out. I know, because I've had to get used to the bitter on my tongue. Had to realize that no matter how much it hurt, it wasn't going to kill me. I wasn't going to let it. And it's only bearable because I've got the sweet to balance it out."

She smiled weirdly, her hand going to the bottom of her stomach. Something sparked with that moment, but I couldn't think of it because she was still talking. "You do too, just in case you haven't figured that." She winked. "At the start, it's hard. These people, they pick at your weaknesses, expose them right to the nerve. It hurts like a bitch. I nearly packed up and went crawling home the first time I felt it. Almost. But I'd felt pain before."

Her eyes went dark, and I knew she was thinking about her history with Killian, with her mom, her crazy murderous dad. Then her crazy murderous stalker who had killed her ex-boyfriend and terrorized her life.

"So I dealt with it. And it stopped being so bad. Eventually."

She reached forward to squeeze my hand. "I know you've felt pain before too. I know you're far too strong and smart to let this best you. And you're not alone. You've got that idiot Sam utterly in love with you. I swear he'd shave his head without blinking if you asked. And his bun is worth three million dollars," she joked. Or I thought she was joking. "And you've also got the rest of us. You've always had us, you know that, right? Since high school.

I'm so glad that life has finally sorted itself out and brought you where you belong. And you belong here. Trust me on this." She looked down. *"And take the damn shoes."*

I took the damn shoes.

And they did make me feel a little better.

Especially when Sam saw them, ripped all of my clothes off and fucked me wearing only the heels.

But now I was filled with dread all over again.

Sam yanked me to my expensively shod feet, his eyes hungrily roving over every inch of me.

I had been tempted to wear some kind of shapeless and tent-like paper bag. Very tempted.

Just like I'd been very tempted to get in a taxi and then on a plane to anywhere but here.

The images in that magazine taunted me as I flipped through the hangers of dresses I'd put in Sam's closet.

Lexie's words had played alongside the ones written in that dreaded article.

It was hard. Extremely effing hard, but I put on my favorite little black dress. It was simple, strapless and tight. It showed all my curves and sucked them in at the same time, a marriage between a dress and a pair of Spanx. Though it showed a lot, it covered most of me, finishing just above my ankles, which was the perfect place to showcase my fabulous new shoes.

I had put on a giant pair of earrings that had tassels so long they brushed the bare skin of my shoulders. My hair was piled up in a messy bun at the top of my head. I'd decided on light makeup and vibrant pink lipstick.

If I was going out, I needed to do it properly. The magazines wanted to call me a whale? Fine, but I was going to be a whale with great style and a contour so sharp it could cut a bitch.

"Okay, I've totally changed my mind," he said, his eyes

traveling back to my face. "You're right. We're not going out. I'll be fighting them off the entire night. Then I'll have to kill someone for coveting what's mine, and it'll be a big *thing*," he said seriously.

I laughed. Genuinely that time, not the fake one I'd been getting extremely good at lately.

Sam glared, resting his hands lightly on my hips. "I'm serious, baby. You look too good. I'm worried about my well-being."

"*Your* well-being?"

"Well, yes. Because I'm obviously going to have to fight every single guy in the joint. And while I do not doubt my fighting prowess or my stamina, I'm still at least going to break a few fingers."

I laughed again, for longer that time.

"Well, you know I am *all about* staying in," I probed.

He squared his shoulders, moving to grasp my hands in his. "No, I have a surprise for you," he said. "And I'll brave broken fingers if I have to. I kind of love you, you know."

"I kind of love you too," I whispered.

And that was it. Lexie was right. The sweet canceled out the bitter.

For a time, at least.

"Do you know what he's doing?" Emma asked as Sam strutted onto the stage.

"Does anyone *ever* know what Sam's doing?"

"Touché."

I glanced at her. She'd been sucking down drinks like they were going out of fashion and she hadn't even begun to slur her words. I'd had one beer and my tongue already felt heavy in my mouth.

That might have been on account of the empty stomach.

She'd been drinking like a fish in an attempt to deal with the death stares Wyatt had been directing her way since she'd arrived two hours ago. She'd studiously ignored him when she'd greeted everyone with hugs and kisses.

"Babe!" she'd half screamed when she got to me, yanking me into her skinny arms. "I'm so fucking happy that you're here and the planets have finally aligned to bring you two together." She glanced between Sam and me, grinning. "I've known it since the start. It was meant to be. Like Romeo and Juliet, you know, without all those freaky suicide pacts."

She had used Lexie and me as human shields throughout the night. And Lexie and Killian had left early, which meant I was the only female left to help her out, apart from Jenna, the band's publicist. She was much like Mark, giving me a handshake and a friendly hello before focusing on her phone once more. Though she was good at her job; not a single photo had been taken of us in the little bar.

It wasn't exactly where I'd expected, not in the middle of Hollywood or with a red carpet, or *any* carpet outside. Just a sidewalk and a rusty sign reading *Alfie's* atop the door. There wasn't even valet parking.

Nor were there any camera-toting assholes, as Sam called them.

Which I thought was by design.

The bar was small, unassuming and had been barely full when we'd arrived. The crowd had steadily grown as the night wore on, but no one really bothered our table. Killian stared anyone down who did so. Then when he left, the residual menacing footprint of his presence seemed to deter most. Sam had kept his chair close to mine, dangling his arm over the back of it casually, stroking the back of my neck every now and then, kissing me when the mood took him.

He was not afraid of PDA, nor ashamed to make sure everyone in the bar knew I was his and he was mine.

A few minutes ago, he'd leaned forward on his chair, mouth going to my ear. "Time for your surprise, babe," he murmured.

Then he'd kissed me. French.

And it seemed that I didn't mind PDA at all.

He parted the crowd like some rock star version of Moses, and they swallowed him back up once they let him pass.

I found myself becoming antsy the second he went out of sight, and I both hated and loved that.

Sam stood up on the stage, the bright lights illuminating every part of him, his ink reflecting with the light, his form carved from the shadows behind him. "All right, team, I'm sure you know me," he spoke softly into the mic.

The returning roar of the crowd was not a murmur. Multiple girls screamed. I winced slightly.

Sam grinned wickedly. "Yeah, you know me. I'm usually the drummer of a little group called Unquiet Mind. But for tonight, I'm here to sing a little song for y'all. Be kind, it's my first time. You're popping my cherry."

More screams.

Sam waited patiently for the noise to die down.

Emma nudged me. "Did you know he was doing this?" she whispered.

I shook my head.

She wordlessly slid a tequila shot over to me.

I downed it without hesitation.

"Be nice to me. I'm not as good on the six-string as my girl Lexie," he said, jostling the guitar on his shoulder. "But I'm *way better* than Wyatt." He winked again.

Then his eyes scanned the crowd. Like I was some kind of magnet and he was metal, they fastened on me, melting away the masses, the screams. Everything was silent. Apart from him.

"This is for my girl. Yeah, I'm off the market and happily so. And also, she's totally and utterly mine. I'll kill anyone who thinks differently." He grinned with half humor, half menace. "And I'm serious about that. I've got a gun and everything."

"For fuck's sake, he's just assured me I'll be doing damage control on that one all night," Jenna moaned next to me.

I barely heard it. Or anything.

Especially when he began to strum, began to sing.

I didn't know what it was immediately, but afterward, I played the original Chris Cornell played live: "Thank You."

And everyone paused. Like, everyone. It was a strange thing watching the man you loved stand up in front of a crowd and have them scream at him. I'd seen it before on television, in the magazines, but it was something else entirely to see it in person.

So there was that.

And then there was watching him literally bring the crowd to a standstill.

Sure, everyone was shocked to see the rogue drummer known for causing trouble and epitomizing rock 'n' roll by behaving badly standing there singing and playing a guitar.

But it wasn't just that. He was playing. Above playing. His voice was indescribable. Husky, low and pleasing, fragrancing the air with the verbal version of his scent.

When you listen to songs, you only half listen to them. I did that. Kind of like I was half living my mind, until Sam. This Sam, singing this song. The power of it and Sam's connection to it grabbed every person in the room like it was an entirely separate beast, clutching them in its grasp, demanding they not just hear but listen.

To feel.

Every single word, every single sentence it belonged to, and witness someone's suffering at feeling this so intensely that their body couldn't contain it. They physically had to put it somewhere, anywhere, so it wouldn't kill them. So they put it into a song.

And he was singing it to me.

Like he'd written it. Like he was feeling every single one of those words. That they were filling him up. That love was filling him up.

The crowd didn't exist. That magazine article didn't exist. Simon didn't exist. The worries about the reality of this working, of how I was going to make *this* work, didn't exist.

It was like his voice, that song, was the audible version of Xanax.

The audible version of Nirvana.

"Okay, I don't think anyone's even going to remember the gun comment now," Jenna hissed happily, the song touching her. Her, someone who, up until now, I hadn't even been sure had a heart. I'd been entertaining the idea that she was one of the latest and most lifelike robots that Sam had bought along with all of his other electronic toys.

Even through my amazement, I barely even acknowledged her.

I didn't have the ability or the emotional capacity to acknowledge anything but the words coming out of Sam's mouth. Out of his heart.

Sam made sure he spent a lot of time letting me know what I meant to him. Trying to tear down the walls I'd created, that the world and my shitty circumstances had created.

Among other things, I worried he'd get sick of trying, decide I was too much work. That I wasn't worth it. He literally had girls falling at his feet. Easy girls. Girls who would give him everything he needed, everything he wanted without difficulty.

Without drama.

Without the inconvenience of my feelings and the reality of them. Because that was what true love really was—an inconvenience, constantly informing, impacting and changing your path in a way you never could've expected. And it would ensure that your life was never your own as long as the other person existed and as long as that love existed.

No matter how many times he said things to the contrary, that always lived there in the corner of my mind, embroiled with my self-consciousness I'd nurtured my entire life.

That song, him singing it to me in front of the bar, in front of the world, it did something that his private words could not.

It changed something.

Changed everything.

It didn't wipe all my worries and insecurities away completely—nothing could do that. Humans couldn't exist without insecurities and worries. It was part of our nature.

But it shrank them. Substantially.

So I could breathe around them.

I didn't even realize he'd stopped singing until the roar of the small crowd started ringing in my ears.

Until the crowd parted once more and spat him back out.

And then he made it to me.

Yanked me into his arms.

Into his universe.

"You get it now, babe?" he murmured, the softness of his voice cutting through the screaming of the crowd around us.

I looked into his eyes. Into his universe. And I saw that it was me.

I was his universe. So it was okay for him to be mine.

"Yeah," I yelled back to him. "Yeah, I get it now."

One Week Later

"This is all kinds of fucked up... just the way I like it."

It took me a second to tear my eyes away from the ruthless torture scene captivating the sickest depths of my imagination.

Sam was standing in the corner of the living room, arms crossed and grinning at the screen, then at me.

Wyatt and I had discovered our mutual love for *Game of Thrones* and he had come over to shoot the shit with Sam, who had gone away on a phone call and we decided to have a mini marathon in his prolonged absence.

"What is this and why haven't I watched it?" he asked.

"Because your attention span is that of a gnat and you couldn't follow the storyline if you had Gina's panties to lead the way," Wyatt snapped. "Now shut the fuck up, we're trying to watch."

I couldn't help but grin slightly at Wyatt's words. A grin that turned into a full on giggle as Sam stomped over to Wyatt and clipped him on the back of the head. Wyatt's head dodged as he tried to move to watch the scene. Sam held steady.

"The only one that gets to talk about my woman's panties is *me*, got it?" He glared at Wyatt, who glared back and then nodded. Not because he actually agreed but more likely because he wanted Sam to get out of his way.

And he did. By making his way over to me and effortlessly lifting me from my spot on the sofa so he could sit with me in his arms.

He kissed the side of my neck.

"I will be inspecting those panties in great detail when this shit is done, just FYI," he whispered.

My stomach dipped with desire, chasing away hunger pangs.

I sucked in a breath, eyes on the screen.

"Okay," I whispered back.

I'd gotten up to get water when it happened. One second I was talking to Wyatt about the possibility of a Catlyn Stark reincarnation while Sam muttered about "being surrounded by total fucking nerds," the next I was staring at a blurry ceiling without any knowledge of how I got there.

Since I was staring at the ceiling, my fuzzy mind still logically thought I should have been lying on a cold and uncomfortable surface, that surface being the ground, since I was staring at the ceiling and all.

That was not the case. In fact, I was encased in a both warm and comfortable cocoon of muscle that was hard and soft at the same time.

Then I was no longer staring at the ceiling, I was staring into the eyes I recognized. The face they were attached to was slightly blurry, but I recognized it as Sam. He was stark and chiseled while the rest of the background around him was like a fuzzy television screen in between the channels.

His features were contorted into pure worry, as if the carefree smile of before had never even existed.

"Gina," he demanded, his voice shaking with urgency.

I didn't answer because my tongue felt limp and swollen in my mouth, I wasn't completely sure I could form words with it.

"Babe?" he probed. "Talk to me."

In slow motion, his head moved to someone who existed in that world between the channels.

"Wyatt, where the fuck is that ambulance?"

A low and muffled voice replied.

It was like I was only tuned into one station, the Sam station, the rest was just static.

Somewhere in the middle of the static reply I began to regain comprehension. Ambulance. Me on the ground. In Sam's arms.

Fuck.

I struggled to push my lead limps up, but like my tongue, they were too heavy to use for their intended purposes.

But now my tongue felt a little better, a little more usable.

"No ambulance," I slurred. "I'm fine."

Sam's eyes, still swimming with concern, narrowed slightly. "Despite the fact that when a woman utters 'fine' it is accurately the signal of the upcoming apocalypse," he clipped. "You fainted. Were unconscious for four minutes and fifty-one seconds. You are not *fine*," he spat the word out.

"You counted?" I blinked, the world coming into focus.

His eyes narrowed further. "You collapsed. Out of nowhere and were unresponsive in my fucking arms. Motionless. Of course I fucking counted. You tend to take note of the period of time when you can't fucking *breathe*."

I stared at him in shaky wonder. I couldn't fathom his words completely yet they warmed up all the spaces that had been chilled to the bone seconds before.

"You're getting in the ambulance and I'll hear no fucking protest from you," he declared.

So I gave him no fucking protest.

"Okay, you're totally fine," the doctor informed me after glancing through my chart.

I smirked at Sam in triumph.

He glared right back at me, and then at the poor doctor, who didn't even know the existence of the 'fine' debate.

"If she was fine, she wouldn't have fucking fainted," Sam clipped.

"Sam!" I chastised. "You can't swear at a doctor."

"I can when he's not fucking doctoring," he countered.

"You don't faint out of nowhere."

The doctor didn't even blink at the exchange. I guess he worked in the L.A Emergency room after all, a cursing rock star was likely one of the more boring cases he'd had for the day.

"No, a person doesn't," he agreed, scanning the chart again. He focused his eyes on me. "Your blood sugar was dangerously low. Which was likely why you lost consciousness. Do you suffer from diabetes?"

I shook my head.

"When was your last meal?"

Shit.

"Ummm," I drew out the world trying to think of a lie.

Though I may have mastered the art of the fake laugh while I was here, I was yet to master the lie.

Hence Sam directing the death glare he'd been treating the doctor to at me. "Gina," he demanded. "You have to think about the last time you ate?"

"I don't know, it's been a stressful couple of days," I snapped.

He gaped at me. "Couple of days?" he repeated. "How the fuck have I not noticed? Why the fuck haven't you eaten in *days*?"

He hadn't noticed because his recording sessions conveniently worked out to last for long periods of time, so whenever he was chowing down on takeout and tried to offer it to me, I could murmur something about a big lunch with Lexie or Emma.

They weren't exactly lies. I usually had been hanging out with either of them, and when I did, they did have big lunches. I just didn't. I picked at a garden salad and made sure to keep the conversation going continuously so they didn't notice the fact I hadn't eaten anything.

Simon would have been proud.

Sam was watching my face and didn't let me craft my lie in my head, let alone attempt to tell it.

"It's because of that fuckin' article, isn't it?" he hissed through his teeth. "I'm going to burn that fucking publishing office to the ground."

He sounded dangerously serious.

"No, I told you, I've just been busy," I lied.

"Cut the shit," he ordered harshly. "It's because that poison settled in your fucking mind and *I didn't even fucking notice.* I've been too busy with stupid shit." Guilt saturated his tone.

"Hey," I said. "It's not your fault. I just... wanted to drop a couple of pounds," I said meekly.

He squeezed my hand to almost the point of pain. I could see it. His battle with fury and love. His urge to unleash that dragon.

But then his hand slackened. He lifted both of our intertwined fingers so he could kiss my palm gently, lighter than a feather but somehow heavier than anything that I'd ever held there.

"Out, Doc, now," he hissed, not moving his eyes from mine.

"We'll keep you in here for another couple of hours, get you back to normal, then I'll be back to check on you," the doctor said, not perturbed by Sam's harsh command.

The soft footfalls and the closing of my door signaled his exit.

Sam hadn't noticed any of that. Or he didn't let on, anyway.

His focus was on me.

"Baby, the thought that you somehow believe you need to change a single thing about yourself breaks my fucking heart," he whispered. "Makes me want to break the kneecaps of every fucker in this universe who had a hand in that shit," he seethed. "You. Are. Perfect."

I didn't let his eyes go, but couldn't let his words penetrate. Not all the way at least. "I'm a size twelve, Sam," I said back, my voice harsher than I'd intended. Most likely to mask my pain and embarrassment. "I have stretch marks, cellulite, and flabby skin. I'm not perfect. You're perfect. You're photoshopped but in real life. And that's what you should have beside you. Someone like that. Someone suited to you." I poured it all out quickly, like a verbal Band-Aid, hoping that it would hurt less.

It didn't.

The pain in Sam's eyes mirrored my own. But it was different. More carnal.

I expected him to immediately fight me on my words, try to convince me I was wrong. But he was Sam, so he never did what was expected.

"I used to do this thing," he said, looking outwards, eyes away from me. Actively looking away from me. He never looked away from me. Not when we were together. When we were together, every aspect of his being was focused on me. The simple aversion of eye contact signified the magnitude of what he was about to say.

About to confess.

"I'd see people," he continued. "Anyone, a guy driving past me on the highway in a plumbing van. The family eating at McDonalds when I sneak in to get myself a McFlurry." He winked at me. "And I do love McFlurrys." The joke fell short. It didn't work as a mask anymore, not now that mask was lying on the ground at our feet and I saw that face, his real face, in all its beautiful reality.

"Heck, even when I was on stage, in front of thousands of people who were there for me. For us. I'd imagine I was any of them. That I was living in a skin that wasn't mine. It didn't matter whose it was, just as long as it wasn't *mine*."

His eyes finally flickered to me.

"The music, the girls, the booze, the screaming crowd, the fat bank account... my band, my family. It's *everything* to me. It's exactly what I imagined, I dreamed of. *I* was exactly who I'd imagined. You know how kids say what they want to be in kindergarten? Like astronaut, fireman, fucking Harry Potter? Well, I said rock star. Even then. And look at me now, world, four-year-old fucking Sammy." He held his arms up in the air, presenting himself to God, to the world, to the past. "I am everything I dreamed of." He dropped his hands. Only for a second. Because then they were raised, grasping either side of my face, pulling me to him, up out of the bed.

"And even then, even when my fast life was bursting at those moments, felt empty. So much so, I'd do whatever the fuck I could to transplant myself out of it all. To something simpler. Fucking easier. Fucking harder. I don't know. I didn't know why I wanted to Freaky fucking Friday with some dude who literally dealt in shit for a living. I just knew it was something that I couldn't control." A grin tickled the edge of his serious face, cracking the marble of it. "That and my utter electric sexuality." The crack repaired itself as he stared into the depths of me.

"And it scared me, babe. More than I was willing to admit. And I worked so fucking hard to try to convince myself I had everything. When, even then, I knew, deep down beyond the bullshit, I *knew*. I had nothing, because I didn't have you. I missed you before I even knew I needed you. Before I even knew I loved you. And that makes me wonder if I didn't love you all along. Since that moment in junior high when I saw you walking down the corridors wearing a pink scrunchy in your hair and those terrible sandals with flowers on them, reading some book not noticing the world around you."

My heart skipped a beat. About five of them. I knew what he was telling me. He'd known me. He'd seen me.

And he wasn't done.

"Maybe it was when I saw those girls made you cry. Maybe it just took me a fucking long time to realize that all I've been wanting to do is escape into that world you made and make it *mine*. Make you mine. And at the same time take you out of it and show you the world. Give you the world." He leaned forward and kissed my head, his hands running down the sides of my body. "I'm gonna give you the world," he promised. "First, I'm gonna work every single day for the rest of forever to give you something else. To give you the *true* image of who you are. *What* you are. Beauty. Unique and special." He moved his hands back up to caress my jaw. "And I know it's gonna take some time to chip away at years of lies. Lies you told yourself, and that people let you believe. But baby, I've got time. We've got time. I believe we've got forever."

His words were a statement and a promise. And so much more than that. They didn't fix it all, but they did a fricking great job at beginning to.

I slowly nodded. "Forever," I agreed, on little more than a whisper.

"For right now, we're going to get McFlurry's," he said, eyes glowing.

Three Weeks Later

We were having a girls' night. It was after a considerable amount of debate with Sam, and—from what I'd heard from the two other girls involved in girls' night—both Killian and Wyatt too.

Apparently each of the men *did not* have good feelings toward the sacred tradition of girls' night.

I didn't even have a particular kind of feeling toward it either.

I'd never strictly had a girls' night. Unless you counted *Game of Thrones* night with Pria, which you couldn't really since Garth was always in attendance too.

And in high school, I hung out mainly with retirees who were in bed, teeth out and sedatives in by 8:00 p.m.

The only reason why girls' night had been allowed by three very protective and slightly deluded males was because it wasn't located anywhere that anyone could get kidnapped by a crazed stalker. That statement was verbatim by Sam.

And he hadn't even known about the various texts I'd been getting from Simon, which had started around the time I'd arrived in LA.

It had been over a month and he had yet to stop.

They varied between pathetic groveling or aggressive insults. The number of pathetic ones was dwindling, the aggressive ones increasing. It was getting ugly. Nasty.

And although I didn't want to admit it, scary.

I planned on calling the phone company to block his number.

I didn't have the great desire to add that to the already heated argument we'd had about the whole thing. To have any kind of conversation, heated or otherwise, about Simon with Sam.

I was sick of it.

Entertaining his ghost. Letting it seep into what Sam and I had. Despite a couple of moments, the time I'd had existing within his life, his Sam Kennedy life, I was happy. There was a place for me somewhere. Somehow, I fit.

Maybe because I stopped trying to think I had to fit in

somewhere. Into something. Whether it be a size twelve dress or what I thought a size six beauty would do. I just *was.*

In the fakest place in the world, full of actors trying to make millions out of creating fantasy, I found my truth, created my reality.

And it was good.

No way was I letting anything touch that. Letting Simon touch that.

Plus there was no imminent threat. Simon was halfway across the country and nowhere near stupid enough to do anything beyond texting. Not with charges pending against him and having already lost his badge.

Despite the town rallying around him, because of his badge and his carefully constructed reputation, he was facing real prison time. I knew Sam—or more accurately, Sam's very expensive lawyers—had everything to do with that. And he wouldn't find the same understanding if he went to prison. Inmates didn't tend to like cops in there.

Or so I'd heard.

The texts were Simon's last-ditch attempt to try to exert power over the last person he deluded himself into thinking he had control over. To get to me.

He wasn't. He wasn't even coming close.

I had a lot of things to be happy about, ecstatic about. Namely Sam. And a lot of more important things to worry about. Namely Sam.

After the way things blew up after the bar and the public outpouring of support for us—for *me*—he'd been pushing me more to move in with him.

He saw that I could handle his lifestyle, that his lifestyle could handle me, and he wasn't wasting time to make sure everything became permanent. After the incident that put me in hospital, he made sure we ate together, three times a day, no matter what. Not that I needed him there to assure me to eat. I was done with that. Trying to cut myself up so I could fit somewhere that I wasn't meant to be. I was still insecure, still caught myself in photos and cringed. But those were split seconds. The rest of the day, I believed I was what Sam told me I was. What I'd known I was, somewhere, deep down.

He had been dragging me around real estate showings for the past week and a half.

When he wasn't recording, of course. And that was often.

Not that I minded.

I missed him, obviously, but I was good at entertaining myself. I liked my own company.

I kept myself busy. Read. Hung out with Emma a lot. We were becoming very close. She was the exact opposite of me: loud, confident, crazy. On the outside, at least. Sometimes I saw glimpses of insecurity I recognized and demons I didn't.

They were much too dark for me.

She wasn't usually in town for this long—she was an arts dealer who traveled often—but she was here for "a stretch." She made it sound like it was a jail sentence. Which may or may not have had something to do with Wyatt, despite all her efforts to ignore him, avoid mentioning him and pretend she wasn't utterly in love with him.

He was doing the same.

Sam had snatched me away from Emma's yesterday and took me to the first house I actually liked. It wasn't an ostentatious mansion that made me feel uncomfortable like the rest of them had been. Empty, but full of expectations and image and built to entertain people. Entertain the surface. All surfaces encouraging the cold taste of fantasy.

And for once I didn't want the fantasy.

I wanted soft and curvy surfaces, like the ones Sam was encouraging me to love on myself. The ones that invited reality.

That would keep me warmer much longer than fantasy would.

It was smaller, on the beach out of Hollywood and away from the entire lifestyle.

"So, what do you think?" Sam asked, eyes going around the empty room that was overlooking the ocean, only five minutes away from Lexie and Killian's beach house.

It was perfect. The floor-to-ceiling windows covered three of the four walls, one of them a sliding door opening to a large balcony.

"It would be the perfect library," he said, mirroring my own thoughts.

But my thoughts were mingled in fantasy. Despite how I'd been living the past two weeks, I had to get back to reality.

The cold one first, and then maybe I'd get the softer one.

"I already own a home, Sam," I informed him, even though he already knew that. "And I already have a mortgage, which I'm going to have to get myself *employed* to pay."

Saying it out loud only made the issue more pressing.

The media circus had tripled since the serenade at the bar.

Most of it was positive and supportive, shaming the publication that had published the ugly article. The publication that was quickly losing circulation and readership.

I didn't know how much of that had to do with Sam buying a substantial number of shares in the company.

"Sam, that's a waste of money," I'd complained when he told me.

He eyed me. "Anything to fix what cost you a fucking second of suffering, caused you a moment of pain, is priceless, babe. It's worth every fucking cent I have in the bank. I end up poor with you, happy when I die? That's a life lived right. I want to be on my deathbed and not count the items I own, the money in the bank. I want to count moments. Ones I create with you. Happiness I create with you. I'm already a fuckin' billionaire, babe. In your smiles. In the times I've made you laugh. Made you happy. Right now, I bite it, I'm done. I've accomplished everything I need to."

When he said that, I'd stopped complaining.

But I'd also gotten panicky and emotional at the thought of him being "done."

"Sam, that's one of the sweetest things I've ever heard," I whispered. "But you promise right here and now that you stay with me till I've accomplished everything I need to. And I'm warning you, it's going to take forever."

He'd beamed at me. "I promise, baby."

With that promise made, it was as if the world sensed our happiness and wanted to fuel it for once, not squash it.

I'd received an outpouring of support from women everywhere, writing to me, telling me how it made them feel good to see someone *real* and beautiful. How I'd inspired them.

Me.

Inspiring people.

I even had a multitude of offers from clothing companies to be a model.

Me.

A *model*.

I'd laughed the first time Mark mentioned it, assuming it had been a joke.

When he hadn't laughed, I got that it wasn't.

And they weren't even "plus size" labels.

Apparently they wanted to move away from perpetuating an unhealthy body image toward their consumers.

I hadn't accepted any of them, despite Sam's and Lexie's gentle encouragement.

Despite the number of zeroes on the shoot offer.

It might have paid my mortgage with enough left over to

buy my own mansion, but it would've cost more than I had to give.

I was willing to show a little bit of myself, the tiniest little bit that I had to being attached to Sam, but I wasn't going to give all of it. I was willing to be in the spotlight, if not slightly to the left. I wasn't ever going to be comfortable in it. Thrive in it. The center of it, anyway. I could handle slightly to the left. Not the middle.

That was not my thing.

And neither was teaching toddlers, as it seemed. It was painfully apparent that I wouldn't be able to go back to work there. Robyn had called me saying as much, then told me she was sending me all the cards the kids had made to say goodbye.

I wasn't as disappointed as I thought I would be. I'd miss my kids for sure, but Sam had been right. It was me living that uncertain life. The one in between the pages. The one I wasn't living for myself. It was the unassuming one I'd been living for... I didn't even know who.

I didn't even know what I wanted to do with my life. I knew I wanted to finish my master's. I wanted to work with teenagers like me, help them, teach them.

I had enough money for about six months' worth of mortgage payments if I was careful.

Not that I needed to be. Sam refused, flat-out *refused* to let me pay for anything.

I'd tried.

Multiple times.

It had insulted him.

"Babe, you give me enough. You give me everything. This is all I have to give you. This life has turned it upside down, so at least let it pay for our fuckin' dinner."

So I relented.

It was clear that he considered restaurant bills to be in the same realm as house mortgages, based on his next statement, back in the present. He waved his hand dismissively. "Oh, I'll take care of that," he said. "Mark's already on it. I think you need to sign some shit."

I stilled.

"You'll take care of it?" I parroted.

He must have sensed the danger in the air, as he regarded me carefully. "Yeah, babe. It's no big deal. And if you think about it, I'm the reason you lost your job. I'm the guy trying to get you to uproot your entire life and move out here. It's only logical that I take care of it."

"It's logical for the man I've been dating for only two months, at a stretch, to pay my mortgage for me?" I clarified. "That's on the insane side of logical, Sam. Even for you."

He narrowed his eyes. "I'll ignore that because you're obviously upset," he quipped.

"Everything's a joke to you, Sam," I hissed.

His eyes held none of the humor that I'd decided was tattooed in his irises, as characteristic to him as the ink that covered his body. Without it, he looked like a stranger. At the same time, he was more familiar to me than anyone on this earth.

"Almost everything," he replied, nodding. He stepped forward.

Like we were doing some of stupid coordinated dance, I stepped back.

The air turned sweet and sour at the same time as this exotically beautiful predator stalked its prey.

"Only way to get through it is to treat it like a joke. Life, I mean. Because that's all it is, really. Someone, somewhere, is holding a fuck of a lot of invisible strings, controlling us on a whim. And most of the time, that fucker has a sadistic and cruel sense of humor. Most of the time it's a joke. A dark one, to be sure, but a joke all the same. And you've got to laugh at it, the grand old joke, because the only other option is to let it destroy you. I'm not too fond of destruction, babe." His eyes burned into mine as he took another step forward. I was too enraptured by his words, his eyes, his *everything* to retreat.

"Well, not until recently. Now I'm praying to Kurt Cobain for a particular brand of destruction. And I'm looking right at her."

My anger and reason disappeared with his words, as it seemed to do when he did things like this. He knew this, and he continued.

"Babe, I plan on you having my last name in the very close future. Fuck, I'll even take yours if that's what chicks are into these days. I don't care. As long as it's written on paper and tattooed somewhere on my body that you're mine forever, I don't care."

It was safe to say the argument had fizzled out rather quickly after that. Rather, I'd melted into a puddle at his feet and stupidly let him pay my mortgage. I still didn't have it in my feminist self to regret it.

I didn't even break out in hives or anything when I realized he meant a wedding, and what a spectacle the aforementioned wedding would turn into.

In the spirit of Sam, fuck the world.

So yeah, we'd had more than enough speed bumps to worry about my asshole ex trying to inject himself into my life.

He was failing anyway, and he would fail.

He'd get the picture eventually and move on to torment some other poor girl.

Sam clutched my neck, pulling our foreheads together as we sat in his car outside Emma's apartment complex. "You call me the moment you start to get even the slightest vibe that things are getting kidnapping-y."

I swallowed my smile when I realized just how serious he

was. "And what kind of vibe would 'kidnapping-y' be?" I asked.

"I don't know: white vans, men with pantyhose on their head. You know, the usual," he said, scanning the quiet street as if he was expecting a pantyhose-wearing man to jump out of a white van and snatch me out of his arms.

I kissed his head. "I'll be sure to keep vigilant," I reassured him.

"You do that. Or better yet I'll just come with you. Much safer," he decided.

I smiled at him. "It's girls' night, remember? No boys allowed."

He grunted. "No good has come from girls' night. I don't like this. Being away from you. I've got a bad feeling about it."

"That's because you're convinced we're going to be having pillow fights in our underwear and you'll miss out on watching," I quipped.

His eyes bulged. "*I knew it*," he hissed. "I'm definitely coming now."

I giggled and put my hand on his chest. "You're not. Now go and have your boys' night. Pillow fight in your underwear and take pictures." I winked.

Sam still looked uneasy.

I kissed him hard on the mouth, intending it to be closemouthed.

Sam did not have that same intention.

We eventually detached, both of us breathing heavily and me feeling ready to abandon girls' night altogether.

I found my sense eventually. "Nothing bad is going to happen, I promise."

Thing with promises like that, they were self-fulfilling for the exact opposite.

About how everything bad was going to happen.

And destroy everything in its path.

Chapter Twenty

"**I**'m pregnant," Lexie blurted the moment Emma set down margaritas.

I gaped at her, only half surprised, remembering the moment in the shoe store when she rubbed her stomach. I'd had an inkling then.

Emma was full-on surprised.

She did not react in the way I imagined a best girl friend would react.

But then, Emma did not react in a way that *anyone* imagined. It was kind of her thing.

"Now? You had to announce this *now?*" she snapped. "Why couldn't you be pregnant after we all get sloshed on margaritas? Now I have to wait nine months for you to get sloshed on margaritas. Probably more if you breastfeed." She pointed at her. "Don't breastfeed."

Lexie grinned up at her, not at all perturbed by her friend's unconventional response to her happy news.

"It's not going to be nine, more like six months," she corrected, cupping her still-flat stomach. "We wanted to wait."

I got why. Because they were bracing. Her and Killian both. Even though they'd both endured about a hundred times more heartbreak than any human deserved, and finally got that happiness, they were cautious. Expecting something to tear through it and destroy it all over again.

I reached over and squeezed her hand. "I'm so happy for you, Lexie," I breathed. It didn't escape me that I sounded the same way Meredith had that day in the grocery store.

Lexie smiled back at me, not saying anything. Not needing to. She just squeezed my hand back.

Emma was not smiling. She was glaring at Lexie. Or more precisely, Lexie's stomach.

"Of course," she snapped. "Of course you're three months along and skinnier than me after eating half a cheesecake."

She then gave Lexie another look. A longer one. No words. Like the visual version of the hand squeeze Lexie had just given me.

No words necessary.

They shared that look long enough for Emma to say everything she needed to without actually having to say it.

Then she stomped back to her small but nice kitchen.

Her apartment was a much smaller version of Sam and Wyatt's mansion. Tastefully and expensive decorated. Small, without personal touches apart from a framed photo of her and Lexie on the coffee table in front of me.

"I always keep a bottle of champagne in the fridge," Emma explained, opening her fridge to reveal a couple of rogue condiments and a flickering bulb in need of changing. She paused, her arm halfway into the empty chasm that would not be so in my house.

I always had condiments, of course, but a lot more than that, and a lot of various types of food to put with them. I glanced at the outstretched, tanned and tattooed arm. The muscles of her bicep were smooth and defined, not an inch of fat, not even that jiggly bit underneath.

"In case of emergencies," she continued, yanking out a very expensive-looking bottle of champagne. She lifted it with a grin. "Or Tuesdays." She set it down and began the process of

opening it. "And now we get to use it for its intended purpose."
She beamed at Lexie. "Celebration."

Lexie beamed back. "Babe, I appreciate this, you." Her eyes
moved to me. "And I appreciate you," she whispered. "More
than you know. You've made one of my favorite people in the
entire world happy. Actually *happy*. And though he's the one
who looks the happiest of us all, he was the most miserable.
Until you."

I blinked away my tears at her words, what she'd offered
so freely. "The same goes for me," I admitted. Sam had given
me not just him and his love, but the opportunity to grasp on
to everything that I'd been depriving myself of. The friends I'd
been distancing myself from because of their proximity to him.
Sam didn't complete my life though, as much as I'd love for that
to be the case.

It was good that wasn't the case.

One person was not meant to complete another person.

Despite whatever romance novels said.

Which was maybe so many romance novels ended in
death.

Because they portrayed love that burned too bright, too
fast. That didn't let anything else exist but love. And concentrated love, like pure alcohol, would kill you if continually consumed without something else. Without the mixer.

Girlfriends were the mixer. You needed them, to survive
this life. And Sam gave me that too, without even knowing it.

I'd been only half living before. Between the pages. And I
needed a man who loved me to sleep next to at night.

But I also needed girls' night.

"He makes me laugh. And he makes me cry."

Emma's eyes twinkled. Danced with love. Too much of it.
And too many more swigs of it might kill her.

"Only men who can make you laugh so beautifully can

make you cry so painfully," she said. "Just like the ones who love you the hardest can hurt you the most. Destroy you, more accurately. It's life's little Catch-22, and it's a fucker."

The room descended into silence, the weight of Emma's words settling on us despite the fact that we were happy.

Maybe it was *because* we were happy. And because we knew that we were with the people who were going to guarantee our infinite happiness. And our infinite destruction.

Emma shook herself out of it.

"Enough of that," she declared, pouring three glasses. "We're celebrating."

I took mine from her.

Lexie did not. "Dude, you cannot celebrate a pregnancy announcement with a glass of alcohol."

Emma looked at her, then to the glass she had outstretched to her. "True. *You* can't," she agreed. She downed the glass in one gulp, setting it down on the table with a clang. "But I can." She drained the second glass.

We watched her, both Lexie and I. Me gingerly sipping the champagne that I decided I liked.

Lexie watched her more intently. With more knowledge behind her eyes. With more worry for her friend and the demons she was hiding.

Emma stared at us and at nothing, twirling the glass in her hands.

"Dude, if you find yourself pinning depressing-as-fuck quotes on Pinterest, then he's not for you. Someone worthwhile makes you forget depressing quotes even exist, and if you see them, you stop reading at the first line because they're so fucking sad and you're so fucking happy. If your finger even hovers above that mouse, kick him to the curb. Because relating to someone feeling shitty means you, in that moment, were feeling shitty, and no man, not ever, is worth you feeling like that for even a moment. We girls make ourselves feel like crap enough without letting a man do it too. Also, you don't want that bitch Sarah from high school knowing you're in a bad place."

I didn't really know who she was talking to, because she was in the company of two people who weren't in that position at all.

But I realized that was another story altogether.

One she wasn't ready to tell yet.

But it was coming.

For now, she was living in fantasy and demanded we talk about possible ways to combat the ankle swelling Lexie might get.

And we let her live in that fantasy.

But reality was coming.

For all of us.

I knew something was wrong the second I walked into the house. All the warmth and happiness of before was snatched away the moment I smelled the air.

It was bitter. A dumb thing to think, maybe, but I could just *tell* something wasn't right. And it wasn't because I was drunk. I'd stopped at the one glass of celebratory champagne Emma and I had shared.

She'd finished the bottle.

Lexie dropped me off so I could surprise Sam.

For a start, it was quiet. Far too quiet. It was *never* quiet. Sam always had music playing. And more recently, Sam was always playing music, experimenting with his songs, sometimes with Lexie and sometimes just with me. We were usually naked.

But tonight, nothing.

No way could he be asleep. He texted me an hour ago telling me to take off my panties and put them in my purse.

The aforementioned panties had dampened at such a request and now were sitting in my purse.

"Sam?" I called, my heels echoing on the marble floor as I ascended the stairs.

Everything was silent.

Eerie.

"I'll be silent when I'm dead."

I don't know why the statement Sam had said in passing weeks ago floated into my head at that precise moment, but it filled me with utter dread.

I'd once reveled in silence. Lived in it.

Now I wanted to get rid of it more than anything.

I tried to talk myself out of it. Maybe this was part of whatever Sam had planned for tonight.

So I sucked in a breath and headed to the bedroom.

The closed door was another omen. Wyatt had taken up residence in another mansion down the street, so Sam insisted on an open-door policy, considering it was just the two of us.

Despite the dread in my bones, despite the fact that I was expecting it, or something like it, I still lost my breath when I opened the door and entered the room. I swore the world tilted on its axis the minute it all came into focus, bile filling my mouth.

It was it.

The black hole that was going to suck in my entire universe until I was left with nothing.

Until I was nothing.

"Genie, so glad you could make it," Simon said with a grin.

He was grinning because he was standing in the middle of the room with a gun pointed at Sam.

Sam's eyes lazily went to me, then widened rapidly. The

way they did it sickened me. Like in *House of Wax* when they were frozen in their bodies, unable to express their horror with anything but their eyes.

That's what was in Sam's.

But it hadn't been there before. When he was alone in the room with the madman with a gun.

It was only when I got there.

His fear wasn't for himself.

It was for me.

Laughable, really. Because I'd just entered a room that contained my abusive ex who'd tried to rape me and I didn't feel an ounce of fear for myself.

All of my terror was reserved for the man in the center of my room, in the center of my life.

There was something wrong with him, the way he was struggling to move from his spot on his knees, his body jerking with effort, limbs limply hanging around him.

"Thumbelina," he slurred. The words were saturated with the same fear that lived in his eyes, but it was muffled under some kind of film. Something that was thickening his tongue.

I stepped forward, forgetting the gun, intending on going to him, to Sam. To help him. To save him.

Simon pointed the gun at me. "Tut, tut, tut," he said, shaking his head. "You stay there." When I kept moving, made it apparent that the prospect of a bullet wasn't going to stop me, he pointed it at Sam.

I immediately stopped, glaring at Simon. "What did you do to him?" I demanded.

Simon grinned wickedly, his eyes cold. "Nothing. Apart from the heroin I injected him with." He laughed. "I highly doubt it's his first hit. He's scum, after all. And scum inject their blood with more scum. And now it's in you." His eyes roved over my body as if it was covered in filth.

"Why did you shack up with scum, Genie?" he asked, scratching his head with the barrel of his gun.

He'd gone off the deep end.

Breaking into Sam's house, drugging him and then threatening us with a gun was evidence of that. But the emptiness filling his eyes cemented it. Craziness was a gaping hole in whatever made up the human mind. Everyone had it. Sometimes it was what made them the most interesting, like Sam.

But they had more, depth to mix it with.

Simon didn't know more.

He didn't have more.

Just that black hole that craved to suck up anything and everything it could.

"You broke up with me. *Me*," he continued, circling Sam. I realized my mistake now, showing my weakness. Showing that fear of death or pain wasn't what was going to give him whatever he wanted. No, I exposed my ultimate weakness.

Sam.

He grabbed on to it, using the gun pointed at Sam's head to command my attention. "I was sure you would come crawling back eventually. I waited. Patiently. There was no way you could find better than me," he scoffed, shaking his head. "I *knew* you'd realize that." He glared at Sam. No, not a glare. The sucking gaze of pure evil. "And you would have. If *he* hadn't come into town." He pointed at Sam with his gun and then kicked him viciously in the ribs.

Sam emitted a garbled grunt, his body twitching.

The blow may as well have hit my own ribs. "Stop!" I screamed.

Simon glanced up at me casually, like this was just a regular conversation.

"I'll do whatever you want," I told him. "*Anything*. Just leave him alone." I paused. I needed to take the attention away from Sam. This was no longer the story where the man in the white horse could save me. The man was pumped full of heroin. That in itself worried me about the prospect of an overdose. He was white. Almost translucent.

The knight couldn't save himself, let alone me. So I had to save him, if I had any chance to save myself.

Even if it meant sacrificing myself.

"He's not the reason I didn't come back to you," I said, tearing my eyes away from Sam with great difficulty. I worried that if I stopped looking at him, he might just slip away. I'd see him and he'd be still. Nothing moving. No sound.

No nothing.

But I had to look away, focus on the madman who had the power to take it all away from me. Focus on how I was going to take it back. "*I'm* the reason. It had nothing to do with Sam. It had everything to do with what a loser and a bully you were," I hissed, planning on antagonizing him enough to put his murderous focus on me.

Sam's eyes were flickering, his body twitching. Mine locked with them for a second and snatched a moment of his terrified lucidity of understanding about what I was doing.

"No," he protested, the word barely audible.

I focused back on Simon, who luckily hadn't seen any of it. His crazy was fixated on me.

He did not need to know that Sam might have been regaining motor skills.

"What?" he demanded.

I continued my glare. "You heard me. It wasn't because someone better than you came along. It's because I realized on my own that I *was* better than you. And you're just a sad, sick man with an inferiority complex and a small dick," I spat. My survival instinct was at a zero at that point. It didn't matter to me as long as Sam had a chance.

"You bitch," Simon hissed, lifting the gun.

I got it then. The Romeo and Juliet thing, the die for you kind of love. The kill for you kind of love. Because I was willing to take the bullet that was going to be heading for me any second. I didn't *want* it. I wanted to live to be old and gray and have a lifetime of excitement with Sam. But I also didn't want my lifetime to be full of a huge gaping hole where Sam should've been.

No matter what I used to think, I didn't want a lifetime of solitude.

"Solitude is for the lonely or the damned."

The words echoed through my ears. And I got them.

If that bullet hit Sam, took away my noise, my universe, I'd be damned. Completely and utterly.

So I didn't move.

And then I watched in horror as Simon's face changed from naked fury to pure, sick satisfaction.

A gunshot echoed through the room. The pain I expected radiated through every inch of me. I didn't even know how I stayed standing.

But I did. I did, and I watched in horror as Sam's body jerked with the impact of the bullet entering his body, blood pooling quickly around him.

Too quickly. You didn't bleed that much, that rapidly unless something was bad.

Unless it was the end.

End.

I didn't think then. Just acted.

I didn't even remember how I got the gun from Simon. Aspect of surprise, maybe. The last thing he expected me to do after he shot the man I loved was charge at him and wrestle his gun from him.

I was the broken, beaten and victimized version of myself

in his eyes.

I didn't see myself through his eyes.

I saw myself through Sam's.

That's what made me successful, most likely.

I pointed the gun at Simon and he smiled.

Not just in insanity, but with lucidity.

The very last thing he expected me to do was empty the chamber into his rancid and evil body.

But that's what I did.

Without hesitation.

And when that was done, I sank to my knees, the gun clattering to the floor as I fumbled through my handbag for my phone.

I found it and called 911, my other hand pressed to the gushing bullet wound in Sam's chest.

"No!" I screamed. Or tried to scream.

It came out as a strangled whisper.

"Sam, please. You can't die. You're here for a good time and a long time, remember?" I choked out. "You're here for us and me and that lifetime you promised."

His body twitched as I robotically told the dispatcher what had happened and the address.

She responded just as robotically, telling me units would be there soon.

I watched my hands turn red. "Soon isn't enough," I murmured. "He doesn't have soon. He doesn't have *now*. And we were meant to have forever."

Now I got why so many love stories ended with blood.

Because forever didn't exist.

"I know you said you're ready to leave, that you've lived enough," I whispered, my voice almost as broken as my soul. "But *I* haven't, Sam. I haven't lived even half enough. You said you'd give me anything, Sam, so give me my other half. Give me my universe."

It was the only thing I'd asked for, truly asked for from Sam.

He'd given me everything else. Without hesitation.

But he couldn't give me this.

When visiting loved ones in a hospital, people always seem to comment on how the injured party "looked so small." That's all my mother kept saying when my father suffered his heart attack last year.

"He's not a waifish man. Swims every day, and he has a weight set in the garage that he uses almost every night. He's no pipsqueak. But that bed, that gown. It's *shrunk* him." The way she said it made it seem like it was a shortcoming, suffering a heart attack. That it was his fault for not looking how she wanted him to look while in a hospital bed.

She'd been sobbing it to her friends later that night when they'd brought over casserole and wine. That's what good friends did, after all. Not that that was what they were, but they wanted to *look* like it. That was Mom's life, a game of images, of surface. Of what looked the best. Who looked the best. Pity she didn't have any marketable talent; she would've been perfect for Hollywood.

That's what I'd thought had upset her the most. That Dad, with his gray pallor and labored breathing and disheveled hair, hadn't looked *right*. He wasn't playing his part right. He wasn't supposed to suffer from a heart attack that meant she'd actually have to be the loving wife and take care of him instead of just pretending to. He was supposed to work enough so she could do minimal hours in the law firm where she worked as a secretary. He was to wear his hair clipped short, styled so it was tidy, neat and complimented his angular and masculine features. His suits were always to be classy, made to look more expensive than they actually were. He was meant to keep his affair with his own secretary under wraps, kiss Mom at the end of every day, compliment her lipstick and take care of her. Pretend he cared about the fucking pantomime she called her life.

I hadn't factored into that.

Nor did I factor into the situation with my "small-looking" father. Despite the fact I was a woman facing the mortality of her parents. Despite his detached affection toward me, he was my father. He sneaked chocolate to me when Mom wasn't letting me eat it, which was always. Brought a separate lunch to school when mom told the cafeteria I had allergies and could eat nothing but salad. Brought me a book from every city he visited. He'd usually already read it on the flight home. And he'd talk to me about it when we were done.

I had been upset then, seeing him in the hospital bed. But the kind of upset that suited my life with him, my relationship with my father. Slightly warm, but mostly cold. Detached.

But it wasn't the case with Sam. He didn't look small. He took up the whole room. Swallowed all the monitors and the sterile smell so it was just him.

His tattoos vivid color against the drab and gray room.

He was full of life.

Even when he wasn't.

Even when I wasn't.

I didn't have a single thing hooked up to me, keeping me alive. I had no life-threatening injuries, apart from a couple of scratches.

But I didn't feel alive.

I didn't feel anything.

With my father, I'd been upset, even if it wasn't as completely as I should've been when a daughter was faced with her father dancing between life and death.

He hadn't died. He recovered quickly and went back to his miserable life with my mother.

I reasoned it might have been because I didn't feel enough pain that I'd managed to feel it at all.

But seeing Sam dancing with death, after the doctors told me it was most likely his last dance, I felt nothing.

Not a single thing.

I was empty inside.

Because I couldn't feel the pain that Sam's death would bring. It would kill me. A part of me knew that. The part of me that was making sure I was experiencing an emotional wasteland seeing the man I loved being kept alive by machines.

Because of me.

I was sure that once even those machines couldn't do their jobs and that terrifying and horrifying future came to pass, I'd feel it.

But for now, he was still here, radiating life even in death. So I owed it to him to find a way to keep myself together.

My soft footfalls echoed in the room as I gingerly made my way over to Sam.

Sam's body.

Sam wasn't in there. The doctors told me that.

"We can't promise you anything. No one can. But we can tell you it's going to take nothing less than a miracle to get him awake and coherent."

"Awake and coherent."

That was the doctor's definition of life.

They obviously knew nothing about life.

About death.

My shaking hand settled atop his stationary one.

The tables had turned. I was the one whose hands couldn't keep still, who couldn't stand the static version of life.

He was the stationary one.

The one immersed in quiet.

And he was right.

Quiet was death.

And it lingered there, in the room, for days. Taunting me with its silence, with its ability to snatch my universe out from under me.

From around me.

Sam danced with it for days.

With the entrance and exit of every single person who loved him.

Who needed his loud presence in their life.

There were a lot of them.

I barely saw them.

Barely knew they existed.

I knew they talked to me. Or tried to.

You couldn't hear a thing when you were damned with solitude.

And then I witnessed it. The most beautiful movement of Sam's hand that I'd ever seen.

It started with a twitch so small I was sure I'd imagined it.

Gone insane and created some form of retribution out of the fragments of my destroyed mind.

Then it was more than a twitch. It was a squeeze. And then it grew, the motion continuing until the doctors spoke of miracles and the faces of Unquiet Mind stopped being so tortured.

Sam danced with death.

I danced with hope.

Or battled with each of them.

One of us won.

"Told you," Sam croaked when they'd yanked the breathing tubes out of his throat and he was finally conscious and lucid enough to speak.

Those two words were whispered. Barely even rippled the sound waves. But they almost ruptured my eardrums with their sound.

"Told me?" I repeated finally, through my tears.

"Fairy tale is real," he mumbled. "But they got it wrong. The man doesn't save his princess. His princess saves him."

And I did.

I'd saved him.

I lost a lot of sleep over almost losing him. Even after he fully recovered. Even after he put a ring on my finger and then our son in my belly.

I did not lose a single wink of sleep over the bullets I'd expended saving him.

Not a single second.

There wasn't a neatly wrapped-up ending for a multitude of reasons. Mainly because this, us, everything we'd been through was nowhere near the ending. It was nowhere near the beginning either. It was somewhere in the middle. We had a lot of life to live, and not all of it was going to be easy. We weren't going to be happy the entire time, but we would be living.

And we'd be together.

The rest would sort itself out.

I was terrified.

Which meant I was finally doing something right.

I was finally living.

Epilogue

"So, my girl doesn't particularly like the stage, though she's *fucking born* for it," Sam screamed into the mic. The crowd screamed back.

I could taste the energy in the air, the way the pulsing masses were feeding off Sam, off his energy, off everything that was him and Unquiet Mind.

"Do you know what he's doing?" Emma yelled at me, hands over her massive baby bump. Even nine months pregnant, the woman still somehow rocked a tight black dress, ripped fishnets and combat boots. She looked different than she used to, with most of the bitterness and pain ripped from her eyes. She glowed with pregnancy, and happiness. Tainted happiness, that was for sure, with everything that she'd gone through, and was still going through. There was no such thing as pure happiness, though. You couldn't know true happiness without experiencing profound suffering.

I knew that as well as anyone.

I jostled my son in my arms, kissing his inky head, inhaling that delicious baby smell and adjusting the headphones shielding his tiny ears from the noise.

Though it didn't bother him. Our son was like his father. He lived his life loud. And fast. Which was a nightmare when he started crawling, then walking. But Sam happily lived loud and fast with our two-year-old son, trading whiskey bottles for baby bottles without a blink. That didn't mean he didn't rock. That he wasn't still Sam Kennedy, the rebel drummer in Unquiet Mind. But that Sam was left on the stage. Sam Kennedy, the husband, father, and friend was for everything else. And he was so much more than what everyone thought he was. But that was good. He gave me what no one else got. He gave me Sam. The universe.

He also dressed our son in all black and in baby Docs he got specially made. My baby was currently wearing a tee shirt with the famous Nirvana album cover on it.

I smiled at Emma, mind going back to that night, all those years ago when Sam sang Chris Cornell to me. "Does anyone *ever* know what Sam's doing?"

Her eyes twinkled. "Touché."

"Now, she may be born to it," Sam continued into the mic, once the crowd's screams had died down. "But I'm rather glad for her reluctance, since she's so fucking beautiful. I don't like the thought of all you perverted mother fuckers leering at her."

Again, the crowd roared in response.

But Sam wasn't addressing them. He wasn't even looking at them. His eyes were on me and our son, standing at the side of the stage. They swam with mischief and that love that had only grown more intense with every passing day. It still gave me pause, every morning when I woke up to see that naked love on his face, watch it stay there until I went to sleep in his arms.

"But she's going to be more famous than me soon, my wife." He grinned wickedly at me. "Always knew she would set the world on fire. And she has. I *know* you've read her books, and if you haven't, you can't consider yourself a true Unquiet Mind fan," he yelled. "Because we're not just a band." He glanced to Lexie, who was shaking her head and grinning. Then to Wyatt, who flipped him the bird then put all his focus on the side of the stage, to the woman beside me.

Finally, Sam's gaze touched on Noah, who saluted him with a sly grin. Sam's attention went back to me.

"We're a family," he yelled.

The crowd screamed in response, the sheer weight of the sound echoing in my ears. Though as if Sam was their conductor, they settled down to near silence so he could continue.

"My family is the band. Is you." He nodded to the crowd. More screams.

"But my *universe*," he said, no longer yelling, but the words seemed to echo in the arena. "My universe is my wife. My son. So I'm gonna get them to come out here and I'm gonna sing them a little song."

My cheeks flamed and I glared at Sam, still smiling. I'd gotten used to his spontaneity, his way of taking me out of my comfort zone so I could live beyond the lines of my insecurity.

"Come on, baby," he cooed. "You know you want to. And you know Zeppelin would be so mad if Mommy didn't take him out."

As if they'd planned it, my son began to wriggle in my arms, pointing to Sam.

"Da da," he cooed in his baby voice.

"Traitor," I whispered to my son. Then I kissed his head and did what I always did. Let Sam lead me out of my comfort zone.

The screams vibrated in my bones as I walked out on stage. I didn't focus on them, if I did, I would likely hyperventilate. Even after years of being a rock stars girlfriend turned wife, turned best-selling author, I wasn't used to the spotlight.

Initially, that's why I'd published under a pen name, not wanting my book to become successful because of who I was married to. Sam hated that. He understood, but he hated it. And when I hit the *USA Today* best-seller lists and had my first book optioned for a movie, he almost burst with pride.

"You didn't even need me, babe," he said, teasing.

I regarded him soberly. "I'm always *going to need you."*

"Good, 'cause I'm never letting you go."

As soon as I was within reach, Sam snatched me into his embrace, being careful of Zeppelin's tiny body. The moment his lips touched mine, the screams silenced. The world silenced. We were in our universe.

Then we were in everyone else's as Sam let me go.

His eyes didn't leave mine, and he took our wriggling son into his arms, position him so he could still speak into the mic. Zeppelin immediately calmed in his father's embrace, smiling toothlessly at the crowd in front of him. It didn't bother him at all. He was born for the stage.

"Now, this isn't one of mine," he said, making sure Zeppelin's headphones were secure. "I'm going to borrow from my son's namesake to sing my wife a little song."

The wave of noise hit us following Sam's words.

He was still the rebel drummer of Unquiet Mind, but he was also the co-songwriter. He'd already won two Grammy's for his lyrics. He sang in albums (which had gone platinum) and on occasion, live. The fans loved this. Just when I thought Unquiet Mind couldn't get any bigger, they did. They were a pulsating life force that was taking over the world.

Not that that mattered to me. It was just the one man, now two, counting Zeppelin, that made up my world.

Sam's eyes held mine for a split second longer, as Lexie started to strum.

And he began to sing "The Rain Song" by Led Zeppelin.

He didn't sing it for the masses, for the fans, for anyone but the baby in his arms and for me.

Me.

The girl who'd loved him since she was a teenager and the

woman who'd love him until he was old and gray.

And he did what he'd promised to do years ago. He showed me what he saw, what I was to him, and what I was to myself.

Showed me the universe I'd created in his eyes. The utter undying devotion in his soul.

He did it that beautiful day in front of thousands. Then he did it every day after in front of no one but each other.

Sam's Playlist

"Come As You Are" - **Nirvana**

"Heart-Shaped Box" - **Nirvana**

"One More Light" - **Linkin Park**

"Help" - **Papa Roach**

"Comfortably Numb" - **Pink Floyd**

"In My Time of Dying" - **Led Zeppelin**

"Thank You" - **Chris Cornell**

"The Rain Song" - **Led Zeppelin**

Gina's Reading List

The Dark Tower Series - **Stephen King**

The Bronze Horseman - **Paullina Simons**

The Name of the Wind - **Patrick Rothfuss**

The Sword of Truth Series - **Terry Goodkind**

The Handmaid's Tale - **Margaret Atwood**

The Year of Magical Thinking - **Joan Didion**

Angela's Ashes - **Frank McCourt**

The Lord of the Rings - **J.R.R. Tolkien**

The Wind in the Willows - **Kenneth Grahame**

Watership Down - **Richard Adams**

Acknowledgements

This book took a lot out of me. A lot. I put my heart and soul into Sam and Gina. I put my heart and soul into every book, which is why I'm rather hard to be around during the writing process. Luckily I've got some special people who kind of like me enough to forgive me for my writing insanity. And my regular insanity.

Mum, you'll always be my hero. Because of who you are and who you taught me to be. I wouldn't be doing this writing thing if it wasn't for all your encouragement and constant support. Even when I'm a total nightmare. Which is a lot.

Dad, you'll always be in here, even though you're not around to read it. I know you're watching over me, sometimes in slight panic, I'm sure, but I know you're there. Without a doubt I wouldn't be the woman I am today if I didn't have my dad when I was a little girl. I miss you every single day.

Taylor, when I began writing these books I didn't *really* know what I was writing about. I knew what I'd read in my favorite books, watched in my favorite movies. But never *felt* it. Until you. You made me not just write a love story, but live one. And I continue to. Each and every day. Forever and then some, babe.

My girls, Emma, Polly, & Harriet, what's life without girlfriends? My life is not and will not ever be complete without you ladies. We don't need to talk every day to be each other's soul mates. That's totally what you are, by the way. I'm a lucky girl to have four soul mates. Love you, babes.

Caro, I probably would forget I was meant to write the words and do the things if it wasn't for you. I'm so blessed to have you in my life trying to organize my crazy ass.

My betas, Ginny, Amy, Sarah, and Andrea, you ladies continue to make my stories better. I couldn't ask for a better team to have my back.

And finally... you. Yeah, you, the reader, none of this would be possible without you. I continue to be blown away by your kind words and continued support. Thank you for reading my books, you don't know how much it means to me.

About The Author

Anne Malcom has been an avid reader since before she can remember, her mother responsible for her book addiction. It started with magical journeys into the world of Hogwarts and Middle Earth, then as she grew up her reading tastes grew with her. Her obsession with books and romance novels in particular gave Anne the opportunity to find another passion, writing. Finding writing about alpha males and happily ever afters more fun than reading about them, Anne is not about to stop any time soon.

Raised in small town New Zealand, Anne had a truly special childhood, growing up in one of the most beautiful countries in the world. She has backpacked across Europe, ridden camels in the Sahara, eaten her way through Italy, and had all sorts of crazy adventures. For now, she's back at home in New Zealand and quite happy. But who knows when the travel bug will bite her again.

Also by Anne Malcom

UNQUIET MIND
Echoes of Silence
Skeletons of Us

SONS OF TEMPLAR
Making the Cut (#1)
Firestorm (#2)
Outside the Lines - A Novella (#2.5)
Out of the Ashes (#3)
Beyond the Horizon (#4)
Dauntless (#5)

THE VEIN CHRONICLES
Fatal Harmony (#1)
Deathless (#2)

GREENSTONE SECURITY
Still Waters (#1)

73767549R10200

Made in the USA
Columbia, SC
06 September 2019